Traitor of Redwinter

THE REDWINTER CHRONICLES
VOLUME II

Traitor of Redwinter

ED McDONALD

TOR

TOR PUBLISHING GROUP
NEW YORK

TRAITOR OF REDWINTER

Copyright © 2023 by ECM Creative, Ltd.

A Tor Book
Published by Tom Doherty Associates / Tor Publishing Group
120 Broadway
New York, NY 10271

www.tor-forge.com

Tor® is a registered trademark of Macmillan Publishing Group, LLC.

The Library of Congress Cataloging-in-Publication Data is available upon request.

ISBN 978-1-250-81174-5 (hardcover)
ISBN 978-1-250-81176-9 (ebook)

Our books may be purchased in bulk for promotional, educational, or business
use. Please contact your local bookseller or the Macmillan Corporate and Premium
Sales Department at 1-800-221-7945, extension 5442, or by email at
MacmillanSpecialMarkets@macmillan.com.

First Edition: 2023

Printed in the United States of America

0 9 8 7 6 5 4 3 2 1

For Casper Fox Robert Morgan

Traitor of Redwinter

Events That Have Passed

Should it have been a while since you last entered Raine's world, a brief summary of key events that have transpired so far is given below. A glossary of characters, clans and terms is included at the end of the book.

Raine was born in the High Pastures, bleak and unforgiving highlands in the far north of Harran. Even as a child, she could see the spirits of the dead, a curse that carries a death sentence if it were ever to be discovered. At seventeen, having abandoned home years before, Raine found herself besieged at Dalnesse Monastery.

Raine helped a wounded girl named Hazia into the compound, but Hazia's mind had been taken by something dark and terrible. It was only the intervention of two Draoihn, Ulovar and his nephew Ovitus—magic users, spell casters, warriors who had been pursuing her—that prevented the rise of Ciuthach, an ancient demon. Raine discovered a trance rising in her mind, and together with Lord Draoihn Ulovar LacNaithe, banished Ciuthach.

Raine was taken south to the city of Harranir and the fortress-monastery of Redwinter, heart of the Draoihn's power. Ulovar used his power to draw a scar across Raine's mind, to allow her to cope with the things she had endured: she felt no grief, no empathy thereafter. Denied a chance to train as Draoihn herself, Raine became a servant. The luxury of this newfound life drew her in, even as she feared her grave-sight would be discovered and resented her low status. There she befriended a number of the other apprentices, including Esher, a young woman with whom she became close, as well as Ovitus's older cousin, Sanvaunt.

During those unhappy months, Ulovar's enemies sought to frame him for causing the monster Ciuthach's rise from the darkness. An attempt was made to kidnap Ovitus, which Raine was able to foil by shooting his attackers dead. However, a group of cultists led by Kaldhoone LacShale, a clan lord who had been cast down for the same grave-sight that Raine possessed, manipulated her and eventually set demons against her. Raine killed one, and Sanvaunt another, though he was grievously wounded. How Sanvaunt prevailed remains a mystery. The numbing scar in Raine's mind burned away.

Raine tracked Kaldhoone down and prevented him from drowning Ovitus. In the battle beneath the city, Raine invoked the ghost of a dead man, and fed it power. Ovitus dragged Raine from the collapsing tunnels, and together they were able to present Kaldhoone's head as the evidence needed to exonerate Ulovar. Despite all of this, Raine and Ovitus's fledgling friendship lay in tatters after she discovered he had misrepresented their relationship.

Through all of this, Raine has been watched, guided, punished and humiliated by the Queen of Feathers. Just who and what she is remains unknown.

JUST A DREAM

I am dreaming. I will not try to pretend otherwise. I am me, but that carries less certainty here. I am Raine, but I am the Queen of Feathers. It is her dream, and I drift inconsequential, a presence riding her existence, a burr that found purchase on her raven-wing cloak. We are the same. I don't think she's aware of me. I don't exist yet. It's long ago, but this is where I am, dreaming, so it's today. Time means even less than I do.

Why should it? Everything is one. That's what the Draoihn say.

A woman stands close by. Her face is drawn, exhaustion marks the slump of her shoulders. The gown that glows around her is a mass of gold and silver. If there was ever a dress like it before, there will never be one like it again. A great arc of spines rises out from the back like a peacock's display, or a banner. Perhaps it is. The majesty of her gown, of her bejewelled rod of office, seems to dwarf the woman that stands surrounded by these treasures, as if she fell through the neck of the gown and found herself wrapped in them. This is what it feels like to be grand, to become mighty, to become apart. She is part of nothing. Only the Queen of Feathers stands beside her, I stand beside her, and together the two, or three, of us watch the final day of a war.

'They betrayed me,' the Riven Queen says, for the glorious golden woman could be nobody else. 'I raised them on high, and they brought me ruin.'

'You betrayed them first,' I say, and I feel the petty meanness in my words. She's looking to me for succour, for forgiveness maybe. I am not going to offer her any.

We look out, us two, or three, across the field where the Riven Queen's army is being driven into the earth by the forces the last Draoihn have scraped together to match her. They are small in number, but they have found new, desperate strength, and they cut a path through the Riven Queen's army. It is an implacable display, a vengeful advance of steel and magic and death. Their enemies are not all human. Many are not even alive. They fall beneath the scythe just the same. The Riven Queen's power has been sundered.

'All this time, all the help you gave,' the Riven Queen says. 'Everything I learned from you. How did it come to this?'

'They have all said this, at the end,' I tell her. The Queen of Feathers tells her. We both tell her. 'I don't have an answer. I just have to keep trying.'

'You already know how it ends,' the Riven Queen says. She tosses her sceptre into the mud. For all that it's a fortune, it's worth nothing to her now. There is no running from this. She has marshalled the most terrible forces the world has seen in centuries. But she is going to lose nonetheless.

'I know what happens,' we say. I say. The Queen of Feathers says. 'But I don't know how. I thought you would be the one. But I appear to have made an error of judgement. This isn't it. But maybe it's a start.'

I wake from the dream now. I remember it piecemeal thereafter. The fear is what lingers, a trapped memory I'm unable to release. It is not the hideous nightmare things that Hallenae, the Riven Queen has summoned. It is not her alliance with the Faded Lords, who despite their terrible power are being brought down one by one, banished back to their nether realm. It isn't even the legion of corpses that fight at her behest.

It's that when we look at her, when the Queen of Feathers looks at her, when I look at her, the tired woman wrapped in a dress of gold and spines is me.

The stories of this age begin and end with betrayal, and mine is no exception.

It was midsummer when the bodies began to fill the ditches and the flies swarmed.

'How many, do you think?' Castus asked. He sat high, a slender figure atop a tall horse. I'd got down in the mud; I wanted a closer look.

'Looks like an even dozen,' I said. Flies in the air, flies landing on my hands, flies hoping to reach my eyes. The dead were off the road, down a goat track, slumped and tangled with one another in the trench.

'You sure you want to do that?' Castus said. No, I wasn't. But I needed a closer look.

I half-slid down the bank and into the ditch. It was dry, everything was dry, the grass was baked yellow and the leaves were turning crisp on the trees. It was a summer for dying things. I reached out to touch the face of one of the dead, but despite the day's savage heat, he was cold. He'd been in his twenties. Not so old. Not old enough to die. His throat was a ruin, the blood that had cascaded down the front of his shirt was brown, and dry as the land around it. The dead man had been wearing a night shirt. The flies hummed loud, clogging the air, clogging nostrils and mouths. Poor bastards. The people, not the flies.

They had been dead long enough to reek, not long enough to rot. I should have felt a little more—"poor bastards" wasn't much to offer them. I suppose I didn't think of these folk so much as people, as people-who-had-been. Since I'd been a small child, I'd seen the souls of the dead. I'd risen from a death of my own, then another, first throttled, then drowned. But there were no ghosts here. Only the insects, billowing clouds of flies, and the silent, graveless bodies. Without a ghost, without a soul, it's all just so much spoiled meat.

'Light Above, the stench of it,' Castus said. He put a handkerchief up against his nose, but I doubted it would do much good. On the road he'd got into some kind of pissing contest with Sanvaunt about who could see the furthest. Both men were Draoihn of the First Gate. They'd mastered the trance of Eio, and proven their dedication to the Crown. As an apprentice, I could hold the trance steadily, but I was glad not to use it now. Eio could sharpen the trance holder's vision enough to spot a field mouse at a thousand paces, let you sense the slight twitch of a muscle that was about to uncoil. But the First Gate was so much more than that. It expanded one's consciousness out, out, into the whole misery and glory of the world around. The bodies had been ditch-dumped a half mile from the road, and with the First Gate drumming its rhythm, Castus had inhaled that stench like a fist to the nose. He and I had broken off from the rest of the group to investigate. There was a bet on whether it was just some dead cow, mouldering in a ditch. But it wasn't, and it was horrible, and with only the First Gate to our names, there was little we could do to change it.

Had we been able to trance beyond the Second Gate we could have turned the dead flesh to stone, or liquified it with a touch. With the Third, the Gate of Taine, we could have burned them. There was nothing that Fier, the Fourth Gate of the mind, could have done to pry into their thoughts now, and they were long past the point when the Fifth Gate of healing could have helped them. That just left Skal, the Gate of Death. The Sixth Gate. And I didn't think they needed much help in that arena.

The sun beat down from a cloudless sky, punishing the living and dead alike.

'Who do you think they are?' I asked. Seven men, five women. Only the one had been dressed for bed. The others wore shirts, tunics, breeches. Nothing denoted them as being special, save the savage manner of their deaths.

'I think they were unlucky,' Castus said. 'First casualties of Arrowhead's ambition, I guess. Stop touching them, you use those hands to eat with. That corpse smell won't wash out easy.'

I ignored Castus and laboured hard enough to roll one of them over. My suspicion was confirmed, and it didn't sit easy.

'Hands were tied behind their backs,' I said. 'Executions. Why bring them all the way out here?'

'Well that's not good,' Castus said. 'I guess Arrowhead didn't want the townsfolk to know what he was doing? Maybe these were the town's leaders. You'll probably find the mayor in there somewhere.'

His assessment didn't sit right with me. I looked up and down the ditch at the poor, dead, trussed-up people. No, they weren't a town council. They were too young. None of them looked past thirty. They'd been helpless, slaughtered like swine, and there were rules in conflict, even for the likes of Arrowhead who was doing his best to foment unrest and was stopping short of outright rebellion against the king, and Redwinter, by a hair's breadth.

It wasn't war. Not yet, anyway, but it was the fronting of war, the way that two drunks square up to one another outside a bar that should have closed hours ago, that moment of posturing before the blows start to fall.

'Can you give me a minute here in private?' I asked.

'If you're thinking of taking up looting, I disapprove,' Castus said from behind his bunched handkerchief. 'They don't look to have had very good taste.'

'I just want to say a few words,' I said, which was honest. 'They deserve a blessing to send them on their way.' Which was also true, but not what I intended.

'So?'

'So go away. It's a private thing. You're too full of yourself to take it seriously. You make everything seem . . . juvenile.'

'Fair,' Castus said, and turned his horse back towards the road where the rest of our ambassadorial delegation awaited our return. I waited until he was a little way off, then slowly took a deep breath. It was supposed to be calming, but I regretted it immediately. The rot in the air filled my mouth, slithered across my gums. I coughed it out and spat until I'd emptied out what I could. I watched Castus move far enough away, his attention caught by angry nesting birds calling and swooping, and then I began.

Sometimes we act on instinct. Sometimes things can be forgiven when they happen automatically, a knee-jerk reaction to something out of the ordinary. Like when I'd fed my strength into a ghost to topple Kaldhoone LacShale. I hadn't known what I'd been doing, not really, and I'd been desperate. We forgive those things. Or we should. This, what I was about to do, I should perhaps have feared more.

People fear what they don't understand, but this was more than that. There is a finality to death that forms a constant in our lives. People live, then they are gone. To see the dead confuses that. It makes people afraid, and the price for that is to be stoned, or hanged, or burned. Fear evokes the highest of prices for its victims. To speak with spirits or command souls is to press close to the other worlds, the Rivers of Skuttis where the damned are taken, the thin veil of the Fault that separates one reality from another, and the Night Below, where demons dwell. Sometimes I wondered whether, had I never discovered this power, I would have been the same as the rest of them.

Sanvaunt knew the truth about me, but he hadn't turned me in for it. If our situations had been reversed, I hoped I would have been like him. I wasn't sure I had his goodness, though. Especially in light of what I was about to attempt on these stinking bodies.

This thing I was about to do, this disrespectful, wretched thing, I'd learned from the book. Not just any book, of course. It was a book that offered words I didn't recognise, and when I whispered them to the night they tasted like corroding metal on my tongue. They buzzed in the air, and gave it substance. They were things of history, perhaps they were part of the history of our world, but they'd given me ideas. I'd told myself I wouldn't use them. I'd told myself I wouldn't go back to that dark place, that I'd already stepped too far down a road I didn't want to travel. But that's the thing about making yourself promises. They aren't promises at all, they're just a way to alleviate whatever shitty thing you're feeling at the time. We tell ourselves, "No more of that," but that's just helpful for a few moments. The temptation comes and we jump right back in. Drink, rose-thistle, Olatte leaf, gorging on food, it doesn't matter. We all crumble at the first hurdle.

I checked one more time that Castus had moved far enough away before I placed my hand on the dead man with the hole in his throat. I began to say the words. I'd read them in the book, though I could never have written them down. They were ideas more than actual words, like colours you've never seen before. I hadn't tried to memorise them, but they flowed like a tune. There are seven spheres to existence, radiating out from us. There is the self, and there is the other. There is energy, and there is mind. There is life, and there is death. As a whole, we say there is a seventh, which is all of creation, but that is mere philosophy. As I gave voice to my song, I traced two circles. The sixth, the encompassing one, and just one more within, occupying half the diameter, isolating the sixth sphere from the others. A Sixth Gate within a Sixth Gate. I sought knowledge from only a single dimension of existence. It was death, obviously.

I wasn't good at this. I'd tried it before when one of the house cats died, and that hadn't gone well. My heart was thumping away, and even if the heat of the day had made me sweat, this drew more. I spoke the words, as best as I understood them. Maybe it didn't matter if I only got some of them right. Distantly, internally, I heard a grinding, droning sound, like the dry turning of an iron wheel, as I looked into the empty void where a spirit should have lived.

I only got a few moments. A glimpse of the young man's last few breaths. He'd struggled at the end. Shouted, just one shout among many. A distinctive accent. And then there was a face, stark and porcelain white in front of his, so thin she could have lived through famine. And then she opened her mouth, and her teeth were jagged yellow points. Most of his last moments were fear, and terrible pain, but he thought of a woman before he died. Resentment that he'd not get a chance to live out his life with her. And that was it. Done.

I shuddered, fell backwards against the ditch wall, found my breath coming fast and hard. I'd only had an image of that face, that dreadful, pale-eyed face, but it had been enough. Human? I thought so, though there were things that walked in human guise. But to drag these people out here had taken more than just one sharp-toothed thing. For a moment I had the impression of blood in my mouth. I spat, but it was only my imagination.

It had only taken a few moments. The man's dead flesh was still cold beneath my hand. *Idiot Raine! You said you wouldn't do this again! Promised yourself!* The regret was intense. This was the last time. What had happened to me that I'd grown so cocksure that I'd do this stupid thing fifty feet from Castus—a fully fledged, oxblood-wearing Draoihn? I mean sure, it was Castus, and he seemed to take his duties about as seriously as he did everything else in his life, which was to say not at all. But still. I hadn't needed to do that. But like any addict, I'd just wanted to, so I'd taken the risk. Power is like a river, and restraint is the dam that stops it from sweeping you away. If you don't allow a little water through, no matter how dangerous that trickle might be, the dam will surely burst. No matter that even if Castus suspected I had the grave-sight, things could turn on me quickly. Those things were stones, pitchforks, and burning torches. I wanted to leave it all behind me, but I had to do it sometimes. Didn't I?

I could not have a life while the dark hunched over me. I felt it, slowly circling me. It didn't want to be still. I would find an answer. I would unlearn what I knew, and I could try to have what everyone else took for granted. Ordinariness. The book, secreted in my pack, held the answer, the means to free myself from these urges. It had to. I had to believe that.

'They were Brannish,' I said as I climbed out, eager to make some noise, as though something different might chase away what I'd just done. 'My bet is they're the Gilmundy governor's men. The foreign garrison.'

The Brannish ruled an empire to the south of Harran, and generously allowed us to govern ourselves—with the requisite tithes, governors and garrisons in place to bleed us dry. The garrisons weren't popular—nobody wants to see their oppressor's boot planted firmly in the middle of their town. But little was likely to bring wrath down faster on one's head than slaughtering a garrison. This was madness.

'How'd you figure that out?' Castus asked.

'Tattoos,' I lied, and since Castus was never going to climb down into the ditch to take a look himself, it seemed a safe enough claim.

'I thought Arrowhead was just expelling the Brannish governors and their men,' he said. 'This doesn't bode well for our negotiations.'

'No,' I said. 'Corpses rarely do.'

·   ·   ·   ·   ·   ·

Across a mile of heather and tumbledown land, sat upon both the northern and southern banks of the River Gil, Gilmundy looked much like any other market town, save for the grey-and-yellow banner that had replaced the king's. There was no wall, and few buildings rose to two storeys. The governor's residence, the mayoral estate and the church spire looked down across the thatched roofs, the triumvirate of power—or they had been.

'Is this really a good idea?' Castus asked. The rest of our small contingent had got stony-faced about the dead Brannish soldiers, but it hadn't changed our course of action. Faces were set gravely, backs were pricked up straight.

A group of men in northern clan colours moved along the road to meet us. Five riders to match our number. We reined in along the sun-baked road to await them. Summer had risen fast and hard across the country, and rain felt a long way away.

'Remember your manners, if you can,' Sanvaunt LacNaithe said. He turned those sleepy-lidded eyes on Castus LacClune. 'Better yet, don't speak at all.'

'I've already had enough of this business for one day,' Castus said. 'I didn't even touch them and I can't get the smell out of my nose.' It sounded like whining, but Castus's nonchalant disdain for the world was all part of a carefully cultivated façade. Where Sanvaunt was dark, Castus was fair.

Where Sanvaunt was unshaven, Castus kept his face smooth—despite what appeared to be yet another monumental hangover. I considered them both my friends, but there'd been bad blood between Clan LacNaithe and Clan LacClune since before they had names. Regardless, the five of us were all here together, so an effort had to be made to get along as best we could.

There shouldn't have been such inter-clan conflict among the Draoihn, but that was the way of it. We weren't like other people.

'I'll handle it,' the only other woman in our group said. She was less imposing than the men. They were fighters, wearing mail beneath their oxblood, but Liara was better dressed for a day in court than she was for battle. Red curls formed a bonnet around her head. Liara LacShale had passed her Testing earlier in the year, and her choice not to wear the Draoihn coat was a different form of intimidation. She was even more scornful of Castus's nightly excesses than Sanvaunt, and that in turn knocked onto me when I joined him, which had been more often than not of late. 'Let's see if Arrowhead comes in person,' she said.

'He won't,' I said. 'They'd be carrying his banner if they did.'

'Best leave it to the Draoihn, Raine,' Colban, the last of our delegation, said. 'It's not our place to talk. Just to watch.'

'I wasn't made to be a butterfly on the wall,' I said. 'I doubt they sent me just to look pretty.'

Colban was middle height, medium build, with ordinary brown hair. His features were even, and sometimes I thought he had the most average face possible. Nothing was small, or large, or pronounced, or weak. He was unexceptional to look at in nearly every way, the kind of young man you wouldn't notice passing you on the street. We were both apprenticed to the same master, and I'd pondered more than once about exactly why the two of us had been sent on this mission. For all the noble blood running around, we were all mighty young. Sanvaunt was the oldest at twenty-four, Liara and I were only eighteen and Castus and Colban were somewhere in the middle. Draoihn or not, and as capable as Sanvaunt and Liara had proven themselves to be, they were inexperienced to be spearheading a negotiation that could determine the fates of thousands. Castus was heir to another of the three great clans, but even the most loving parent—which he certainly did not have—wouldn't have been able to recommend him as a negotiator.

'Want to run lines while we wait?' Sanvaunt asked Liara. 'We've got ten minutes before they get here.'

'I think we should focus on the matter at hand,' Liara said. 'I need a clear head.'

'If I have to hear you two pretending to be imaginary people even one more time, I'll honestly have to take up drinking,' Castus said. 'I'm serious this time.'

'They're good lines though, aren't they?' Liara said. 'You should come see the show when it's done. Better yet, I'll give you a part. First ass from the left.'

'I would make a fabulous ass,' Castus said.

'You already do,' I said.

The five horsemen approached at a steady pace, horses stepping a non-threatening walk, but they were armed and armoured. The warrior at their fore wore a full suit of armour, plates polished to a silver-bright sheen that caught the midday sun. He must have been baking in there, so he must really have wanted to put on a show. The other men were clan warriors, mail-clad and bearing the devices of the High Pastures upon their shields.

I knew that I shouldn't have, but I slipped my hip-flask from my pocket and took a little swig. An acrid, nauseating flavour ran down the back of my throat. Given a minute, I'd feel a little surge of energy, of alertness. Confidence too, but I wasn't intended to do the talking and I'd need to remember that. Rose-thistle helped me get through the day after another long night spent reading by candlelight, but it was renowned for making tongues billow in the wind.

Ah, there it was. That little lurch in the world that made it all that much brighter without ever entering a trance. I slid the flask back and felt that I'd got away with it.

'I have the floor,' Liara said. 'Interrupt me and I'll run lines all the way home.' Liara could make even Ulovar laugh, but she took her duty seriously, didn't trip over her own worries when it came to business. She was a rising star in Redwinter, and that was no mean thing to say. Our fortress-monastery was more than just a centre of learning. It was a place of power, in all the ways that mattered, from the ancient artefacts hidden in the Blackwell, to the secrets locked in dry old tomes in its libraries and the deadly warriors it put into the field. Redwinter awarded no crowns, but it made and unmade kings all the same.

The armoured lord rode two lengths ahead of the rest of his party. They were all men of station, but this suit of silver marked him as something special. The helm had a full face plate styled to look something like a playhouse mask, the mouth hole either mournful or snarling. Runic sigils had been engraved across the surfaces. It was Draoihn-made, forged by Redwinter's artificers. My bow, which I had stolen from the Blackwell and kept, was slung in a holster on the rear of my saddle. She wasn't strung, but she strung herself with moonlight when I asked, and I'd named her Midnight. The armour that this lord wore might even be proof against her arrows.

'I see LacNaithe and LacClune represented,' he said, his voice all metal within the helmet. 'But I think Van LacAud was expecting someone a little more . . . experienced.'

'Redwinter should be grand enough for you,' Liara said. 'Who am I addressing?'

'Braman of Dulceny,' he replied. Lack of a title suggested he'd climbed up through the ranks. That made him dangerous. Not many could afford Redwinter armour without being born to it.

'Well, Braman of Dulceny. You know why we're here,' Liara said. 'I assume you're our escort.'

'Of course,' he said. 'You'll understand that this is a difficult situation for all involved.'

'Difficult for the people of Gilmundy,' Liara said. 'But our negotiations should not be so complicated.'

'You'll understand if I ask you to surrender your weapons,' Braman said. 'Difficult situations, and all that.'

The corpses we'd come across said *no*. They'd be disarming me over their own dead bodies before I handed them Midnight. She was mine, I'd earned her, and no bow could match her. I thought it might come to blows at this very earliest point if Braman was foolish enough to insist. That took guts. There was something about him that told me his calm was solid but thin, and the violence that lay beneath could be called upon at any moment. It was the arrogance that told that story. What kind of man dared to order Draoihn around? We were the keepers of the Crown, we commanded fire and stone. Well, some of us did. A handful. The rest of us were still pretty dangerous and laws were of relative rather than absolute importance to us. But then, Braman was probably not his real name, and I'd have sent a Draoihn to treat with Draoihn. His visor remained lowered: if LacAud's streak of rebellion was ended with words, we'd all probably go back to pretending to be friends, but it's the lower caste of warriors whose transgressions are remembered. When a clan lord like LacAud took possession of another's town it was a border dispute; when a common man tried the same it was only common thieving.

I'd shoot the other men first. Midnight would come out, and I could put an arrow into at least two of them before anyone realised. I didn't fancy my chances against Braman's armour—there were diamonds blended into the fibres of the steel. I'd leave him for the actual Draoihn to deal with.

My mind hadn't been the same since I'd killed Kaldhoone LacShale and his followers in the undercity. Eight months had sped by me. Cursed to see the dead, they'd had a right to be angry, but their anger had made them bitter. Cruel. They'd lied to bring me to their side, then tried to force my master to execute his own nephew. They'd inadvertently nearly unleashed a monster on the world. They had paid for it. I destroyed them all. And now, never knowing quite whom I could trust, I never stopped looking for threats, to the sides, in the shadows. Always working out the sequence in which to deal with enemies, making sure I had an exit at my back, covering all the angles. I hadn't killed anyone since that day, but calculating and assessing the world around me gave me some measure of control over what had happened. It did nothing to lessen the dreams, or the night-screaming. But it kept my heart from beating wildly out of control to know how and when I'd need to act, if I did. Maybe this was what I'd been sent here for.

'We are here on a diplomatic mission, from Redwinter, by order of Grandmaster Vedira Robilar, with the backing of the loyal members of the Council of Night and Day,' Liara said. 'An insistence that Draoihn be relieved of their weapons could only be taken as an indication that your master, who as you'll recall sits on Redwinter's Council of Night and Day, has chosen to relinquish his seat and now considers the Draoihn to be his enemy. I strongly recommend you rethink your position.'

Liara LacShale was young, short and roughly the shape of an apple, but when she spoke, people listened.

'As you wish,' Braman said. 'Nobody's looking for bloodshed today. But you can't blame a man for trying.'

'The only thing you're trying is my patience,' Liara said primly. 'Lead on.'

Braman didn't like that. There was no face to see beyond his mask, but he sat motionless for several moments, and that stillness felt like a threat. But then he laughed, an unforced, natural sound bouncing around the tinny confines of his helmet.

'Quite so!' he said. 'Trying. I like it. Come, then. You're quite safe.'

Of course we were safe. We had three Draoihn, and though Colban and I were only apprentices, I liked to think we could hold our own too. I nudged my roan mare, Conker, to follow after our small escort, and flapped my arms up and down like a chicken. I was unused to the heat. Not a cloud in the sky, and the morning sun already had me slick with sweat. I could smell myself, which is seldom a pleasant experience. Funny that someone else's sweat can induce a tingle whereas one's own is just a reminder that you need to change.

. . . . . .

Gilmundy was a town like many I'd seen, a trade confluence where the great north road between Harranir and Dulceny intersected with the River Gil, which flowed east to west across it, all the way down to the LacClune seat of Clunwinny on the coast. Ostensibly the town belonged to the king, but the king was very old, his son was away fighting another king's wars, and his clan had lost most of its power, so like any wise ruler he'd left it to the vassals to sort things out for themselves. I tried to count fighting men as we passed through the streets, but I gave up quickly. The reports that had come in suggested a warband five hundred strong, and I didn't doubt them.

Light Above, but it was hot. Unseasonable early summer would lead into a blue-skied late one and I'd already had enough of it. I wasn't made for this kind of weather. I was a northern girl, and as much as I complained about it, rain and fog were a lot more comfortable for me than a heatwave. It had seemed fun at first, sitting on the porches of the gaming houses that Castus frequented, sipping chilled mead and wine, letting the aches of my training bruises soak away in the alcohol. But on the road, riding beneath that relentless ball of fire, I longed for winter to return.

LacAud had taken over the mayor's house on the north side of the river, but we made a diversion first to the Brannish governor's residence. No sign of any soldiers there, but then, I hadn't expected there to be. No governor, no 'peacekeeping' garrison. The occupiers, as many liked to call them. I liked the look of the place. It had white-washed, straight stone walls, and a good door. It wanted to be a small fortress, which in a way it was. At least the Brannish had been taken out to die—ghosts stayed close to their bones. My nights were restless enough without a haunting.

We'd been supposed to find those bodies. Billeting us here was all part of the show.

'Arrangements have been made for you to freshen up,' Braman said. 'Van LacAud will send for you when he's ready.'

'He should see us now,' Liara said. Braman's metal face was unchanged.

'Van LacAud is a Draoihn of the Second Gate, and a member of the Council of Night and Day,' Braman said. 'Not to mention he's actually lord of his clan, while this delegation is made of . . . you. I understand what the grandmaster intends, but honestly, we expected Ulovar LacNaithe.'

'He had better things to do than deal with this nonsense,' Liara said. 'But we'll play the game.'

I wished that were true. Ulovar would have been here on the fastest horse available to him, had he been able. Clan conflict served nobody, and murmurs of unrest over the succession of the Crown were muttered on every street. Ulovar wasn't well. He'd tried to hide it from me, from everyone, but he was always tired. Slower than he had been. My heart ached to see it.

There is a way that people speak about their parents, a bond that I'd never really understood. It stems from knowing that there's somebody out there who loves you relentlessly, that nothing could ever take that from you. I'd never felt it with Mama. I'd longed for it as a child, but she'd resented me so greatly that by the time I absconded, I knew that unconditional love wasn't there. Ulovar was not my father and he had never tried to be, but he'd taken me in, and done his best to help me. When grief and horror had threatened to overwhelm my sanity, he'd drawn a scar across my mind, cut me off from the pain. He'd given me a chance, recognised something in me that he thought was worthy of more. He'd offered me a life when I'd had nothing left. And that was as close as I thought I'd ever get to feeling what others took for granted. When I'd first met him, he'd been so strong, implacable, a rolling boulder that came to rest only when it willed. It hurt to see illness stealing that power away from him.

We were ushered inside. Crossing the threshold felt like stepping into a dead man's shoes. The whole place had been scrubbed and cleaned, like a spare bedroom made ready for guests. A pair of loaned retainers were ready to wait on us after Braman and his warriors left us at the door. It was a sparsely furnished, hard-edged sort of place, the kind that a proud commander takes satisfaction in having his people live in, and his people muttered about having to endure. Our escort left us there.

'Making a bit of a show of it, aren't they?' I said.

'Looks clean enough,' Castus said. 'I always sort of wanted to have a look inside one of these places. See how the Brannish do things. It's a little disappointing.'

'He's throwing it in our faces,' I said. 'He ejected every garrison in his land. You think it's meant to arouse patriotic sympathy, or is it a warning?'

'Maybe both,' Sanvaunt said. 'Or maybe they just had the room to spare.'

'I wouldn't take anything Arrowhead does at face value,' Liara said. 'He's a crafty old wolf. Sly, and audacious. It's a bad combination.'

'Do you think it's true, what they say about him? That arrows can't touch him?' I asked. It was a point of particular interest for me.

'It's true,' Sanvaunt said. 'And not just arrows. He's spent his life weaving incantations around himself to cover every attack. You'll feel it when you're close to him. Like a kind of lifting of the air around him. We've made jokes along the road, but what we're doing here is important. Best behaviour. Courtesy. Don't promise anything we can't deliver.'

'I'm not even sure why Colban and I are here,' I said. Sanvaunt looked away. He knew more about that than he was saying, but we hadn't talked much on the road. Last time I'd travelled with a LacNaithe man it had resulted in rumours going around about me, and we both felt it. He was protecting me, in his standoffish way. We'd kept a distance, although my gaze tended to rest between his shoulder blades as we rode. He had fantastic shoulders.

Liara and I were led to the room appointed to us, and that felt a little awkward. The night terrors came more often than not, and I often awoke screaming. I dreamed of burning eyes, of cold, wet, dead places, of the fleshless hands of the dead. Ulovar had used his Fourth Gate to free me of grief and empathy after I saw my friends cut down at Dalnesse Monastery, cauterising the mental wound, and whether it had been right or wrong to take that from me, it had worked. For a long time I had turned a blank face to the world, protecting myself, escaped into a void. Months on, after the scar left my mind, the dreams had flooded me, and at first, people had come to check on me. After a month, they just left me alone. Liara was unlikely to get a good night's sleep sharing a room with me.

Water had been warmed for a pair of copper bathtubs. It was only lukewarm, but that was better than the steaming Redwinter baths on a day as hot as this.

'You ever fear that you're going to get into a bath and the water's just going to turn black?' Liara said as she undressed. 'I swear I'm more sweat than person at this point.' I smiled weakly at the joke, but I felt too nervous around her to join in. What did one say to the daughter of a man after you drowned her father? I stripped off and sank into the tub. The water was scented, and I felt my muscles begin to relax. My thighs were sore as a whipped backside: riding a horse all that way was no joke. But as I felt the relaxation coming over me, I immediately began to tense up again, looking for my weapons, checking the door, figuring out how far the drop from the window was. I should have checked the window before I got in. I had to fight down the urge to get out and check it.

It would have been so nice to just be a normal girl.

'Why did they send us?' I asked.

Liara had settled her head back against the rim of the tub, her eyes closed as she breathed in the steam.

'Because the north is in the grip of the sheep sickness, there'll be famine come winter, and LacAud is trying to force subsidies and concessions from parliament to alleviate it. That's what he says anyway.'

'That's not what I mean,' I said. 'Why us? You, Sanvaunt, Castus, me, Colban. That horse turd Braman was right—none of us have the rank to negotiate properly with Van Onostus LacAud.'

'You've hit the nail on the head,' Liara said. She opened her eyes, rested her hands one over the other on the rim of the bath and rested her chin atop them. 'Sending someone with real clout would make this a bigger issue. Everyone wants this over and done before autumn, and that means making light of it. So they aren't sending their biggest horses, they've sent foals instead. But Sanvaunt, wildrose he may be, has standing in the clan, and Ovitus is off in Brannlant so he was the only choice. By sending Castus they show that LacNaithe and LacClune stand together in this.'

'They make sense,' I said.

'But "why am I here," is that what you're asking?' Liara said. 'I'd love to believe that I was sent because I'm good. But I'm not naive. My father was a traitor, and I'm a reminder to LacAud of how Redwinter deals with those Draoihn who put themselves before the Crown. And to negotiate with a traitor's daughter—I'm an insult. You're here for the same reason. Or as a threat. You killed him, after all.'

She talked about her father bluntly. She had to, but I knew it hurt her. Whatever else he'd been, Kaldhoone LacShale had been her father, and for people who actually have fathers, apparently that's important. I'd never met mine, and I didn't really care to.

Onostus LacAud intended us to wait. It was a flex of his arm, a game played to show who was in charge here. So it was a surprise when evening rolled around, and a summons arrived for me, and me alone.

'I don't like it,' Sanvaunt said. 'Decline.'

'I agree.' Liara was troubled. 'It stinks of game playing. Splitting up's a bad move.'

'I'll go,' Castus offered.

'I won't,' Colban said. He was a bit of a dour sort of fish, keenly aware that he was outranked. Colban Giln liked to do things in their allotted order, as if following due process made more sense of the world. But the more I learned about the world, the less order and sense there appeared to be to any of it.

I'd spent ten minutes thinking about it.

'I'm going,' I said. 'At the very least, it lets me get a look at him before you have to start negotiating.'

'I don't like it,' Sanvaunt said again. Trying to protect me, I supposed.

'Try to bring back a bottle of something Kwendish,' Castus said. 'The cellar here is all Brannish stuff. Dreadful.' Sanvaunt shot him a scathing glance.

'Raine, if you're really going to do this—you need to be careful,' Liara said.

'I can handle myself,' I said.

'Nobody doubts that. But don't give him anything he can use. Arrowhead is a ruthless man. He'll be looking for you to slip up, to take every advantage. Even a little knowledge can be put to dangerous use. If you go tonight, it's his game you're playing.' I smiled, my lips made thin.

'Don't wait up,' I said, and headed out to go and meet the man who threatened to destabilise the country.

The day had finally cooled. There was an atmosphere of distrust across the town. Too many warriors from the north, with their hook-ended northern accents, their unfamiliar breacan, and of course, their spears and blades. But life went on and people still had to go about their business. A troop of children filed out of a school. The idea of schools for children still seemed odd to me. They should have been at home with their parents, learning a trade, but I suppose they got to learn their letters. Mama had thought herself so special for her learning in that distant village that I'd never seen, and set out to make her fortune. She hadn't known that her literacy was considered only marginally above average down in the south, and had been too proud to return home to the village she'd abandoned. In my childhood, we'd come all the way down to Harranir as she sought out whatever it was she thought would fix the disillusionment. Most likely we'd passed through Gilmundy as travellers ourselves, but I had no recollection of it.

The mayoral residence was three storeys tall, surrounded by courtyards large enough that the higher levels could just have sprawled across the ground if they'd wanted to, but political life is often as much about show as it is practicality. It was all in good repair, and when I approached alone, the warriors on guard duty were ready for me. I was nervous, no doubt about that. It wasn't just the bodies we'd found off to the side of the road, it was all of it. I was invited to dine with a man of power, and I might have grown used to the likes of Ulovar and Ovitus but when you're born low, the aristocracy might as well be a different species. Moreover, I'd been singled out. I'd come dressed for dinner. Liara had refused that we give up our arms, but I could hardly bring a bow to the dining table. But I wasn't defenceless— Lady Datsuun and her equally unpleasant son, Torgan, had been drilling me in both armed and unarmed combat three times each week for most of the last eight months. I hadn't missed those lessons on the road, but I was glad that I'd had them now. The wiser part of me knew that eight months of hard work didn't make me a match for LacAud's warriors, even the least skilled of whom had to have more experience, and advantages in strength, but the more belligerent bit of me liked to believe I could handle myself.

I expect that the mayoral residence was considered opulent by the people of Gilmundy. Compared to the luxuries of Redwinter, it seemed parochial.

'I wasn't sure you'd come. I'm glad you have.'

Onostus LacAud was not at all what I had expected. A popular leader, I'd always imagined northern red or dark hair and a pale complexion, but his bloodline was half Kwendish. Pushing sixty, his skin had a rich warmth that seemed out of place for the most powerful clan-lord in the desolate northern territory. He was tall and heavy in the face and gut, but his bulk was worn with a kind of pride that said he didn't care. Every finger bore a silver ring inscribed with ancestral patterns, not a gemstone in sight. Sixty was too old to stand on a battlefield—it's a place for those young enough not to realise just how much they have to lose. He'd seen enough of it, though, and had earned himself the name Arrowhead, which he played into eagerly by wearing a coat sewn with all the bent arrowheads that had struck, but failed to hurt him.

'I don't like to pass up a free meal, my lord,' I said. Onostus gestured to the opposite end of the long table. It was much too long a table for two diners to sit and converse, but that's apparently what we were going to do. A couple of the men who'd ridden out to meet us stood guard at the doors, while fifth-rank retainers were stirred into motion.

'Eat, sleep and dance when you can, hard days will come soon enough. That's what my father used to say,' Onostus told me. He had a confident expression, bordering into cocky, but then I was in his town, surrounded by his men, and about to eat food that he'd also decided was his but had probably belonged to the mayor a few weeks ago.

I could feel his protections in the air, even from all the way down at the foot of the table. Arrowhead was a living legend, much loved in the High Pastures despite his mixed heritage. Such things were still frowned upon there in a way that didn't seem to matter in the south. Impossible to kill, that's what they said about him. The incantations he'd woven around himself had a presence of their own in the air, like strings tied around erratically shaped frames. I felt the little press of them against me, not against my skin but more against the me that inhabited it. They were ideas rather than physical matter, but I could tell that there were many. Dozens of them, lying one atop the other. Enchantments, spells, protection after protection layered like the lines across breacan. He'd earned his nickname after taking an arrow straight to the head. That first arrowhead had been set into glass and he wore it on a thong around his neck.

'You're going to have to give it all back, you know that already,' I said as a loaf of brown, seed-sprinkled bread and a jar of fish paste was set out in front of me. Simple, but pungent.

'We'll see, we'll see,' Onostus said. 'Gilmundy is only a talking point anyway. But there'll be time for all that tomorrow. You're probably wondering why I asked you here alone.'

I stuck the knife into the grey, jellified fish and smeared it across a broken crust.

'I'm not going to play guessing games,' I said. I bit into the bread and chewed. The fish paste was fishy. Funny that. I wasn't overly fond of fish, but it made a change from mutton. 'You tell me,' I said with my mouth full.

'I prefer directness. I hope your friends are just as straightforward,' Onostus said. 'Truth be told, I just wanted to get a look at you. You're supposed to intimidate me, I suppose? Raine the Draoihn Slayer. Kaldhoone LacShale's Bane, the apprentice who took on a Draoihn of the Fourth. Few others can claim such an accolade. I thought it best to take your measure before talks begin. I didn't expect to be alarmed, but a cautious man avoids surprises.'

I tore off another piece of bread and scooped more of the fish paste onto it. Eat when you can—good advice in times like these.

'You're certainly cautious enough,' I said, gesturing towards his coat of arrowheads with my paste-smeared knife. The fish was really coming up rather more strongly than I'd have liked. Perhaps it was time to slow down. As if sensing my wish, one of the retainers moved to pour wine for me. 'Let me understand how it works. You cast a spell on yourself, and it made you immune to arrows?'

'Arrows was just one,' Onostus said. I could see he was happy to talk about it. One doesn't wear a coat advertising invulnerability without being proud of it. 'Although it isn't just arrows. That first charm affects swiftly moving objects of a particular size.'

'No good against a tree falling on you, then?'

'No, no good at all. But that was only the first. I crafted another for trees, boulders and the like after a mangonel stone struck a battlement twenty feet from me. I've another for horse trampling, and obviously there are protections for swords, axes, fire and the like.'

'Why are you so scared?' I asked. It was a silly question, but it's fun to needle lords when you can get away with it, and Onostus LacAud seemed to be in a talkative mood. I was still hungry but I decided against any more of the fish paste. I had to share a room with Liara and it didn't seem fair to subject her to that much fish breath.

'Afraid and prepared are not the same thing,' Onostus said. 'You've certainly got some pluck. It's the north in your bones, I think. You can travel hundreds of miles south, but the granite of our mountains never leaves us.'

'Come on now, I'm not going to fall for the romance of northern siblinghood,' I said. 'We all happened to get born in a barren stretch of land

and because of that we're kin? If I've learned anything since I left the High Pastures it's that kinship is something you earn. Blood may be thicker than water, but nobody wants to be thick.'

'Whatever you think of your countrymen, you're one of us,' Onostus said. For a moment there was flint in his tone. He didn't snap at me, but he came close. A man who loved his lands, despite his fancy name and mixed heritage. 'The north would bleed if only it had the water to spare. The spring heatwave brought the radish sickness, decimating every flock it touches—and its reach has become long. We burn carcasses in piles that fill the sky with oily black smoke. Ewes and rams, even the lambs, the wool falls from them in slimy tatters. There will be famine come winter, and poverty will flood us with mouths we cannot feed. The babes will die first when their malnourished mothers cannot produce milk. The young will flee to find their fortune, and they will fail and become beggars and whores for the south.'

'And Gilmundy will change that?' I said. His words were hard-spoken, passionate. He had the right of it too.

'Subsidies will change it,' Onostus said. He regained his composure and clicked the rings on his fingers together. 'The south must support the north in times of hardship. What use are our tithes to the king and parliament if times turn hard and we starve?'

'I wouldn't know,' I said. 'I'm still just an apprentice. It's not me you need to persuade.'

'No,' Onostus said. Retainers came out to clear away the fish, which I was glad about. A second course arrived immediately—boiled mutton with neaps. Bland, but bland was all right by me. The only problem with mutton is that it's, well—very muttony. 'It's the LacNaithe wildrose and the LacClune heir I'm supposed to negotiate with,' Onostus went on. 'Although from what my man Braman tells me, it's Liara LacShale who intends to do most of the talking.'

'She's smart,' I said. 'You'd do well to listen to her.'

'She may be, but she's barely out of swaddling,' Onostus said. 'Although the same could be said of you, and I was there the day you tossed Kaldhoone LacShale's head into the middle of proceedings in the Round Chamber. But you were rather beaten up that day.'

'You would be too if you'd had to fight a Draoihn of the Fourth Gate.'

'It has fascinated the upper echelons of the Draoihn,' Onostus said. He gestured at his arrowhead-covered coat. 'Although, as you'd imagine, it holds a particular fascination for me. How did you do it? Did he let his guard down? Did you take him by surprise?'

I paused between forkfuls of muttons. It was overcooked, dry and tough. I laid the fork down on the plate.

'Murder is like a late-night party,' I said. 'If you weren't attending, you don't get to hear about what happened there.'

Onostus grinned. He had most of his teeth, but he'd lost an incisor on the upper right side and the rest were yellowed.

'So it was murder rather than battle?'

'I've come to understand there's little meaningful distinction between the two,' I said. I wasn't willing to give him anything. He wanted to know if I could bypass his protections. That's what I'd been summoned here for. I was a threat. *Here is the girl who felled Kaldhoone LacShale, a Draoihn of four gates. How will you fare with just two, Onostus LacAud? You are not as untouchable as you believe.* 'Would you say you gave battle to those poor bastards from the Brannish garrison?'

'The Brannish occupy our land and reap from us in times of plenty and times of famine alike. I will not have the people forced to give over what little produce remains to them to King Henrith of Brannlant. He can go boil his arse for all I care. The time has come to throw off their yoke of oppression. I am leading the way, but others will follow.'

'They'll follow you right into a grave,' I said. I wasn't meant to be negotiating, but I'd had a nip of rose-thistle before I entered and my tongue fancied doing some wagging about. 'Rebellions have launched before, and have crashed down into the cemetery just as yours will.'

'I'm hardly a rebel,' Onostus said. 'I have ancestral claims to Gilmundy, and Prince Caelan, who should by rights be here asking for his town back, has been away fighting with the Brannish and the Winterra for more than twenty years. A whole generation has grown up and had babes of their own without seeing their lord's face. I've freed them from Brannish oppression, and all without spilling Harranese blood. I do not think you'll find my people ungrateful.'

'But you understand why I'm here,' I said. I sat back in my chair. 'And Apprentice Colban Giln. You understand why he's here as well.'

'Giln,' Onostus said with distaste. He waggled a finger around in his mouth to work on a bit of gristle. 'You're intended as a threat. He's just an insult. One of my brood sired a wildrose on a penniless Clan Giln girl and had to marry her. A great disappointment to all. Yes, the grandmaster has hand-picked you all rather carefully. Thought I expected to see Ovitus LacNaithe among you.'

'He's away on business in Brannlant,' I said. 'While you're fomenting rebellion here, he's shoring up support there.'

'Acquiescing to our overlords. How noble,' Onostus said. His eyes carried a hint of mischief. 'You must be missing him.'

My appetite had turned as dry as the mutton. The old rumour. It didn't matter that I'd been vindicated. Where there was smoke, there must be fire, that's what people believed. What was true to most just came down to which version of events they'd heard first. Ovitus had whispered that he and I had been romantically involved, and he'd let it spread unchecked. It probably hadn't helped my cause that he'd half-carried me into the Round Chamber at Ulovar's trial. The people who mattered knew the truth, but even mention of it still left me as cold as if a bucket of ice water was slowly being poured down my back. Ovitus had never apologised for that lie, and that rankled at every mention of his name.

I stood up, the heavy chair scraping across the tiles.

'Did it work?' I asked.

'What?'

'Do I frighten you?'

Arrowhead's smile spread between narrow eyes.

'I gave up on fear long ago,' he said.

'Funny,' I said. 'You spend your whole life trying to protect yourself from every conceivable harm. I'd say it was fear that drives you.'

'Maybe,' he said. 'But you don't frighten me at all.'

I turned to go, and standing in the doorway was a vision of the Night Below itself.

She was a woman of indeterminate age, but she hunched her shoulders like she sought to swallow her own neck. Her hair was long and black, but her skin was unnaturally, unhealthily pale and her bones sought to escape a thin film of skin.

I stopped dead and reached for my First Gate, let it pulse around me. The world intensified, and I only saw her more clearly.

The woman's clothes were sewn with small bones. They covered her thin frame in dull, yellowed hardness. They pierced her lower lip, her ears, there were even sharp spikes of bone thrust through the skin of her forearms.

Serpent tattoos wound between them, coiling darkly across ivory skin. She stared at me, irises pale as her skin, and as her jaw quivered and her mouth juddered open, I saw the spikes of yellow teeth that had torn the Brannish man's throat out.

'That girl is cursed,' she said in a heavy accent, a voice like the ripping of meat. 'Death rides her shoulders.'

I quivered with readied energy. My muscles had turned hard and I found myself in a fighting crouch. I had only my belt knife, but drawing it in Onostus LacAud's presence could be enough to sign my death warrant. Was that what this was? A trap?

'The grandmaster finds it amusing to thrust her beneath my nose,' Onostus said.

'She is death-marked,' the woman said.

'Fine for you to say, all covered in bones,' I shot back, but my voice was a whisper and by any standards it was a weak retort. I doubt she went around like that all day with any kind of qualms about it. 'What are you?'

'My sled-mother named me Akail,' she said. 'I am the drinker of blood. I am the chewer of bones.'

'Those sounds like bad life choices,' I said. 'You should consider a better career.'

'We should kill her now,' Akail grated. Sinew ripping from bones.

'There'll be no killing today,' Onostus said. 'So dramatic, Akail. Rein yourself in, please. This isn't the tundra. We go about these things with propriety here. Kindly step aside so that Raine may pass.'

From the look the bone-pierced woman was giving me, I didn't think that mollified her very much. I had the terrible, gut-burrowing feeling that Akail saw something different in me, and it could only mean one thing. She saw the tunnel that lay at my core, that grinding, turning emptiness. The Sixth Gate.

I let my First Gate drop. I put on a smile. And I walked past her, walked past her neck-tearing teeth, heart pounding, sweat running, with all the calm I could muster. Sometimes it's all about the show.

It was only natural that the rest of my group wanted to hear everything there was to tell about my dinner with Arrowhead, and naturally I gave them the details. We gathered in the garrison's mess room and sat around the table like conspirators. Or prisoners. Maybe both.

'What advantage did it give him?' Sanvaunt asked. 'That's the question we need to ask ourselves. He wanted to see Raine, and Raine alone. Why?'

'It's her courtly etiquette,' Liara said with a grave expression. 'She's legendary for her table charm.'

I picked up a reed-woven coaster and tossed it at her. I heard her Gate open a crack while the disc was in mid-flight, and she caught it with a crooked smile. I stuck my tongue out at her.

'See?' Liara said, and she had a point.

'Powerful men get the horn for famous women,' Castus said.

'It wasn't that,' I said.

'May I suggest something, my lords Draoihn?' Colban offered. They nodded that he could. His deference frustrated them sometimes. Ideas were what was needed, not subservience. Colban was fretting. He hadn't liked what I'd had to tell him about his own role. 'Why would he want to look Raine over? She's not even fully Draoihn. She doesn't even have the training I have, lowly as I am.' He didn't look at me when he said it. He'd been training for his Testing for years, and his resentment was clear.

'Because she has her own legend,' Sanvaunt said. He didn't avoid my eyes. He had these sleepy-lidded eyes, like even when he was awake he was half in a doze. There was something knowing about that, like he only had to be half-present in our world to act as fully as the rest of us. *Tingle, tingle.* 'She's the least in training, but her story is bigger than any of ours. He wants to know what he's dealing with. The worst thing that can happen in a negotiation is to find yourself unprepared and on the back foot.'

'Do you think he sees you as a threat?' Liara asked.

'No,' I said. 'The wards he has around himself are like those magnet irons we looked at in training. It's like there's an area around him that just repels everything. I think he got what he was looking for.'

'Then we backfooted ourselves by sending you there,' Liara said. 'We shouldn't have let you meet him on his own terms.'

'Refusing would have been a sign of weakness,' I said.

'It's late,' Sanvaunt said. 'I'm going to bed.'

'No running lines tonight?' Liara said.

That damned play. It came up in every spare moment. Maybe it was daft that in these troubled times, in an occupied town and with a rebel at our doorstep, Liara would suggest practising lines for a theatre production, but it's doing the small, ordinary things that helps us find a place of calm. The play that Liara and Sanvaunt had written together, *The Demon of House Croak*, was about a frog who became a man, and was due to be performed in one of Harranir's playhouses later in the summer. It was somewhat unfair of me to feel envy that Liara got to share something so personal with Sanvaunt. I'd discovered his hidden romances when I'd been raiding his room back in winter, and rather than remaining a secret between us, that discovery had led him to share his passion with Liara. They were just friends. Sanvaunt and I were just friends too. There'd been a bit of gazing across the table, and I'd certainly watched him enough on the practice court, but between my gruelling training schedule, Sanvaunt's need to take on more of his uncle's duties and the other things that lay on my mind, there'd been no time for exploring. It was for the best, I told myself. I didn't need distractions just then.

'An hour, no more,' Sanvaunt agreed. 'I could use practice on the last two scenes.'

'I think I'll walk around the town a little, with your permission,' Colban said as he rose from the table. I could see by his expression that he wasn't at all happy with the way things had played out at my dinner.

'Same,' Castus said.

'I don't think that's wise,' Sanvaunt said.

'If LacAud wanted to get at us, he's had ample opportunity,' Castus said. He hadn't had much else to contribute. 'And frankly, sitting in here is probably more dangerous than the alehouses of Gilmundy. I'll buy the first round. Raine?'

'I think I've had enough company for one night,' I said. 'I'm just going to read a little.'

'Suit yourself.'

Whilst it was true that I'd done enough socialising, I had other things to attend to. Liara and Sanvaunt went to his rooms to run their lines. I waited for the door to close, and then I fished the book from my pack.

In the weeks after I rescued Ovitus and freed Ulovar, by lamplight I'd scoured the shelves of Redwinter's libraries for an answer to the curse that had only grown stronger within me. The Draoihn did not record the dark skills of the Sarathi except descriptively, in histories; the books that could have taught me were long since burned. But then, deep in the library's bowels, I found it. Found it like it had been waiting for me all those years, ready to push itself from its hiding place between books on dream duels and other magics long since abandoned. The Ashtai Grimoire. A codex of the laws of death. It didn't exist in Redwinter's records, and I'd checked them more than once. It had to be centuries old. What exactly it was, I couldn't have said, it wasn't as simple as just any book. But I knew it was what I needed if I was to live to see twenty. Though not if it was found in my hands.

The pages of the Ashtai Grimoire were always cold to the touch. Its cover had been slashed with a blade at some point, a bent-angled rip through the early pages. Part of the text seemed to be journal entries, written in different hands. Others were treatises on incantations and spellcraft, illegible and confusing. I couldn't tell if there were three writers or more, sometimes the script would shift into a different style even in the middle of a word, when the words were readable at all. There were similarities to all of the styles, but enough differences that I couldn't be sure. At times the writer seemed to be reeling from some great injury, at other times she almost sounded excited as she described the things she had learned beyond the Sixth Gate. Some pages recounted only a terrible, drifting melancholy and nothing of relevance at all. I often took several attempts to understand what she was trying to teach me, but it was all there. Symbols I couldn't decipher, words I didn't grasp. Spells of spirit, spells to talk with the dead: the magic of the Sarathi. There were other, darker things in the book. The summoning of creatures whose names the Draoihn had banished from the world. I found Ciuthach, the demon I had helped to vanquish at Dalnesse Monastery, described just as I'd seen him. I had not lingered on that page.

I didn't need those things. I just needed to know how to make it all stop. Visions of the dead had brought me nothing but pain, but I felt it calling to me. The tunnel's draw was strong. I didn't want to go further towards it and yet, it pulled at my edges. I had to cut myself off from the source, or I'd bring about my own destruction, or end up one of the cold, hateful dead things the book described.

'Not coming to visit me tonight?' I said into the dark of the candlelit room. I waited, but the Queen of Feathers did not appear. Some nights she came. Most she did not. I had no control over her, and I knew that beneath her calm visage there lurked a furious temper and a child-like cruelty. But I knew she could help me to learn the things that nobody else could.

Beneath the streets of Harranir I had lost control in a moment of desperation, and given a dead man the power to kill. At first I'd told myself that I'd never touch that power again, could never abuse the dead like that. It wasn't just that it was forbidden. There was a life waiting for me in Redwinter, but if my brush against the Sixth Gate was detected, there were three outcomes: those that saw the dead were stoned, those that meddled with them were hanged, and those that sought to learn the forbidden Sarathi lore met the pyre. I was fit for all three.

The book offered me words I didn't recognise, and when I whispered them to the night they tasted like corroding metal on my tongue. They buzzed in the air, and gave it substance as they pried at the stone I had rolled back across the Sixth Gate in my mind. I didn't need a Path of Awareness or Serenity to meditate into that place as I did the First Gate. It always lay there, slowly grinding against my edges. But I still went on reading, and whispering, and filling myself with death sentence after death sentence. The others couldn't hear the tunnel, no more than they could see ghosts. They hadn't bought that privilege as I had with my two deaths. I told myself that if I understood it, I could control it, and then I would be free. It's funny the things we let ourselves believe when they suit us.

Liara and Sanvaunt's hour became two, then three. I'd expected as much. Finally, the door rattled as Liara tried to enter. I'd latched it from our side. I wrapped the Ashtai Grimoire in an inconspicuous hessian sack and stowed it safely in my pack before I admitted her. It was dangerous to carry it around, but would have been more dangerous to leave it in Redwinter where an inquisitive, well-intentioned servant might have tried to give it a clean.

'How goes Lord Croak?' I asked.

'Bless him, I should have cast Sanvaunt as the toad demon,' Liara said. 'He looks a bit like a toad.'

'He does not,' I said.

Liara gave me a wide-eyed, open-mouthed smile, and I reddened. She laughed at me, and went to stow her sheaf of papers away in her travel pack.

'He's nervous about it,' she said. 'He hasn't performed before.'

'Frankly I'm amazed he has the time,' I said. 'Ulovar's placed so many of his duties on him, and he's always going off to train with that new mentor of his, Draoihn Firean.'

'Better Sanvaunt than Ovitus,' Liara said, and I had to agree. It had been a relief when Ovitus had headed off 'on business,' whatever that secretive business was about. 'It's a kind of relief for him, I think. Sanvaunt isn't very good at relaxing. He feels like he needs to be working on something all the time. This play—it's a way for him to relax and work at the same time. It challenges him as well. Acting doesn't come naturally to him.'

'So why not give him the toad part?'

'Because he's cliff-drop handsome and that isn't going to hurt the audience numbers,' Liara said. 'But then, you knew that.'

'Have you ever met Draoihn Firean?' I asked.

'No,' Liara said. 'Apparently he's very old, and doesn't get out much.'

'What does he teach?'

'The Second Gate, I suppose?' Liara said. 'I never heard of him except from Sanvaunt.'

'You think I should ask him to help me along too?'

'You could,' Liara said. 'But there's time for that after your Testing, whenever that comes. Focus on your First Gate. That's all you need to worry about right now.'

If only that were true. I drew the covers up over myself and nestled down into what was proving to be a very comfortable bed.

I woke to a sound. A startled jerk awake in the night. There was darkness all around me, the street beyond the window was quiet. Not one of my usual nightmares. I woke screaming often enough these days. Sometimes I remembered the dreams, sometimes I didn't. None lingered now. What I'd heard had probably been my own screaming. I could hear Liara's slow, gentle breaths. At least I hadn't woken her. I rolled over, tugged the blanket up around my chin, and closed my eyes.

I heard it fully this time. A real scream, a man's scream that had me throwing back the blanket and sitting bolt upright. It was so loud, it was as though it were in the room with us. Liara didn't stir, not even on the third time. And then the ghost stepped through the wall.

He was green and white, formed of gossamer wisps, translucent and empty. So empty. He was medium height, middling build. An ordinary face, so ordinary you wouldn't notice him if you passed him on the street. He staggered on unsteady legs, ghost-hands pressed to his chest, where the wound that had killed him didn't appear.

Colban.

He stood at the foot of my bed, and he screamed. A rattling, ululating scream of fear and breaking, a scream that only I could hear. His eyes met mine.

For many people, their greatest weakness lies in not wanting to make a fuss. Even in the face of uncertainty, they feel a need to pretend that things are still ordinary. When a drunk sways up to them at a bar, they go along as though it's an ordinary conversation, even when their instincts are telling them to run. When they're sent into battle, they do it because they're used to following orders, no matter that the arrows are about to start falling. It's the same instinct telling them to lie still when a predator comes near, hoping that through inaction or disbelief, everything might simply remain unchanged. Birds have never learned this. Birds fly at the moment they hear a sound. Ulovar had told me that the way to be ready to take flight was to have a phrase, like a code that you say to yourself. And when you say it, you know.

The time is now.

I leapt out of bed.

'Get up,' I said. 'Get up, wake the others. We have to go. Now!'

Liara stirred blearily. By the time she was sitting up taking in what I was doing, I had my bow in hand. Midnight flexed, her smooth, silver-threaded limbs forming curves as a string of silvery moonlight formed.

'Where did you get that?' Liara asked, the dregs of sleep clouding her understanding of how perilous our situation had just become. I wasn't supposed to have the bow. I'd stolen her from the Blackwell, and I kept her wrapped and hidden. But this was no time for hiding. Dressed in my nightshirt and with a fistful of arrows in hand, I opened the door and swung into the corridor, seeking targets, looking for the fallen. I ran along the hall, pounding on doors and yelling at everyone to get up.

I dashed through the building, corridor to corridor, a fire-hardened arrowhead leading the way. The garrison seemed secure. No sign of Colban's body, no sign of him at all. The doors were locked, the small windows latched and secure.

'What's going on?' Sanvaunt asked as I ran back up the stairs, taking them two at a time.

'Time to go,' I said. 'Grab what you can carry. We're leaving. Right now.'

'What happened?'

'No time,' I said, and that was a helpful way of stalling any further questions. 'They're coming for us. It's a double cross.'

'I think we need to know a little more . . .' Liara started.

'Just trust me,' I said. I fished the muddy bottom of my mind for a lie. 'I heard something out there. I think Colban's dead, and Castus is probably gone too. They're gone, and we go. Now.'

Sanvaunt pursed his lips. He knew what I was. He'd never shared my secret, but he'd known what Hazia had been, and he knew what I was too. He trusted me. Nodded.

'We go.'

I didn't know how much time we had. I didn't know how many of them were waiting for us, out there in the dark. Perhaps they'd picked Colban and Castus off because they'd been out there alone. An opportunity spotted. But Colban Giln was dead. His ghost had gone. How it had got here, why it had returned, I didn't know. But he was gone. It wasn't just some night terror, that wasn't how dreams worked. I was sure of it. I had to be sure of it.

Was I sure?

The time is now. Act fast. Worry about it later. It's just that voice in your mind telling you to lie flat and maybe it's all going to be all right. That voice saying not to embarrass yourself. The voice that gets you dead.

Sanvaunt and Liara threw on their travelling clothes, belted their weapons and were ready in a matter of minutes. I watched the front door, listened for sounds at the back. It all seemed quiet and dark. We lit no candles, gave no sign that we knew something was up.

'Wait,' Sanvaunt said. He eased past the First Gate, his trance subtle, reminding me of the steps he took on the practice court, and pressed up against the door frame. He closed his eyes. 'There are men out there,' he said. 'I can smell them. Oil. Leather. Iron. They're armed, across the street.'

'How many?'

'Six.'

Liara came back from the back of the garrison.

'Five at the back door,' she said. 'Light Above, they've penned us in. Why? They took Gilmundy without bloodshed. Why start it now?'

'Could just be keeping watch on us,' Sanvaunt said. I shook my head.

'No. The cellar's on the west side. They won't be watching the cellar door.'

'They might be.'

'Only if they think we know they're out there.'

'Why would LacAud do this?' Sanvaunt said. 'It makes no sense. He has to know it'll bring the great clans down on him like thunder. Not just the clans, but the king, and Redwinter too.'

'We can figure it out later,' I said. 'Right now we have to move.'

'We need to get to the stables,' Sanvaunt said. 'Without horses we're easy prey.'

Liara nodded. I nodded. It was decided as swiftly as that.

We slipped down into the cellar, musty-smelling and stocked with barrels and crates of rations, and on the other side, a ladder leading up to a trapdoor that would open onto the street above. They had no reason to think that we'd go this way. All three of us worked our Gates, but listening and smelling up and out into the night was a tough task. Stinking bodies on open moorland was one thing, picking out people amidst a town's myriad odours was another altogether. I sensed nothing.

'I'm not picking anything up,' Sanvaunt said, and Liara agreed. He blew out a breath, drew back the bolt and eased the trapdoor up. Cold night air flowed down into the cellar. The stars were out, crowding the clear sky. Sanvaunt laid the trapdoor down slowly, quietly, and one by one we climbed out into the darkness of the narrow alley between the garrison and a cooper's shop.

'As soon as we go for the horses, they'll see us,' I said. 'We can't risk it.'

'We have to have them. No choice about it,' Sanvaunt said. He drew his sword three inches out from its scabbard. It slid easily. 'Be ready.' He started down the alley, and then we all heard it. It was an open Gate, quiet and soft in the darkness. There was a Draoihn out there. It wasn't Castus's heartbeat trance. Colban's, which I'd heard over and over in daily lessons in Redwinter, was a steady plod. This one was light, the ticking of a water clock. *Tick-tock, tick-tock, tick-tock.* And then it was joined by another, *DHUM-dhum-dum, DHUM-dhum-dum,* the banging of a loose shutter in the wind. We all froze. We all stood silent. The Gates were open for only a few moments, and then rescinded into the night.

'They're listening for us,' Sanvaunt whispered. 'I think they know.'

'They heard me shouting,' I said. 'I messed up.' I eased past Sanvaunt, around towards the front of the blocky, whitewashed building and took a glance around the corner. They were on the opposite side of the road, hidden behind a wagon that had been parked obtrusively opposite the main door. We'd have to go past them to get to the stables.

'We can't reach the horses,' Liara said. She was as serious as the grave now, her usual jokes cast aside.

'Then we leave them,' Sanvaunt said. 'We head to the river and steal a punt. They won't expect that.'

It was as good a plan as any. Colban's scream was still echoing in my head. How had he come to me, when he'd died somewhere else, off in the town? Another thing to figure out later. It didn't have to make sense to be true.

'The side alley, over there,' I said. It cut between the cooper's and the low house that lay alongside it. 'You two first,' I said. 'I'll bring up the rear.'

We stepped as quietly as we were able. The night was quiet, but a dog started barking somewhere off between the streets. It was as good a cover as we were going to get. My mind was racing. Was this something I'd done? Had I given something away when I went to visit LacAud? If he'd wanted us all dead, then why not detain me there, why not poison my wine? Sanvaunt was right. Politically, militarily, LacAud was making a blunder of colossal proportions. We were leaving much behind, but the Ashtai Grimoire nestled safe and cold against my spine in my pack. We didn't speak as we wound through alleys that stank of piss and rat droppings, seeking the river. The alleys ran out and we were forced onto a major road, the same road that we'd rode in on, but by then we'd left the garrison behind. The mayoral manor lay on the far bank, over the fifty-foot-long wooden bridge. We moved west along the waterfront, then tucked away between a warehouse and a fishmonger's.

'Maybe we should go after LacAud now,' Sanvaunt said. 'Maybe that's our duty.'

'A good way to get killed,' Liara said. 'Besides. We can't touch him, not with those wards. And if he sent men who can access the First Gate to watch us, I'm willing to bet he has more.'

'Traitors,' Sanvaunt said, and there was more disgust in that word than I'd thought he'd ever have been able to muster. 'Deserters from the Winterra, maybe.'

'Or just northerners who've chosen to fight for him,' I said. 'It doesn't matter. All that matters is that we get out of here now, or we'll end up like Colban.'

'How do you know he's dead?' Liara asked again.

'I just know, all right? I felt it. And those men were watching to make sure we didn't leave. I just have this feeling.'

'This is a lot to gamble on a feeling,' Liara said. Everything along the banks seemed quiet. Lamplight glowed in a window here and there, but for the most part, the people of Gilmundy were long abed. I judged the hour to be a little past midnight, but I was only guessing.

'There's a sailing boat moored a little way down the wharfs,' Sanvaunt said. 'That'll do.'

'Wait,' Liara said, catching Sanvaunt's arm as he made to step out again. 'Hear that?'

Again we fell into our trances, and I caught it now. Faint, subtle, a distant series of waves repeating on sand, but it was faster and more urgent than I'd ever heard it before. I knew that trance.

'Castus,' Sanvaunt, Liara and I said at the same time, and maybe we were all surprised to recognise it so immediately that we stood for a moment, unsure what to do. And then Castus came spilling around through an alley on the opposite bank. He skidded on the stones as he made to turn, slipped—or it seemed like he slipped—and then something caught a glint of reflected light as it hurtled from the alley and sped out across the water. An arrow. It struck the fishmonger's shop to our right, quivering in the wood as Castus began to run along the waterfront. His sword was out in his hand, but half the blade had broken away.

'Untie that boat!' I hissed. 'Do it now. Go!'

Sanvaunt and Liara scrambled down a ladder that led onto the wooden jetty where the sailing boat was moored. I didn't follow. Instead I firmed my trance in my mind. I could hear them now, clattering down that far alley in pursuit. I knelt, drew a fistful of arrows and nocked the first. I waited, but I didn't have to wait for long. Warriors in mail hurtled out of the alley's darkness. The first had a sword, and I drew on him but a bowman came second, and I changed my aim even as he was putting an arrow to the string. Thirty paces to the river, forty across, another twenty or so on the far side. Little light, no wind to account for, a moving target. I drew back on Midnight, felt a little twinge of pleasure from her as I raised her to account for the arc I needed, predicting the target's run, and then *thwack*, the glimmering not-string thumped against my bare forearm and the arrow was loose in the night. I knew I'd hit before I'd released it. A better archer than I would have struggled to make that shot without the First Gate, but in the trance of Eio, I sensed it all. I knew where he'd be when the arrow made it across the water, *dhum-dhum-dhum, dhum-dhum-dhum*. I could almost sense it strike home before it landed.

The bowman was knocked back, colliding with a stack of pottery, shattering the quiet of the night. The arrow had found its target, but he was mailed and the shot was long and I couldn't tell whether I'd wounded him. It didn't matter. I drew the second, and this time I went for the lead man as he looked back over his shoulder to his fallen companion. My mouth was a hard, set line, both eyes were open, judging the arrow's arc by feel as much as sight. The less you think on these things, the better your body responds. I loosed and this one was solid, striking him just below the ribs. Midnight had an easy draw, but she was more powerful than she looked. He hit a window ledge as he went down.

Castus had seen us now. I targeted my vision on him, swooping it in close and I could see a grin spread on his face. There was blood on his cheek, in his hair too, dark smears in the shadowed night, but I didn't think it was his own. And still more men were coming out of the alley, three of them. I loosed two more arrows in quick succession, but they'd seen me now and they weren't idle amateurs. They found cover behind dockside crates, or the low wall running above the drop to the jetties. I sent enough arrows at them that they didn't pursue.

Time to go, and as I dropped down onto the wooden decking, I heard the distant barking of dogs. Sanvaunt and Liara were in the boat already, pushing off, and I ran for it. An arrow from the far bank went three feet wide of me as I leapt from the dock and landed in the shallow boat, my sudden weight sending it rocking. Liara and Sanvaunt took the oars, and I found more arrows and sent them back at the men on the shore.

'More coming,' Liara said. I turned, looking back the way we'd come and there were new men there now, men on horses. I'd fallen from my trance when I jumped—it wasn't easily held when there was running and bounding around to do—and so they were mostly just dark figures in the night. A splash near the far shore had to be Castus, diving in and swimming for us. The current was strong here, and Sanvaunt and Liara strained at the oars. Another arrow splashed into the water beyond us as Castus caught the side of the boat. I let Sanvaunt drag him up and turned back, loosing arrows into the dark as they tried to keep pace with the boat.

'Can you work a sail?' Sanvaunt said between pulls on the oar. He was stronger and taller than Liara, and his drags were turning us to the left. Castus spat water and shook it from his hair.

'Is there anything I can't do?' he said. 'Of course I can work a sail.'

'Then shut up and do it,' Sanvaunt said.

I was running low on arrows. I tried to refocus on Serenity and Awareness, the meditation paths that would lead me through the First Gate, but my heart was pounding and it wasn't at all like focusing in the quiet of a Redwinter meditation room. I loosed arrows just to keep them cautious as Castus worked ropes. He had been born on the coast, at Clunwinny, and seemed to know what he was doing. I wouldn't have had the faintest idea. But I had a good idea about how to put arrows into people, even without Eio pulsing in my mind. Unfortunately a quiver of twenty-four arrows had seemed like plenty, and now I was down to just six.

That's when I saw him, at the head of the horsemen. The warrior in the silver-shine armour, the face plate glowering like a surly theatre beast. I drew back, tried to account for the rocking of the boat and loosed at him. It was one hell of a shot. A shot that I should have been proud of. The moonlight string thrummed as it bit against my forearm, the arrow soared across the space, and there was a faint, tinny sound as it pinged against Lord Braman's helmet and bounced away. Draoihn-worked armour indeed, what a pot of shit.

The boat picked up speed, the sail catching and the oars working, as the swiftly flowing river carried us west. North and south, the buildings crowded close to the water, impeding pursuit on both sides. The horsemen drew rein. Lord Braman watched us go, a starlit silver figure, ghostly in the night as the river bore us out of Gilmundy.

'So,' Castus said, slumping down against the narrow mast. 'How's your night been going?'

4

'This thing doesn't go any faster?' Sanvaunt asked.

'Of course it does,' Castus said. He was doing something with rope. Never underestimate how much rope there is on a sail boat, or how important it is to do things like, I don't know, spleen the wingle or untangle the haddock wench. 'I'm just waiting for the experienced crew to come aboard, and we'll be shooting down the river like a quarrel.'

'Fair point,' Sanvaunt acknowledged.

The world was quiet out here. The river flowed swiftly, and Castus's waves-on-sand Gate susurrated against the peace of a summer night. There was little light to see by, but the river seemed to be content to guide us for the most part. I sat at the stern, Midnight resting across my knees. I'd named her for her colour, a blue so dark as to be nearly black, the silver threads in the wood as clear as falling stars. I didn't think I'd killed either of the men I'd hit—no ghosts. They might succumb to their wounds later on. They'd been enemies, and they'd been hunting me, but I hoped they'd live.

Eight months had passed since the night I'd tracked Kaldhoone LacShale to his subterranean lair, and on that night I'd slaughtered more people than I could count on one hand. It all felt distant now. As soon as Ulovar's innocence had been proven, I'd been put into a gruelling training regime. Mornings practising my Gate with the other apprentices, trying to understand incantation with Palanost, afternoons with Lady Datsuun, who loathed me, and her son, Torgan, who loathed me more. Then there were Ulovar's history and philosophy lessons, and statecraft, and war, and the frustration of my linguistics tutor. I'd had so little time to stop and think about what I'd done, and perhaps that had been Ulovar's intention.

They hadn't even been the first people I'd killed. I didn't like to think on them, though I found my mind wandering to it in idle moments, and then I'd find food sitting cold before me, or that my bath water had grown grey and stale. Those thoughts weren't really anything. They didn't have words. They were just kind of empty. I didn't think anyone could kill another person and come away entirely unchanged. It wasn't easy. No matter which side they were on, those men back in Gilmundy had probably just been following orders, just as I had. They obeyed their lord because they'd been born to do so. Probably.

'They'll pursue,' Liara said. 'And I daresay they have a ship with a bigger sail than this. We won't get away on the river.'

'Fast horses could catch us,' Sanvaunt agreed. 'Although if I remember right, the hills rise up around the bank ahead. We might have no choice but to fight.'

'I'm ready!' Castus said, lifting his broken sword. 'Bloody useless Brannish steel.'

'What happened?' I asked. 'How did it start?'

Castus sagged down, dropping his broken weapon into the bottom of the boat.

'We found a tavern that didn't seem likely to close,' Castus said. 'Colban was going on about all his Testing preparations like he always does. On and on and on. Wanting to know the secret to passing, like he always does. Did. We drank, and then at some point these men just came into the tavern. I knew straight away that something was up. They just had the look.'

'Killing men,' I said. Castus nodded.

'Killing men,' he agreed. 'They just marched right up and stuck a sword through him. I was already running before he hit the floor. There were two out back, but I did for them and left half my sword jammed through a ribcage. Then I just started running.'

Somewhere off towards the bank, a toad croaked into the night.

'You knew they were coming,' Liara said. The question was directed at me.

'I heard something,' I said. I needed something to tell them now. None of it made sense to me. By Castus's account, Colban had died on the north bank of the river. Ghosts usually stayed close to their bones. Somehow his shade had made it all the way back to the garrison. Maybe he'd been so intent on warning us that he'd broken the normal rules, whatever normal rules were these days.

'What did you hear?'

'I heard a Gate opening,' I lied. That seemed to make sense. 'And not one of ours.'

They had no reason not to believe me. I felt a fool for having believed Onostus LacAud meant us well. It hadn't been so very long ago that I'd been eating at his table. But why afford us the most defensible building in the town if they meant to close in during the night? Why not hit us on the road, far from help? Sanvaunt had standing in the LacNaithe clan, but Castus— Castus was the LacClune clan heir. An attack on him was a direct assault against one of the three greatest clans of Harran. Arrowhead might as well have raised the war-pipes and blown them himself.

'Try to get some sleep if you can,' Sanvaunt said. 'We need to sail through the night, but it'll be a long day tomorrow. No point in all of us being wrung out.' He handed his hip-flask of rose-thistle to Castus. 'You'll need to guide the boat. I'll watch the water.'

It was sound advice, but there was no sleep to be had for any of us.

* * * * * *

It is a terrible thing to feel hunted. There are no amount of glances back over your shoulder that can make you feel safe. Every sign you look for tells you that the pursuit is closing in. After a while, you see faces in the clouds watching you, and the rustle of a water rat in the reeds becomes the clatter of drawn weapons. The lack of sleep didn't help.

I saw the Queen of Feathers for a time that night. She appeared along the bank, vaporous and blue, a silent ghost watching quietly as she glowed in the dark. She didn't try to speak to me—not with other people around. I gave her a nod once, and there was a slight creasing around her eyes, which I took to be approval.

Sanvaunt and Liara discussed whether to ditch the boat and cut straight across the moorland or to keep riding the river all the way to Clunwinny. Castus outranked them both, but he didn't like to lead. Clunwinny meant the safety of his father's warriors and an armed escort home, but every mile west carried us a mile further from Redwinter, and we had news that needed to be shared. The answer presented itself by luck, and sometimes you just get lucky. Past a small village whose name I never learned, a horse fair was in session. They were selling hill ponies for the most part, but between them Sanvaunt and Castus had sufficient coin to acquire six sturdy palfreys. All three of my remaining companions were Draoihn; they could have commandeered horses as they saw fit if necessary, but paying for them meant less talk would flow out of the fair. They chose not to show their oxblood coats and money changed hands instead.

We rode fast, changed the horses whenever an opportunity presented itself, and saw no sign of anyone following us. If they'd tried to chase us down at all, we saw no sign. A week later, forging hard to the south and east along forest roads and lesser-travelled paths, we passed through a mining town where a group of Brannish recruiters talked loudly around the well. They sweated beneath their banner of orange-and-white checks displaying the rampant Brannish hare. Foreign soldiers serving a foreign king, collecting the young and the dispossessed, the poor and the desperate, to travel south into Brannlant, then east towards places exotic and dangerous: Russlant, Faralant, Garathenia and beyond in a conquest that had been slowly grinding kingdoms beneath its wheels for generations.

The north was full of those whose flocks had been decimated by the radish sickness, and the tradesfolk who relied on them. A bit of soldiering might have put food in their bellies, but Arrowhead had determined that the Brannish would find no more levies there, and the king was going to need to raise men of his own if Arrowhead was intent on full-scale rebellion. The recruiters were going to find their jobs a lot harder if we needed our own young people to die at home instead of abroad.

Two young men, fifteen or sixteen, their shirts heavily patched and worn thin at the elbows, looked puzzled by a document one of the Brannish recruiters held out to them. They probably couldn't read it. A standard contract of service lasted six years. The Brannish would be filling them with ideas about returning home rich and buying land of their own, bags brimming with conquest silver, but I'd never seen a poor man return rich from war. I'd seen plenty of men and women living cold and rough on Harranir's streets, some missing something visible like an arm or a leg, the rest missing something less visible but somehow worse.

They looked us over, but they could sense that we weren't for them. Sanvaunt, Castus, Liara, none of them had the look of a person who could be exploited. Those who would form the front lines of King Henrith's conquests didn't own horses. Perhaps in a year those two young men would be breathing desert dust and eating animals I'd never heard of, or maybe they'd be lying in a fortified ditch somewhere, peppered with arrows and losing their ghosts. Still, the presence of the Brannish seemed to be setting the world back to normal. The road had felt hostile ever since we'd joined it, but finally we were heading into the heartlands where the king's thails watched the roads. I got my first good night's sleep in a week.

Eventually, after what seemed an unbearably long time, Harranir and the mountains that provided its valley loomed larger ahead of us. Sanvaunt had fallen into one of his brooding moods, his mind seldom far from future events and possibilities. There'd been no more recital of theatre lines. Liara's good humour had fallen into quiet sadness. She'd lived with Colban Giln in the greathouse for most of her teenage years. She felt his loss the most keenly. Colban and I had not been close, and it didn't seem all that real to me, even though I'd been the one to see his shade. He'd been a part of my life, briefly, and now he wouldn't be. I did my best not to think of it.

Castus just drank his way through it. He picked up bottles of wine whenever we stopped. Money ran low, but he always had a drink to hand.

'I don't think those two like me very much anymore,' Castus said, nodding towards Sanvaunt and Liara at the fore. He rode alongside me often, finding the atmosphere brittle.

'Did they really like you to begin with?' I said.

'Nobody likes me except you,' he said.

'Huh,' I said. 'I wouldn't be so sure about that.'

'About them not liking me, or do you not like me?'

'Should I?' I said.

'Oh, let's just skip on to the part where you do. Nobody seems to want to drink at night anymore, but we both know you'll hit the taverns with me the moment we reach Harranir. That's the thing about me, Raine, I'm a terrible bastard but I'm also extremely loveable.'

'You're half right,' I said, and I wasn't sure which side I meant.

A lot of Castus's front was pantomime. It was hard to get to the honest part of him, if even he knew where to find it, but at least it was an openly worn mask. And yet he veered between the light-hearted bantering and deep, sullen moods where he barely spoke. I sometimes wondered what could seat him so low in the saddle. He was in pain, I thought. Something had wounded him and lodged inside.

'What now?' I asked Sanvaunt as the city came into sight, brown and grey, smoke-stained and alive. He'd been sleeping less than any of us and maintained a tired, tattered look around his edges. It made me want to stroke him and put him to bed, which would have annoyed him more than anything else in the world.

'Parliament will convene to talk about how to quash this revolt. LacAud's representatives will already be briefed ahead of our arrival and will no doubt have their own way to turn the truth into mud. The king will make his judgement. Messages will go back and forth, and if LacAud doesn't surrender Gilmundy, he'll face a real army.'

'Will he be stripped of his titles?'

'It takes a people to strip a man of his clan, not just the word of a king, but these events will make LacAud's seat on the Council of Night and Day difficult. Waging war against the north would be costly. Every step a soldier takes outside his home buries coins in the dirt. If Arrowhead was deposed, we'd only see vengeful kin take his place.'

'He should pay for what he's done,' I said. It didn't seem fair, that people could die and we'd all still have to be friends afterwards. But there was little fairness in the world.

Only the weak insist that life be fair. Castus had taught me to believe that. It didn't sit easy with me.

'No clan but LacAud can hold the north,' Sanvaunt said. 'Nobody would bloody want to. Arrowhead's right when he says that the sheep sickness has devastated the north's economy, but he's burned any sympathy the rest of the country could have had for him. Our best bet would be for one of LacAud's many children to sneak forward to rebel against him, someone who has enough support in the north to take it from him.'

'But they can't, can they?' I said. 'Not with all those protective wards he has around him.'

Sanvaunt nodded thoughtfully.

'Makes you wonder whether he's had this kind of ambition all along, doesn't it?'

'You know, this really wasn't as much fun as I thought it would be,' Castus said as his horse pushed forward to join us. 'Things I'm looking forward to, in order: a trip to the bathhouse; some food that I can actually bear; a bottle of something red; the spin of a gaming wheel. Things I'd like to avoid: mornsong, noonsong and evensong in church; getting a bollocking from the grandmaster; stacks of letters to read through.'

'Yeah, your life is just so damn hard,' I said, unimpressed even if I'd been thinking along similar lines.

'Honestly, getting out on the road felt like a holiday.'

'You'll need to try to remember what tact is,' I told him. 'A holiday? People died, Castus.' His face hardened. He drifted back behind the shine of his eyes.

'People die all the time.'

'And you still have it easy,' I said. 'I'll be back to apprentice training in the morning, and Lady Datsuun most afternoons. I've never slept so little.'

'I know,' Castus said. 'Hence necking rose-thistle every night.'

'I'm not addicted,' I said. 'I just need a top-up now and again. You try undergoing two hours' training in the practice court and then another four getting beaten black and blue by the Dharithians. Lady Datsuun doesn't go easy on me, and her son is even worse. I actually think he hates me.'

'Torgan Datsuun hates everyone who isn't Dharithian,' Sanvaunt said. 'But he's the best.' Sanvaunt had a proud veneration for his former instructors, and hated hearing anything said against them, but he was tight-lipped around Castus. The old clan rivalries lay deep as marrow. LacNaithe, Lac-Clune, LacAud: put three great clans in competition to put a candidate on the throne every time a monarch dies and what else will grow but grief? Add in all of the lesser clans and their blood-ties and allegiances to the greater, and our winds carried old tales of betrayal. The moors were shaped by the bones beneath them, the roots of trees grew twined around swords long fallen. Centuries of anger, of slights both perceived and real, of raids and grudges whose beginnings were deep and dark as lakes.

'My father had the terrible idea of sending me to them,' Castus said. 'I lasted two days before I refused to go back.'

'They didn't hit you hard enough,' Sanvaunt muttered. He put his heels to his horse and rode out ahead, the way he always did when he wanted time alone.

'Some of us don't get a choice,' I said.

'You'll appreciate it in the long run. Most apprentices get picked up when they're a few years younger than you and have trained on the practice court daily ever since. I started learning swordcraft when I was ten. Ulovar's giving you a run through the rapids, but it's good for you.'

'I know,' I said, but even thinking about Lady Datsuun's gruelling practices and the aches that followed seemed to make old bruises swell. 'I still come out of it battered like an apple thrown down the stairs. We've been gone two months and I swear some of the marks still haven't faded.'

'And what about you?' Castus asked. 'You and him, I mean. I seem to remember we spent a long night talking about Ditch Water LacNaithe over there. He asked you to walk out with him, didn't he?'

I had been dreading Castus bringing this up.

'Two days before we got sent to Gilmundy,' I said. 'I think it's forgotten now. Other things just took over.'

'Nobody has forgotten it, not even me. It's a big deal for him to ask you to go play with him. A pair of wildroses on parade, think of the scandal! He was fun when he was young, but I think they Tested all the fun out of him. What'll you say if he asks you again?'

'I'm still thinking about it.'

And the truth was, on the road to Gilmundy I'd thought about only two things: the forbidden book in my bag, and Sanvaunt LacNaithe's suggestion that we go to some silly party together down in the city. He'd been gentle, put it out to me casually, like it was something I could turn down if I wanted to. I'd told him I'd check my training schedule, although I knew I could have made it. Why was I so reluctant? Sanvaunt turned heads everywhere he went, he was brave, smart, and he knew how to work. And he'd carried my secret for me without asking anything in return. He'd given me time, lots of time, after I killed Kaldhoone LacShale and all those men. He knew about my night-terrors—he'd probably heard them often enough. I didn't know what it was that was holding me back. When I tried to think about it, my mind squirmed away like a worm avoiding the hook.

'Don't take too long to think about it,' Castus said. 'Sometimes it's best to just make a decision, even if you can't guess the outcome. You can never know what'll happen. Life is short, and we're meant to make mistakes. We just have to try to keep their effects from spilling onto everyone else.'

I didn't like being pushed, but a pushing Castus was better than a morose one. We had an easy camaraderie when that frost wasn't upon him. He was easier to talk to than other people. He didn't want or need me to be anything.

'Is that why you're always slouched so low in your saddle?' I said. 'Too many mistakes?'

His eyes glazed over, and the smile he wore was as manufactured as a player's mask.

'You can never make too many mistakes in that department,' he lied. But just as it had woken up, I'd killed his good humour. Me and my waspish tongue.

Redwinter sat on its plateau on the mountain above the city. Walls rose twenty feet high, white marble and rose-coloured quartz gleaming in the light of a golden hour. I remembered well my first arrival, armed Draoihn all around as Ulovar was led in under arrest. Sanvaunt and Esher had been there too, and Ovitus. It had been overwhelming, too big to grasp in some ways, but the strangeness of the situation had overwhelmed those kinds of concerns. My return was different. I knew that the path leading up between the pines was haunted by snatterkin, little hidden folk spirits that made peculiar sounds but meant no harm. I knew that the gates would open onto broad swathes of garden and practice courts, and the greathouses of power-ful clans. I had fought there, had come close to dying there, and I had struck a bargain to grant a single favour.

'Welcome home,' the Queen of Feathers whispered in my ear. I looked for her and found nothing but wind.

Redwinter was bigger than many small towns, its sheer size causing it to feel empty even by day when the retainers—servants, groomsmen and gardeners, smiths and servers, carpenters and cooks, engineers and entertainers, and every other type of tradesperson imaginable—outnumbered the Draoihn many times over. The greathouses, mansions with pretensions to being small castles of widely differing design, lay towards the perimeter wall. The Round Chamber, seat of the Council of Night and Day, sat squat and low in the centre of the grounds. Beyond it lay the library, the baths, the armoury, dozens of smaller dwellings and off on a spire of rock connecting to the rest of the plateau only by a narrow bridge of stone, the Blackwell, where I had made my bargain and sealed my fate.

I breathed in the familiar smells. Summer flowers around the yellow-baked lawns, manure from the stables. We were home.

Castus had galloped on ahead of us two hours before we reached Redwinter, heading into Harranir on 'business,' though I suspected he was heading towards a period of heavy intoxication in one of the gaming houses. He outranked all of us, but his mood had sunk low as home grew larger. He'd left the rest of us to bear the burden.

By contrast I felt a sense of ending, and of resolution as we passed through the gates and back into the familiar. Funny to think of this place as home, but home it was, for now. Perhaps I shouldn't have begun feeling this place was safe, but it seemed safer here than it did out there.

The LacNaithe greathouse was all straight lines, cut black stone rising three storeys high. The ivy lay green against the dark stone, clan colours proudly displayed. It was a brooding, joyless structure with a single tower rising high above the roof, as austere as the man who owned it, my sponsor and master, Van Ulovar LacNaithe. But for all its dark grandeur, I felt it welcome me. I had a certain empathy for the house; bleak, more than half-empty, rife with secrets.

First Retainer Tarquus was outside tending to a flower bed. It was far beneath his level of responsibility to be doing so, but he enjoyed gardening even if he'd never admit it.

'Welcome home, Draoihn Sanvaunt, Draoihn Liara,' he said.

'It's good to see you, Tarquus,' Sanvaunt said. Grooms emerged to take our horses without being called for. Tarquus wore a pleasant smile, but he hadn't risen to his rank by missing details.

'Is Apprentice Colban following after?'

'No. He's not,' Sanvaunt said. 'He won't be returning.'

Tarquus said nothing for a few moments, processing the finality of that statement, but he was a good retainer, and it wasn't his business to ask here in public view. I still saw the stiffening of his posture, the adjustment in demeanour.

My saddle-sore buttocks left the saddle eagerly as I dropped down from my horse and stretched my back. I was a better horsewoman than I'd been, but it can't be overstated just how sitting a horse drives splints through your whole body.

'Welcome home, Apprentice Raine,' Tarquus said gently. 'I'm glad to see you back safe and sound.'

I gave him a smile and a nod. I hadn't been very nice to Tarquus when I first arrived at Redwinter, and he'd treated me with a good deal more courtesy and respect than perhaps I'd deserved. He didn't seem to hold it against me—not publicly anyway. I'd resented being a servant with every part of my being, and yet I valued Tarquus and all of his staff so much these days. They were worthy of respect, from the servant-head who kept it all running, down to the youngsters who scrubbed mud from the floors. I should have been more grateful for the role I'd been given, but all I'd seen was another cage. I'd come to see that becoming an apprentice was a cage of a different sort. The servants' lives may have seemed tedious, mundane, but it was Colban lying dead and abandoned in the north.

I slipped inside the greathouse and headed straight for my room, my saddlebags slung over my shoulder. It looked exactly as I'd left it, though the absence of dust indicated that it hadn't gone untended. Even after more than half a year, I wasn't used to people quietly entering my space. The retainers never appeared to dust and polish when I was there, but with the training regime Ulovar had set for me and my extracurricular studies, I seldom managed more than five hours' sleep each night.

I ate alone in my room. I would be summoned to give my account, no doubt of that, but Sanvaunt would be first, then Liara. I had a rare moment of solitude. Most of the other apprentices were out on a field trip on the day of our arrival, a training exercise that involved harmonising their trances under different levels of duress while Draoihn Hylan put them through various ordeals. I was glad to have missed it. Those exercises pointed out the gulf in ability between us. Gelis and Adanost were clumsy in their trances, while it was hard to tell with Jathan as he found it hard to take much of what we did seriously. Esher I avoided at those times. I couldn't bear to watch her fail. In the quiet of a meditation hall she could flicker in and out of Eio at will, but when she was being watched her trance often buckled. I feared what that might mean for her future, and I hated hearing Hylan mocking her failures.

I latched the door, opened the Ashtai Grimoire in the quiet of my room and read about a spell that had been used in the war against the Riven Queen, a shadow shield that had absorbed a barrage of arrows, protecting the Sarathi beneath from Maldouen's forces. It wasn't written in Harran, but a sister dialect that I understood easily enough. The ink had a bronze cast to it, but the diagrams were impenetrable to me. It spoke of containment jars and woven amulets, and using bone to draw a soul back from the Afterworld. The book wasn't a guide written in order, and it assumed knowledge the way I'd have assumed an archer in training would know what a quiver was. It didn't seem to be intended to be read from front to back, and I had yet to find the same page twice. As usual, I closed its covers confounded.

I was not an idiot. I knew just how dangerous this was. A good apprentice would have taken it straight to the librarians, or better yet, left it untouched as they raised the alarm. I had seen firsthand the danger that a book can hold. That I had been the one to find it—I knew how unlikely that was. The frost-cold pages of that book had wanted to be discovered.

I had used it, to reach into the dead and pry truth from a body on the road to Gilmundy. I'd seen into that poor, throat-torn man's life, just as the book had said I could. I'd sensed the rending of flesh, and his terror, and his regret for all he hadn't achieved. That was the thing with pressing close to death. The illusion of night and day, the turning of one easy point of existence to another, gets shattered. You remember that you're finite, you will not go on forever. Life is an illusion, just a momentary patch of cloud drifting through a sky that was there before, and will be there when you dissipate into nothing. I read the book, and I tried to learn, because it was there, and I wouldn't always be. Knowing it left me feeling detached from myself, and cold.

I was summoned to attend Ulovar shortly after a mornsong that followed a sleep plagued with dreams of another woman's life. I was guided not towards his reception room or study, but towards his own personal rooms. I'd never been inside them before, and despite being tired and saddle sore, I was slightly intrigued. I slipped inside the door, and found the lamps set low. Larger than life paintings adorned the walls, austere-looking men and women of the LacNaithe clan looking down in oils from stormy backdrops, riding magnificent horses and clad in fashions long since fallen from use. A crystal chandelier overhead was lightless, and though the hearth was cold, the heat of the day had already made the temperature uncomfortable. Ulovar sat in a high-backed, padded chair beside the broad, tall windows. He wore a soft robe lined with fur, slippers and a warm hat despite the oppressive heat in the room. When I saw him sitting there, wrapped in softness and seeming small in his oversized chair, for the first time I thought he looked old. He had a bull's physique, even if he wasn't the tallest man. He was only in his mid-fifties, but age had suddenly rushed in and wrapped itself around him. His eyes caught the light, red as blood. He pulled at his fingers as if to rub warmth into them.

'Come. Sit down, Raine.' He sounded exhausted.

'You have something I can catch?'

'I do not believe so. But you'll sit when you're instructed to regardless.'

I did as I was told, taking the plush armchair across the little table in front of him. Daylight slanted down through the west-facing window, catching the dust as it drifted slowly in the warm air. A game was laid out on the table, tiles and horses carved from ivory vying for domination of a series of hexes. I didn't like being told what to do, even if that seemed to be my lot in life, but from Ulovar I accepted it.

'So. Gilmundy,' Ulovar said. 'I've had it from Sanvaunt and Liara, but I understand you went and enjoyed dinner with LacAud before things went wrong. I'll take your report on it now.'

I gave him what I remembered. Ulovar had the grace to lower his eyes when I mentioned that Colban's presence had been perceived as an insult. Perhaps he'd miscalculated and sent him into certain death. I didn't think so, and said as much, but Ulovar was nothing if not a shoulder for every responsibility he could heap upon himself. He'd eat the blame. I told him that Onostus had Draoihn in his service, and about Lord Braman in the silver mask, who kept his face a secret. And I told him of Akail, the black-haired, ivory-skinned woman who named herself blood-drinker.

'And then it all went to the hounds,' I said finally.

'Do you want to talk about it? You will have feelings.'

'Everyone has feelings,' I said.

'Not always.'

There had been a time when my mind had been cut apart by a scar of his making, my empathy and despair forced away. Ulovar had opened his Fourth Gate and cut away the grief, the sorrow that had threatened to over-whelm me after the massacre at Dalnesse.

I shrugged.

'What do you want me to say?'

I saw it in their eyes sometimes. Liara, Sanvaunt, even Esher. I didn't doubt that they cared for me, but they knew there was something wrong with me. They heard my terrors in the night. For a time they'd asked how I was, but I had no answers for them, and they'd let the questions rest. I didn't want to be pitied. What I needed was to feel that some part of me, any part of me, was normal. That I fit in among them. I couldn't bear to be broken anymore. And if I couldn't heal the normal way, I'd fix myself. I had to empty out the curse that made me different and then perhaps I could just go back, back in time to be—whoever I was meant to be, and not this simulacrum.

'I want you to tell me what you feel. A member of my household did not return. You've spent months around him. You ate with him, trained with him. Perhaps you were friends.'

'We weren't close,' I said. I could feel that I was being difficult, or maybe that Ulovar wanted me to feel more for Colban than I did. But I'd already lost so many people before I ever set foot into Redwinter, I was used to it. Like many things that made me uncomfortable about myself, that too was best buried.

'Other people died, too.'

'People are always dying.'

'And yet it is no easy thing to take a life.'

I just shrugged. 'Maybe it shouldn't be. But sometimes it's not so hard. I sent arrows at people who were trying to kill us. They'd earned them.'

'Sometimes these feelings arrive late, Raine,' Ulovar said. 'And sometimes we don't know what we're feeling, or why. You fought bravely, and righteously. But that doesn't mean it has to sit well.'

Ulovar looked drained, and unwell. I made no comment upon it; nothing would have grieved him more.

'I accepted my rightful place as an apprentice,' I said. 'I never imagined it would be a life of peace.'

'You are not yet full Draoihn,' Ulovar said. 'There is no guarantee that you will pass your Testing. There are no free passes. Ovitus approached his first Testing with confidence and surety. That was an error, as he learned to his cost.'

It was a point seldom spoken of in the greathouse that Ovitus had been given his Testing just before his departure for Brannlant, and had returned to the greathouse under the shame of failure. Nobody knew how or why he'd been found lacking, but a cloud of anger had surrounded him for days. He would be given a second opportunity—Redwinter did not callously throw away its apprentices over a single failure, we were much too rare for that—but he'd felt the bite of humiliation.

'I know,' I said. 'I'm training hard. And if I get a chance to stop this—to end what started in Gilmundy—then I'm going to take it.'

'Be careful what you wish for. You might just get your opportunity,' Ulovar said. 'Ours is a life of duty, and danger. And loneliness, at times. It is not suited to all. Do you understand why I sent you north while others much closer to their Testing remained here?'

'You said it was because I know the northern customs,' I said. 'But I know I was sent as a threat.'

'That was an afterthought, in truth,' Ulovar said. He rested the tips of his fingers against the edge of the table and pushed against it, bending them back at a right angle to his palm. He winced as his knuckles cracked. 'I sent you because you've the mettle to do what needs doing, when the time demands it be done. You've proven yourself before. I see in you a side that neither of my nephews will ever possess.'

'Sanvaunt is good, and loyal,' I said. 'He knows when to act.'

'He would have made an excellent van if he wasn't a wildrose.' Ulovar nodded. 'And I have hopes that Ovitus will rise to the challenges that authority will place on him. Perhaps failing his Testing will be the spur he needed to rise to greatness. I want you to love this clan as I do, Raine. I want you to share our values and our loyalties. I hope that when my time is over, that you will remain part of it. A clan is more than its leader. And our clan will have need of those like you, and Liara, and even Esher if she can learn to overcome her self-doubt.'

In the fading light I saw how dry Ulovar's skin was, flaking between his eyes. His cheeks looked sunken, as if he'd lost weight while I'd been on the road. He flexed his fingers again.

'Are you sure you're well?' The question annoyed him, as though he'd have preferred I pretended I hadn't noticed. A man's pride is a dishonest beast.

'I am not as young as I once was,' he said. 'My fingers take pins and needles, turn numb at the tips. Do not worry yourself. It is your wellbeing that I wish to attend to. You and your role in the clan.'

'You made it my job to worry,' I said. Ulovar grunted. The whites of his eyes had turned scarlet the day that he banished Ciuthach back into the cursed book, and they had never healed. His stare was a disconcerting, blood-filled weapon. But while it would have been foolish to dismiss his bite, Ulovar's bark was too commonly displayed for it to concern me. I held his gaze until he put his pride back in his pocket.

'Redwinter's cells are cold, and deep,' he said, looking out of the window. 'I never quite feel my full self these days. Redwinter's cells taxed me more than I would have wished. And lately, my Gates are not as responsive as they once were.' He leaned forward slowly in his chair to lift a cup from the table. I could see that even that movement was difficult for him, so I moved to take the cup. Ulovar growled low in his throat to still my hand. 'I'm not an invalid,' he snapped. 'Not yet. We all need some rest from time to time.'

'You don't have to pretend,' I said. 'Not around me.'

Ulovar took the cup, drank its contents quickly and rested it in its lap.

'We carry too many of each other's secrets already,' he muttered. 'My sons preferred the simplicity of a sword and a battlefield to leadership and administration. Sometimes I think they had the right of it.'

I most certainly did not agree. His eldest, Ulovir, had died in a duel eight years ago. His younger, Ulovaine, had fallen in battle. Redwinter would never have made the son of LacNaithe's van serve in the armoured ranks of the Winterra. Ulovaine must have volunteered. The sword was a simpler way of life, but it was nothing to aspire to. There is little wisdom in informing a person that you mean to kill them, even less in formalising it within a circle of rune-cut ash trees, and least of all across the madness of a battlefield.

But despite the grief he fought to keep from his stone-ground features, somehow the old warrior before me had a sense of pride in his sons' deaths. Even though they'd been pointless. Even though they'd lost.

'We will have guests in the greathouse soon,' he said, changing tone, banishing the unwanted. 'Visitors from Brannlant.'

'Brannish ambassadors in Redwinter?' That was not ordinary. Ulovar kept a handsome townhouse down in the city for social functions, a dust-filled, seldom-opened manor.

'In Redwinter. It's important that there are only good impressions.'

I smiled.

'You want me to keep out of the way?'

'I want you to make a good impression. Treat them with the same—no, more—respect than you give me.'

'I can do that,' I said. 'Who are they?'

'I'm going to keep that to myself a little longer,' Ulovar said, and despite the dry skin and the blanket, the deeper lines around his eyes and the slowness in his hand, there was still a hint of something lighter there. Like a burden of some kind was about to be lifted from his shoulders. The slight hint of a smile nudged at the corner of his mouth. 'But do treat them well. They're friends, allies and more. Cause them no trouble. But be watchful. Listen. You'll remember that.'

'I'll remember.'

He nodded, still smiling, a quiet, secret smile so rarely seen that for a moment I felt as though it reached out and embraced me entirely. The warmth of the fire became the warmth of something shared, the closeness of the walls became a closeness of another kind, and I felt it land within me like a lead weight. I didn't deserve this. No matter what I'd done and what I'd showed myself capable of, I was not a LacNaithe. I was barely even of Redwinter. At my core lay secrets that I could never share. Ulovar had known that his ward, Hazia, had possessed the grave-sight, just as I did. Hazia's power had led her to breach the Blackwell, there to steal the torn page of a book that had raised Ciuthach, a devil of the Night Below, and damned her. But she hadn't meant to do it; coercion, and the power of the Fourth Gate, had overpowered her mind. Even at the end, she'd been unwilling. But I'd gone so much further than just seeing the dead that had he known, not even my master and guardian could have turned a blind eye. I'd fed a man's spirit, given him the strength to kill. Briefly, I had brought him back from the dead in a dark parody of life, to save myself. I'd pried into a dead man's final moments. And I knew it was only the beginning. I heard the groaning of turning iron wheels in my sleep. The road I'd walked out onto did not have an end that I could see.

If the Draoihn knew what I was, I would have faced Kaldhoone LacShale's fate. Blinded, hobbled, dumped to drown in the harbour—though maybe they'd do a better job of ensuring that the drowning actually happened in the future. I didn't deserve Ulovar's trust. Not anyone's.

'Do you smell that?' Ulovar asked sharply, an edge to his voice.

I smelled nothing—hardly surprising given the amount of rose-thistle I'd been numbing my senses with lately—so I dropped into Eio on instinct, and suddenly what might have been the slightest touch of bitterness at the edge of awareness blossomed into my nose. Woodsmoke, like a farmer burning chaff from his fields. Ulovar's trance followed my own moments later. Slow on the uptake.

'Fire?'

I was up and out into the corridor moments later, the smell intensifying, carried down the corridors from the eastern wing. Fire is a constant threat to all houses, and a careless candle could bring down a fortress faster than an army. I ran down the hall, the caustic woodsmoke thickening, then clouding in the hall. I rounded a corner and nearly collided with Esher, who skidded and thumped into the wall. She was soot-smudged and her hair was wild. Not the way I'd planned to meet her on my return.

'Fire!' she choked out, her voice raw. 'There's fire in the east wing!' Her fingers clenched tight around my arms, panic in her eyes.

'Is someone getting water?' I demanded sharply.

'I don't know!'

'Then get water! Have everyone bring buckets!' I shouted at her, shaking free. For a moment she just stared at me, her teeth locked and manic, her blind left eye catching the glow of orange flame around a corner up ahead.

'Sanvaunt's trapped,' she said. A surge of fear washed through me, chilling despite the corridor's heat.

'Go!' I gave her a slight push to get her moving, and under orders she sprinted off, shouting at the top of her rasping lungs.

I headed around the corner and stared into an inferno. No unattended candle had caused this. The wood-panelled walls were alight, curtains roared in ragged rushes of yellow fire, the carpet was ablaze and thick dark smoke roiled through the air. I staggered back, away from the heat, and there I saw Sanvaunt's lean silhouette down the hall, cut off by the blaze. He swatted at the flames with a cloak, as if it could cut a path through sheets of fire. The heat was forge-like, a solid wall. With horror I realised that the fire was not just between him and me, but lay behind him as well. Sanvaunt was cut off at both ends of the corridor, trapped between the raging heat of twin blazes.

'Sanvaunt!' I screamed at him as he beat at the fire. The cloak he was swatting at the flames smouldered red in a dozen places. He looked up at me, half blinded by smoky tears. He didn't know what to do. How could he?

I ran back into the previous room, pushed the bust of a long-dead ancestor from a side table and dragged it back to the burning corridor. Flipping it over, I took hold of the legs. Maybe I could use it to smother the fire that covered the floor, the blackened carpet and even the burning floorboards. If I pushed it down the hall, perhaps—perhaps—perhaps—

The heat was too much for me. It emanated from the walls, rippled like a pool across the ceiling. Even if I made it to him I'd be scorched and seared.

'Get back,' Sanvaunt shouted, choking on smoke and falling to one knee. Then weaker, 'Get back.'

I wouldn't let him die. I *wouldn't*. He'd asked me to go to a party with him and I was going to *go*, I was going to hold onto his arm and dance and no fire was going to take it away from me. I gathered myself, ready to drive the upturned table down the corridor if it cost me every hair on my head and half the skin besides.

'Hold.'

A heavy hand on my shoulder. Ulovar had caught up with me. He pulled me back, fingers slipping as he tried to grasp me. Over the rush and roar of fire-devoured wood, I could hear the triple trance emanating from him, three open Gates twined together like strings of beads, somehow each one part of the other. In that moment he was stronger than he should have been, his Second Gate empowering his muscles to drag me back as if I weighed nothing. And then he raised his hands high, and slowly brought them down in a wide circle.

The fire in the ceiling died first, hissing briefly and then gone. The fire around the walls went next, dissipating and sputtering out where moments before it had roared with fury. Lastly, the billowing flames across the floor flickered their death throes and slithered down into the floor. I felt the cold issuing backwards from Ulovar, as his Third Gate tore the heat from the corridor, and even a few feet behind him it was like being struck naked by the depths of a winter gale. I staggered back further, trying to put distance between myself and the sudden freezing chill. It lasted only moments, but my nose and lips turned numb. Smoke filled the corridor, dense and black and impenetrable. For a few moments there was silence, and then the crash of something heavy hitting the floor.

I got down low, low as I could, and crawled forward. The ruined carpet flaked into brittle pieces, as cold now as a frozen lake. I found Ulovar, and he was nearly as cold as the air around us. My breath steamed into the drifting, choking smoke. He'd lost consciousness, his trances silent. Many more thrummed throughout the greathouse now.

Sanvaunt staggered through the clouds of black and grey, coughing against a hand pressed across his mouth. He was streaked in soot and his hair was singed.

'Help me,' I said weakly. Ulovar was a dead weight on the ground, mouth open, bloody eyes half closed. 'Help me.' Together we lifted Ulovar LacNaithe from the ground, and carried him from the ruin of the hall. He weighed more than I'd thought he could. More helping hands arrived to bear him into bed. His skin was milk-white, and I couldn't tell whether he was conscious or not. All thoughts of the ruined corridor were left behind as the true heart of our household was surrounded by worried faces.

'Send for the grandmaster. She can heal him,' Sanvaunt said, before he began to cough like the night was in his lungs. His face was washed with fear. But it was at those words that Ulovar's hand batted clumsily out to catch him by the wrist.

'No,' he said, voice grating like sandpaper. 'I don't need Vedira's help.'

The chorus of relief around the room from the gathered apprentices, Draoihn and retainers seemed to force Ulovar's eyes open.

'This isn't a circus show,' he choked out. 'Everyone get out. I took a lungful of smoke, that's all. Go and see what damage is done.'

Relief seemed to empty me out. I'd feared, really feared for a moment. Hearing Ulovar ordering everyone around almost overcame my concern for just how bad he sounded. At first nobody moved.

'You heard him,' Sanvaunt said, and he sounded like he'd been swallowing gravel. 'Go secure the east hall. Make sure there are no embers. Get to it, swiftly now.'

'Can I stay?' I asked.

'Everyone but Sanvaunt, out,' Ulovar grated. 'Bring me water.'

It wouldn't have paid to have made him ask me a third time. I filtered out into the hallway, shaking, the aftermath of the panic-rush ringing through me, the soreness of my skin where I'd gone too close to the fire. I'd been about to try to run through it. I felt scorched. I fumbled inside my jacket pocket and fished out my silver hip flask, and took a swig of the rose-thistle within, the bitterness sending a rush of nausea through me. Given a few moments it would bring my senses up higher, push some energy through the marrow of my bones, but it would also dim the pain in my nose, my cheeks, my fingers. I shuddered and retched a little.

I found Esher sunk down against the wall in a nearby corridor, crying softly.

'Everyone's all right,' I said, kneeling beside her. It was the first time I'd seen her since I'd arrived back from the expedition to LacSpurrun's lands. Soot-streaked, singed and shaking from both the sudden panic of the fire and the rose-thistle running through me, I hadn't imagined it like this. There was anger behind the tears.

'I did nothing,' Esher said blackly. 'Nothing.' Her words simmered with regret and her anger was turned inward at herself.

'It wasn't your fault,' I said.

'That's not what I mean,' Esher said. She closed her eyes and laid her head against the wall, breathed out slowly. 'I didn't know what to do. I *panicked*. I was useless.'

'I don't know what anyone else could have done,' I said. 'How did it even happen?'

'I don't know,' Esher said. She dashed furious tears onto the sleeve of a ruined dress. She would have looked stunning in it in most any other circumstance. For one absurd, jealous moment I wondered what she and Sanvaunt had been doing together in the east wing. The hot spur of jealousy rose like a wave, crested and died. Esher was my friend, and so was Sanvaunt, and there was nothing between them like that. They'd been separated by fire if nothing else anyway. 'It happened so suddenly. One moment we were walking along and the next fire just spread across the carpet, all around us.'

'Around you?'

'In front of us. Behind us, too.'

I'd seen a Draoihn throw fire on more than one occasion. But I hadn't heard the Third Gate opening, not as I had when Ulovar opened his, and it took the Third to manipulate it. I reached out a hand to Esher, and she gripped it hard as I pulled her to her feet.

'I was looking forward to feeling safe again when we got back here,' I said. Esher swept pale hair back from her face.

'This is as safe as it gets for us.'

6

The clans could vie and scrape at one another, but a threat within Redwinter was a threat to all. Armed Draoihn scoured the house, trances thrumming and thudding as they searched for every possible sign of an intruder.

I tried to find Esher, but she'd retreated behind a locked door and ignored me tapping at it. The rest of the apprentices, Gelis, Jathan, Adanost, me and Little Maran gathered in one of the sitting rooms and traded wild theories on the cause. Nightcrafters and Sarathi seemed popular, but I wasn't going to tell them that conjuring fire wasn't within a nightcrafter's power. Jathan treated my scorched skin with a cooling salve. Gelis gave me willowbark tea, and trimmed a lock of my hair that had been singed brown. Little Maran sat looking startled and more than a little afraid. They were new to Redwinter, but this was new to all of us.

'House is clear,' one of the Draoihn told us eventually. 'No sign of any intrusion. Just an accident.'

'Didn't look much like an accident,' I said. The Draoihn shrugged.

'We combed the place top to bottom. There's not so much as a flea in here we haven't found. Doors and windows all seem secure.' He assessed the worried faces. 'Your van has posted guards. You're safe. Best to get some sleep if you can.'

One by one we retired to bed. Easy sleep was seldom my ally, but that night was different. The wash of charcoal odour permeated every corridor and room, acrid and accusatory. Draoihn patrolled the corridors, heavy boots clomping reassuringly along the hall. The rose-thistle kept me up even after tiredness should have claimed me. Too tired to study, too fraught to sleep, I sat and stared out of the window and watched the rise of dawn.

The house's occupants were gathered together again at first light, Liara leading without any of her usual humour. The cause of the blaze remained a mystery. There was no sign of an intruder in the greathouse, and any stray candles had been destroyed by the fire. Nobody had heard a Third Gate opening before Ulovar's. Nobody had been seen coming or going. Neither

Sanvaunt nor Esher could explain how rapidly it had blossomed around them. Whatever reassurances were provided, uneasy fear filled the house.

'Keep your eyes and ears open,' Ulovar said when I called in to see him. He refused to stay in bed, and sat instead by an open window. 'I don't think even Arrowhead would be so bold as to strike at me in Redwinter, nor would he be fool enough to think fire would hurt me. But we have more enemies than the northern clans right now.'

'Maybe you weren't the target,' I said.

'Anyone capable of infiltrating our home would surely have poisoned our cellar, or used a knife. I can't justify someone being so capable, and yet so incapable at the same time. Sometimes, it's only an accident.'

He looked haggard, working at his numb fingers. Eventually he seemed to forget I was there, and I saw myself out. Ulovar would recover, but even though I'd seen him work more impressive magic in the past, sapping the heat from the corridor had taxed him. Everyone felt his pain. We were a strange family, but a family of sorts nonetheless.

Esher was conspicuous by her absence. I eventually found her on the Pheasant Lawn, striking blows against a wooden post with a training sword. She was dressed in a sleeveless cream-coloured shirt and a knee-length kilt of green-and-black LacNaithe breacan, her arms bare to the morning sun and her hair coming loose from a hastily woven braid. Each blow from the wooden sword caused the post to quiver. She was working through one of the cutting drills Master Hylan taught, alternating angles at speed. She might have had trouble holding her trances under pressure, but there was no doubting her prowess with a training sword. Many held her the best among the forty-odd apprentices in Redwinter.

'You missed breakfast,' I said. Esher lowered the wooden beater as I approached and offered her a bowl of strawberries. Her right eye was sore with broken veins, while her cloudy, blind left eye was pink around the edges. She looked not to have slept any more than I had.

'I'm not hungry,' she said, ignoring the bowl.

'Didn't get much sleep?' I asked.

'Not much at all, lately.'

'Sit with me a bit?'

'I need to practise.'

Esher usually had a sunny outlook, and it hurt to see her looking so grave. Whatever was going on, no matter how hard the sessions with Lady

Datsuun or how frustrated I got in the meditation hall, she was a ray of sunlight in a place where suspicions and troubles found us all in equal measure. When I was around Ulovar I felt old beyond my years, the Raine who had killed a dozen and more people, the Raine who had suffered and been hardened by loss. Around Castus I dispensed with those cares, his irresponsible spirit letting me forget about them in bursts of careless hedonism. But with Esher I just got to be a girl. Amid all the iron and threats and hard decisions, she refused to let go of that side of her life and made it worth living. I always came away from time with Castus feeling some sense of chagrin, but with Esher I just got to be.

'Everyone's all right,' I said. 'Ulovar got it under control. These things happen when you build your house from kindling and badly laundered rugs.'

'I'm glad,' she said. Her voice was pulled taut as a tightrope walker's wire.

'You don't sound glad.' I reached for her hand and she had to steel herself to let me take it. Her skin was sweat-slicked, and I wondered how long she'd been out here, battling imaginary enemies as the summer dawn filled the day. 'You got to skip dawnsong. That's a better start to the day than most.'

She pulled her hand away.

'I should make the most of dawnsong attendance,' she said. 'I might not have that many left.' She turned around and delivered a tremendous overhand whack to the post, then stood facing away from me, her shoulders rising and falling.

'It was frightening,' I said. 'I know that. It's all right if you were scared.'

'I was scared,' she said, in a tight, hard voice. 'But I'm used to being scared these days.'

'What does that mean?'

'You wouldn't understand.'

'Why not tell me and let me see if I do?'

Esher turned, tossed the practice sword down and picked up a strawberry from the bowl, and took a tiny bite from the end. She always ate them the same way, never removed the stalks first. Just ate up around them until there was a disc of ragged-edged red attached to a weed. The juice put colour on her lips. I hadn't realised how pale she looked until the colour brought out the contrast.

'I'm not like you, Raine,' she said. 'You're already a legend around here. You know what to do when things turn dangerous. You took on Kaldhoone LacShale all by yourself. You don't know what it means to be afraid.'

Sometimes you see what other people think about you, and the hurt comes out of nowhere.

'That's me all right. Made of stone,' I said. My voice had turned flinty. I took one of the strawberries from the bowl and plucked the green stem away, tossed it and put the whole thing into my mouth, like it was a challenge. It was a little under-ripe, hard, but still sweet.

'I didn't mean it that way,' Esher said, though it wasn't clear to me what she had meant. But the weariness in her tone, in her eyes, melted the annoyance from me. I reminded myself that I hadn't come out here to bicker, or to be upset. I'd missed her in the weeks I'd been away. I'd thought of her often. There had been moments where things had started to get blurred between what we were to each other. I'd never been so close with another girl as I was to Esher. We trained together, lived beneath the same roof. We wore each other's clothes as a way of approving of each other, of sharing something that we didn't share with other people. And when we laughed, we laughed so hard and so wild that it caused people to stop what they were doing and look over to check what was going on. But there was something else that lay in the middle of all that, and I don't think either of us knew if we wanted it, or what it would mean if we did, or what would happen if either of us was willing to show that we both understood it. Or if one of us was wrong, or didn't want it.

Our training kept us so busy, so tired by the end of a day that it was easy to just keep on delaying having to face it. We'd successfully avoided having to acknowledge it for a long time, and that had just become how things were.

I tried to smile at her as the morning sun began to spill across Redwinter's red-veined, white-marble walls. It would be hot today as every day was hot that summer, but the breeze had a depth of freshness to it that was a welcome change from the smoke-tinged air inside the greathouse. Esher couldn't find a smile of her own, so I stepped in and took her hands in my own.

'I've been afraid my whole life more or less. I was afraid of my mother, and I was afraid of running away. I was afraid of being too young, and just as afraid of becoming a woman. I was terrified in Dalnesse, frightened of Redwinter and scared by practically everything that's happened since.'

'But you don't freeze,' Esher said. She blinked her eyes, turned her head so that strands of hair fell across them. 'You act.'

It was true that she'd been in a panic when the fire flared up. But I hadn't been caught up in it from the beginning, I'd known from the smoke what I was running towards. But I couldn't deny that she was right. Esher took another piece of fruit and nibbled it away from the bottom up.

'It's good to be scared,' I said. 'Fear helps us. It means we act right.'

'Not if it means you're no help to anyone,' Esher said. She drew a long, frustrated breath, made a wordless sound of frustration in the back of her throat. 'I saw the fire and I just stood there. I stared at it, into it. I looked at Sanvaunt and I couldn't think of anything to do at all. He was shouting at me, but I couldn't hear him. The fire just mesmerised me, and all I could think was that if I didn't move, somehow it wouldn't know I was there. I was useless.'

'It was a shock,' I said.

'*You* weren't shocked. You're always ready for anything.'

That wasn't true. My own plan, driving an upended table across the floor, might even have been a worse idea than doing nothing. I forced my arm around Esher's shoulders and pulled her warmth against me.

'The important thing is that nobody came out with more than some light burns,' I said. 'Nobody got badly hurt. The house is still standing. Whatever you did, it wouldn't have made any difference.'

'That's not the point!' Esher said hotly, shrugging my arm away. 'I'm three months from my Testing, and I'm still freezing up. I helped bloody Ovitus abduct poor Castus. Either I jump in too quickly without thinking things through, or I do nothing at all! I'm not good in a crisis. I don't have what it takes to be Draoihn. I'll be Tested, and I'll be sent back to my mother's kitchen.' She shook her head. 'Even if I pass, they'll pack me off to the Winterra.'

Most Draoihn apprentices ended up in the Winterra, it was true. They were Redwinter's military arm, and they'd been fighting for our Brannish overlords for decades. The apprentices tried not to speak about it, every one of them hoping they'd be chosen for some other aspect of life as a diplomat, a teacher, a cartographer, and for the very lucky few who managed to open the Second Gate, artificing or more. There was a Winterra draft once a year for apprentices who had ascended to become Draoihn, and she wasn't the only one of Ulovar's apprentices whose mind it was on. I pulled her close, and her shoulders shook a little with silent tears. I let her have those moments, let her tears draw out the poison. Sometimes it's good to cry. It empties us out and lets us start over.

'Do you remember the first thing you ever said to me?' I said when I felt my shoulder was sufficiently damp. 'You levelled a sword at me and said: 'Don't interfere, *Fiahd*, or I'll cut you in half!''

I got the laugh I wanted.

'You didn't seem all that tough.'

'I'd already helped kill a demon. And I'd put an arrow in Haronus Lac-Clune,' I reminded her.

'Well, you didn't seem it. You just looked cold, and ragged, and exhausted and too pretty to be involved in trouble.'

Tingle, tingle. Light Above, she could bring it out in me even when she was tear-stained and savaging herself with her own self-doubt. I felt suddenly self-conscious and stepped away.

'If it helps, the real dangers don't always come with bells and ringers attached,' I said. 'Your First Gate is strong. You could do it before we even met.'

'But I won't make the Second Gate,' Esher said. 'I've been trying for nearly a year.'

I couldn't argue with that. None of Ulovar's apprentices had been making progress in that direction, myself included. I couldn't bear the thought of Esher being sent away to live a life on the front lines of the Brannish king's conquests.

'There's still time,' I said. 'Doesn't Ulovar say that sometimes it comes all at once, a moment of awakening and realisation and *bang*, the Gate opens and you're turning grass into wood and smoothing the lumps out of your porridge.'

'But for nine of every ten, it never comes at all.'

I realised that I wasn't helping.

'Do you know why I eat them this way?' Esher asked, holding up the end of a strawberry. She took a breath. 'When I was a little girl, I put one in my mouth whole. I felt the worm inside, and spat it out. I cried for an hour. It was this ugly, pale little thing, squirming on my apron. Half of it was gone. I spat and spat and I couldn't find the rest of it. I didn't know whether it was inside me already. I made myself throw it up, and I still couldn't find it.' She held up the green fronds of the stem. 'So I take little bites. Just in case there's a worm inside. It's fear, Raine. Even in a strawberry, there's fear.'

I ran my tongue around my teeth, as if inspecting them for grubs. I'd eaten my share of wormy biscuits, had picked the weevils from my bread. Somehow it seemed different when Esher spoke about it.

'Well,' I said. 'Means you've probably eaten fewer worms than I have. Personally I don't eat anything that doesn't have at least one worm in it.'

'That's disgusting,' Esher said, but I got a smile back on her face, even as she dabbed her eyes. We linked arms, and we walked, and I told her everything I could about my journey to Gilmundy and back, and left out all the bits where I'd tried to kill someone or drawn the truth from a corpse.

.   .   .   .   .   .

There would be many meetings and gatherings of the people who controlled the money that controlled Harranir to decide what to do about Onostus LacAud's ambitions, but I wasn't one of them. I returned to my studies.

The days ran to a tight schedule, and there was some comfort in rejoining it. Dawnsong was followed by breakfast, after which we meditated for two hours and tried to push the limits of the First Gate—or for the newest arrivals, just tried to keep it steady. I didn't feel like I needed those sessions anymore, and was quietly confident in my ability to hold the trance in most situations. But our second session of the day, for those able to hold a steady trance, was now incantation, and that I actually looked forward to.

It was Draoihn Palanost's turn to lead us, as happened every third day. I looked forward to hers more than the regular sessions with Ulovar or Roth. Everyone said that Roth was too old to find a rapport with the apprentices, but he'd been doing it for forty-five years and nobody was going to put him out to pasture. Ulovar approached our daily lessons as he did everything, working by routine, by principle and by following what had been written down long centuries before he was born.

Palanost was different. Esher and I were sometimes referred to as 'the tall girls,' on account that we were of a height with a lot of Redwinter's men, and those men didn't much like the idea that they were short, but Palanost looked down from higher even than Sanvaunt. She took a different approach to Ulovar and Roth, like the things she taught had me at the centre. She wasn't asking me to impose concepts onto the world, her teaching guided us to find union with it.

In meditations we all sat together, a discordant clatter of thumping trances filling a high-ceilinged hall, but for incantation, we were shown the basic principle before being sent to small cells, windowless and lit by pale blue-white cadanum globes. The walls were smooth black stone, the type that had been used by those that had built Junath, the undercity beneath

Harranir. Apprentice rumours said they chose dark bricks to mask soot and blood from incantation attempts that had gone wrong, but nobody had managed to achieve anything so grand as a deadly explosion.

My incantation equipment was arrayed before me. A variety of quill pens with inks of red, gold, blue and green, a stack of thick parchment sheets, a metal ruler, a book of arcane designs and sigils that could give us focus, and devices for trigonometry that looked more like they should be used for surgery than art. And lastly, a small vegetable pie.

The task that Palanost had set us was a simple one. We were to crack the pie lid without touching it. She'd shown us how to do it. The problem was, what worked for her wouldn't work for everyone. That was the thing with magic. Everyone's trance was different, and their perception of the world was different too. The way that Palanost's incantation was formed was a good starting point, it laid out the basic premise, but I had to find my own way to break the pie apart.

I set to, determined that for the first time, I would finally get to break the delicate crust. I dipped the gold ink, and started with a sigil array that was to describe the target of my focus. The first step was to create its representation, turning the paper into a kind of bridge between me and the humble, doomed pastry on the desk. The gold didn't feel right, and I switched to red, and then green. The words didn't follow lines, I wrote in circles and triangles.

Palanost came by. She'd been born in Murr, down south where they argued that the Light Above was divided into three somehow, where it was hotter than even our freak summer and they spoke like every word was a punch coming out of the throat.

'Good,' she said. 'I can see it on the page. You're angry at it, and that's coming through.'

'I'm not angry,' I said. 'I just want to break it.'

'Are you sure?'

'I'm angry at a lot of things. The pie would be low on the list.'

'Ah,' Palanost said. 'See these straight lines here, spoiling your curve? You need to separate the anger you're feeling from the incantation. If it doesn't belong here, why would you include it?'

'I need to start over?' I said, angry at time wasted.

'You do. There's still too much of *you* on the page, and not enough of the object,' she said. 'Try throwing in some blue. It might help.'

She left me to it for a while as she visited other students. I knew that Jathan had never had any luck with incantation, but Esher had broken her pie lid years ago, and had even managed to light a fire. The problem was, she could only replicate it here, as though the little black cells were part of the equation. The calm of the environment suited her. Some Draoihn came to master incantation, and for others it never worked at all.

I started over. I reimagined the pie and tried to distance myself from it. I pushed into Eio for a little while as I considered it, but that just made me feel closer to it so it didn't seem like a good idea. But after a while, I thought I had a pretty good idea of it down, and so it was on to the second part of the incantation—change. I'd stabilised it in the world in another form, so now I had to sigil it to be different. For that I decided on a single rune. The breaking would be instantaneous, and it would be harsh. One stroke would be enough.

Palanost returned. She studied my work, at times checking references to the sigils I'd written and how they interacted across the chaos of the page. She traced a dark finger around one of the triangles.

'It's a bit odd,' she said eventually. 'This is your breaker? What is it?'

'I couldn't find the sigil I needed in the book,' I said. 'But I think it's better. For me.'

Palanost didn't seem sure. What I'd drawn was fairly complex, overlaid across the entirety of my construction. Jagged lines and rippling waves flowed out from a central stem like some kind of nightmare squid.

'Well, it's what you drew. The sigils are foci, but they can be shaped as we want. It's worth a try. Are you ready?'

'I'm ready.'

'Now's the time for that anger,' she said. 'It might serve you well here.'

I tranced into Eio again. I felt the world around me, tasted the salt-spice flavour of Palanost's skin. Smelled the mouse droppings in the corner of the room. The world was glaringly bright. Everything in the world is one, it's just divided, but ultimately it's divided by nothing. By absence. And since absence is nothing, everything must be connected. Me, the paper, the ink, the pie, all of it. I just had to make the world see that I was as much the subject as I was the object.

Dhum-dhum-dhum, dhum-dhum-dhum. My trance pulsed soft and deft. I was me, and I knew my body from every bone, to every hair, to every tiny mite living on my skin—almost everyone has them, they just don't know it.

And I felt the silly pie in front of me, and the paper and the ink, and the way that they all interacted and all existed as part of my consciousness, which was the same as me, which was the same as all of them.

I activated my nightmare squid as I made myself part of that as well.

There was a thump in the air, soundless, lacking substance, but a change had taken place. I wanted to punch the air; it was the first time I'd managed anything at all with an incantation.

'What did you do?' Palanost asked in that throat-punch tone. The pie sat intact on the desk before us. It hadn't broken after all. 'What's that smell?'

It rose slowly, but it was deep, and it was nauseating. Sweet and rotting, it began to fill the confines of the chamber. I didn't know what I'd done but something had gone wrong.

Palanost picked up the pie and broke it open. What had once been stewed vegetables poured out onto the desk, slopping into a gooey pile of stinking rot. The smell intensified and I held a sleeve up to my nose.

'This breaking sigil, where did you learn it?' Palanost demanded. She lifted my work from the desk before the rotten slop could spread into it.

'Nowhere,' I lied. 'I just improvised.'

'No more improvisation for you,' she said, and all her gentle warmth was gone. 'Just what's in the book. Understand?'

'Yes, Draoihn Palanost,' I said.

'Clean this up,' she said.

She folded my page and tucked it within her oxblood coat, then turned and stalked from the room. My incantation lesson was over for the day.

'Well done,' the Queen of Feathers whispered into my ear. 'A first step.'

'Go away,' I said. I'd disappointed my teacher. Maybe even scared her a little. I didn't quite know what I'd done, but it hadn't been good. I should have known better than to experiment with the things I'd found in the Ashtai Grimoire. I felt a coldness settle in as I realised that I might have just disclosed what I was on paper. Whatever my intentions, I was aware of just what I'd been pushing into. I'd told myself I could lay a finger on that darkness, that it wouldn't bleed into my skin. And now I'd drawn a Sarathi rune, and it had flowed from me like a signature. I knew it in my heart: I had passed beyond the Sixth Gate a long time ago.

How had I leapt from the First Gate to the Sixth? The Ashtai Grimoire said that the Sixth stood apart from the rest. It lay beyond the physical realm, opening only for those that saw the dead—those that had died at least once. I'd died twice already, once when my birth-cord strangled me, and again when I drowned as a child. Such brushes with the veil had led me close to the tunnel. Draoihn only reached the Fifth Gate, Vie, the Gate of Healing, through mastery of the first four. But death was an easier step to take, provided you'd already died enough.

It wasn't supposed to be that easy, but I understood the mechanics of it in a way that perhaps nobody else in Redwinter did. On the day of my birth, Mama's birth-cord had wrapped itself around my neck and I first emerged into the world without breath on my lips. The midwife got me breathing, but my mother had sometimes said in rare moments of what I'd thought to be affection that I'd been dead before I'd ever been alive. Then, years later, as a child I'd managed to fall in a pool and drown. Resuscitated, the air forced back into my lungs, the grave-sight had intensified, or maybe that's when it began. But it was the journey into death and back that gave the grave-sight, and that second death had only strengthened it. Sometimes I had to ask myself: what would a third death do?

Probably best not to find out.

I had given strength to spirits at the cost of my own. The Sixth Gate was nearly as much of a mystery to me as it was to everybody else. What could it achieve? I wondered that in treacherous moments. The book spoke in riddles around the Drinker's Bite, the Witching Skin, the Banshee's Wail. How would it feel to call forth a bog wraith, or summon a shadowed blade? These were the magics of the ancient Sarathi. Once I had read in the book about a spell called Soul Reaper, and I'd slammed it shut with a sudden pounding heart. I had not dared to open it for two weeks after that. But in moments like this, when I sat silent and utterly aware of every part of my body, filled with the physical world all in the tight space around me, I sometimes felt that I could sense my own spirit. I could feel the life force within me, and I could feel it in others too. Spirits, maybe, but housed within flesh, bound to bone. One with them, as Palanost kept on reminding us.

I had no choice but to read the book. I needed to learn more about myself, about what I had opened, but I was afraid to know more. The Sarathi, those Draoihn who had opened themselves to the Sixth Gate, were legendary for their betrayals, first of the Draoihn from whom they came when they sided with Hallenae, the Riven Queen, and then the day they'd brought her defences down so their enemies could destroy her. The word *Sarathi* was steeped in treachery. Was that part of what the Sixth Gate led to? I didn't fear what I could do: I feared what it might make of me if I let it.

I had to know. Had to protect myself. Forewarned is forearmed, wasn't that what they said? I had known too little to understand Kaldhoone LacShale's plans, but it wasn't just that I felt an urging within me to open the Gate. It wanted to open whether I willed it or not.

And why shouldn't I delve a little deeper? The Ashtai Grimoire had come to me, hadn't it? I could never have found it, not if it didn't want to be found. At times the things I read horrified me. I didn't want to be *that*. But if I could just understand them, if I could just know what I was doing, how the tunnel was bleeding into my world, I could control it. To keep it at bay was a responsibility, it had to be. After all I'd given up, after all I'd sacrificed for everyone else, why not go just a little further?

I would read the book. I would listen to the Queen of Feathers, and learn what I could from her.

May the Light Above have mercy upon my soul.

* * * * * *

I was looking upwards, towards clouds that seemed too perfect against the blue. I wasn't sure what I was doing on the ground, but I felt oddly calm. I was out of sequence somehow. Something had just happened but I didn't know what.

A face obscured some of the view. A man. A foreign man, whose dark hair was slicked back with oil and bound in a tail, whose tattooed skin had an umber cast. I didn't recognise him. He didn't look happy with me.

'You hit your head.' A woman's voice from nearby. Her face appeared above me alongside his. She was small, thin, the same race as the man, but less of her face was tattooed. He said something to her in a flurry of syllables that meant nothing to me. 'He says you should lie still. Not move.'

The clouds didn't move. Clouds on a ceiling. Not real clouds at all, just paint on paint on wood.

'I'm fine,' I said, but my voice felt a little distant. Speaking a little harder than it should have been.

The man gabbled something that was too fast and too distant from real words for me to understand. He sounded infuriated rather than concerned. Should he be concerned? I didn't feel terribly worried. It was quite nice on the ground. My right ankle hurt.

'Master Torgan says to lie still on ground a little while longer. I will bring you honey in water. It will be good to drink after you bump your head.'

Ah. Torgan. The clouds, of course, were the ceiling to the training studio that formed part of Lady Datsuun's townhouse. I wriggled my ankle around. It was sore, but didn't hurt too badly. Nothing broken. It came to me that the man above me was Torgan, and the woman was Ibaqa, the interpreter. Their faces hadn't fit quite right for a few moments, and I was almost reluctant to accept that I was still in the Dharithian townhouse. I was made to lie still for a few minutes, and then Torgan helped me to sit up. He was a powerfully built man, clean-shaven, and he would have been beautiful if not for the constant grimace of distaste he wore whenever he looked at me. From his cheekbones up, his face was covered with an artfully drawn tattoo that signified his clan—no, his *House*, as the Dharithians had it. Ibaqa's tattoo ran in a strip across her face, just below her eyes, indicating her rank as a lifelong servant. It was hard to work out through the translator whether Torgan's dislike was of me personally, or of women, or of Harran's people. He had sneer enough for it to be all three.

I might have felt more comfortable with it had the way he insisted we train somehow imparted some of that ire. If I'd been able to feel it through some form of cruel tutelage, some sort of abusive thrust of the stick, or if he'd taken pleasure from sending me tumbling to the ground. But while I often came away battered, he didn't do it egregiously. That would have been beneath him. Maybe that's what made me so uncomfortable around him, knowing that he hated me and yet I was too far beneath his notice to abuse. His mother, Lady Datsuun, sat on a chair on a high dais so that her head was always highest in the room as she watched. She didn't spare me any cruelty whatsoever. The Dharithians had some funny ideas about status and rank, even more so than the Harranese and the Brannish.

After he made me drink the honey water, and sit for a while, Torgan helped me to stand and put me in a chair.

'How did I end up on the floor?'

Ibaqa looked to Torgan, they spoke, and she gave me his words in the Harran tongue. She must have been there all along, must have seen for herself, but she didn't give me her version. That wasn't how things worked here among the Dharithian exiles. Her role was to translate, so that's what she did. Lady Datsuun's household had travelled a long way to escape the purges of an empire-breaking civil war. Their homeland, said to stretch halfway across the world, didn't appear as much more than a word and an arrow on even the largest maps, thousands of miles away. Sanvaunt had tried to explain that it wasn't just bitterness that caused their disdain. Dharithia held to a caste system that placed non-Dharithians at the very bottom, even Draoihn. Even kings. Datsuun herself had been married to a great war leader, and would never speak to me directly. They lived among us to survive, fled far from home, but to abandon their xenophobia would be to dismiss their own heritage. Dharithia sounded like a shitty place to live.

'You do it badly, fall to the ground and hit your head,' Ibaqa said. 'He ask if you feel it in your head?'

I didn't, which was a little concerning. The floor was strewn with a thick padding of rushes, but I was surprised there was no feeling to the impact. I shook my head, and there was no dizziness.

'How long was I unconscious?' Another flurry of exchanged words.

'Only a second or two second,' she interpreted. 'He is not concerned. The LacNaithe clan girl has a thick head, good for bouncing from the ground.'

It was a compliment, of sorts. I didn't receive many. Torgan's way of teaching was not short on pain. He didn't spare me blows from the cane, and certainly didn't shy away from bruising me. The day I'd gone back to the LacNaithe greathouse with two black eyes had raised a number of eyebrows and some voiced concern, but perhaps my pride made me foolish. I valued those little mementos of my time spent training. I was years behind the other apprentices. Castus was a devil with a blade, had been training under a master since he was ten years old. I'd been trying to play catch-up for just six months. Everyone wants to believe that they're the hero, that the enemy soldiers will be thuggish and swing wildly with crude swipes, but the truth is that most highland boys and girls were playing with stick and shield long before they grew hair under their arms. Mama hadn't wanted me to engage in such rough sport. She hadn't liked it when I ran around, as though it reminded her that it was my birth that had twisted her inside and given her so much pain when she walked.

The deeper voice that always made the hairs on the back of my neck rise up sounded from across the room. The sound of it was so alien, and I glanced her way before snapping my head back. Lady Datsuun was nothing special to look at. A small woman in her fading years, Dharithian, bald, her face a mass of dark ink, her lips painted black as her son's hair. I was not to look at Lady Datsuun. Ibaqa had tried to explain it to me once, and while complicated, essentially it came down to not having the right breeding to be able to look on one born to her station. Ibaqa translated for me now.

'Lady Datsuun, may the moon ever bless her name, says you should not move too fast for a while. Instead she would like you to recite the names of the twenty-two common poisons, their giveaway signs, their effects and potential remedies.'

My ankle was growing more painful. I must have twisted it when I fell. Torgan moved obediently to his mother's commands, clearing away the thick wooden canes we'd been training with. The poisons I was well familiar with. I came here four days of every seven to learn to fight, but Lady Datsuun's methods of fighting were not those that were familiar to most of Harran. To help memorise the poisons, I'd separated them into those that grew in Harran, of which there were nine, those which could be located in dubious markets, of which there were five, and the eight which belonged to the Dharithian Empire, so far to the east that its people had likely never heard of Harran, or even Brannlant.

'Hecksfleet, otherwise known as Spouse's Remorse, is found growing on the banks of streams near to freshwater swamps. It has pink flowers, and smells like ripe peaches. It isn't poisonous to deer, which seem to like it. When the flowers are dried . . .'

It was a moribund sort of recital, but truth be told, I was glad to know it. More than one of our client kings in Brannlant had historically perished after 'bad humours' were found in his meal. It wasn't the Harranese way of doing things, although I didn't think that knives were all that much better than deadly flowers.

I recited them to Ibaqa with what I thought was absolute perfection.

'You said Hecksfleet has pink flowers. Lady Datsuun says Hecksfleet only flowers in pink in alternate years. She would like you to perform forty press-ups, so that you remember in future.'

I almost looked over at her. Almost. I restrained myself in time, knowing that doing so would only add to my burdens. My ankle, twisted when I fell, protested viciously as I flattened myself against the ground, planted my knuckles and began. I didn't think anything was broken, just sprained as I went down. Forty press-ups was a lot for me, after the fifty I'd started the afternoon with, and the cane-play that had gone on before I'd knocked myself out.

Torgan hated me. I hated him back, but I hated his mother even more.

Sanvaunt practically worshipped her, spoke about her like a favoured grand-mother, and that made it all the worse.

When I was done for the day, Ibaqa led me to the door. My horse was always waiting for me there beside a mounting block, as though they couldn't wait to be rid of me as soon as the allotted time was up.

'Good practice today,' Ibaqa said. They would be Torgan's words, not hers. I didn't think I'd ever heard any of Ibaqa's own. 'He says it is good to be knocked out in practice. Now you know what it feels like. Recover faster next time.'

'I've been killed before,' I muttered. Ibaqa nodded.

'Recover faster,' she said, and shut the door in my face.

7

By night I woke screaming, and then I delved cold pages for the secrets of the dead.

I didn't like to read from the knife-scarred book in my bedroom. The two things seemed too distant from one another. Within my grandiose chamber, I had my goose-down bed, my dresser with its growing array of glamours, the walk-in closet with more tunics, skirts, breeches, pants, doublets, dresses, coats, dining coats, prayer robes, formal robes, and socks than one person should ever really need, the ever-laid fire, the silvered looking glass and Midnight hidden on hooks beneath the bed frame. The book didn't belong here, and it slept hidden beneath the floorboards. These were the things of Apprentice Draoihn Raine LacNaithe. The book belonged to another girl, Raine Wildrose of Dunan, the girl I had been and would always be somewhere in all these frills and frippery. They wore different faces, but they were both real. The book was just for one of them.

Liara's room was past mine along the corridor, Gelis's was just before. They had both come running when they heard me screaming to begin with. Somehow the dark things got inside me, invaded me during the night where I couldn't keep track of them and chase them away with resolve. I remembered things, but they were never as they'd been. Sometimes it was Lochlan I saw, and sometimes his ghost, his big trusting eyes. We hadn't been dissimilar in age even when he died, less than a year ago. I felt a thousand years older than he would ever be. Sometimes it was Sister Marthella, hanged by the neck until she was dead. Other times it was the watchman, sitting alone in the night on a crate at the entry to the undercity. I'd put an arrow through him, and then I'd finished him with Esher's sword. He'd been so ordinary. I couldn't remember him accurately in my dreams. He was just the idea of a person, faceless, a nobody blending into the dark. Others were less common: the two men I'd shot dead in the woods, the cult of Those Who See burning in the dark, but never Kaldhoone LacShale. I don't know why. Sometimes I simply dreamed of corpses.

They weren't dead in the dreams. Sometimes they were ghosts, but they were still there to walk and talk. I would always be doing some mundane task with them. Drawing well water, baking bread, shoeing a horse. And then I would remember they were dead and the smell would hit me. It is hard to dream a smell, but I did it. And then I woke screaming.

Liara and Gelis didn't come running anymore. I must have woken them sometimes, but I was bad company in the middle of the night, sweat-drenched and panting hard. I knew it was no end solution for the dreams, but rose-thistle fought them back. Sometimes I didn't sleep until the dawn was already warming the horizon, the acrid poison taste ever at the back of my nose. By the time I was ready to sleep my body insisted on collapse and put me down. It didn't stop the dreams, it just meant I had less time for them. Every week I needed more for the same effect. My line of credit had grown heavy with it.

On the road to Gilmundy, nobody had mentioned my night-terrors. We'd found inns to stay at, or lodged as guests with the wealthy, but their rooms were never far enough from mine that my friends couldn't have been woken many times. But the road had been good for me and the dreams had plagued me less often. It wasn't every single night. Sometimes there was just nothing, and that was the greatest of pleasures.

More time awake through the night was more time with the Ashtai Grimoire. The summer nights weren't so cold down in Harranir as they were in the High Pastures, but I still wore a fox-fur ruff around my neck to ward off the cold. Keep your neck warm and it tricks the rest of the body—you learn that early in the north. I could sit up atop the meditation tower for hours without anybody knowing I was there. I delved into the secrets it held, at once horrified, disgusted and intrigued. Sometimes I wondered who had tried to attack the book with so feeble a thing as a knife. Had they delved as I did, and become afraid of what they saw? Had they lashed out in rage against it? I had encountered an impervious book before. Perhaps someone had tried to destroy it and failed.

After Gilmundy, I knew I'd already delved too greedily, and too deep. I'd started into a great dark space, the walls slick and untouchable, and it tugged on me, bidding me come further in. The tunnel didn't lead to a happy ending.

There had to be a way to cut myself off from this power. Some of the dead were dangerous, and some of them knew that I was a source of life for them, just as they were a source of power to me. Once I thought I was getting close, when I read that power could be transferred from the bones of one to another, but the book described Unthayla the Damned drawing power to herself, not giving it away, another dead end. If there was an incantation that could hide me from the dead, or that could keep them from me, I was yet to see it. Those things I had tried to decipher were far, far too complex, strange words and geometric designs were required, an alignment of stars I didn't grasp, not to mention the ritual ingredients. I resigned myself that I had seen the dead for as long as I could remember, and they weren't going to go away.

'Is that what you'd really want?' the Queen of Feathers asked me that night. 'To lose it all, when you've already come this far?'

'I've gone too far already,' I told her.

'You're unlocking it, piece by piece,' she told me, and she sounded pleased. It was like that with her sometimes.

The Queen of Feathers didn't always join me, and I couldn't remember the first time I'd delved into the twisting pages, but she'd been there the first time. I could feel her sometimes, behind me, silent, watching over me as I descended into the secrets of the past. She didn't speak to interrupt me while I read, but I knew she was there all the same. I felt her that night. I hadn't known it before, the sensing of things such as she, but since I'd torn the tunnel open before me, somehow I knew.

I didn't know how to open the Sixth Gate, to trance into it as I did Eio. Each time I closed the book I told myself that tomorrow I would find the solution, the one that would drive away the spirit world. But when I opened it again the next day, I read with fascination about the eyeless dead, about spirit locks and binding, about shadow faces and all the dark spells the Sarathi had worked as they'd helped Hallenae conquer half the world. They had been Draoihn who broke beyond the Sixth Gate, corrupt and evil, wielding power as lieutenants and generals. And I read about her, Hallenae, as well. The Riven Queen, the great terror whose rise ended the Yanni Dominion and began the Riven Age, and whose defeat at Solemn Hill marked the end of her age and the beginning of another. Some of the book's authors had admired her. Loved her, even. I read about Unthayla, a Sarathi who had severed her own soul from her body and hidden it before trying to take the Crowns for herself. She nearly succeeded.

It is a bitter thing to understand that you are rotten at your very core. I hadn't been born this way, the tumbling leaves of fate had made me what I was. Desperation guided my fingers to turn page after page. I needed to know that they weren't all twisted, evil things, because if they were, then that meant that I was too. I hadn't asked for this. I hadn't wanted any of it. If such wickedness was preordained then I was already lost and nothing would make any difference. But if I could learn these things—not to use them, just to learn them, know them, feel them—then I would know that corruption was a choice. I could isolate that darkness from myself, and I could still be me.

And yet more than once, those we called Sarathi, the treacherous Drao-ihn of the Sixth Gate, had attempted to take the power of the Crown for themselves. Before the Crown's construction, they had served Hallenae the Riven Queen in a war she had come so, so close to winning. A blind child named Maldouen turned the Sarathi against her at the very end, and he re-paired the tears she had made in the world and banished the things of dark-ness back where they belonged, locked in the nether realm by the power of his Crowns.

There is a part of every person that tells them that they are different. That they will somehow succeed where others failed. We have to believe it, or we're merely raindrops running down a window, set on a course that cannot be avoided.

Every time I closed it I told myself I was still just looking for a way to escape the curse that lay upon me.

Every single time.

·   ·   ·   ·   ·   ·

I had forced myself to grow accustomed to Grandmaster Robilar. She was seldom seen around Redwinter's grounds, keeping to the quiet of her own greathouse, requiring those that did her bidding to come to her. She left only on rare matters of state, and I had never seen her in the bath house, or taking a quiet turn around the gardens. There was a power in that, I thought. Everybody knows who she is, but few have access to her. By keep-ing a distance she became half myth, although she was fairly mythical in actuality. So despite trying to make myself feel like knowing she was within Redwinter's walls was normal—*ordinary*, even—being summoned to see her was still like being told that a dragon wanted to take tea with you. Ro-bilar scared me more than any dragon could have, though. I was totally confident that dragons weren't real, which was fifty percent more than I could have said about the grandmaster.

A servant brought me to her. There was a strategy in requiring everyone else to come to you; it gave them the walk, occupied more of their time, and it forced them to look at all the things you'd lined up for them along the way. I waited in a hallway hung with vast paintings. There were the usual religious scenes, Our Lady of Fire scouring the unrighteous down into the freezing rivers of Skuttis, and the blind child, Maldouen, defeating the Riven Queen at the Battle of Solemn Hill. There was a portrait of a slender man with a short beard, wearing a cap with a pair of pheasant tail feathers thrust through it. There was something about the way he'd been portrayed, his eyes so dark in such an ordinary face that it made me shiver. But despite the artistry of the oils and the great scope of the canvases, it was a smaller portrait that caught my eye. Smaller than the huge, wall-covering pictures anyway, but still a good eight feet wide. Two figures stood atop a windy moor. One of them was a young, dark haired Robilar, perhaps twenty-five, wearing a kilt and a sleeveless jerkin of outdated design, with a falcon perched on one hand. She was athletic, pretty. But there were significant differences. Her nose showed a slight kink; her hair was sleek but fine and flat. Somehow, I recognised more of Robilar in her crone's guise than I did of her in the bouncy-haired form she more often displayed. There was a hardness to her, as though even at that young age she'd been possessed with utter determination and authority. But the fair-haired woman in the portrait was no less cut from hard, glassy lines. I didn't see a family resemblance in their features, but the expressions were matched. The artist had depicted her with an oxblood-red coat slung over her shoulders and what at first I thought was a fur ruff, but was in fact a stoat curled around her neck.

'My sister and me,' Robilar said from behind me. I jumped at the sound. 'Atop Hennock Tor. We stood for that portrait for nearly four days.' I was nervous to turn around, but it was just the youthful version of her, late twenties, a light summer dress.

'Your sister was Draoihn too,' I said.

'She was. One of the strongest.'

Robilar admitted me into a comfortable parlour where taxidermy animals fought for space around the walls and bade me sit.

'You had pets?' It didn't seem like her at all to want an animal's companionship.

'Familiars,' Robilar said. 'They were outlawed shortly after that was painted. I enjoyed my falcon, but there's too much danger in giving that much of yourself over to something else.'

'What was your sister's name?' I asked.

'Alianna,' Robilar said.

'And the man there. The man with the feathers in his cap,' I said. 'Who was that?'

Robilar made a grunt, part laugh, part scorn.

'He's the one who broke my head open. The Remnant Sul.'

'He looks so ordinary.'

'The greatest of our enemies often do. The ones who stand out are more easily dealt with.'

'Why keep a portrait of him?'

'Not every piece of art must speak of glory. He was an enemy of a different time, and it serves me well to remember in my power that all can be toppled. Speaking of which, let us cut to the matter at hand. Give me your account of Gilmundy.'

I knew that Ulovar had already told her everything, but I'd still expected to be summoned. I told her what I could, and truthfully. She'd had two centuries of practice to figure out when someone was lying to her.

'What did you make of LacAud?'

'Clever,' I said. 'Dangerous. More confidence than he should have.'

'Does he desire the Crown for himself?'

'I don't know. I don't think so.'

'I watched that man grow from a child into the man he is today,' Robilar said. 'He is paranoid. Bold. A good war leader, and not without vigour. But try not to hate too hard. LacAud will make peace, and then we must all be friends and sit around a table together.'

'After what he did?' I said. My hands turned to fists.

'Do not be simple, Apprentice Raine,' Robilar said firmly. 'Clans have warred with one another and chafed at each other's borders since before they knew what borders were. Land disputes are the bedrock on which every nation grows.'

'But Colban died,' I said.

'People die all the time,' Robilar said, and I heard my own words echoing back at me. I heard their ugliness, not without shame. 'Guilty and innocent both.'

'Maybe I'm wrong,' I said. 'Maybe he does want the Crown.' I said it because I wanted her to feel the anger I felt. Wanted her to see LacAud's betrayal, his murder of Colban Giln, as darkly as I did. I wanted her to turn her retribution against him. If anyone could kill Onostus LacAud, it was her. But Robilar had dealt with girls like me for many normal lifetimes. My anger breezed past her like blown seeds.

'For himself? No. Onostus is many things, but he knows that no Draoihn can ever hold the Crown. To do so would be to invite catastrophe into the world. But for one of his Gateless children, perhaps? It is to be expected. King Quinlan is not long for the world now. When the succession comes, every great clan will select a candidate and grasp at the kingship. The Crown does not want to be controlled. Many who try to bear its weight perish, or are driven mad.'

'Why would anyone accept it?' I asked. Robilar smiled.

'Someone must. If the Crown goes uncontrolled, the Fault that separates us from the Night Below will collapse. The Riven Queen and the Faded Lords who fought beside her unleashed such magic that they weakened the Fault, allowing terrible things to cross over. The world itself became unstable. Without the binding power of the Crown, unspeakable horrors would emerge. You have only glimpsed the least of those nightmares, Raine. The succession ensures that only the most powerful can take it, so that its preservation is absolutely, utterly understood by our highest powers. King Quinlan has borne it far longer than most, but memories are short.'

I had been born to a mountain clan, far, far away from the noise and the politicking of the capital. Ulovar supported Clan LacDaine, and King Quinlan's heir, Prince Caelan. LacDaine was not the mightiest of clans, but Ulovar valued their character, their stoicism, and ultimately, their sense of duty. He didn't need to seat a king on the throne to feel he had done his, and so when the votes were cast in parliament, Caelan would be the first to attempt the succession.

'If Arrowhead wanted to push his own clan's candidacy, then striking at us doesn't make sense. He can't muster enough votes to win parliament alone.'

'Indeed,' Robilar said. 'LacAud vote for LacAud, LacClune vote for Lac-Clune, and LacNaithe will vote for Prince Caelan. Between LacNaithe and LacDaine, they will win. Lacking the strength to destroy them, Onostus LacAud can only have a real chance if he can garner support from another great clan. So why attack both LacClune and LacNaithe?'

I wasn't sure whether I was being asked for an opinion. Robilar paused long enough with one eyebrow arching like a bridge for me to decide that I was.

'Weakening the other clans would strengthen his candidate, surely?'

'It would—except clearly, had he been successful the most likely course would be for LacNaithe and LacClune to put aside their differences to ensure that LacAud fails. Ovitus LacNaithe is not the iron-soul that his uncle is, so Merovech LacClune would dominate their alliance, which is the worst outcome LacAud could imagine. Merovech LacClune hasn't half the honour in your master's thumbnail.'

'Then I don't understand it,' I said. Robilar's lips tweaked a smile.

'Neither do I. That's what makes this all rather fascinating. I am looking forward to LacAud's arrival.'

'His arrival?'

'Following such a spectacle he can hardly fail to show up to discuss matters. He will come alone, I expect. He has woven such charms around him that he fears nobody, and of course I am obligated to remain impartial in these matters.'

'You could kill him,' I said. 'You have more Gates than he does.'

'Blades will not cut him, arrows will not pierce him,' Robilar said. 'I have wondered from time to time whether he has proofed himself against poison as well. It is a paradox, is it not? The more things he makes himself immune to, the more interested I am in testing out the ones I don't know.'

'But you wouldn't,' I said. 'You're impartial.'

'I am impartial,' the grandmaster said and I felt spiders climbing across my entire body. 'Now tell me how your studies are progressing.'

*   *   *   *   *   *

It was time to say goodbye to a fallen comrade.

A service was held for Colban in the cemetery yard outside the church. There was no body to bury, and it was unlikely that it would ever be recovered. Many of the apprentices came, and those retainers from Ulovar's household who had known him. Ulovar clearly wanted to lead it, but after saying a few words of praise for Colban's bravery and diligence to his studies, he accepted a chair and sat heavily.

Sanvaunt took over. He looked none the worse for his brush with fire, having miraculously escaped without so much as a burn. He had begun trying to grow in a beard on the road, but like many men in their twenties, it was more a dark haze of stubble than real facial hair. I liked it on him nonetheless. He'd dressed up in full battle regalia, a mail hauberk with steel plates harnessed across his shoulders and a rich cloak in green and black. His hair was a mane of thick, dark curls around his handsome face.

'Colban Giln came to us seven years ago,' Sanvaunt said, casting his voice loud. 'He was the son of tin miners, and he spoke often of the sisters he'd left behind when he joined us. He was good with words. Good with a pen. He was nineteen years old when he fell, serving his clan, serving the Crown, and doing his duty to Harran. He will be missed by all that knew him.'

They were good words, and there were tears. Apprentice Gelis had been closest with him, and her eyes were red and raw through the ceremony. Since there was nothing to bury, she'd selected some of the personal possessions he treasured most, and they were buried in a small hole in the ground. Some of the others took turns offering stories of time they'd spent together. I hadn't been close to him, but when it was my turn, something was expected. I occupied a strange position among Redwinter's community. Everyone knew who I was, after I'd bounced a head across the court-room floor last winter. Sanvaunt nodded to me and gave me a smile of encouragement. I had nothing prepared. I took a deep breath and stepped out in front of everyone.

'On the way to Gilmundy, Colban told me he was looking forward to his Testing,' I said. 'It seems unfair that he trained all this time and won't get to try.'

Expectant faces all pointed in my direction. I was supposed to have a point to make. Was supposed to say something profound, maybe that meant there was peace to be had from some form of poetic justice. But there wasn't. The real world doesn't make sense the way that stories do. Not everything means something, and there's nothing fair about who lives and who dies. They still needed me to say something, so I dragged in a long breath as though I was feeling deeply emotional, which I wasn't.

'The Crown matters,' I said. 'All else is dust.'

It was the mantra the Draoihn lived by, but it didn't seem very comforting in this situation. Esher gave me a pained look.

'What I mean to say,' I went on, 'is not that Colban didn't matter. I mean that we were doing the Crown's work, and he gave his life to bring peace to the land.' We hadn't. 'He gave his life to defend justice.' He had been murdered. 'He was Draoihn.' He hadn't been Tested, so that wasn't true either. Despite the blatancy of my exaggeration, that all seemed like I'd been saying the right sort of thing. It was tiring to have to feign all that emotion, tiring and pettily annoying that I'd had to participate. Nobody had held a ceremony for Lochlan, or the sooth-sisters, or any of their dumb followers. I raised a fist. 'Let's all try to live more like Colban did.'

Everyone seemed pleased, or at least seemed to feel like I'd said enough of the right things to be able to merge back into the crowd. Esher lowered her eyebrows at me as she stepped past as if to say 'Come on, that was rubbish.' She was going to take a turn though. She'd dressed up pretty for the occasion.

'Colban once told me that he liked me in this dress,' she said. It was a beautiful dress, sky-blue with bands of gold running over the seams. 'He told me he'd like to see me out of it as well, but only because Jathan made him.' She smiled, and she laughed, and despite how absurdly inappropriate that was, it raised smiles and a handful of lives. 'But that was Colban, wasn't it? He didn't mean anything by it, he just said things like that. Dumb things. I don't want to make out like he was some great hero,' she said. 'He was just one of us. One of us training to be apprentices, one of us who lived in the house, one of us who breathed the same air, ate the same food, walked the same paths and heard the same snatterkin on his way up the mountain.'

Esher faltered for a moment, closing her eyes and raising her brows as she regained control. When she opened them, Ulovar gave her a slight nod of fatherly approval. She cleared her throat and continued.

'When we're taught the trances, we're told that everything is one. And that means that he's not really gone, since we're all connected. Maybe it's hard to see it, but he's still with us in spirit. In our hearts. I'll always have my memories of him, and you have yours. So let's remember him tonight, and know he's still here, somewhere in the walls, the ground, and the air. Praise be to the Light Above.'

The prayer was mumbled around the gathering, and that was pretty much it for Colban Giln. It was a quiet send-off for a quiet apprentice. As orderly rows of mourners dissolved into little clumps, I went to make my escape but found Sanvaunt in my path.

He looked absolutely regal, I had to admit. The panoply of war suited him, and I was beset by that excitement that comes over you every time you're in close proximity to someone you want to see naked, like there was a charge in the air.

'Walk with me,' he said, and offered me his arm.

There was always a little thrill for me when he did so. Taking a man's arm is like holding his hand, except it's less showy for everyone else. I didn't need his help to walk, but there was something fun for both of us in pretending. I knew Sanvaunt liked it too.

We walked a way out from everyone else, and I ignored Esher making dumb eyes at me so that I wouldn't start to giggle. We stayed on the gravel paths, away from tall hedges so that nobody could say anything untoward. One might have thought that two seasons on from the events that had brought me to Redwinter, we might have progressed further along the road that sought to connect us, but schedules were difficult and there had been talks of marriage alliances for Sanvaunt. He'd brushed them off so far, or at least Ulovar had, and I'd wondered what would happen when Ulovar finally decided that the deal was good enough. Sanvaunt and I were both wildroses, born out of wedlock, which seemed to matter a good deal more in the south than it did in the northern High Pastures, but a LacNaithe bastard was still a high choice for the young noblewomen of lesser-ranked clans, and that he was Draoihn, and unbearably handsome certainly didn't hurt.

'We need to be extra vigilant right now,' he said, and for a moment I thought he was referring to the spark that lay between us. 'Ulovar is weaker than he looks.'

'Quashing that fire took a lot out of him,' I said.

'It shouldn't have,' Sanvaunt said. 'It should have been easy for him. He's weakened in a way that I don't understand. Like his body is starting to fail him, but his Gates are failing too.'

'I didn't know that could happen,' I said. Sanvaunt shook his head.

'It doesn't.'

The path led us past the LacAud greathouse. Its usual occupants had left Redwinter months ago, forewarned of Onostus LacAud's plans, no doubt.

'You came through it unscathed,' I said. 'I'm glad you weren't hurt.'

'No,' he said. For a moment he wasn't present, I could feel it in the slackening muscle of his arm, but he blinked and came back. 'One moment I was just walking down the hall bringing my uncle a few books from the library and then—I felt like I was choking. Like I'd already breathed smoke. And then the fire just came up. It happened so fast, I can't explain it.'

'The carpet had been cleaned with some kind of flammable chemical,' I said. 'I heard the retainers saying that.'

'Maybe. But short of soaking the whole thing in oil, I don't know what could have done that to it.' He paused. 'I think it came from me.'

That, I had not expected.

'You found the Third Gate?'

'No. It was different. Like the fire just poured out of me.' There was something more there, but he struggled to go on. 'It happened once before. The night we fought the Mawleths.'

On the night that Kaldhoone LacShale tried to drown Ovitus, Sanvaunt and I had fought against a creature of the Night Below, summoned to try to take me out of the equation when I would no longer follow LacShale's script. Sanvaunt had told me to run, and I had. How he had vanquished that terrible corpse-like creature I didn't know—nobody knew, in fact. But I remembered seeing what had been left of his sword, the blade melted and fused as if in a forge.

'But you don't remember what happened.'

'You don't remember how you killed your Mawleth either,' he said. He gave me a smile. Such sleepy-lidded eyes, such a well-aligned jaw.

'And nobody believes either of us.'

'Well, that's just how it has to be,' I said. We both knew that there were secrets, but I was happy for us each to keep our own close. I had always suspected that Sanvaunt could in fact access the Second Gate and the Third as well, and that he'd called on it to destroy the Mawleth. That he chose to keep that secret was his prerogative, though why he'd want to I couldn't fathom. But people get to choose what parts of themselves they share. If he had the Third Gate, he would have used it to stop that fire.

'The flame came that night too,' he said. 'It came without warning. I thought perhaps that it was something you did. I was fighting the Mawleth, and it had me hurt. Badly. I thought I was done. My sword was doing nothing against it. Then there was this ringing sound, like nothing I've ever heard and there was fire all around me. Was—was it something you did?'

'None of it was my doing,' I said. 'I ran a long way off. I couldn't even see you among all those locusts.'

'Are you sure?'

'Positive. There were probably two dozen Draoihn in Redwinter at the time who could have used the Third Gate. They'd come for Ulovar's trial. Maybe one of them helped you.'

Sanvaunt didn't look convinced. His face was hard, and serious.

'It felt like you,' he said. 'I can't explain it any other way. It just felt like it was you and it was me. I've heard the Third Gate enough times to know that wasn't it. But when it happened, it felt like you and me. It's the only way I can describe it.'

I didn't know what I could say to that. I'd been on the far side of Redwinter's grounds, running for my life and heading to the Blackwell, or maybe I'd been inside the Blackwell, depending how long Sanvaunt had been able to hold his ground for. Maybe it wasn't very healthy to have found him fighting that thing so attractive, or that I got the tingle thinking about how he'd told me to run off like one of the damsels in distress he wrote about when he thought nobody else was looking, but the Mawleth wasn't the only things his skills set on fire. I struggled a little with that sometimes. My first lover, Braithe, had wanted to control me and I'd allowed it because I thought that it was how I was meant to be. He desired me to dominate me, but with Sanvaunt—how to even express it? When I thought about him alone in my room with my fingers working beneath the covers, I wanted him to take me, roughly and forcefully, but only with him knowing that I wanted to be taken, to see him desire me so much that he just forgot the rest of it for once. To let him have me as I was, to discard all the propriety and circumstance and status and let us just be bodies. It was just make believe. Maybe my mind played it that way because it was the last thing that would ever happen.

Honestly, what an absolute mess we all are when you boil us down to the bones.

I saw a narrow alley between two storage buildings and wondered what would happen if I told him to drag me down there and have his way with me. I cleared my throat instead.

'It was a strange night,' I said instead. 'Will it happen again?'

'I don't know. But it wasn't you?'

'No,' I said. 'I wish it was. Then I could tell everyone that I saved you.'

'You saved the clan,' he said.

'At least I let you look heroic,' I said, and he smiled, and it was melting, and alas, that alley was a way back behind us.

'I'm going to keep hold of Ulovar's responsibilities here,' Sanvaunt said. 'He needs rest right now. But I hope that there'll be time for other things too.'

The party he'd invited me to. Ah. Of course I wanted to go with him.

But there was something different about walking quietly through the grounds and going out publicly together that cooled all those alleyway thoughts. It was so public. It would mean being seen, and spoken about, and everyone's preconceptions and judgements. After I'd learned about the blatant lie Ovitus had spread about me sleeping with him I'd grown suspicious of the way that people looked at me. Those closest to me knew that it had been untrue, but I knew there would always be those who would continue to believe I was a social climber. A slut who bedded men for position. I felt no shame about going to bed with someone if I wanted to, but that was my business and nobody else's. I saw people undressing me with their eyes. Sensed the old men thinking, *'Can't really blame him for taking her for a tumble, can you?'* The violation of it was like creeping poison on my skin.

I steered the conversation away, and we spoke of the events up at Gilmundy, once again sticking to those that were safe to share.

'Can you do something for me?' Sanvaunt asked.

'Probably.'

'Try to get a sense from LacClune as to how their people here have received news of Gilmundy. Ulovar wants to know what their response is likely to be before he has to address parliament tomorrow.'

'Castus doesn't take all that much interest in affairs of state,' I said. Sanvaunt quirked an eyebrow at me.

'That's what he likes everyone to think, but I've known him a long time. He's smarter than he lets on.'

'I didn't say he wasn't smart.'

'He's a burning haystack of resentment despite being one of the most powerful men in Harran, but one day Clan LacClune will be his. I'd say we should dread that day, but the rest of his clan are generally worse.'

Sanvaunt was disapproving of Castus, as he always was, and I was still disapproving of Castus as well so that was easy enough.

'I thought befriending him was disapproved of,' I said.

'Situations like this are precisely why Ulovar doesn't mention it,' Sanvaunt said. 'Truth be told it would be good for all concerned if LacNaithe's next generation were on better terms with LacClune. Ovitus scuffed that badly, but the Crown is best served when we all work together. Ovitus will return from Brannlant soon, which will only make things harder.' Sanvaunt didn't need to mention that Ovitus and I had not been on good terms when he left.

'There's always something to look forward to even during a crisis,' I said sourly.

'I don't need to mention that he's going to be van of Clan LacNaithe one day, do I?' Sanvaunt said.

'No more than I need to remember it,' I said.

We didn't speak for a little time, and I wasn't sure if the silence made me feel closer to him, or whether it was uncomfortable, but he was working up to saying something. The longer he took the funnier it became, until he could see the quirk at the edges of my mouth, holding back a smile.

'Just spit it out,' I said eventually.

'It's nothing really,' he said. 'I mentioned there was going to be a social gathering. There's a poet up from Murr, an orator really. She's going to be performing at Thail Cullada's townhouse, and there'll be drinks, and probably a band and some dancing. I thought you might like to go. To see some culture, get out for once.'

'I get out plenty,' I said.

'Excursions with Castus are hardly culture,' he said, then realised that he'd criticised me. I didn't really mind, even if it sounded a bit superior. It seemed a long time since he'd asked me to walk out with him and I hadn't given him a straight answer. Maybe it rankled at him that I'd spent so many evenings with Castus. Maybe I liked the idea.

'You aren't wrong,' I said. 'I don't know anything about poetry.'

'I don't think you have to know all about something to enjoy it,' he said. 'Will you be my guest?'

'I'll have to see how things pan out,' I said, but I smiled at him so he'd know I meant yes.

'You let me know,' he said, as if he was asking nothing instead of something huge.

Our circuit had come to an end, leaving us back at the greathouse. I let go of his arm, but my fingers remembered its warmth for hours after.

I knew where the heir to Clan LacClune would be. There weren't that many options.

I found Castus in the gaming den, a smoky, badly lit hall near Harranir's ironworking district. His doublet was darkened beneath the armpits, but he didn't seem to notice his own dripping sweat as he stood beside a roped-off, straw-strewn area in which a pair of heavy-bodied men were thumping the hell out of each other. The humidity was thick, aggressive, body heat stacking atop summer's glare, the air damp with perspiration and heavy with regret and lost wages.

'You have a bet on?' I asked, shoving in beside him. Castus stared at the fight blankly as he always did in this place. One of the men belted the other in the face, eliciting a cheer from the crowd. Castus's expression didn't change. He swilled some terrible, watered-down vintage in a smudge-covered glass.

'On one of them,' he said.

'Which one?'

'I don't remember.'

There are few places sadder than a place where men come to lose money over other men fighting for their entertainment, but Castus managed to make it an even more morose experience. He came here and drank alone, or joined one of the wild parties in the back—I had only walked into that lavishly furnished back room to see what people were getting up to the one time, and one look had been enough. The parties didn't seem to give him any more pleasure than the drink.

He was a little drunk, but only a little. He offered me the bottle of wine. I took a cup and found it to be better than expected. Castus got very upset with bad wine.

'What's the point if you don't remember?'

Castus shrugged. He was good at presenting a face. That self-assured smile, the cocky strut in his walk, the way that everything seemed wryly amusing to him. Those were all there, cast in yellow and shadow by the smoky light of the lamps, but there was something more to him that night. Or something less. Perhaps it was just the way he huddled as if the noisy den was filled with bone-biting cold rather than a throat-clenching heat, or maybe the shadows caught longer in the hard lines of his cheekbones, but something was different.

'Well,' I said, feeling that uncertainty that comes with knowing something isn't quite right but not knowing how to talk about it. 'I got sent to find out what LacClune are going to do next. Want to share?'

'Still waiting to hear what my father thinks,' he said. 'If he thinks anything of it at all. Figured I'd just watch some men get bloody and lose some money.'

'You don't seem to be finding it all that interesting,' I said.

'It isn't,' Castus said. One of the boxers had the other in a chancery grip and was ramming his fist into chin and nose, but both men were tired and the blows lacked force. It probably wasn't their first bout of the day.

'You came here to be alone,' I said. 'Want me to go?'

'No,' he said quietly. 'I'm glad you're here.' He reached out and put his hand over mine. He had big hands, long fingers.

'Are you sure?'

'I'm tired of being alone,' he said.

'Sometimes I feel that living in this place there's never time to be alone at all,' I said. 'You have more friends than I've had bruises from Master Torgan.'

'They aren't my friends,' Castus said. 'Not really. We go and we drink, and we talk through the operas, and they come and drink my father's wine in the greathouse. But they don't know me, do they? They don't know anything about me.'

'What's there to know?' I said. I smiled to try to siphon some of the melancholy out of his spirit. 'You're a cocksure overachiever with erratic taste. I'm pretty sure they know the gist.'

'That's what they see,' he said. 'They don't see what I really am. What this place has made me. What it's made of us.'

The boxer who was getting pummelled went down to his knees, and the victor backed up, surrounded by the usual cheers from those who'd backed him, and muttering from those that hadn't. Boys and girls came forward to sweep the straw back into place. The winner helped the loser to his feet, and half carried him off to the benches.

'What do you mean?'

'People are dead, Raine,' he said. 'Colban was right there in front of me, and I didn't stop them. He should have saved himself. It wasn't my responsibility. But whatever I do, people keep on getting killed.'

It was a surprising turn of face for Castus. I'd once seen him stab a growling drunk with less remorse than most people felt when squashing a spider. On the road he'd seemed so glib about it all.

'You're not to blame for that.'

'Aren't I? If I hadn't taken him off into the town, maybe it wouldn't have happened.'

'That ambush had been planned before the sun even rose,' I said. 'You know that. The grandmaster, the council, they all know it, I'm sure.'

'I won't mourn those people who deserve to die,' Castus said sadly. 'But not everyone does. I'm tired of my choices leading to people dying on my behalf. I'm tired that it doesn't matter if I feck it all up, everyone just goes on treating me the same.'

'You act like you don't care at all,' I said.

'Isn't that what everyone expects?' he said. He swirled the wine around in his cup, but its rich flavour had lost its appeal for him. 'It's like the idea of me matters more than who I am, or even what I do. But they don't care about us. Not really.'

'Ulovar cares,' I said, and felt a twinge of sadness, like I was remembering a glorious summer now that we were entering winter. 'He's not as stony as he seems.'

'And what about you?' Castus asked. 'Do you care?'

'I ended Kaldhoone LacShale and his plot. I ended Ciuthach, with a bit of help. I might only be an apprentice, but I won't forget what Arrowhead tried to do to us. He'll die screaming, and it's his head I'll bounce across the flagstones next.'

It was a bold claim, and one that I was in no position to make, even without Arrowhead's plethora of wards and charms. Castus allowed himself enough smirk to laugh it off. But I meant it.

'I don't need vengeance,' Castus said. 'I just want someone to know me. I had someone once, a friend so good we were closer than brothers. I loved him. But he's gone now. I miss him. I miss him so, so much, and the worst part? He wouldn't have liked me, not now. Would have thought me vain, and selfish, and cruel.' His words seemed to catch on his teeth, and then the sentiment seemed to draw back into him, as if he'd released a breath he hadn't wanted to share and sought to claim it back. 'Do you know what the last thing my father said to me was, the day he headed back to his estate? "Send word when you get around to putting an heir in someone."'

'If you do, you probably should.'

'That's not the point,' Castus snapped. 'I don't make it much of a secret that I don't turn my sheets that way. It's out there for everyone to see, and it's still like being invisible. I'm just tired of everyone else pretending that I'm whatever suits their goals the most.'

He drew his hand back. Rubbed at eyes grown strained in the weak, pastel-blue light of the cadanum lamps, dried by the heat.

'I understand,' I said.

'You think you do?'

'It's not just boys I like,' I said, letting it sigh out of me like a breath held too long. I regretted it immediately. Castus looked up from beneath a fringe of pale hair, a slight crook to his lip, a hook to his brow. That cocksure smile, lighting up his face. The mask returned. He wanted to be seen but maybe he'd worn this face so long he'd forgotten he didn't need it.

'Do you now?' he asked. I blew out my cheeks and poured myself wine. Mistake, or liberation, or both at the same time. I didn't know. But now that the brick had been pulled free, water began to pulse through the dam.

'Maybe. I don't know. It's confusing,' I said. The words came out of me like I was shaking an open box, letting my unseen bric-a-brac tumble onto the table in front of us. 'I don't know what I think. Most of the time, in fact.'

'It's Esher, isn't it?' he said. For a moment I felt all of the muscles in my face collapse, muscle and skin hanging loose on the bone.

'I didn't say that.'

'Coyness is deeply boring,' he said. And just like that, his face locked into that self-assured blankness, the one that only distributed needling mockery, overconfidence and glib remarks. 'Tell me everything. Don't skip a detail.'

'There's nothing to tell,' I said, and ventured nothing more.

The next fighters were getting warmed up. They didn't have the look of the professionals—their ears and noses were in too good a condition. They were northern boys, driven down south by famine and disease. They weren't waifs, or gentle, they were working men, and I was sure they'd done their share of scrapping—who hadn't? But I doubted this was the work they'd expected to find on southern streets. A city is like a wildfire. It burns everything inside it, devouring, and the smallest are always the first to catch light.

'I kissed her once. Esher.'

My stomach fell down into my shoes.

'You what?'

'Oh, don't look at me like I've kicked your puppy down the stairs. We must have been thirteen or fourteen, it was years ago now. I hadn't figured out that she lacked the requisite equipment to get my cart moving, and the reverse may well have been true. That isn't how I knew, though.'

'Then how?' Four, five years ago—I still felt a hot ingot of jealousy sizzle within my chest. It wasn't just that he'd kissed Esher. It meant nothing to him, just a toe dipped in water that hadn't been to his liking. He'd had something I wanted, and to him it meant nothing. Nothing at all.

'I didn't always know myself the way I do now, Raine,' he said easily. 'You think I haven't got to know women? I've known a *lot* of women.'

And that annoyed me too. I'd only had one lover, and he'd been a terrible piece of shit, and Castus had been with a bunch of women, and he didn't even like them. It seemed a terrible injustice in the world for our scales to have been so poorly balanced, a reminder that while he was the son of Van Merovech LacClune, heir to vast lands and fortune, I'd been traipsing the north under a threadbare shawl, stuffing my shoes with hay to keep my feet warm in winter, gone late to the market when the traders got down to the bottom of their apple barrels so I could buy the squashed fruit at a discount, and also that he'd kissed Esher and I hadn't, and that just seemed like the most grotesque unfairness imaginable. Was there anything, anything at all, that he hadn't had first?

The bookies began making the rounds, handing out coloured wooden chits in exchange for real money. There were northerners in the crowd as well, people who'd decided to take a risk with the last of their money in the hopes of doubling through and making enough to keep their families in beds and soup. I knew, deep down, that all of them would be on the street come winter.

'I thought it was Sanvaunt that you liked?' he said, cutting into the growing silence.

'I suppose you've had him as well, have you?' It was the lengthening, deepening silence that told me that the edge I'd flashed had not just missed its mark, but made everything so much worse for myself. 'Light Above,' I said, not just hurt but angry now. 'Oh, come on. *Really?*'

'Calm your cheeks down. It was years ago, and I'm pretty sure he was just trying things out.' Castus shrugged.

'But he likes *men?*'

'No, I can say with some confidence that he's straight as a board. But even the straightest boards can be flexible in the right season. Honestly, we were just kids and it meant less to either of us then than it apparently does to you now.'

'It's just annoying to think you've . . . done things with him. With both of them. And it's even more annoying that it means nothing to you.'

Castus wrinkled his nose at me.

'I can understand that. But you're new here and the rest of us have been living here for years. We've grown up together and there aren't that many young people up in Redwinter to begin with. It would be weirder if there wasn't some incestuous spit-swapping from time to time. What did you think, that everyone was a virgin? I never took you for judgemental. Crazy, and dangerous, and cold as a prick in winter, but judging people for having tried a kiss or two when we were just kids? Come on. That's not you.'

It all made sense. He was right, and I was being stupid and nothing he said indicated that he'd done anything wrong. If I told Sanvaunt all about Braithe, would I expect him to turn quiet and start spitting venomous little thorns at me? There were some old folk who believed the Light Above frowned on sexual practices out of wedlock, but with Linny Seed tea so widely available it was a belief that had fallen out of fashion even before my mother's time. So the truth of the matter was, I was just jealous. It didn't even make sense to be jealous over two people at once, especially when I'd never done anything with either of them and ah, by the freezing rivers of Skuttis my head felt like it was getting so full of nonsense thoughts and powerful, directionless emotion that I wanted to crumple into a ball, like so much torn-up paper.

'Are you going to parliament tomorrow?' I asked, suddenly feeling a need to change the subject. Castus reached for the wine and refilled his own cup.

'Maybe. Uncle Haronus will make all the decisions. What could I add?'

'You could speak on Colban's behalf.'

'And where would that lead?' Castus asked. 'To war with LacAud? More bodies on the pile for the sake of my name?'

'There are already bodies on the pile,' I said. 'Take some responsibility. People are relying on you.'

'They keep on doing that,' he said. 'And they keep on ending up dead.'

The fight started. Everyone seemed to be losing.

9

Parliament made its usual parliamentary noises, the ineffective bleating of sheep that had somehow avoided the slaughter and were too old to produce anything but turds. Venerable lords of lesser clans denounced LacAud's claim on Gilmundy in the strongest possible terms without criticising Van LacAud himself, and declared their utmost support without giving any actual guarantee of money, warriors or action to come. More information was needed, more people had to be consulted, Onostus LacAud's arguments had to be given the consideration due to a venerable van of such station. It would be winter before anything was sorted out, at which time the weather would lock everyone into their homes, and men could sharpen their swords beside the fire while hoping that everything would have blown over by spring. The world seemed to be on fire; I had never known the sun so angry. Winter's cold fingers seemed a faraway caress.

I wanted to make a plan. I wanted to go north again, but this time with spears and Draoihn and all the things that would undo the humiliation that being forced to run had brought down with it. But whatever fame I'd earned doing my little murders, I was no war leader, and for now I had to be a good little Draoihn apprentice. We all thought of the Winterra as the fate to avoid, but as I seethed for Colban, and all of us, I began to wonder whether war was in my blood after all.

On yet another burning morning I made it out of bed with only a few minutes to spare, throwing on the thick, starched grey robe, whose hood would hide the hollows of exhaustion beneath my eyes. Participation was expected of every apprentice, but I hated wasting time every day singing praises to the Light Above, which I was pretty sure didn't care about us one way or another. And yet, there was a sense of calm in the routine. When I was part of those pointless rituals and their daily observances, when I dressed like the Draoihn and joined their number, I felt that I was part of something, maybe for the first time in my life. Mama had run me around the highlands, never managing to stay one place long enough to lay down roots, and I'd run from her into the sooth-sisters' cult, where I'd never belonged either. Redwinter was home now, and it's a fool who treats their home without respect.

Esher, tall and golden, greeted me with a yelp of excitement, a sisterly hug and a kiss to the side of my head. The panic that had threatened to overwhelm her on the night of the fire had been interred somewhere for now, and she shone as brightly as ever, but I knew that the dark thread of self-doubt still lay under her skin. Liara followed a few steps behind her, sober and looking serious. In our flight from Gilmundy we'd grown closer again, but her father's death at my hand would always exist between us, like a stone beneath the mattress, a lump in what had been a growing friendship. It didn't matter that he'd been a traitor, that he'd tried to kill me too. Not everything makes sense.

'Life didn't feel right while you were both gone,' Esher said. The three of us linked arms, as friends will in their first years of school. Liara walked three steps to our two, being much shorter than the Tall Girls.

'Am I under arrest?' I said, thoroughly outflanked.

'Yes,' Esher said. 'For your own good, so you don't go running off again. I miss you too much when you're not here.'

'I'm glad we're back safe. All that running, I felt we'd never stop,' Liara said. Whatever her thoughts about her father, she hid them well. She had to. It couldn't have been easy to grieve her father a second time, and unable to do it publicly. Tears for a traitor—and a dangerous, murderous traitor at that—would have been problematic.

'Well, I have you both back now,' Esher said brightly. 'I intend to keep you here from now on. The place just isn't the same when I'm on my own.' Her smile was a dazzling flash of straight teeth. She'd applied her glamours before leaving the greathouse, something she did every morning without fail. Nobody ever saw Esher of Harranir without her warpaint. I'd heard some of the other apprentices making fun of her behind her back over it, but it's a short drop from admiration to jealousy. Liara rarely bothered with glamours, if at all, but she radiated a different kind of confidence.

'It seems quiet,' I said. 'The greathouse feels half empty.'

'Ulovar takes up half the space, and Ovitus the rest,' Esher said. 'Whatever business called him down to Brannlant, he's taking up space somewhere else.'

Esher was not good at hiding the residual anger she felt on my behalf.

Ovitus's lies still rankled, but holding on to that kind of grudge felt like taking poison and expecting someone else to die. For Esher, the poison was worth it. I knew she didn't trust her tongue when he was near. But Ovitus had been gone from the greathouse for five whole months. He'd made some noise about having important business with important people and then just up and vanished away. It was a tactical manoeuvre on his uncle's part, I thought. After his lies about me had been discovered, the air had turned uncomfortable around him. Since he was destined to lead the clan, nobody could speak his shame aloud, but that didn't mean he hadn't felt it in their eyes.

I knew I should let it go. I didn't want the poison. But perhaps Esher was just the one who was being honest.

Ovitus hadn't apologised to me as I thought he would. Maybe he felt that dragging me out of the undercity as parts of it collapsed made us even. It didn't. It counted for something, no doubt about that, but he had work to do if he wanted my respect again. The sting of his deception still hung from my eaves like a bat. Eight months had dulled the impact, and people could learn from their mistakes; I had. The whole thing just felt so exhausting, so needless and so petty. I had bigger concerns than someone casting aspersions about my past.

And yet the question always arose in me: when will it happen again?

'He's going to be home soon,' I said, and facing that brought up all those feelings I'd been able to ignore for five months. The huge church rose before us, spires thrusting upwards like candles of irregular length.

'Maybe he's bringing home a Brannish princess,' Liara said.

'More likely it's a troop of priests to tell us why we've been singing the hours the wrong way,' I said. I thought that infinitely more likely.

'Or an entire household of sentient self-loathing,' Esher said. A Draoihn from the LacClune household heard her and smirked at us over his shoulder.

'Anyway,' Liara said.

'*Anyway,*' I chorused with Esher.

'It's a shame you missed moon-horse night,' Esher said. 'I felt like I was close this time!' I felt a pang of envy. On the full moon, we girls would head onto the moor and attempt to tempt forth moon horses. It was as much about whisky and freedom as it was about actually bringing forth those fae steeds from the hidden realm, and nobody was fool enough to mount one even if it came. I'd only seen them summoned once, but the memory of those beautiful, sleek creatures, ephemeral and ghostly, was one I treasured.

'You were?'

'I really was!' Esher said. For a moment a burst of radiant energy lit her face, and Light Above, what a face. I wanted to lick it. I was aware of how weird that is, but there was so much joy there. 'I think I understand how it works. What the moon horses want from us, or what they come for, at least. I'd seen one of the Winterra recruiters in Redwinter that day, and—well. I'll show you next time.'

'I'll try to come,' I said. The rigors of Lady Datsuun's training and the sleepless nights often left me exhausted, but it was nice that they still asked.

Sanvaunt was at the church doors, talking with Apprentice Raddesia. She was annoying. Tanned Brannish skin, pretty, good at things. She laughed at something he said, which was odd since I never really thought of him as funny, and twizzled a bit of her hair around a finger. A jealous surge that he was being funny with someone else dropped down on me like sleet, so I stuck my chin in the air, made sure my arms were most firmly linked with my girls, and stalked on into the church. I hoped he'd notice.

Dawnsong passed, training passed, and so did the long hours of trances, incantation and the longer hours at Lady Datsuun's house. Nobody went easy on me for sake of my schedule. With Ulovar abed, Draoihn Palanost now took all of his lessons. I felt a twinge of guilt when I overheard other apprentices whispering that she was the better teacher. I was more cautious in incantation now. If I'd seen it in the Ashtai Grimoire, I didn't draw it. And so I achieved little.

Lady Datsuun had taken to making me drink some kind of thick, noxious green liquid every afternoon before I began sparring with Torgan. It reminded me of soggy cabbage, and that may have been a principle ingredient. Some days she took my face in her hands and stared into my eyes.

'Pupils are too wide,' the translator, Ibaqa, told me. 'She does not like that you drink the rose-thistle.'

'I don't like it either,' I said. 'But it means that I get hit less.' The fresh bruises I came away with argued differently. When the other apprentices trained under the armsmaster, Hylan, he made them move slowly, never truly landing a blow on one another, duels conducted at half speed. The Dharithians did not believe in going slowly. I came away sore, but when I probed my tender points after I was done for the evening, I savoured those little pains. They were making me stronger.

'Have you ever been punched hard in the face by a man?' the translator asked.

'Slapped, yes. Punched, no,' I said. So Torgan hit me hard in the face. He was hard-bodied, built from coils of hammered steel, and the force of his blow rattled my brain in my skull. It hurt a lot. I was sick for a while in a bucket whose purpose had previously gone unspoken. My vision swam for hours after and my legs were unsteady.

'Lady Datsuun says, now you know what it is like, and will not be paralysed by shock,' Ibaqa told me. 'She says no point training only for circumstance of training room. Learn to fight when you have only one leg, one hand, from your back, blind, punched. All good practice so no panic when it happens.'

I nearly fell from my docile horse's back three times on the ride back to Redwinter.

'Concussion,' Liara said after taking one brief look at me. 'That bloody old woman, eh. I'll let her know you won't be training for a few days.'

'Datsuun is a royal bitch,' I said. Liara smiled.

'Not far off. She was the wife of a high-ranking general in the Dharithian Empire. There was some kind of changeover of power there, and her family were forced to flee. She may still think of herself as a woman of vast influence, but the truth is she has her little household of indentured servants and whatever money she brought with her, but she's nobody.'

'That's interesting, but all I really want to know is whether I can get out of her lessons for a week.'

I got three days, and that seemed like luxury enough. It wasn't enough, but it had to be. I caught up on sleep with dozy afternoon naps and slipped down to the city to drink with Castus in the blazing afternoon sun. Embroidery had taken root as a pastime among all of the apprentices, not so much because they wanted to work on their clothes but because they embroidered their hoops with elaborate messages to one another that were then hung on doors. Mocking insults, mostly, though occasionally they left a kind of embroidered scavenger hunt leading each other around the house. Esher tried to teach me some of the skills she'd picked up, but I couldn't see the appeal. It took hours just to make one of them, and the joke was always done in an instant.

'It's fun because it's pointless,' Jathan explained to me when I finally told the little sewing circle that I was never picking up a stitching hoop again. He had a reddish cast to his skin, thick black curls, and though I didn't see it myself he was as well-regarded as Sanvaunt when it came to his looks. He had a rather worse reputation when it came to his fidelity, but then apparently Sanvaunt had had a sticky fumble at some point with Castus, of all people, and I was still cross with him about that. It didn't matter that it had been four years ago. Jealousy is a knife, and a blade will cut no matter how rusty it gets.

'How is that enjoyable?' I asked.

'Because it doesn't require any thinking,' Jathan said. 'Take a load off. You work too hard.'

Despite his less-than-spotless reputation, one of the things I liked about Jathan was that he didn't try to flirt with me as he did the other girls. Maybe it was a result of Ovitus's lies, locking me off from the beginning, but that was the dynamic that had formed. It was nice not to worry about having to be a woman around him. I could just be a person.

* * * * * *

Life returned to its normal routine. One morning, after a particularly broken night of bad-dream screaming, I slept past dawnsong. Rather than go late to Palanost's lesson and face her disapproval, I went to Ulovar's rooms, where I found him sitting by the window once again. He ran me through a few exercises, though I could see he was tired, rubbing at his neck and clearing his throat often, as if breathing were still hard for him. The effects of smoke inhalation, I supposed, though I'd been in the thick of it longer.

'You aren't getting better,' I said eventually.

'No,' Ulovar said. 'No, Raine, I don't think I am.'

I'd expected rebuttal and claims that he was strong as an ox, or that I should mind my own business. But instead my master stared out of the window. His mask was broken. In the lines around his blood-red eyes I saw something he'd never let slip before. He was afraid.

'Is there anything I can do?'

'Age catches up to all of us eventually. Some are younger than others when it tightens its grip. I had thought I would see sixty. My grandfather lived all the way to eighty, if you can believe that. But I suspect that the Afterworld may come calling for me before winter's zenith.'

I could not imagine this world without Ulovar. He formed our strong centre, the pole around which our dance was conducted. A slow and sombre dance, for sure, but without him we'd just be a tangle of ribbons.

'Perhaps it'll pass,' I said. 'When I was a child, a man in my village lost his mind for nearly three years, and then recovered.'

'Losing my mind,' Ulovar said. He smiled, but it was shallow. 'That's the truth of it. More than you know. But I will persevere. You'll be Tested and made Draoihn before I lie down in my grave, I promise you that. After everything I did to you, and everything you did for me, I owe you that much, Raine.'

'Can the grandmaster not help?'

'She has tried,' he said. 'Don't share that. I don't want to be the subject of gossip. But even with her Fifth Gate she couldn't fathom the cause. And that means it's simply age. I am not ill. I'm just worn through, and the road of my life is reaching its destination.'

'I think you're ill,' I said.

'You always want to fix things,' Ulovar said. 'Sometimes, that's not an option. Enough maudlin talk. Without looking behind you, tell me the order of the items laid on the tea tray.'

It wasn't easy to enter the trance with those thoughts weighing upon me, but I did as he asked. Seeing me progress comforted him. He wanted to know that things he had crafted would continue after he was gone.

The day of Sanvaunt's invitation finally arrived, on one of the rare rest days when I was required for nothing at all. Murrish poetry was all the rage in Harranir, seen as exotic and 'good culture,' but it wasn't of much interest to me. But then, that was hardly the point.

I was weary from sleepless nights and mental focus with Palanost, battered and bruised from training, and wanted only to go back to bed and lie in the thickness of the blanket, swamp myself in the luxury of goose feathers. But as the afternoon crept forward, I still found excitement growing. I hadn't quite said yes, not with words—but I was going to. I put on a full face of glamours—I had the hang of it now and rarely had to start over—and put on a light linen dress of cornflower blue that showed as much leg as I could get away with and a pair of ankle boots that were either mine or Esher's, it was no longer clear. My legs were all bruised but he'd just have to deal with it. I looked myself over in the mirror and tried braiding my hair, well past my shoulders now, but decided on a low ponytail instead. Eight months since Ciuthach, and my hair had remained that shade of winter ice blue-white. I was stuck with it, but I didn't think it looked so bad. The knife scar across my cheek and nose I could do nothing about with any amount of powder and paint. I told myself that Sanvaunt liked me or he wouldn't have asked me to go with him. It was just some stupid poetry. Maybe he thought it would be educational.

I was angry with him for having fumbled around with Castus years ago, and just as annoyed that Castus had kissed Esher when they were barely teenagers, which wasn't terribly fair, but I still found ways to tell myself that I'd been wronged. So I delayed long enough to be a little late before I went looking for him.

I couldn't find him anywhere. I didn't want to have to ask after him, not all dressed up as I was. The other apprentices were terrible gossips. But eventually I had no choice and asked Tarquus.

'I believe he has already left for the city,' he told me, without casting a single look at my attire. 'He won't be back until late.'

I felt my stomach sink. I'd gone through all that trouble for nothing. Sanvaunt had asked me to go with him, and then he hadn't even waited for me. Had he forgotten that he asked me already? Had that pretty vixen Raddesia usurped me? I let anger stoke the hurt and raged into one of the sitting rooms, the one with the foot bath, and found Esher and Liara there. Liara was trying to teach Esher the harp, which hadn't been going too well by the sound of things. I threw myself down into a chair that was far too comfortable to suit my mood.

'He's gone off without me,' I said crossly. 'After all that thinking and worrying about it, he's just buggered off without a word.'

Esher plucked a pair of strings together, creating a sharp, jarring sound that made Liara wince.

'Who's gone?' Liara asked, 'And where have they gone, and why has it brought this extremely fortunate interlude to Esher's lesson?' Esher scowled at her back.

'Sanvaunt asked me to go to some dumb poetry show with him. But he left without me.' I folded my arms across my chest and stuck my chin down as I slunk back into the depths of the chair.

'He asked you to walk out with him?' Esher asked, her scowl forgotten. 'He actually asked you again? And you didn't tell us?'

'He said there's some Murrish poet down in Harranir, with dinner and

drinks and dancing,' I said. 'I was planning to go, but he just went without me.'

'Why wouldn't he wait for you if he asked you? That's not like him,' Liara
said.

'I don't know!'

'But you told him you'd go?'

'Well, he asked me.' I slid down deeper into the plush cavity between the
chair's arms. 'He didn't say there was a time limit on the response.'

'Didn't he first ask you before you went to Gilmundy?' Esher said. She
dragged her fingers along the strings, sending a peal of bright notes into the
sitting room's stuffy gloom.

'And again a few days back.'

Esher struck the strings flat, killing their peal.

'Then you should have told him yes or no. You can't expect him to just
wait around hoping. If you aren't interested in him then there are plenty of
girls around who'd gladly take your place.'

'Well, he should just have taken one of them then, shouldn't he?'

'Maybe he did,' Esher said. Liara evidently felt too uncomfortable to
comment. I glowered at Esher, then felt bad for it and snarled at the carpet
instead.

'It's bloody rude,' I muttered, but Esher was prepared to turn her musical
frustration on me.

'Are you sure you aren't just feeling annoyed because you've let someone
else go with your beau?'

'Mean,' I said. 'And he's not my beau. He just asked me to go with him
once. All right, twice.'

'Did you want to go?'

'I don't know. Maybe? What's the point? I don't have time for any of that
these days anyway.'

'No,' Esher said, and I found her face hard to read. 'I know you don't. But
if it's Sanvaunt you want, then you have to do your part of the work too. You
left him dangling in mid-air for weeks. Sometimes you have to play your
own part. Life's not a river running in one direction with you as the destination.'

'I haven't had time to even think about anything like that,' I said, keenly
aware that I'd been thinking about it a lot. I was getting angry, but it was
hard to tell now whether it was directed at Sanvaunt, at myself, at my training

schedule, or at Esher for—well, just for being Esher. 'It feels like I'm being judged,' I said.

'Nobody is judging you, Fiahd,' Esher said, turning her eyes back to her strings. 'But if he'd asked me, I'd have said yes straight away.'

Maybe it wasn't fair to feel such a surge of heat coming up all across my face. Maybe it wasn't fair that Esher's words bit into me, as though I'd lost two things rather than just one in the space of an hour. But fairness rarely had anything to do with the world, and the thought of Esher and Sanvaunt together chilled me. Maybe she'd aimed that deliberately.

'Raine,' Liara said quietly, 'if you did want to spend time with him, why didn't you just tell him yes? Are you sure you didn't forget to answer him because you didn't want to?'

I didn't like the truth that welled up inside me. It wasn't the weariness of too many late nights, or that I felt I looked like dinner's leftovers, mottled and bruised, or that the last time I'd allowed myself feelings for a man it had ended with a slap to the face and my whole world falling apart. Perhaps they formed parts of it, but there was something much deeper, something that had held me back until the absolute last moment, and had only reached to seize it as I saw it slipping from my fingers. It was an answer that lay with Redwinter, and the Ashtai Grimoire, and what I was and what I was becoming. What I had been for what felt like an impossibly long time now, though it had been less than a year. I'd once thought that the grave-sight would always be the worst thing about me, but I knew now that I was wrong.

How could I share myself with someone when what I had to share rotted things from the inside out?

'You get to make your own choices,' Esher said. 'Nobody owns anyone else's feelings.' She meant it well, but her previous words were still cold in my bones.

'You're terrible at the harp,' I said, and stormed out of the room.

* * * * * *

The next morning, Ulovar forced himself from his confinement. Had he not been such a proud man, I would have expected to see him walking with a cane. Instead he was dressed in his finest, a lace-cuffed frock coat, his best kilt in the black-and-green LacNaithe breacan, with a decorative court sword on his belt. The flesh was falling from him, and when he came to join us for breakfast, the atmosphere among the apprentices was nervous.

'Yes, I'm still a little under the weather,' Ulovar lied. His voice was thin and hoarse, as if a scarf had been tied too tight around his throat. 'You've all had a cold before. No need to make anything bigger of it. I want you all turned out in your best, without those morbid expressions on your faces. Our guests arrive today.'

I had at times had my doubts about the rest of Ulovar's apprentices' commitment, worldliness and common sense, but they did scrub up well. A healthy line of credit and servants on hand will do that for you. Ulovar had even brought in a man and a woman from the city to help us to get ready, so whoever was arriving was clearly important.

I had come to enjoy dressing in the city fashions, but not today. The secrecy made me nervous. Someone was coming to join our household—and whoever it was we were supposed to impress them. I had uncomfortably wondered whether Ulovar was bringing one of his former protégés home to take over the running of the house. What would that mean for us? The rules might change. Our line of credit might dry up in the hands of a less generous host. Our training might intensify under a battle-hardened, one-eyed old dog, and on top of training with Torgan I didn't think I could take that. And a little of me wondered that new eyes might see more than Ulovar's did.

But most of all I worried that Ulovar was asking for help, and that he needed it.

Esher was stunning in a dress of summer green that left her pale back exposed. Liara's shirt was as crisp and white as its pearl buttons, and her red curls were piled up atop her head like treasure. Jathan, who was handsome whatever he wore, was resplendent in contoured grey. Adanost had ceased wearing his earrings after Castus LacClune had torn two of them from his ear, leaving it ragged, but his scarring seemed to suit him. Gelis had dressed to match Ulovar, and even our newest recruit, Little Maran, looked like they'd been painted by a master. I didn't talk to anyone, hadn't spoken to anyone after my storm-out the day before, and they all let me be.

Sanvaunt was absent. I couldn't bring myself to find out if he'd come home after the party. I had no right to ask, and nobody was offering to tell me. Maybe he was off about his duties. Maybe he was crying to himself softly in some garden, thinking of me. Maybe he was in the bed of some beautiful, more grown-up, more cultured woman. A woman with fewer scars. A woman who didn't wake screaming in the night. A woman who didn't carry a death sentence inside her.

Anger is the ugliest of emotions. It is the team of dogs that drags the sled of shame. Midmorning, we lined up outside the greathouse to wait for our mysterious guests. As the procession made its way through Redwinter's gates and across the vast grounds, the secrecy was finally explained. There had to be sixty people in the procession, with twice as many horses. It wasn't just our own household who gathered to see them, the occupants of others came out to murmur and gawp, servants and all, to bear witness. The guests approached in a riot of colour, greens and yellows, purples and white, but flying overhead on a banner that required two men to hold aloft, was the royal orange-and-white checks of Brannlant. Twenty footmen in mail and helms led the way for a whole train of servants, dignified elderly retainers of station and young page boys and girls on ponies. Someone was playing a warbling, nasal tune on a brass instrument of a type I'd never heard before.

Two riders stood out, grand as they led the procession.

Ovitus had transformed himself, and the weight had fled from his bones. He seemed taller with the excess forged away, or perhaps that was this new posture he'd adopted, back straight as a spear. His face still retained a heaviness to the cheeks, but a light beard had come in, and it suited him well even if it was half fuzz. He was dressed differently as well, no longer swathed in shapeless shirts, but wearing bright-polished mail, a surcoat of green and black with the LacNaithe wyvern roaring boldly across the breast. His Draoihn longsword was belted heroically across his back, and he'd swept his hair from his face with oil. Half his previous size, for the first time I thought he looked like a van-in-waiting. Impressive even. A wolfhound that seemed as much wolf as hound padded along below his horse, its long grey fur a little ragged, a little dull. An old dog, but its eyes were bright. It trailed behind him a pace, stopping when he drew rein.

As for the woman—well. Some people exist just to remind you that you're a mere mortal. Dressed for a palace ball rather than the road, a mountain of white, yellow and pale blue silk and lace flowed from her side saddle. She sparkled in the summer morning light, a fabulous necklace of silver and precious stones almost too dazzling to look at half-covering her chest, a glittering brightness against the rich dark of her skin. A wire net cast pinpoint stars of light from her black hair, as did the jewels at her ears, her fingers, even her slippers. I could have bought a town with half of them. It was hard to tell whether she was naturally so dazzling or whether it was simply impossible to look ordinary wearing so much splendour.

Ovitus dismounted in front of the open-mouthed apprentices before assisting the vision down onto a mounting block. He led her a few steps forward, then made a short bow to his uncle. He seemed relaxed—possibly for the first time in his life. It wavered for just a few moments as he took in Ulovar's failing health, but he brought it back for the show.

'Uncle Ulovar,' he said formally, gesturing towards the jewelled woman. 'It is my pleasure to introduce Mathilde Wendlan of Brannlant, daughter of King Henrith Wendlan the Second, my beloved and future bride.'

'Feck me,' Esher whispered. 'He *did* bring a princess home.'

10

The LacNaithe greathouse was alive with people and sound and excitement as it had never been since I'd first laid eyes upon it. Instructions sped between the Fourth Retainers who ran the kitchen and laid out rooms. The LacNaithe staff of thirty was about to be swamped by the Brannish visitors.

'He's getting married?' Esher whispered to me, taking my arm. 'He's actually getting married—and to *her*?' It was too big for us to remember the previous day's fight, the excitement washing the morning clean.

I thought I heard Liara mutter a heartfelt 'Light Above be praised.'

We dissolved back into the house ahead of the servants. It seemed only appropriate that this was a cause of celebration, even if Ovitus and Ulovar were still outside. Someone brought up a keg of cider and another of wine. Apparently it was acceptable to start drinking before lunch if something this momentous was taking place. I joined in alongside them. I didn't necessarily feel like celebrating. I felt a sense of discomfort at the events the world was showing me, distant from the riot of bright eyes around me. It was hard to put a finger on it, until I eventually came to understand that what I was feeling was injustice.

When I first came to Redwinter, I had lost everyone I knew. I had faced off against Ciuthach, a deathless thing rising from the grave, and Ulovar had cut a scar across my mind to protect me from my own grief. I still sometimes asked myself whether he'd been right to. But I was here now, and it was better than being consumed by the overwhelming pain of sudden loss. Ulovar had housed me, partly out of guilt, but also because he'd needed me as a witness. Brought into this strange world as a young woman with no power, no status except that which the master of the clan gave me, and Ovitus had quietly told lies about me. He'd told his cousin Sanvaunt that we'd been lovers on the road, and then he let the lie fester. Sanvaunt's father had been a social climber who'd bedded his mother seeking position and he'd feared me to be the same. It is no easy thing to have your name cast into the mud like that. I'd kissed boys before, and I'd had a lover. But those were my decisions, and if people thought less of me for that then that was their issue. But I had been painted as some kind of sexual plaything by a man of vast power and wealth, and I would never accept that.

Seeing Ovitus there with his betrothed princess wife-to-be felt like a vast wave of cold water sweeping over me. It didn't affect me, had never had call to affect me, but Ovitus didn't *deserve* a beautiful, royal-blooded wife. He'd been a shit. He'd been a shit, and he'd never apologised for being a shit, and now we'd all be expected to be impressed and excited and to treat her as the lady of the house. Which she would be, I supposed, if Ovitus didn't relocate to Uloss Castle in the LacNaithe heartlands, or leave us all for Brannlant, which I hoped he would. I couldn't bring myself to go and play at refinery and listen to poems with a man I actually liked, and here Ovitus was marrying the daughter of our overlord.

It hadn't been me that exposed Ovitus's lies about me. One day, he would lead Clan LacNaithe, and my fortunes seemed aligned with theirs. To reclaim my name sounded simple enough, that I could have just spoken freely about it—but I needed Ovitus's favour, and how often is a woman believed on such things anyway? I had to let him come to apologise in his own time, or what was it worth? A forced apology is no apology at all, and if I pressed the matter I risked his heels digging in. Unless something steered fate's prow to a new course, one day he'd be giving me orders, and just now I didn't have a tiller in my hands. But now—this was bigger than just the clan. Brannlant had conquered our country of bracken and blood feuds just over a century ago, and in my tiny mountain village we spat at the name. The Harranese paid them tithes, supplied them with warriors, and though they kept governors around the country to keep us in check, they let us have our own king, keep our own ways. It was a model of conquest that had Porient, Faralant and Russlant under their yoke. Brannish conquest suited the Draoihn; the Brannish held another of the Crowns, with three more beneath the distant lands of Osprinne, Khalaclant and Ithatra.

The Crowns confined the greatest of evils to the hidden realm, and the Brannish royalty were the most powerful of its guardians. And Ovitus was going to become part of that.

'She's a stunner all right,' Jathan said. 'Who'd have thought it? Our Ovitus, sliding into the Brannish royal family.' He raised his pewter tankard high, sloshing cider over the rim. 'To Ovitus and Princess—wait, what was her name again?'

'Princess Mathilde!' Liara said, raising her own tankard up high to clash against Jathan's, and everybody but me joined in. I drank to mask my lack of enthusiasm.

'She was pretty dazzling,' Esher said. 'Did you see her hair? The way it curls? Half of her was all covered in jewels, but I'd die for hair like that.' The rush of jealousy burned colder, but I tried to summon life into my face. I nodded, smiling like the world wasn't rushing around me in a tornado of conflicting emotion.

'Your hair is beautiful,' I said, but I didn't intend her to hear me, and she didn't.

My thoughts flashed to an image of Esher and Princess Mathilde walking arm in arm across the Magpie Lawn, laughing, becoming best friends. Beauty drew beauty to it, didn't it? Esher was the most beautiful woman I'd ever seen, except perhaps for the Queen of Feathers—if she was indeed a woman, and she was too otherworldly and fierce for her beauty to be attractive. Why wouldn't Esher and Ovitus's wife-to-be want to become close friends? Of course they would. And I'd lose my best friend, and more than that I'd have to see her with someone else and that was just as bad as Sanvaunt going down to the city without me.

Everyone else drank, and all I wanted to do was throw myself into the nearest well and lie staring up out of the dark water to see whether anyone even noticed that I was gone. But I kept that smile plastered onto my face. I should be happy, like they were happy. I should be one of them, exulting in the surging fortunes of the clan.

It was only a matter of time before Ovitus came to find us, but it took longer than I'd anticipated. I'd found my drinking stomach and probably had more than was good for me by the time Ovitus and Mathilde entered the dining room. Mathilde had changed from her thick, fluffed-out silks into a simpler, but no less refined woollen dress of grey and white. Her hair was free of its net, arrayed as a halo of glorious black curls. King Henrith had taken a Murrish wife to broker peace with the one nation he couldn't conquer, and that lineage had dominated in his daughter's appearance.

Mathilde beamed at us like she owned us. She sort of would, one day.

'My friends, how I've missed you!' Ovitus declared from the doorway, all martial and still wearing his mail. The old Ovitus would have just walked in, slumped down in a chair and begun lamenting how tired he was, but this stranger just stood smiling quietly. There was no doubt that he was feeling proud, but he wasn't doing too bad a job of hiding it. He scratched at the ears of the big grey dog that followed at his heels.

Scarcely needed introductions were made. Brannish royalty glowed in our midst. Mathilde's father was overlord to our king. It would never, ever, ever be a good idea to do anything that could displease her. Not even a little bit. A younger woman was introduced as Lady Dauphine, Mathilde's cousin and courtly companion. Dauphine smiled coyly, far more comfortable among strangers than I was in my own home, while the rest of the apprentices thrummed to be introduced, not a shred of caution amongst them. Jathan practically leapt from his chair to be first in line to kiss the royal glove. I went last, even behind Little Maran.

'Your grace,' I said as I air-kissed her glove. I wasn't going to actually kiss it where everyone else had. Gross.

'You must be Raine,' Mathilde said. Her Brannish accent was strong, but her voice was warm and princessy. 'Ovitus has told me all about you, and the ordeals that you went through together. It's an honour to meet such a great warrior.' And she curtsied to me. For a moment I stood stock-still, not knowing how I could possibly respond to that. She adjusted the situation for me, by laughing. 'Come, we should not stand on ceremony too greatly if I am to be part of this clan. If not for you, I would never have met my darling Ovitus. I've heard how you helped defeat the demon of Dalnassy and foiled the cult that tried to harm him. All Brannlant owes you a debt, in making our ever-tighter alliance possible.'

It had been Dalnesse, not Dalnassy, but it was the effort that counted. I couldn't even find words to respond.

'Raine,' Ovitus said warmly. He gave me a polite bow. 'I confess I've not had any option but to regale Mathilde with your deeds.' Up close, I saw then that he'd been scarred during his absence. His face bore a jagged rip from the base of his jaw up to just below his eye. It had been stitched neatly, but it was a scar he'd wear for the rest of his life. It made him look older. More serious. Many months ago, Hazia had slashed her knife across my face, but it wasn't just my face that wound had changed.

'The honour is all mine,' I said, snapping my treacherous hand down, finding my tongue and offering a bow. 'Service to Redwinter, and all that.'

He smiled at me, and for just a moment I thought I saw something else there behind his eyes. Nerves. He hadn't known how I'd respond.

'And this is Waldy,' Ovitus said, patting the head of the tired old dog, who licked at his hand with a very long pink tongue. 'An old dog, but one to whom I owe my life. We were on a boar hunt, and—'

'Perhaps that story can be saved for later, dearest,' Mathilde said. 'I hope to be friends with all of you,' Mathilde continued, removing her exclusive attention from me, and I stepped aside gladly.

'Shall I show you the grandmaster's residence next?' Ovitus asked.

'Surely, we must have time for a drink with your brothers and sisters?' Mathilde said. 'Let us wash the road from our throats.'

Servants followed Mathilde and her cousin into the room, two women of an age with her, a much older woman wearing a widow's knot in her hair, and a man who was very clearly her royal guard. His sheer size was imposing, maybe six foot ten, clean-shaven and with hair cut as though a bowl had been placed over his head. He didn't look like he'd need the swords at his belt to deal with trouble, his hands would be enough for that. He took a position behind Princess Mathilde's chair, seeming to see us all without ever having to meet anyone's eye.

The apprentices quietened down, more ready to listen than speak. Ovitus sat quietly, happy in the glow of his newfound prestige. Mathilde more than made up for him. She knew something about everybody—little facts and details which could only be the result of studious preparation. She asked Adanost about the horses he was breeding, and told Gelis that they shared a love of Haddat-Nir era poetry. They'd been happy to kiss her hand when she'd entered, and by the time Ovitus quietly insisted that they needed to pay visits to the other greathouses that LacNaithe associated with, they would have eaten out of it had she asked. Jathan would probably have licked it, and I wondered whether someone already needed to remind him that Mathilde was engaged to his future lord.

'What a thing this is,' Esher said when the royalty had left the room. 'The house will change now.'

'It changes everything,' I said. 'LacNaithe has allied directly with the royal house of Brannlant.'

'King Quinlan is old and unwell, and there'll be a succession before too long,' Liara said. 'Whoever LacNaithe puts its strength behind will be nigh-on guaranteed to take the Crown. I wouldn't have believed Ovitus capable of pulling off something like this. How did he persuade King Henrith to accept him as a suitor so quickly?'

'He's the van-in-waiting to Clan LacNaithe,' I said. 'There are few men more powerful in Harranir. It makes sense for Henrith to continue firming up the alliance. Maybe Ovitus will put up his own candidate for succession of the Crown.'

'Clan LacNaithe will support the king's son, Caelan LacDaine, and Clan LacDaine, as it has for many years.' Sanvaunt had appeared in the doorway. He was dressed for riding, mud on his boots. He'd gone out to meet the procession. Not some other woman's bed. 'They kept this news quiet somehow, but it'll be reaching parliament around now. This alliance all but seals Caelan LacDaine's first right to succession in stone. LacAud's ambitions will die with it.' He walked across the room and sat down in an unoccupied chair in the middle of the table, avoiding those that had been vacated by the engaged couple. The head chairs sat empty as though they had been permanently claimed.

Amidst all this excitement, my first thought on seeing Sanvaunt was whether he'd enjoyed the stupid fancy-people party, and if he'd taken stupid Raddesia in my place. Here we all were in our finery, looking dashing and styled, slugging back drinks, while he'd been off putting things into place. He worked so hard, and the only thing I could have given him—a little consideration—I'd managed to squander. It wasn't like I knew what the future held, I didn't even let myself daydream it. But I'd let him down, and while I felt morose and vented my anger on those around me he'd gone on doing what he did, fixing all the things that needed fixing, asking for little. He really had asked me for so little.

Grudgingly, when the disappointment and self-flagellation had died away, I'd had to admit that Esher had been right. I hadn't said yes. Princess Mathilde had said yes to Ovitus, and the world had changed. I'd kept my thoughts to myself and my world had stayed the same.

I fled the greathouse. I could not bear it.

The quiet I could handle, and a big house is usually quiet. But there was so much joy and carelessness all around me, and it didn't seem real. It was too far from the rest of my life for me to feel a part of it, and none of it sat well with me. But there was something more than that, something I couldn't share with them.

I found my way to the LacClune greathouse, the last place the other Lac-Naithe apprentices or retainers would be found, and one of only a few who hadn't immediately sent representatives to offer congratulations.

'Had enough already?' Castus asked with an arched eyebrow as I disturbed what seemed to be a morning nap, reclining in a sunbeam.

'I don't know,' I said. 'I just needed a place to be.'

'There are better places than this,' he said. 'There's a whole party of new folk out there, and impressive ones at that. None of them are interesting to you?'

'Interesting how?'

'In whatever way you find things interesting. It's your life.'

I sat looking down at my hands for a while. Three of my knuckles were split and scabbed. My wrists were still ringed with dark bruises from Torgan's demonstration of wrist locks. It was quiet in the LacClune greathouse, and I liked it here. By the time I was finished examining my hands, Castus had settled back with his eyes closed, and I realised that maybe I was intruding on time that he wanted for himself. I'd come here for solitude, but I was invading his. Still, I lingered. There was too much noise outside, too much change and the prospect of even greater changes to come for me to be comfortable there.

'Something's eating you from the inside,' Castus said. 'I'm not saying you have to talk to me, but whatever it is, talking to someone is usually a good idea.'

Should I tell him that I was annoyed at him for kissing Esher, years before

I ever even met her? That I was angry at Sanvaunt for going to a party without me, when I'd failed to accept his invitation? That I knew both of those things were absurd, and it was even more unfair that I felt that way about both of them at the same time?

'How many people have you killed?' I asked. The question just came out of me without me meaning to ask it. It had been in there, though, not at the surface but somewhere deeper. Hiding from the part of me that listened to itself. It had been there a while, quietly taking up space, long before Gilmundy.

'Strange thing to think about, on a day like today,' Castus said. But his face softened. 'Are you hurting over shooting those men in Gilmundy? It was them or us, Raine.'

'It's not that,' I said. 'I can handle that.'

'You sure?'

'Yes,' I said firmly. It was true, and still it was something that I wished people would stop asking me. They trained us to do this, and then we were meant to feel bad for having done it. I wouldn't feel bad. I had made my peace with the blood on my hands. I still didn't want to be asked about it, because I knew they wanted me to say that it had damaged me somehow. I rested my chin on my fists, my elbows on my knees. 'I just want to know how many.'

Castus sighed. He kicked off his blanket.

'You think it's a lot?'

'I don't know. That's why I'm asking.'

'Probably more than I should have,' he said eventually. 'You know, when I was a child, there was a Draoihn who'd served my father all his life. Sometimes he was around the estate, and then he'd go off for a while, and he'd come back. I asked him the same thing once. You know what he said? 'Keep going long enough and the answer to that question will become the same answer you give when people ask you how many people you've slept with.''

'How's that?'

'Around twenty, you just stop counting.'

I didn't think I'd stop counting on either front, but it seemed that somehow I had managed to get life very wrong if Braithe was the only person that I'd slept with but I'd severed at least thirteen souls from their bodies, and that wasn't even counting demons. I would have felt better if the numbers had been reversed; at least then I'd have been having more fun, although I don't know how much fun I'd ever had in Braithe's bed. It had just felt important to me back in those days to be seen as an adult, to show the world that I was no longer a child. Looking back through the haze of blood, charging headlong into an older man's arms had only kept me a child longer. Being a child had felt like containment and I'd thought being seen as a woman would have freed me. I was far from that now, and yet I was still lumped in with the apprentices. They seemed even more distant than the fragile child who'd convinced herself that Braithe's blows were for her own good.

'Have you stopped counting?' I asked. It wasn't clear to me which quota I was asking about. Castus smiled, but it didn't make it all the way up his face.

'I always guessed what life had in store for me. I made sure never to start.'

Which was another way of telling me to mind my own business, and perhaps I should have. I didn't feel any better.

I found my way to the baths, to the library, watched another group of apprentices training on the practice court. They were distracted, as well they might be on a day with royal visitors in Redwinter. I dawdled my day away until night had overtaken the world, and even when I returned to the greathouse I was reluctant to put myself inside its walls. This was my home, I reminded myself. I had as much right to be there as anyone. But the prospect of so many people, so many introductions and explanations seemed overwhelming. Perhaps most of all I wanted to avoid Mathilde. She thought of me as someone special, had heard my legend before she'd ever laid eyes on me. The Draoihn treated me with a combination of respect and hastily averted eyes, but to her my actions last winter had made me a hero. I didn't know how to feel about that.

I went into the greathouse's gardens, ten-foot-tall hedges spiralling and winding around one another, and at length reached the crooked old tree with the little door where Tarquus claimed one of the hidden folk lived. I had never seen it, if it even existed. I sat there a while as the evening cooled and I began to wish for a coat, but still I remained, my skin turning cold, hunching my shoulders.

'I guess you were looking for a quiet space too.'

Sanvaunt stepped from the shadows beneath a hedgerow arch. I'd not heard him approach. He walked as though he didn't want his footsteps to intrude on anyone else's space, like his existence wasn't meant to impose itself too firmly into the world. Like a shadow.

'I thought I'd found one,' I said. 'How is everything going in there?'

'Jathan passed out about an hour ago. Gelis was sick down the back of the red divan. Ovitus seems to be about as happy as a pig in mud, which is hardly a surprise. His bride has changed her dress twice, and the cellar ran out of wine.'

'Sounds like a hoot,' I said.

'It's general chaos. If my uncle was up and about, I suspect it would be a more sober affair.'

'He went back to bed?'

'Ovitus and Mathilde went to visit him, but not for long. He's no better than he was.' Sanvaunt came across to my bench and sat at the opposite end, space enough for the empty space that lived between us.

'He's not getting any better,' I said.

'Not yet he isn't,' Sanvaunt said. 'Master Firean says that rest is the best thing for him just now. Maybe he did push himself too far putting out that fire. It took too much of his strength.'

'There was a time I thought him the strongest man I'd ever met,' I said.

'He is that,' Sanvaunt agreed. 'The fire was stronger than he could have known. Hotter.'

'You say that like there's more to be said.'

'I just can't explain how it happened,' he said. 'Not taking so fast as it did. It was so sudden. I just felt this rush of heat, and it was right there.'

'But nobody was badly hurt at least,' I said.

'Not unless you count Ulovar.'

'It's wasn't your fault,' I said.

'I don't believe that. Firean is trying to explain it to me. He knew, somehow. It was me, Raine. I did it.'

'Who is he? This Firean you call "master"?'

'He's been here since I first came,' Sanvaunt said. 'I think he knew something was strange with me. He sought me out. He's old, and impatient. But he makes time for me. It's good to have someone different to learn from.'

There was a rustling in the undergrowth as some small night creature—or one of the hidden folk, if you believed they really did live in the garden—passed by on its nightly foraging. We stayed very still, the sounds of ongoing revelry in the greathouse muted behind its thick stone walls, watching the dark. A musical troupe took up a lively tune. Someone cheered. The quiet took over the garden, leaving me unwilling to break it, uncertain what to say as all the thoughts I'd been holding in swam in misguided spirals through my mind. So many things that I'd run through my head, things that I wanted to say, things I'd told myself didn't matter or weren't true. I could barely keep a grasp on a single string of thought before the next came to the fore. The chill of the night was gathered deep, the darkness swallowing us so that all I could make out of Sanvaunt were the gleams of light catching on his thick, curling hair. When he reached across and put a hand on my shoulder, he caught me off guard. I was too surprised to flinch, too engaged by the warmth of his hand through the thin fabric of my shirt to want to move.

'What are you doing?' I said quietly.

'We don't seem to connect, do we,' Sanvaunt said, his voice barely disturbing the night air. 'It feels like we're the sun and moon, never quite in the same place.' He sighed and took his hand back. The place where he'd touched me felt colder than before.

'Sometimes there's an eclipse,' I said. I'd read about them.

'Once every few hundred years maybe,' Sanvaunt said, and I felt more than saw his smile in the dark. 'You missed a good party. The poet was good. I think you'd have liked her.'

'I was busy,' I said, more on instinct than because it was true. 'And I was really tired.'

'There'll be other parties,' he said. 'One night doesn't make the world.'

'Doesn't it?' I asked. I bit down on my lip, expecting him to ask me to go on. But he didn't. He didn't push into it, and I realised as my mouth started moving that I'd wanted him to. 'Everything changed that night with Kaldhoone LacShale. Nothing has been the same since.'

'I don't disagree.'

I looked over at him and for a moment I knew that he had his own secrets from that night. I'd never told anybody about breaking into the Blackwell and claiming back my bow, how I'd called on the Queen of Feathers and promised to grant her one favour, or how I'd defeated Kaldhoone LacShale by empowering the spirit of a dead man to drag him into the water. Those were things that I'd take to my grave. But Sanvaunt had defeated a Mawleth, a demon of the Night Below, leaving his sword twisted and ruined. It shouldn't have been possible for a Draoihn of his ability.

'How's the training going?' he asked.

'It's a nightmare,' I said, realising for the first time that I truly felt that. I'd not allowed myself to consider it too closely.

'It is,' Sanvaunt said. 'Training under Lady Datsuun was the hardest thing I've ever done in my life. Have you got onto running up walls yet?'

'Nobody can run up a wall without magic,' I said.

'You'd be surprised what you can do if you work hard enough at it.'

'Go on then. Run up the garden wall over there.'

The low light from the greathouse caught in Sanvaunt's eyes. I felt amusement on lips the darkness hid from me.

'Why should I run up the wall if you're going to stay down here?'

'I just don't believe you can do it.'

'Not good enough,' he said. 'What do I win if I make it?'

'What do you want?'

And for a moment that question hung between us like the swinging arm of a grandfather clock, swaying backwards and forwards, ticking away the empty moments.

I want you to kiss me, is what I wanted him to say. Just say it and be honest, and let me lean in and kiss your damn mouth.

'If I make it, you have to come with me next time I ask you to go somewhere,' he said. He began to stretch his legs out, moving with that swordsman's elegance. 'It has to be worth that at least. Do we have a deal?'

'What if it's somewhere boring?'

'Even if it's coming to listen to Ovitus going on about how happy he is with Mathilde for three solid hours, you have to come and pretend to enjoy it.'

'What do I get out of this?'

'You get to see me run up a wall.'

Why was I resisting? Maybe because resisting is what I did, and because I could handle a kiss in the dark where I didn't think I could handle being seen out in public on Sanvaunt's arm. Didn't want to think about what people would say about two wildroses stepping out together. After what Ovitus had done, the thought of people whispering about me left me cold. And yet . . .

'Okay, it's a deal. But only because I want to see if you can do it.'

'Watch me,' he said. 'I could do twice that height.'

Sanvaunt stretched his arms and legs, jogged a couple of times on the spot, and then ran at the wall. It was at least fourteen feet high. There was no way he could reach the top. And yet he went for it all the same. A brief sprint and then he jumped, kicking off against the wall, once, twice, three times and then he was leaping, arms stretched out to grasp the top of the wall—and he came up short by the width of a few fingers. He came down just as fast as he'd gone up, kicking off the wall again, staggering and falling backwards. He even made falling look elegant.

He hadn't made it, but Light Above, it didn't matter. If I'd wanted to kiss him before, seeing him run up there had firmly solidified the idea in my mind and ringed it in steel. I'd seen a lot of weird things among the Draoihn, but it was different when there was no magic involved. He picked himself up from the ground, dusting mud from his breeches.

'You lose,' I said.

'I can't believe I just tried that, in the dark, just to impress you,' he said. 'I think you should go with me anyway.'

'We'll see,' I said. And he came to stand near me, breathing deeply, which I put down to the exertion he'd just displayed, but wasn't quite sure if that's all there was to it. Five feet away, a step, three feet.

Kiss me, damn you! Take me here and now!

The sounds of raucous laughter and drunken hooting came from beyond the hedgerow that walled off the garden. The celebrations were breaking their bounds, revellers spilling into the gardens to gaze at the stars, or to undress each other behind the bushes. Anyone could be out here, watching. What would they say about me if they saw me here with Sanvaunt?

I always suspected Ovitus had been telling the truth! She shamed him for nothing.

She had one LacNaithe and then the other—that's a real social climber for you.

A pretty girl like that knows how to get what she wants from men, there's your proof.

'I have to go.' I turned and fled out of the enveloping darkness and into the greathouse's light. Nothing was easy. Nothing was ever simple and pure and clean.

Does he know she's a murderer?

Did he know she was Sarathi?

I practically ran into the greathouse's dining room. The party had long since moved on. I took the nearest unfinished cup of wine from the table and downed it, before seeking out a crowd in which I could lose myself, and be observed being what I wanted people to think I was.

12

The party went on through the night, which was terribly exciting for every-body. Through the dark hours I wondered whether Ulovar slept, or if he could hear the music, the laughter and the clashing of cups. I wondered if he silently objected. There was certainly cause for celebration from Clan LacNaithe's perspective. The clan's heir had finally chosen a bride, and his choice brought with it an alliance that could only elevate the clan's standing across the country. But it wasn't what our house had been, and perhaps it was a sign of greater changes to come.

The greathouse was predictably quiet the next morning, and my head seemed to be the least sore. I trudged across to the church in my starched grey robe to sing dawnsong, feeling conspicuous that I alone of the Lac-Naithe apprentices had made it. The pews around me stood empty, even as the chanted songs of praise to the Light Above echoed from the arched ceiling. I kept my hood up, so that nobody would know which of Ulovar's apprentices had fulfilled their duty.

Peace never lasts long. If life teaches us anything, it should be to never expect anything to remain calmly the same.

A night of raucous drinking was to be followed by a more sober lun-cheon that nobody was in any fit state for. Trestle tables filled the Rookery Garden, which had no more to do with rooks than the Magpie Garden did magpies. The retainers set it up as if the promised wedding had already arrived, LacNaithe household staff worked alongside Princess Mathilde's vast entourage, laying everything out with well-practised good humour. She seemed well liked among the people who worked for her. I didn't trust her, of course. Trusting anyone who could glow at people that hard was a recipe for disappointment.

A stretch of the soon-to-be-trampled Eagle Lawn had been left clear for entertainers, and someone—Tarquus I suspected—had laid out name cards around the edges. I walked around the rows of tables twice, until I was sure that my name wasn't there. I found Esher, Jathan, Gelis, even Little Maran, but my own was nowhere to be seen. Draoihn from the other greathouses had been invited to join—even Haronus LacClune, whose shoulder I'd once put an arrow into and was as close to being our enemy as another Draoihn could be, had a place. My name was missing. Guests filtered to their places over the course of the morning, and bottles of wine so clear you could see right through them were issued as streams of merchants arrived at the gates to deposit freshly ordered cargo. Hogs had been slaughtered before dawn, roasting over pits, filling Redwinter's grounds with a thick, savoury smell. I could see Ovitus's loping wolfhound, Waldy, had escaped the house and sat near the pits as if he might sneak in and steal a pork leg away when nobody was watching, but the cooks already knew his game.

Ovitus and his bride-to-be arrived together, her hand daintily perched in his like it was a songbird poised to break into music. She wore orange and white today, while Ovitus was handsome in LacNaithe green and black, a frock coat over breeches in the Brannish fashion. I hadn't yet adjusted to the changes that had taken place, not just in his appearance but in his demeanour. The way he spoke to the retainers, offering them a smile and a word whenever they approached to ask his opinion, and the way he seemed to be at the head of organising things. He mirrored Princess Mathilde. Had he learned this new charm from her? It seemed unlikely, as I couldn't imagine the bumbling, self-doubting, moonstruck young man I'd first met having the ability to bring such a major victory to fruition. As I watched them taking their seats I caught glimpses of the old Ovitus now and again. A nervous laugh, or a dreamy gaze towards Mathilde. He was besotted, but maybe finding love had pulled something up from his roots. Maybe it had been there all along.

Or maybe, this was all her idea and she'd blasted the old away with a gust of charisma, a pretty smile, a ruthless plan lurking behind it all. There was intelligence, preparedness behind her sparkling eyes and dresses worn like armour. Perhaps this—the marriage, the alliance, even Ovitus's shift in mannerism—had all been conducted at her doing. Or just as likely her royal father, Henrith the Second of Brannlant, had set her on this path. I sighed. She was going to be around for a long time. It would be best for everyone if I could find a way to be comfortable with it all.

'Where are you sitting?' Esher asked. She'd dressed up pretty, in a scarlet gown that was as much statement as it was clothing. She wasn't the only one of Ulovar's apprentices to do so; Jathan had found a vivid orange military jacket somewhere, cut so that it only came down to his ribs, displaying his tight abdominal muscles through a shirt that could have doubled as gauze.

'I don't think I'm sitting anywhere,' I said.

'Oh,' Esher said. Her face fell, reddening in embarrassment for me. 'I'll go and talk to Ovitus now, I'll make him set you a place. It must be an oversight. He can't have meant to—'

'Don't,' I said, laying a hand on her arm. 'It's not a problem. Ovitus and I haven't really spoken, not since—not since it all happened. Maybe it's right that I'm not part of this.'

Jathan snorted.

'I really doubt Ovitus had a hand in the seating plan. We'll be able to tell whether he planned the menu by how bland the food is. I doubt a few months abroad have given him a taste for anything that hasn't been fried into oblivion.' He flashed a grin and a tilt of his chin towards a Brannish retainer, whose blush implied that in the brief time she'd been in Redwinter, Jathan had shown her more than a little hospitality. He chuckled as she hurried on with a basket of napkins.

'Careful with your jaw there, Jathan,' Liara said dryly as she joined us. 'Stick it out in the wind too much and that fluff you think of as a beard will blow away on any slight breeze.'

It was true. He probably should have shaved. It would probably be the first time he'd ever needed to shave it, but like many young men, he was proud of the smudge of dark hair he'd managed to grow. He was lucky that he had a face that wasn't ever really going to get judged by those things. Colban had worn something similar on his face as we rode north to Gilmundy. He hadn't carried it off with nearly such style or beauty. He'd been a quiet presence around the greathouse. Sometimes it felt like he wasn't gone at all, that he might just walk in and sit down to dinner. But there was no nameplate for him around the table either.

'Ovitus is waving at you,' Esher said. 'I'll talk to him. I'll go now and say something. It's just a mistake.'

'Leave it,' I said. 'Maybe it was.'

I walked the length of the trestle tables to the head table, mounted up on a platform that put the happy couple and key guests a couple of feet above everyone else. I noted the seating arrangements as I went. The highest-ranking Draoihn had all been given places of prominence, but so had powerful people from down in Harranir, guests yet to arrive. Politicians and merchants, thails and priests. The invitations must have gone out the day before. Maybe even before that. Ovitus rose before I arrived, stepped down from the platform and offered me a bow that wasn't required.

'Apprentice Raine,' he said. He still had some weight around his face, puppy fat they called it, but again I couldn't help but be impressed by the totality of his transformation. The first time I'd seen him, he'd been riding on a snowy slope while I hid among the trees above him. He'd just been so—*doughy*. It was like he'd lost half of himself while he'd been away, or as if someone had punctured him and just let all the air inside him out. They weren't kind thoughts, but he hadn't apologised.

'Apprentice Ovitus,' I said, offering a bow of my own. I felt suddenly ridiculous. I'd come dressed for a formal occasion, wearing a gown Esher felt didn't suit her. Pale blue, with fox heads embroidered in white around the neck, cuffs and hem, the belt a sash of silver. I seemed to inherit a lot of clothes that arrived that way. A dress suited to a lawn party right outside my home, one which I apparently wasn't invited to.

'Might we talk a little?' he asked. I nodded. He offered me his arm, and I felt suddenly overwhelmed by the gentility of it. I didn't want to take it, but it would have been an insult to refuse him, would have embarrassed him in front of his lovely bride-to-be, even if she wasn't looking. I settled for laying a hand on his elbow, and he led me away towards the Nightingale Garden, which was being used as a staging area for food. Neither of us spoke as we crossed between the retainers, who scattered from our path like startled hens. Waldy followed on after us, wagging his tail, never wanting to be too far from his master and enjoying the summer sun. I was glad this was happening away from the rest of the household, away from observation. I realised guiltily that I'd just considered the forty or so cooks and waiters not to count.

'It's all a bit much, isn't it?' Ovitus said when we stopped beneath a cherry tree. He took out a handkerchief to dab at his brow. 'Somewhat ostentatious for my liking, if I'm honest.'

'It's a special day, I suppose,' I said. Ovitus nodded.

'Everything feels a little different. Well, it is different. I know that. But I didn't know what to expect. Being away, it's all been such a strange time, things have moved so quickly. I feel like I've been swept up in a river and carried off to some beach downstream.' He offered me a smile. He wasn't wearing his eye glasses, and he had to squint at me to focus.

'It's different,' I said. I tried to keep my face impassive. I wasn't going to award him a smile. He didn't deserve that. Ovitus looked uncomfortable. *Here* he was. The uncertain, nervous boy who'd got himself kidnapped and nearly drowned by a cult. He fidgeted his hands together, trying to work up the courage to finally say it. To finally give me the apology that had gone unspoken for eight long months, an apology to acknowledge that pretending I'd fucked him had been to cast every element of friendship between us into the river.

'I meant to talk to you before,' he said. His voice was low, travelling no further than the spread of cherry tree branches. The retainers didn't enter our space.

'It's been a long time coming,' I said. I'd wondered what I would say when he finally said he was sorry. When at long last he mustered the nerve to do the little he could to right that wrong. I'd imagined myself being sharp-eyed and flinty. Had practised dozens of speeches I'd give him, played through in my head and then pushed aside to make room for the next. But now that I found myself here I didn't remember a single one. None of them seemed appropriate, or realistic, like it had been some character version of myself running lines for a play. So instead I just waited.

'Thank you,' he said. 'Thank you for saving me. Thank you for doing what you did. You had to fight for me, to save me from myself. I haven't thanked you, not properly. And you deserve all my thanks. You deserve everything I have.'

I was taken aback. Those voices in my head that had planned their cutting oratory, their razored rebukes, had all taken their leave.

'You pulled me out of there before it collapsed,' I said. My treacherous, appeasing mouth issued words that I'd not intended. Words that I'd never imagined I'd say to someone who'd hurt me the way he had. 'You saved me too.'

Ovitus leaned towards me and put his arms around me. Waldy sensed an occasion, barked and leaned up on his hind legs as he sought to be included.

'And thank you for that too,' he said. The embrace didn't last long. I didn't return it. He stepped back from me, using that sweaty handkerchief to wipe his eyes. 'I'm just sorry it took me so long to say it.'

It hadn't been so very long ago that I'd killed a man. I'd known what to do, I'd known how to act, and I'd acted and the assassin had died with my arrow in his chest. But I didn't know what to do here. Waldy barked again, snuffling at me but I didn't let him lick me; getting slobbered on by a dog is disgusting, and more than that he was Ovitus's dog, and even though he was just a dog that somehow made him feel like an enemy.

'I want you to sit up on the high table with us,' Ovitus said. 'I told Matty and she thought it was a splendid idea. Will you?'

'I—Matty?'

'Princess Mathilde,' Ovitus said. He looked nervously towards the ground. 'My wife-to-be.'

'Of course.' I said it automatically. Not a moment's hesitation. A ripple of relief crossed Ovitus's face.

'I'm so glad,' he said. 'I'm so glad we can be friends again. I never meant for you to have to put yourself in danger for me like that. I'd never want you in danger, Raine. I really, truly mean that.' He stepped back from me and looked over me. 'There's a dress Matty would like you to wear, she had it made for you on the way here. She thinks so highly of you, would you wear it? There's still time to change before the first course.'

I looked down at Esher's dress. Fox heads around the hem. It was one of my favourites. But what could I say? I could hardly refuse a princess's wishes.

'If that's what she wants?'

'She'll be so happy,' Ovitus said. Beaming. Smiling like the Light Above had shone down on him from a sunbeam. 'Come on, I'll have Retainer Elizatte take you inside.'

'You know the retainers' names now?' I asked as he gently took my arm and began to lead me back towards the greathouse.

Ovitus's smile didn't dip for a moment.

'I've had a lot of lessons to learn,' he said, almost wistful. 'About the world. About people. About myself. I can't wait to show you.'

* * * * * *

Formal dining is terrible. Formal dining where you don't get to choose where to sit is even worse. I may have felt excluded and a little burned when I thought I'd been omitted, but to be sat up on the high table, in full view of everybody else, was worse.

The dress that had been provided for me fit well enough. The hem rode a little high, and the bust was more generous than I really needed, but if it had been tailored for me—and I had to assume that it had—the tailor had done a good job blind. The colour didn't suit me at all. LacNaithe black with lines of pine-forest green, the wyvern of the house clear across the breast. My hair stood out stark and white against the dark, accentuating my pale northern skin and even paler hair so that I looked something like a ghost. It was an extravagant piece of work: rows of small pearls ran around the neck, wove patterns across the belt. I had no idea what the shoes were made of, but they too shone like mother-of-pearl.

'We're done,' the tailor said in a strong Brannish accent, having made what minor adjustments she could to the bodice with pins. 'Try not to shake around too much.' I could see her frown in the mirror.

'Not the colour you'd have chosen for me, is it?'

'Can't say too many of your Harranese fashions come down to Brann-lant,' she said. 'It's striking if nothing else.'

'That's a polite way of saying you think I look ridiculous.'

'Not at all,' she said, turning away so I wouldn't be able to read it in her eyes. 'Very striking. Very nice.'

I found my way back to the Rookery Garden, and the high table where wooden arches woven with summer flowers formed a grandiose backdrop. Anyone would have thought that the happy couple were marrying today, and perhaps that was the idea. Solidifying the idea in place for the rest of Redwinter, and the merchants, the politicians, the thail-lordlings and the priests to see. Professional dancers, lithe and muscled, dressed in ribbons of fabric, twirled in synchronised time in the hollow between tables in time to a small, merry string orchestra.

Ovitus and Mathilde took the centre of the high table as was only appro-priate. Grandmaster Robilar sat to Ovitus's right, Ulovar on Mathilde's left. The big bodyguard stood behind the princess, dour and armed, though she hardly had need of his protection here. Suanach LacNaruun, a member of the Council of Night and Day and master of artifice in Redwinter already swayed tipsily between a high-ranking lady from Mathilde's retinue and the speaker of parliament, a greasy man who licked his lips as he watched the dancers twirl. One end of the table was taken by Grand Matriarch Priseda of the church, who sat next to the Brannish ambassador. It was a long table. I wouldn't have been surprised if King Quinlan LacDaine himself had ar-rived to sit beside me, but he was well known to be suffering hard with the natural onset of old age.

Instead I found myself seated at the opposite end of the table to Matriarch

Priseda, and the only dinner companion beside me was the sixteen-year-old girl I'd seen when Mathilde had first been introduced, a cousin. The seat beside her was empty.

'Hello,' I said. The girl gave me a sidelong glance from beneath eyes that held a weight of glamours I would never have supposed could look refined. Like Mathilde, her dark curls framed a sharp little face.

'I've heard of you,' she said. For a moment I wondered how, but I was the only young woman with white hair around so I suppose I stood out somewhat.

'I'm honoured, Lady Dauphine,' I said. I'd done my due diligence before taking my seat. Lady Dauphine Wendlan was Princess Mathilde's cousin, the only daughter of Prince Racaiden Wendlan, the king's brother. Racaiden had been in his grave for more than ten years, poisoned slowly by a wound taken in the Brannish expansion. She sat seventh or eighth in line to the Brannish throne.

'I don't like the food here,' she said, though nothing had yet been served. 'It's bland. It's gritty.'

The food in Redwinter was usually sumptuous beyond anything I'd ever tasted. I imagined how Dauphine would have fared on the pottage I'd grown up on in the north and couldn't help but smile.

'We're a humble people,' I said.

'My uncle—the king—says that sometimes,' Dauphine said. I wondered if she might be a little drunk, or maybe this was simply how someone born into royal lineage spoke at that age. 'I was told you killed a demon. You don't look like a warrior.'

'Ever seen a demon?' I asked. I was glad to accept a cup of wine for myself. I had to get through this meal somehow. I delved into the little bag attached to my sash and tried to unscrew the cap from my hip flask one handed. The rose-thistle didn't just drive back tiredness and make me overly chatty: it was numbing, and I figured I might well want to be numb for however long this lasted.

'There are no demons in Brannlant,' Dauphine said smoothly. 'They wouldn't dare. We have magicians who deal with them. They're called Artists.'

I swivelled to the side, took a swig of the bitter, coal-dust-flavoured water.

'What's that?' Dauphine asked.

'Medicine,' I said. 'Keeps the demons at bay.'

She narrowed her eyes at me as if unsure whether she was being mocked or not, but then a ripple of indifference turned her face blank again. But the mask only lasted a few moments, as an approaching figure caught her eye.

'Who is *that*?' she asked.

'Sanvaunt LacNaithe. He's your sister's husband-to-be's cousin,' I said as he paused to exchange pleasantries with a Draoihn who'd worn his oxblood coat. Ill-advised in the seasonal warmth, and not exactly right for the occasion. They laughed at some shared jest, and I glanced at Dauphine to see her biting her lip in a way that didn't leave me comfortable at all.

'He's *gorgeous*,' she said.

'He's got ten years on you as well,' I said somewhat defensively. Technically it was only nine years. 'When he was your age, you were six.'

'What is age but a number?' Dauphine said, her eyes not leaving Sanvaunt for a moment as he stepped up onto the platform. He gave me a smile, and then looked along the row of merry, prestigious people on the high table, up and down, before his eyes came to rest on the one unoccupied chair on Dauphine's left. He took the seat, moving with that gliding ease that came from all those hours spent on the sword court. 'Do you believe that age is but a number, Master Sanvaunt?' Dauphine asked. She held out a dainty hand, a lace glove covering all but her fingers, expecting it to be kissed. Sanvaunt gave it an embarrassed glance. It wasn't customary in Harran to treat children like adults, so he gave it a little shake instead.

'Such wild and outlandish customs,' Dauphine said coyly, covering her mouth with artfully cocked fingers. 'I'd heard that Harran was a place of fierce and rugged splendour, but I have to say I find it altogether exhilarating.'

'Even the food?' I muttered. Rose-thistle likes to loosen your tongue. Dauphine either didn't hear me, or didn't care what I said. Apparently demonslaying was of significantly less interest to her than Sanvaunt's jawline. She didn't speak to me during the soup course, which she left untouched, the meat course, which she managed one mouthful of, the fish course, which she devoured three valiant forkfuls of, but she did manage to make a slight dent in the jelly of sweet summer fruits. Not much of a dent, but then she was pretty small. Built like a little bird.

Sanvaunt spoke to her politely. He laughed at her jokes, making a sound I'd not heard from him before. A forced laugh. She was his cousin's betrothed's cousin, and royalty, so what else could he do? There was a child sat between us, but an uncomfortable pressure still filled my chest. I drank more rose-thistle, which filled me with fast words and hard temper, but with Dauphine so fixated on Sanvaunt I had nobody to spill either onto. One time, scanning the assembly, I caught Esher looking at me with one concerned eye, and I looked away feeling something made out of guilt, shame and anger. What was I doing up here? I didn't belong among the high and mighty. I didn't belong robed in this tough LacNaithe fabric that claimed me for the clan.

I felt the presence of somebody behind me, then a hand touched lightly on my shoulder and a warm breath filled my ear.

'Sorry,' Ovitus whispered. 'Someone had to sit next to her.'

'I've killed enough people,' I said, the rose-thistle finally getting its way. 'I think I can handle this.'

'I know you can,' Ovitus said. 'If it's any consolation, Grandmaster Robilar is hardly a font of levity. I've spent the whole meal terrified.' He went back to the jolly conversation with Mathilde and the grandmaster, and I glowered into my sweet fruit as though I could reduce them to pulp with my mind.

It would not have been a proper feast without a speech or two. I no longer expected Ulovar to make one. He looked weak in his chair, a great fur cloak around his shoulders as if he sat in deep winter rather than the best of Harran's summer sun. It cut me to see it.

Ovitus rose from his seat. I had never taken him for a speech-giver, but with the beaming smile of his princess shining up at him, even he could be infused. I wondered, cruelly, how he would be if his glorious, beautiful rug was whipped from under him. Would the newfound confidence dissolve with it? But he didn't look at her as he shuffled a little slip of paper in one hand, a humble clay cup held up before the gathered, appreciative masses.

'My brothers and sisters of Redwinter, good people of Harranir and friends from beyond our borders,' he began, calling out in a voice that I was expecting to falter, but didn't. 'I am honoured beyond measure to stand here before you today to present my wife-to-be, Princess Mathilde Wendlan of Brannlant.'

Cheers, admiring calls of support, banging of fists on tables. All that stuff. Mathilde half-rose from the table, flashed a white-toothed smile, but didn't rise to her full height, sinking down again with a sincere, affectionate gaze towards Ovitus. I just couldn't quite believe it. Yes, he'd lost a lot of weight, but that had never been the thing that had left him lonely and heart-forlorn. Could a princess really have fallen for him so swiftly? Could anyone?

'I am most thrilled to return at this time,' Ovitus continued. 'And what a time we live in. It is my hope that in but half a year's time, I shall be honoured to call Princess Mathilde my lady wife. But in the meantime, we do not mean to dawdle. We do not wish to sit back and fail to conduct the great works we have planned between us.'

Everybody sat up now. Exultation in a joyous union was one thing, but plans? Leaning forwards, I could see it on the faces of those seated along the high table. *What do these great works mean for me?* they wondered as one. Ulovar's brow flattened out. This was unexpected. Grandmaster Robilar wore a small, knowing smile, though whether she knew anything or was merely pretending to was anybody's guess. Sanvaunt looked nervous. Change was coming on fast, and he was a cautious soul at heart.

This was how declarations of war were made. LacAud's claim on Gilmundy had to be in everybody's mind.

'Firstly, let me reveal the passion with which we have been in discussion about a project of my dearest Mathilde's that we have carried back to Harran with us. For many years, the princess has been engaged in charitable endeavours. Schooling for those children whose parents cannot afford it. Charitable dispersal of excess produce, so that those in need can be fed. Projects to help those former soldiers who served her father so well to find new employment. It is our aim to clean Harranir's streets of the vagrants who fill them, but we will not just move them on. We will find them purpose again. We will give them back their lives.'

I fought back a snort that the rose-thistle thought was an entirely suitable response. For all the likelihood of any of that succeeding, he might as well have promised sun throughout the night and an end to disease. LacNaithe's fortune was great, but even the great clans could not solve all the problems of the poor of Harran. He could have promised to push the mountains back to create more pastureland and had a better chance of achieving it.

'It will not be easy!' Ovitus said, momentarily fumbling around for his paper. Perhaps he'd been expecting a cheer, rather than the slightly puzzled faces. *What's in it for me?* they wanted to ask. Money had to come from somewhere. 'I speak not of the work of a season, or a year, but the work of a lifetime. Of generations. But the work that I and my wife-to-be set ourselves upon will form a bedrock of investment, of redistribution, that will see the future dawn bright for our children, and our grandchildren, and their own children beyond.'

'Hear, hear,' a few supportive or fawning voices called.

'I know it's a bold claim,' Ovitus said. 'But I hope I will see you join me in this endeavour. Prince Caelan LacDaine has shown his support in letters we have exchanged. He too wishes to improve the lot of the common man, and in doing so improve the lives of all. The money trickles down, you see. Take an old soldier from the street, show him how to work again in society, and he not only makes a living but he pays his taxes upwards. In turn, those taxes help his brothers and sisters into work.' He offered a beaming smile, and half managed it. He was nervous about this speech. 'It is not a small task. But it can be done. I—no, *we*—believe in it. I have seen Princess Mathilde's labour-homes in Brannlant, where they take in the poor and dispossessed. They make rope, they make sack cloth, why, they are even given work in tin and copper mines.'

Ovitus was losing them in the details. He cleared his throat, the clay goblet still stretched out in front of him, raised in a toast to himself that had gone on too long as he tried to shuffle his notes in just one hand. Mathilde said nothing, wearing her smile broad and wide as a rainbow. She tilted her head to one side to give people something to look at while Ovitus prepared his next round.

'It will not be easy,' he said, finding his stride once again. 'But then, what do we here in Redwinter know of ease? What does Prince Caelan LacDaine know of ease, fighting so far away with our Brannish friends? Life for the worthy is never full of ease. It is with hard work that we shall prevail.'

Nobody that does it likes hard work, but most of the assembly were nobleborn so it went down well enough. Sanvaunt rose to his feet, raising his own cup up to match Ovitus's. I suppose there are some people who enjoy hard work, maybe.

'Hard work prevails,' he said approvingly. He hid his surprise well.

'Hard work prevails!' Lady Dauphine agreed, standing to join him. I doubted she had seen a day of hard work in her life.

A general call for the glory of hard work rose up from the assembled Draoihn and high-ranking people of Harranir. The rose-thistle made me want to laugh, but up here, dressed in Ovitus's clan breacan and in full view of the audience, I fought it back into the bitter phlegm at the back of my throat. I couldn't really object to what was being said. Old resentment made the words stale before they even reached my ears.

'While I have your attention,' Ovitus called, waving for quiet. 'I would like to share one more piece of happy news. Please be calm, there's no cause for alarm.'

For a moment I thought he was about to reveal that Mathilde was pregnant. But no, they weren't married. I very much doubted the matronly attendant and the six-foot-ten killing man who followed Mathilde around would have allowed any such thing.

Ovitus raised the clay goblet above his head. I didn't know what was happening at first. He placed his other hand on it, standing as though the goblet were a sword raised to the heavens. And then the sunlight caught on it—no, through it—refracted and bounced a thousand different ways.

The trance that emanated from him was nothing like it had been. I had remarked once that Ovitus's trance sounded like a bull strapped all over in pots and pans that had been stung by a bee. Now it was more akin to the gentle buzz of the bee's wings. The cup seemed to shine like a rainbow for a few moments, and then it was clay no longer. Glass.

Not everybody understood at first what they were seeing.

'The Second Gate!' Jathan cried, jumping up from one of the trestle tables and spilling his wine down the shirt of the dignitary on his left. 'He's opened the Second Gate!'

Ulovar sat forward in his chair for the first time, his eyes wide. Sanvaunt came back up to his feet. Princess Mathilde's smile was dazzling ivory, evidently in on the spectacle. The older Draoihn hammered on the tables with the ends of their cutlery. The younger and the apprentices jumped up on the benches, cheering, applauding. The din filled the air. With a grin, Ovitus tossed the glass goblet over the table to shatter in the grass.

'Don't worry,' he said, grinning and waving a hand of dismissal. 'I can always make more.'

I slouched down, well aware that only Grandmaster Robilar and I remained seated. Even Ulovar pushed himself up using the table to join in the congratulations and cheers. Not even Tested, not even Draoihn by rank, and somehow Ovitus has broken through that wall into the Second Gate. I could see the thoughts going across every Draoihn's face. Was Ovitus set to become as powerful as his uncle? Would he reach the Fourth

Gate? The Fifth? What did it mean for the world, to have one who commanded such powerful magic, such wealth, such a powerful alliance with our overlords?

The rose-thistle welled up in my mouth, bitter and acrid. I spat.

'Oh, fucking hell.'

The party went on, and on, but I escaped from my place at the high table and disappeared into the crowd.

'Who'd have thought it?' Liara said when I managed to push in alongside her. 'The unlikeliest of prodigies.'

'Well, I guess we know where all his newfound confidence came from,' I said. 'I wonder if he just—you know, made the rest of himself disappear.'

Liara frowned at me, looking intently into my eyes.

'Maybe lay off that stuff,' she said. 'It's making you mean. Ovitus has his flaws, but he's worked hard for all this.'

I snorted, feeling the bitterness of the rose-thistle in the back of my throat.

'Easy to work hard when you're born with pockets full of silver,' I said.

'Bitterness does not become you,' Liara said. She looked serious, older than usual. Without a ready quip on her lips, there was a sadness about her. I didn't like it, so I pulled over a beaker that had already been used and filled it with wine from one of the many jugs. A boozy wasp made its escape from the rim just in time.

'I guess you're regretting your choices right about now,' I said. 'Could have been you up there on that dais drinking in all that attention.'

'No, that would never have been me,' Liara said. She slid the cup across the table and drank from it, claiming it. Trying to keep me sober, which did nothing for my mood. 'To Ovitus I was nothing but fantasy. He chose me because he thought I was realistic, but unattainable. I was a safe place for him to put his feelings, of which he has many, and of which many are unwise. Mostly he just wants to feel loved.'

There were no more cups in reach, so I settled for the jug and raised it towards my mouth. Liara put a hand on my arm and drew the jug back down.

'Light Above, Raine, the grandmaster herself is here. Show some decorum.'

'Uff.' I got up and stalked away. I was in no mood for Liara's patience, her warmth. Right then I'd rather have gone five bouts with Torgan. It wasn't just Ovitus's advancement through the Second Gate that was tearing at me. It was sitting up on the high table in someone else's dress. It was listening to Dauphine mooning away at Sanvaunt. It was all these people gazing up at Ovitus, so impressed with what he'd accomplished. He'd managed to convince a king to give him his daughter's hand in marriage. How very difficult that must have been, with Uloss Castle to call home, a place in Redwinter, political alliances and an income that never required he lift a hand himself. Who couldn't have achieved what he'd achieved with all that privilege behind him? He'd spent most of his life slouching and mumbling his way through, resting on the strong arms of those with less, and the moment he turned his eyes towards something he wanted it had fallen from the sky and landed in his lap.

And me? I'd fought tooth and nail for everything I ever had. I'd run from home, I'd seen blood in the snow, I'd fought the Night Below and worse. But it wasn't me they were lauding up there on that platform. The rounds of applause, the appreciative glances and murmurs, didn't they all see that he'd done nothing to deserve this other than finally, finally understanding how to use the privilege he'd been born with?

The lie he'd told about me would be forgotten now. Had already been forgotten. I'd been so surprised when he'd taken me aside that I'd lost my tongue as I waited for the apology. I was more than a little drunk, the wine only held in check by the buzzing of the rose-thistle, trapped in a prison-dress that I couldn't remove without casting a slight on the man of the hour. Ovitus had tried to honour me with my seat with the fanciest and most important people, but unwittingly he had only managed to throw up another cage around me.

I'd drunk too much. I'd avoided my friends. By the time bald pates had reddened in the sun, cheeks had reddened with drink and dresses were reddened with spilled wine, I managed to extricate myself from the proceedings, slipping quietly away to my room, with its luxurious goose-feather bed, its neatly folded laundry and all the trappings of this family that I had become bound to. Someone had laid a fire in the hearth—utterly unnecessary in the midst of summer, and the room was stifling. Throwing open the windows allowed the barest channel of air to flow through the room, and I found myself wandering into the halls, going nowhere in particular.

I went to the east wing, where the fire had raged, where I'd felt its heat against my skin. The corridor lay ruined and blackened, the work of rebuilding yet to begin. The beams were badly scorched, but the bones of the house were built from great oaks, and even that inferno had done little more than darken them. The carpets, the drapes, the tapestries that had hung on the walls for generations, all were just so much ash. The rooms leading off to either side of the hall had fared no better, and would see neither guests nor business for a long time. But in the centre of the hall, where Sanvaunt had stood trapped by the flames, something gleamed among the ash. I puzzled at it, decided to take a closer look. I stepped warily, since even if the upright beams had remained in place, the floorboard may have been weak.

Had Sanvaunt really caused all this? It didn't seem probable, but then, a lot of improbable things had happened since I'd arrived here. He said he'd felt like he was choking, and then . . . fire.

The east wing had been made off limits for our own safety, but drink and rose-thistle had made me reckless. Gingerly stepping along the edges of the corridor, holding onto the larger beams where I could, I tracked through the ash leaving footprints behind me and gathering a grey hem around my LacNaithe-breacan dress. Amidst the drifts of ash, I found a rectangle of brass, and another beneath it. Holes down the sides, and between them more of the ash where there'd once been pages. The plates were book covers. I shook the dirt away. The title was in Elgin, one of the dead languages I'd had to study, badly, but apparently not all my lessons had been in vain. *The Eyes of Serranis*. Nothing I'd ever heard of, but books like this weren't uncommon in Redwinter's library. Sanvaunt must have been carrying it when the fire came out of him. I took it with me.

I backtracked out of the dirt and the char. My hands were black with it, my dress much the worse for it too. There was another long night ahead, and much as I longed to stay hidden away, the rose-thistle in my blood was insisting that I move my body. Too much energy, too much buzzing to secret myself away somewhere, too much paranoia and fast temper to be around people for too long. The taste of it wormed its way back up through my throat, bitter and accusatory.

I was approaching the grand staircase when I heard a series of coughs from below. I'd come to recognise Ulovar's growling breaths. I stepped back and away, planning to secret myself in a side chamber that served as an apprentice study until he'd passed on his way to his rooms. The day must have been taxing for him, and he wouldn't want me to see him looking weak. But as the coughing faded, I heard voices.

'It's not yet his to give away,' Ulovar said. He was angry. The slow, heavy stomp of his boots punctuated his words as he ascended.

'He's just excited.' Sanvaunt. No sound of his footsteps. He always did move like a cat. 'It's premature, but he wants to make a statement. To be seen.'

'He can be seen without promising to ruin the clan,' Ulovar growled. He lapsed into wheezing.

'Nothing can happen without your say-so,' Sanvaunt said. 'And the banking house will come to me before they release funds in the amounts he's talking about.'

'Charitable endeavours,' Ulovar muttered, his boots thumping once again, one slow step after another. 'Not even within our own lands. Harranir doesn't need our money. You need to put a stop to this foolishness.'

'I can't overrule him. He'll be my van one day. But I'll talk to him. See if we can find some kind of way forward that lets him make his wife happy without bleeding us dry.' The voices were growing louder as they reached the top of the stairs. 'I don't disagree with his motives, uncle. There are more destitutes on the streets of Harranir than ever before. The northern blight has driven them south looking for work. And there are always the veterans. The country owes them. We have the means to help them.'

A grunt of displeasure.

'A man must cut his own wheat. I'll not see my legacy handed out to the workshy, the drunks and the addicts,' Ulovar grunted. They had reached the top, and Ulovar's breath came heavy. I hadn't realised just *how* weak he'd become.

'It was just a speech. Ovitus has a good heart, he's just a little carried away,' Sanvaunt said. And then I lost their conversation as they turned down a corridor towards Ulovar's rooms.

I stepped out of the study and leaned against the newel post at the top of the broad staircase. I waited. Sanvaunt returned before long: Ulovar's pride could not abide for him to be nursed. Sanvaunt looked good. He always looked good.

'Enjoy your lunch?' I asked. I hadn't intended to sound bitter. It just came out that way.

'Babysitting has never been something I've aspired to,' he said. He saw right through me at once. That was deeply annoying. 'You didn't look like you were having much fun either.'

'Lady Dauphine seemed to be having a good time.'

'She's just a kid,' Sanvaunt said easily. His sleepy-lidded eyes, that steady smile invited me to join him in that assessment. But even if Dauphine was only fifteen, she was still a pretty girl who'd devoured all of his attention. I didn't know how he kept such a calm demeanour if he was hitting the rose-thistle as hard as I was.

'Your cousin's a big man now,' I said. 'Quite the entrepreneur.'

'I suspect his bride-to-be has more to do with all that than he does, but what can he do? He's a young man in love,' Sanvaunt said. 'He's waltzed back here with a solid backbone and a scar on his face, but he's still the same Ovitus he's always been. People don't change all that much in my experience.'

'No?' I said. And then pointlessly, combatively: 'You dropped this.'

I offered him the brass book cover. Sanvaunt looked down at it, all filthy with ash, as were my hands. He reached out, gently, and took it from me. Tolerating my waspishness.

'What mattered was inside,' he said. 'It's just so much metal now.'

'What was it?'

'A book. Master Firean thought it might help.'

'Help who?'

'My uncle. What's happening to him isn't natural, Raine. My uncle knows it. He just doesn't want to believe it. I just don't think we're seeing things clearly.'

'No,' I said. 'Nothing seems clear anymore. It's all gone upside down.'

'You should take some rest,' Sanvaunt said. He could see my spinning eyes. He knew the effect of rose-thistle all too well.

'No, you should take some rest,' I said, and stamped off. It didn't make any sense, but neither did anything else.

.   .   .   .

It was late. Firepits had been lit. Laughter and music filled Redwinter's grounds in a way I'd never seen or heard before. I avoided my friends. There was a sour mood all over me and I didn't want them to see it, didn't want them to ask me what was wrong with me on a day when smiles were more plentiful than I'd ever seen them before.

What *was* wrong with me? It was a question I asked myself, time and time again. Why was I such a scald to the people I cared about? Between merry revellers I could see Esher and Liara sitting with Jathan, Gelis, Little Maran and other apprentices who joined us in the daily classes. They were playing some kind of stupid game that involved throwing dice and then asking each other intrusive questions. A game for children. I didn't belong there.

'You're starting to understand it now,' the Queen of Feathers said. She appeared through the darkness behind me, on the edge of the celebrations. I didn't turn to look at her, but I felt her there, beside my shoulder, watching. I could smell the sooty, musky smell of her feathered wings.

'Nobody understands,' I said. She placed a cold hand against my shoulder as we watched them all from the shadows.

'It is always like this. It is no easy thing to understand that you stand apart,' she said. 'Out here. In the dark. They don't know it, but we're watching them. Waiting for them to turn into threats, to try to stop us from doing what must be done. They would think you less than them, but you are so much more.'

'I never asked for much,' I said. 'I didn't want the sight, or the book. It came to me. I just wanted a normal life.'

'If you had not been open to the book, it could never have found you,' she whispered. 'We are not like them, Raine. We will never be like them, not now, not in the future, nor were we ever like them in the past. It is how I know that you may be the one to change it all. To create. You will do what you must, and this time . . . This time it will finally work. But it is a lonely road.'

'Is this what I wanted?' I asked quietly. 'Is this what anyone wanted?'

'No,' she said. 'But it's what we are.'

JUST A DREAM

I am myself, but I am someone else again. I, we, are older than me, a woman more than seventy. The tatters of our royal costume hang limp from tired limbs. We have been fighting for so long. We have crushed every nation we knew existed, and learned the names of more to bring beneath our domination. The world is young here. It stretches out around me for mile upon mile as the wind gusts and rips at what is left of me. Of us.

I am chained atop a great edifice that I built atop a palace that I destroyed. The empire that once spread from this silver-plated tower was unrivalled before my time. But in my time, I have shown what an empire can be. My name is known from the Southern Sea to the Great North. I have raised the fallons, as my allies asked me to. But where are they now? My enemies have come for me.

I need an ally. I need a friend, just for comfort. But I have long since run out of friends.

'Empress Serranis, you are condemned to suffer eternally for what you have done,' a warrior with bestial features says. He is part man, part owl. He has chosen to be this way, blending himself with the hidden folk. I will not accept such a change. I wish to be me. I have fought a great war to drive them back, to keep from their insistence. But I have failed, as all my kind have failed.

'I have suffered long enough,' I say. 'End it.'

I look for my beautiful ally, the queen who showed me my path, who stepped with me day and night. I look for her raven wings, her coronet of feathers, but she is nowhere to be seen. Not now, not in my defeat.

There are many of them gathered atop the great tower. Kings and queens whose lands I conquered. I look to the chains on my wrists. Chains formed not of metal, but of pure, spell-wrought power. I no longer feel the tunnel grinding inside me. Its silence has become the last blessing I will receive. I look up to the moon, full, fat and golden above us. It bears witness to my final hour.

'There will be no ending for you,' the owl-man says. He is part shadow, his feet fading towards the floor. Murmurs of approval surround me. 'You will

be buried beneath the earth, there to dwell forever. Knowing what you have done. Knowing the souls that you stole for your own ends.'

'Your victory will fade in time,' I say. We say.

'No,' the man says. 'We will endure. But for you, there is nothing but darkness.'

The need wells in me. Just the need for someone, anyone, to be here with me at the ending. I hear hooves, drumming like thunder. Impossible, up here so far from the ground, but they are coming. Ah. Here she is. She never came for me, never felt my need flowing like a river before. She charges down from the sky, her mane a stream of perfect night-light, and I am swept up onto her back. Owl-face shrieks, they all shriek, as I am carried from the tower. I grip her mane and we flee across the sky into the morning.

14

It is easy to desire responsibility until such a time as it is thrust upon you, and then it's very easy to wish you could have just stayed in bed. I'd boasted to Castus that I'd kill Onostus LacAud if I got half the chance. That chance came down on me sooner than I'd imagined. The grandmaster had been right; there would be talking, not battle. Not yet, anyway.

Arrowhead approached Redwinter on foot like a supplicant. He wore his arrowhead-decorated coat over road clothes, and it was a coat that had seen much wear down the years, the leather cracked and pale at the elbows and collar. He wore a longsword as befitted his rank and status, but had no other accoutrements of power. The rings that had sat on every finger were gone, as was his chain of office. He presented himself not as a lord, but as Draoihn.

I was not afraid of him, though perhaps I should have been. Onostus LacAud was big and imposing, but he was soft in the gut and age was creeping across him like wrinkles in a bedsheet. He carried a branch onto which his own upside-down sword-and-hammer yellow-and-grey banner was tied, the traditional symbol of parley.

I stood outside Redwinter's gates to meet him.

'The grandmaster wants you to deliver him,' Sanvaunt had told me. Ulovar had retired to his chambers, and it was Sanvaunt running the house while Ovitus was preoccupied with his bride. He was a little more wary of me now, especially when he could see me jittering about on rose-thistle, which was more often than it should have been. I felt the distance growing there.

'Why? What does it mean?'

'You can ask her after you deliver Onostus to her. She's honouring you for your past service.'

'She's waving me in front of him as a reminder that he failed to kill me,' I said. Sanvaunt had smiled sadly.

'A little of both, maybe.'

Now I stood alone as Arrowhead approached, and he sized me up as he walked the mountain road that led to Redwinter's gates.

'Raine of Dunan. We meet again,' Onostus said easily.

'I'm not allowed to kill you,' I said. I amused him. It made me angry.

'No, I should think not. Grandmaster Robilar awaits me. The time for talk is upon us,' Onostus said, resting the branch against his shoulder. For a moment, the wind lifted the banner into his face and he had to push it aside.

'You'd best watch your step,' I said. 'This is my ground now. You won't catch me flat-footed again.'

I wanted him to know how much I hated him. How much venom I'd spit if I had my way. But he was a powerful Draoihn, and he was invulnerable, and my barbs were bouncing from him as surely as the arrows that decorated his coat.

'Charming. You know, I was walking this ground long before you were born, Apprentice.'

'And I'll still be walking it when you're under it,' I said.

'Well,' he said. 'Being led by you is a punishment of sorts, I suppose.'

'I'm more than you deserve,' I said. I didn't add "my lord" as I probably should have, but I was damned twice and backwards if I was going to honour this man who had seen fit to try to kill me.

'I suppose she could have tied a note to the collar of a dog instead,' he said. 'Come on then. Take me inside.'

I couldn't have hurt him, even if I'd wanted to, which I did. Frustration ground like sand between my teeth. But duty, and self-preservation had to come first. I had some carefully rehearsed words for this, which I'd had to memorise quickly from Grandmaster Robilar's delivered note.

'By the grandmaster's decree, the leader of a rebellion shall not be permitted into Redwinter's grounds nor seek its succour should their rebellion fail. So has it been since the Great Folly in the 677th year of the Crown.'

The meaning would not be lost on Onostus LacAud. The 'folly' which the grandmaster wished to remind him of had been instigated by King Nuncan LacAud, the second major attempt by the Harranese to throw off the Brannish yoke and reclaim independence. Nuncan had been assassinated by the Draoihn, who saw his rebellious spirit as destabilising the alliance between Harran and Brannlant. Both held a Crown, and it was the Crowns that held our world together. Peace between those that held them was more important than sovereignty to Redwinter. LacAud had not held the Crown since. It only occurred to me then that, given that the assassination had taken place some seventy-three years ago, it had been made on the order of Grandmaster Robilar.

At times like those I did have to admit that those dry histories we listened to over dinner were useful.

'Rebellion?' Onostus said. He looked wryly amused. 'How dramatic. I'm hardly a rebel. I'm a loyal servant of the Crown.'

'No point wasting your breath trying to convince me,' I said. 'You already tried to have me killed.'

'Is that what they're saying?' Onostus said, giving little away. I could feel a charge in the air around him, an outward, wriggling pressure from the wards he had written into himself. 'So your job is to turn me back?'

'No,' I said. 'We're going up.'

I had two horses saddled and ready. One was my own black mare, a replacement for Conker who I'd been forced to leave in Gilmundy, and the other was small enough to be a pony. The indignity was not lost on Onostus, but he'd come on foot carrying his branch-banner, so he was already playing the role of supplicant. He mounted without argument.

We rode back along the road and turned off on a path that led higher up the mountain. I was aware of the power of this man riding beside me, and just how great the conflict he had engendered was. Onostus didn't just rule his clan, the allegiance of the north-western clans lay stronger with LacAud than it did Harranir. Onostus was not the most powerful Draoihn, with only two Gates to his name. After the two Draoihn of the Fifth Gate, Robilar and Kelsen, came the four Draoihn of the Fourth—Ulovar, Merovech LacClune, Hanaqin Clanless and Lassaine LacDaine, commander of the Winterra. Beyond them came the Draoihn of the Third Gate, and if Arrowhead wanted to continue his war, he must have had at least a few of them in his pocket.

'How's your master faring?' he asked me as we began the ascent.

'Hale as a horse,' I said. Onostus seemed unconvinced.

'I suppose I'll speak to him soon enough,' he said. My resolve hardened up. I remembered Colban's ghost, crossing far too great a distance to reach me, somehow knowing he could warn me. A last act from a murdered boy. Arrowhead might have presented a friendly face with the security of his banner-branch to protect him, but he had presided over a slaughter. Such was the way of those who hold money, and power. I had a knife. I wanted to hold it. Arrowhead's proximity was like a bush of nettles, one that could sting me at any moment. But the wiser Raine, the one who could keep her temper in control and her flask in her pocket, was winning out just then.

We passed up through the pines and emerged onto a rock-sheltered plateau, the peak rising around us on three sides, where the Shrine of Our Lady of Fire was kept. It was a simple thing, an indentation cut into the rock where a large metal fire-brazier sat for burnt offerings to be made. A small waterfall ran to its left, feeding a cold mountain pool that was banked with rushes and choked with weed. The sun fell in a beam directly onto the grandmaster. She sat on a lawn chair awaiting us with a small, wheeled silver drinks cabinet a little distance away, like a paramour awaiting her lover.

Only today she was wearing her crone face. Her hair was long, grey and tangled, her robe was violently red, and the bands of iron riveted to her head held back an inner fire.

'Dismount, both,' she croaked. 'Apprentice Raine, you will serve us when I ask you to.'

Well, shit on it, I wasn't going to be leaving then. Part of me wanted to go. But part of me wanted to be here, to hear what this monster had to say for himself. And part of me wondered whether the grandmaster might try to destroy him. She was one of the few people who could take a shot at it.

'Grandmaster Robilar,' Onostus said as he dismounted his nag and dropped the banner. He held his arms out as if in expectation of a hug, but the grandmaster did not stir from her seat. All crone'd up as she was, it had been a long shot.

'Sit down, Onostus. We're both too old to be standing around all day.'

Onostus took the only other seat available. I didn't know what to do with myself, so I went and stood beside the drinks trolley. There were a number of different bottles, cut crystal glasses and expensive goblets.

'You have given me a problem,' Robilar said. Her ancient fingers were claws gripped against the arms of her chair, but her tone was calm. 'I am greatly displeased.'

'The failure of our government has long brought problems to the north, Grandmaster,' Onostus said. 'My people are bleeding. They look to me for leadership as we burn our own flocks to halt the spread of the radish sickness.'

'Yes, yes, money and economics and all that,' the grandmaster said. 'I care not if you take Gilmundy. If House LacDaine cannot hold it themselves, they are unfit to lead a candidate to the Crown. Petty infighting over a meaningless town matters not. What matters is your attack on Ulovar LacNaithe's nephew and Merovech LacClune's son. Conflict within Harran is natural. Conflict within Redwinter is not.'

Onostus had a solid face. Wise, dependable. The kind of man you might wish to have been your father if you'd never had one.

'I fear I have been poorly represented before you, grandmaster. I ordered no attack. Quite the opposite, I was there to discuss terms, as I had been the day prior. The contingent sent to negotiate started the trouble. Ask your apprentice there—we dined in peace that very night. Had I wished any of them harm, why would I not strike at them myself?'

'What rot,' the grandmaster snapped. It *was* rot, although from his deeply aggrieved expression, Onostus was doing a very good job of seeming like he was taking offence.

'Grandmaster, I am innocent of action against the other great clans. Yes, I took Gilmundy. And, I have a right to it. But they have penned you a poison letter. I lost several valued men in the cafuffle. Valued warriors, friends who have been with me the best part of forty years. It is the rogue element that must be held accountable.'

He was either a very, very good actor, or he believed what he was saying. I wasn't always a very good judge of people. I'd failed to understand either Ovitus or Sanvaunt's motivations at first, and I'd been duped by Kaldhoone LacShale for far longer than I should have allowed. I'd tried to start distrusting people more, but it seemed a sad way to live a life.

'Raine,' the grandmaster called. 'We will drink now. The orange bottle.'

I did as she bid as Onostus continued to plead his case. There were three bottles, orange, blue and pink. I poured from the orange, smelled something sickly and sweet. Apricots, maybe. I carried it across on a tray—I had a lot of practice at drink serving from my time as a retainer—and the grandmaster took one in her skeletal claw. Onostus took his, drank and made an appreciative face.

'I come here at great risk to myself . . .' he went on.

'You risk nothing,' the grandmaster said. 'Everyone knows you've worked so many threads around yourself to be nigh-on invulnerable.'

'I am not the only one to have done so,' Onostus said, tilting his head as if he tipped a hat towards her. He looked over at me. 'And you have had me led here by a woman who killed a Draoihn of the Fourth Gate. The gesture is not lost on me.'

'I want to know what your endgame is,' the grandmaster said.

'I want the Crown to be taken by my liegeman, Lord Braman,' Onostus said. 'The shame of the past is long gone. It is only right that LacAud enter the succession once again. Prince Caelan has spent his life abroad, fighting wars I do not care about. He doesn't even know his own countrymen, an appeaser to Brannish dominion. I want support for the north before famine costs countless lives through the winter.'

'Would you repeat Nuncan LacAud's mistake?'

'I would see Harranir the strongest it can be,' Onostus snapped hotly, and I had never seen anyone show such disrespect to Grandmaster Robilar. 'How do we best protect the Crown by sending the Winterra out into barren sands, by feeding our young men and women to the meatgrinder only to expand King Henrith's domain? It does not make the Crown stronger. We are equal to Brannlant. We have always been equal.'

For a moment, I thought that the grandmaster might smite him there and then. Onostus might have turned his body proof against blades, but what if she turned him to stone? People said she'd done that in the past, and I could never tell if they were joking or not. But she listened. Said little as he launched into a long rant about past injustices, the strip-mining of the north's best and brightest to feed the Brannish war effort. The unpleasant thing was, it all sounded very convincing when taken at face value. He wanted peace and prosperity, he wanted an end to hunger, justice for the deserving. But all men talk that way, and those that would take it at the edge of a sword are usually just looking for an excuse to wield one. Funny how his aims were so noble, but if successful inevitably led to a swell in his own personal power.

'If you start outright war, I will fight you,' Grandmaster Robilar interrupted him. 'I did not fight the Remnant Sul only to see my country burn in the ambitions of my inferiors. You are Redwinter first, LacAud second. Remember that, Lord Draoihn. You took an oath.' She looked over to me and snapped her fingers, a brittle sound against the gentle trickle of water over stone. 'Apprentice Raine. The blue or the pink next. Choose whichever you think smells the sweetest.'

I turned back to the drink trolley and pushed the orange bottle out of the way as they fell back into discussion of politics, support and opposition. What did I know about the suitability of fancy drinks at whatever this meeting was supposed to be? The bottles had no labels, so I pulled the cork from the blue and took a sniff. It was mead of some type. Probably very expensive. I took the pink and sniffed and suddenly my senses were flooded with memory.

'Hecksfleet, otherwise known as Spouse's Remorse, is found growing on the banks of streams near to freshwater swamps. It has pink flowers, and smells like ripe peaches . . .'

Peaches. Some sort of liquor made from peaches. The pink was a coincidence. It had to be.

Choose whichever you think smells the sweetest.

I have wondered from time to time whether he has proofed himself against poison as well?

There was Hecksfleet in the bottle, its presence masked by peach liquor. It had to be. My mind reeled around the inside of my skull, tried to climb out of it like Sanvaunt running up walls. How was this my choice to make?

The grandmaster wasn't telling me to poison Onostus LacAud. She was offering me the choice. Did that mean that I ought to kill him? Or would I be condemned if I did? This could be a test. A test to see if I would respect a flag of truce. But was that the right option, given the lives at stake, given what Onostus had already done? There was no time to think about it. No time to weigh up the options one to the other.

As in battle, it had to be the choice of a moment.

I was not an assassin. I was a murderer, in a way, but there had always been urgent need. Lives had been at stake *then*, not in conflicts that may or may not arise weeks or months along the road, battles fought in far-off places that I would never even see. And yet the power to prevent those deaths lay in my hand. Or worse, if I poisoned Onostus, would a greater and more vengeful lord arise in his place?

It was too big a decision for me to make. I couldn't decide.

'Apprentice? Drinks,' Robilar said again.

'*What do I do?*' I mouthed beneath my breath.

The Queen of Feathers rose from the lake, visible only to me, the waters unbroken around her. The world seemed to darken, the sunlight failing and shadowed darkness drawing in around me.

'What do you want to do?' the queen asked me. I said nothing. 'Hallenae asked the same when I first came to her. And the answer is the same, no matter who is asking. What would the Ashtai Grimoire tell you to do?'

'I don't care what it wants,' I thought. 'The book doesn't rule me.'

The Queen of Feathers laughed at me. She did that sometimes, and I always hated it. Every time, it sounded like my own self-doubt, my own fears welling up through her throat.

'Are you sure of that?'

'I take the lessons from the book,' I whispered. 'I am not its weapon.'

'Then make the choice you want to make.'

'What fecking help are you?' I shot back.

'I'm exactly what we need,' she said. 'You'll see, eventually, if you're the right one to see it. We both will.'

She made me angry. Light returned all around me as I snatched a bottle from the table and poured.

They talked for another hour. Eventually there was no more to say. Onostus was adamant that Ulovar had set the attack on him, no matter the truth of it. He argued well. I could see how he'd amassed so much power in the north, and I understood why men would follow him. He was impressive, though it galled me to admit it.

'Return to your people,' Robilar said. 'If Ulovar calls for a duel, you will have to fight him, and you do not have the Gates to prevail.'

'Ulovar's duelling days are behind him,' Onostus said. 'Age has come upon him suddenly. He is not the man he was.'

Robilar touched a hand to her broken skull.

'We're none of us what we once were,' she said. 'But that is the way of people.'

'His nephew has passed the Second Gate,' Robilar said.

'The same nephew who brings us into ever-closer alliance with Brannlant,' Onostus said. He smoothed down his coat over his rounded belly as though suddenly thinking of it. 'That one I would relish a chance to put an end to. But I will make no move against him. Not if he makes no move against me.'

'Go, then,' the grandmaster said dismissively, wafting him away with a hand. 'Back to Gilmundy with you. I cannot attest to your safety on the road. Apprentice Raine, see him out. After that, you are dismissed.'

We rode down in silence. Where the path diverged, a man awaited him a hundred feet down the road on horseback. I went cold. That was the man armoured head to toe in bright silver steel, his face hidden behind an ornate face plate that snarled open-mouthed. By the light of day I saw the little

dents in his armour, blemishes that didn't catch the sun. Lord Braman. A
man LacAud would raise to the throne.

Onostus had been lying after all. He'd lied the entire time he spoke to
the grandmaster, and the proof of that was here to see: the very man who'd
sought to kill us in Gilmundy. He'd brought a threat of his own.

'Your man there is a killer,' I said.

'Aye, he is,' Onostus said. 'But he's loyal, and we're all made killers by the
times we live in.'

I gripped my reins so tight the leather dug hard against my skin. Sometimes it takes more strength to remain still than it does to launch yourself
forward. Spells from the Ashtai Grimoire flashed through my mind. The
Banshee's Wail. The Drinker's Bite. Soul Reaper.

'You didn't bring your blood witch then?' Just the thought of that bone-
dressed creature made me want to shiver. Onostus smirked. He could see
how much the thought disturbed me, even more than Braman in his silver
armour did.

'Akail has her place, and her uses. But restraint is not her great strength.
I thought it best to leave her where she cannot be too much bother. Besides,
Redwinter is not overly fond of her kind.'

'What is she?'

'She is something we all forgot,' he said. 'And honestly, had I not needed
her rather unique services, I'd rather things had stayed that way. But I'm a
man who pays his debts.'

'I hope you've prepared your wards and charms,' I said. 'I think you're
going to need them.'

'Cheery sort, aren't you?' Onostus said. 'You'll have to get in line. Thanks
for the drink. It was worth a shot.' He laughed and carried on walking.

It was a relief when things started to go back to whatever normal was. Some of Mathilde's party headed back to Brannlant. I fell back into the routine of singing the hours in church, practising Eio and making attempts towards the Second Gate, Sei, before heading down to Harranir to get pummelled around by Torgan under his sneering mother's narrowed eyes. Ulovar did not rejoin those lessons, nor meals. I saw him occasionally taking a slow, brief turn around the gardens for air with Sanvaunt close by. I saw from his occasional stumble that his knees had grown weak.

I saw Sanvaunt and Liara loading up a pack horse for the ride down to Harranir. A frilled costume protruded from a saddle bag. With everything going on around us, I'd forgotten about Lord Croak and their silly play was finally to be unveiled that evening. I took a deep breath. I knew what I had to do.

'Nervous?' I asked, just to enter conversation.

'No,' Sanvaunt said. 'Not really.'

He was being distant with me. I'd known he would be. Sanvaunt was predictable like that. But I'd prepared the words I needed—that he needed. Ovitus had taught me their importance by their absence.

'I'm sorry. For being a wasp, on the stairs that day.'

Sanvaunt finished checking the saddle girth, straightened and turned those sleepy eyes on me, and I melted a bit.

'These are strange days for everyone,' he said. 'But I appreciate the apology. I'm still flesh and blood. And this isn't easy on anyone.'

'I need to cut down on the rose-thistle,' I said. 'I don't think it's good for me. But I was being jealous, and out of sorts. I'm sorry.'

'I can only take so many batterings,' he said, and I sensed just how tired he was. He looked frayed around the edges, scuffed. But then he smiled at me and that rose-thistle-induced argument seemed to have been forgotten. 'The timing is never right, is it?'

'I don't think we'll ever get easy timings.'

'You didn't say no properly, in the garden.'

I looked off to the side, lips pursed, but I couldn't fight the smile from my face.

'I better think up some more excuses then.'

I left them to it. I was a distraction that wasn't needed.

Ovitus and Mathilde were seldom apart. Their charity project got under-way, and Ovitus even ventured in his uncle's place to parliament. From what I heard, his intentions to feed the hungry and work the needy were met with an even combination of enthusiasm and scorn. An enterprising young woman who clearly saw the benefits of being first among Princess Mathilde's supporters offered up a great crumbling old building near the docks to be the first labour-home. A place to work, a place to sleep, meals and clothing provided in exchange for labour. At supper, when Ovitus occasion-ally joined us to share news on his plans, his eyes shone with a hopeful light.

We apprentices were little affected by his efforts to relieve the plight of the poor. All we wanted to know from him was how he had managed to blunder his way through Eio and into Sei. To open the Second Gate excused one from the call of the Winterra and Mathilde's father's endless wars of conquest. It practically guaranteed a place among Redwinter's artificers, forging stronger weapons and battle cloth that wouldn't tear, retaining the steel from which it was sewn. And if the Second Gate was mastered, there was the possibility of opening the Gates that lay beyond it.

Draoihn Palanost was rarely impressed by our efforts, but she never raised her voice or outright chastised us. She was a gentle woman at heart. She herself had never moved beyond the First Gate, but her command of it was so encompassing that her talents were put to better use here, rather than with a sword.

'You must focus on yourself, and focus on the moment,' she instructed. 'Be one with your surroundings. Be one with yourself first. It is mastery of the First Gate that will allow you to make your attempts towards the Sec-ond. Many of you think you have mastered your trance already, but unless you can tell me what lies beneath the cloth, we are not there just yet.'

Eio thrummed around me, held close, a tight radius. What was under the cloth? I couldn't tell. I had a vague impression of its weight upon the flagstone beneath it, and its covered shape gave nothing away. The faintest sense of movement within. Animal? No. Too routine, we'd seen enough mice and sparrows. I wasn't sure how I was even feeling it, perhaps in the tiny vibrations its tiny movements sent into the floor. I didn't get it that day. It turned out to be a water-driven clock. I thought that should have been easier than the previous day's, which had been a jar of honey. I'd managed to pick out the sweetness in the air.

'I really don't see how this is going to be helpful,' Jathan muttered.

As usual, Palanost heard him all the way across the room. I never knew when she was in Eio or not, her control was so subtle.

'We do not lift the heaviest weights we can so that we can spend our time lifting heavy weights,' she said in her rich Murrish accent. I didn't think Palanost beautiful, but there was something about her that made me want to be more like her. She was so at ease with her body, her height, her place in the world. How freeing that must be. 'We build our bodies so that when we must lift a smaller weight, we do it more easily and more quickly. Will you ever need to sense what mystery object lies beneath a cloth? It is unlikely. But when you want to hear a conversation through a window pane, when you must know what a man is pulling from his coat, when you must assess all of an opponent's details, even as they charge towards you on the battlefield— then your minds, through honing and expert application, will be ready to meet those challenges.' She gave Jathan a pointed look. 'All of them.'

Jathan gave her his most charming grin as she met his eye, and Palanost tilted her head slightly to one side with half-closed eyelids. His charms were as ineffective on her as a butterfly battering against a wall.

'That's all for today.'

I got up, rubbed my backside and began rolling my mat. They could have given us mats that actually had some padding in them. Woven grass made for a poor seat. As we packed up, a bald man wearing a fur-lined robe in oxblood red entered the room, a golden hammer-and-tongs crossed on the left breast. He was in his later sixties but looked whole and hale. Suanach LacNaruun, a member of the Council of Night and Day and the master of artifice in Redwinter.

'I've an announcement, Draoihn Palanost,' he said. 'May I?' Palanost indicated that he indeed may, which was always going to be the case. 'Apprentices. Following the council's discussions, and to ensure the security of the Crown, it has been determined that the schedule for your Testing has been advanced.' Shocked gasps. Fear. Excitement. 'We have great faith in you, and we believe that for many of you it is high past time you were given your opportunity to earn your coats. Therefore, all apprentices with six months of training or greater will be undergoing their Testing no later than the thirty-first day of Somerdhoone.'

Astoundment. Gasps. Eager from some mouths, nervous from others. I didn't gasp. I just stared.

'That's not even forty days from now,' Esher whispered. Her eyes had grown wide. 'I'm not ready. I'm not—'

'You'll be fine,' I told her, reached out and squeezed her hand. She pulled it away and clasped her hands together over her chest.

'May I ask why, Councillor Suanach?' a young man who lived at the LacAud greathouse asked from midway through the ranks. His name was Nygell LacAud, a bookish boy who foundered on the practice court but knew the histories better than any. It was well that he be the one to ask it. None of the LacAud apprentices were direct kin to Onostus, but clan ties were grown in the bones. Suanach cleared his throat.

'It is felt that your journey as Draoihn is being unduly delayed. We have need of good hearts and good arms. It is true that traditionally, an apprentice serves a bare minimum of two years before being Tested, and for those of you whose talents were discovered young, that can stretch to five or even six years.' He gave a warm smile. 'There are those among you I recall arriving here when you were nine or ten years old. It is high time you took your rightful places.'

I put my hand up.

'Apprentice Raine,' Suanach said. He knew me by sight. I'd limped into the Round Chamber and tossed Kaldhoone LacShale's head at the council's feet, after all. It had certainly been dramatic, but not everyone had appreciated the theatre of it all. Suanach had a kindly disposition towards me, though. Like Palanost, he was the type who actually liked to see students succeed.

'I've only been here eight months,' I said. 'Some may have been here for years, but—but I haven't.'

'Rest assured, Apprentice Raine, that the council knows each of your names and would not be advancing with this plan if we did not think you could succeed. Each of you has been assigned a mentor who will take responsibility for your training in the next month. I have a list, somewhere.' He fished in the pockets of his robe, and drew out an ivory scroll case with golden fixings. It seemed too grand a thing to contain a simple piece of paper, where fates had been written just an hour before.

'In alphabetical order . . . Apprentice Adanost of Murr, you will be mentored by Draoihn Roth.' Adanost, two rows in front of me, gave a slight groan. Suanach's eyes flashed up over the assembled apprentices with the hint of a frown. 'Apprentice Beatrand of Dalwinny, you will also be mentored by Draoihn Roth.' The groan was more audible this time. Roth was all rules and hard looks. 'Apprentice Colban, you shall be mentored by Draoihn Palanost.'

There was a disquieted murmur among the apprentices.

'Colban's not here anymore, Councillor,' Palanost said soberly.

'Colban was killed by Councillor LacAud!' Esher shouted angrily.

'Lies!' Nygell LacAud shouted back.

'Quiet, all of you,' Palanost said.

'Ah.' Suanach hadn't the guile to hide his embarrassment. 'One of Ulovar's, wasn't he? I suppose, perhaps with Councillor Ulovar indisposed, that was missed.' He cleared his throat and continued. Collaine, Dunfric, Dynae . . .

'Palanost. Palanost. Palanost,' Esher whispered quietly. But as Suanach reached her name, she received a different teacher, Draoihn Eiden. 'That's all right,' Esher said with some relief. 'He mentored Liara before her Testing.'

'Quiet at the back there, Apprentice,' Suanach called, and it was Esher's turn to reach out and give my hand a squeeze. Several other apprentices were given Draoihn mentors that we didn't know, presumably those linked in some way to the houses who provided their patronage.

'Apprentice Jathan, to be mentored by Haronus LacClune.'

'You can't be serious?' Jathan exclaimed. He was halfway risen to his feet.

'Sit. Down,' Suanach said, exasperated by constant interruption, and all Jathan's easygoing charm abandoned him and he plopped back down onto his arse. It was the worst of outcomes. Haronus LacClune loathed us. He loathed all of LacNaithe. He was a cruel-natured bully with demon-inflicted scrapes across his forehead, and I often thought it was a shame the demon hadn't done a better job. Jathan looked like he was going to be sick. 'Your household allegiances are not important in Redwinter,' Suanach said. 'You are being Tested to see whether you will be true servants of the Crown. The Crown is our life: all else is dust. You would do well to remember that as you go forwards into your Testing.'

'Can't Van Ulovar mentor me?' Jathan blurted. Suanach's eyes narrowed. He was a gentle sort, but even gentle men do not have infinite patience.

'Put aside these petty thoughts, Apprentice,' he said sharply. 'Your Testing will show your abilities and your allegiance. There is not a one who wears the oxblood who has not undergone it, and not a one who is not bound to the Crown above all else.' But he relented and recovered a more kindly expression. 'The vans of houses do not provide mentorship before a Testing. And Councillor Ulovar is still recovering his strength.'

But he wasn't. He was losing it.

There were more names. I seemed to be right at the end of the list. There were thirty-nine of us, or thirty-eight now that Ovitus seemed to have stopped attending lessons, but Little Maran and two others weren't eligible. As my time approached I ran through the options.

It wouldn't be Palanost, or Roth. They each had four, which seemed to be the limit. Eiden and four other senior Draoihn had four as well. Amistaja and Bellise each had three, while Fyrio of Kwend and Haronus LacClune each had just two. That made them the most likely choices. I knew Haronus better than any of them, but mostly because I'd shot him with an arrow and faced down against him on Tor Marduul, and though I don't think he'd ever realised it was my arrow that had pierced him, he didn't like us much anyway. Dedicated Draoihn he might have been, but the experience was hardly likely to be pleasant.

'Apprentice Raine,' Suanach read. My breath had got stuck between lung and mouth. He looked up at me and his face was blank as he read the last name. 'Grandmaster Vedira Robilar.'

I fled the hall, making straight for Lady Datsuun's home in Harranir where none could follow me, brushing off quizzical looks and the murmuring that flowed after me. I had no answers to the questions that would follow, and I sought to avoid them for as long as possible.

What in Skuttis was going on now? Had she been intending this since I poured wine for Onostus LacAud? Or had it been before that? Maybe it was simply spreading resources out, but—I didn't want her as a mentor. She still terrified me. She had powers beyond those of any other Draoihn, and to be in such close proximity to her put my secret so much closer to discovery. That meant stoning, or hanging, or the fire. I tried to make a point of ignoring the ghosts I saw as I passed through Harranir's streets, the fresh and the old, but one man lay unmoving in a doorway. He could have been another vagrant on the streets, and there were many of them, flooding down from the north where work and soon food would be lacking. The ghost sat over his body as if spending one last day being ignored by the city's population.

It shouldn't have been possible that people could end up that way. In the north, communities helped one another. We didn't let people go hungry. It seemed like the more people you crammed into one place, the less care there was to go around. And yet these poor folk were fleeing famine and poverty, their livelihoods decimated by a sickness that had wiped out their flocks. They'd found no succour here. I had nothing but hatred for Onostus LacAud but didn't he have a point? Shouldn't the wealthier southern lands be doing something to help these lost bastards? We gave them nothing in the north, and we gave them nothing when they joined us in the south either. Guilt led me to give every coin I had on me to the hungry souls I passed. It wasn't enough.

Lady Datsuun worked me hard that afternoon, her instructions relayed to her son, and in turn from him to Ibaqa and lastly me. Torgan clearly didn't need his mother to be there, but it was the way of things in their household. I focused into the thick cane in my hand, the wood scarred and dented from thousands of clashes, and tried to let its solidity still the same bubbling un-ease I'd fled from.

'Strike to land with your first intention,' Ibaqa translated. 'Be ready with your second intention if it is parried, and your third after it. You do not strike one blow, you strike blow after blow. Do not stop moving. Do not think you win a point, you never win a point, there are no points. Look for openings and *strike* and *strike* and *strike*.'

It was a familiar exercise, and I let it blank my mind. The Dharithian style of fighting sought to end any confrontation as swiftly as possible. The first strike was usually a cut from the draw, but that was never the end of it. Every blow struck for the head or chest, sword hand and blade leading so that there was no room for the opponent to snipe at wrist or hand. It was not a style suited to duelling to first blood, nor for the cautious fencing I saw the other apprentices engaging in, where bouts could last ten minutes without a blow being landed. The Dharithian sword was swift, decisive, and employed to bring an opponent to their knees as swiftly as possible. It was a philosophy that worked when there were enemies all around you, not just in a duel with rules and limits. If the first attack did not land there was already another flowing on its way. I needed it just then. I wasn't ready for what had to follow.

'Master Torgan says you did not do worse than a beginner,' Ibaqa said after two hours. 'You may rest now.'

'Thanks,' I said, before it occurred to me that it was the first praise I'd received. I nodded my head towards Torgan, but he curled his lip and let forth a string of Dharithian. Ibaqa bowed her head.

'He says you have fallen to pride. No resting. You fight again.'

By the time we were done I was exhausted, smarting from the blows to shoulder, flank and chest where Torgan hadn't pulled his strikes. I didn't mind. I was happy to just feel the aches and weariness in my own body, concentrating on that rather than the fear that wanted to work its way in.

The grandmaster herself was going to mentor me, and me alone, in the brief window of time before my Testing. Perhaps she had elected to take me on because I was the least experienced, the least practised of those who were to face whatever trials the Testing involved. Maybe she just wanted to have me around, the girl who had killed a Draoihn of the Fourth Gate, to serve as a reminder to her enemies. I had no idea what to expect. Those who earned their coats didn't speak of what they had gone through. I suspected that my trance would be put to the test, maybe identifying more covered objects like Palanost gave us. Perhaps history, hopefully not languages. But I was so far behind the rest of them on those things I didn't know how I'd ever match up to the Draoihn's demanding standards.

Would I find myself like Colban? He'd trained as an apprentice for nearly seven years, and it had all been for nothing. He'd been fluent in four languages, and had even penned a paper on the Haddat-Nir kings of old that had thrilled the scholars of the library. If those were part of the criteria, I didn't match up to them.

It hurt to know they wouldn't be the conditions on which I was judged. I already knew my value to Redwinter.

. . . . . .

I cleaned myself up before I left, dressing in drab, simple clothes. Nondescript, light enough for the endless summer heat. There had been too much carousing of late, but tonight was different. Tonight I got to just blend in with an audience, become part of a crowd. I could heckle and laugh, or I could be still and silent among the crowd. It was the night of Liara and Sanvaunt's theatre-play. I was tired, and my mind was abuzz with the recent news, but for once I wouldn't have to do the work.

The playhouse was not one of the larger ones, but pulled a crowd on the fringe. There was no mention of Sanvaunt's or Liara's names on the chalk boards outside—they had adopted performance identities for the show. The doors of the wide hall were thrown open, trying to let out the heat that had built up in the day. It would be sweltering inside.

'Got you, Fiahd!' Esher pounced on me as I waited in line outside. She wrapped her arms around me from behind in the cooling day.

'You got me,' I conceded. Was this a game we played now? I found I enjoyed the ambush, the quiet strength in her arms. 'Excited?'

'Everyone's talking,' she said. 'You'd think Ovitus's engagement would have been the big news of the month but somehow it got trumped.' I'd meant Liara's show, but of course the Testing was on her mind.

'You feel all right about it?'

'Not really. I'm nervous,' Esher said. 'How else can any of us feel? I mean, I knew it was coming at some point. But this is awfully close. Liara knew half a year in advance and Eiden took her out into the country to train for three whole months. They've given us forty days.'

'Eiden's a good pick for you,' I said. 'He's calm. Reliable.'

'He's tough, is what Liara said.'

'Maybe tough is good.'

'Maybe.' Esher chewed on her lower lip, and I could see the question making its way up across her beautiful face, smile spreading between cheekbones that could have cut cloth with a slash of her face. It was impossible not to notice her blue-white, milky left eye. The lid was a little heavier than on the right, and when she smiled it half-covered it. 'It's not me everyone's talking about, though.'

'I suppose they want to ask me if I know why I was assigned to the grandmaster?' I said.

'I expect they do,' Esher grinned. 'I'd say it was an immense stroke of luck, but I don't think luck had anything to do with it.'

'You think I'm lucky?'

'You get to be mentored by the *grandmaster* herself. I asked around and nobody has ever heard of the grandmaster mentoring anybody before. Not in our lifetime.'

'It's hard to feel lucky,' I said. I leaned forwards, elbows on knees, chin on my fists. 'She's terrifying.'

'I remember,' Esher said, but she was all bright with a glow of excitement for me. 'She appeared on Tor Marduul in a blast of blue-and-yellow fire that night we met. And that head of hers.' She made a face, wrinkling her nose. 'But terrifying can be a good thing, can't it? That's what we need at the top of things. Protecting the Crown.'

'Sometimes it feels like the Crown is a very distant, invisible idea and not much more,' I said. 'It's hard to give your life over to something you can't see, or touch. Or understand, really.'

'A bit like being a priest,' Esher said. 'Only there is *definitely* a Crown beneath Harranir, and four more off out in the world. Keeping us safe. That's what we exist for, isn't it? To keep everyone safe.'

I had wondered about that, from time to time. I hadn't been raised on tales of the Crown since I was young as those brought earliest to Redwinter had. The grandmaster had shown it to me in a vision, a vast, subterranean dome filled with twinkling starlight. She already had all the power she could ever want: what need had there been to show me a falsehood? But I'd heard others talking, when ale loosened tongues and night's shadows crowded at the windows. Few had ever observed what I'd been gifted with. It was hard to ask people to believe so fervently in something that only impacted their lives invisibly.

I had seen not only the Crown, but the terrors it held in check.

Without the Crowns, our world would collide with the hidden realm, and the Faded, the demons, the hidden folk, even the dead could return. Our world would be shattered.

I had seen the dead return. I had seen the darkness of demons, and Ciuthach's burning eyes. They woke me, strangled for breath between dreams, and I had seen the nightmares that waited beyond the divide. Man could be a beast, but even at his worst, he is just a beast. There were things out there in the darkness that were more terrible than most could ever have imagined.

'Why do you think she chose you?' Esher asked.

'Maybe she just got stuck with me.'

'As if she gets stuck with anything! She could have palmed you off to Haronus, Fyrio, any of the others. Nothing on that council happens by chance. She has something in mind for you.'

'Can we not talk about it?' I said sharply. Then, 'Sorry. I know it's strange and hot news, but for now, I just want to enjoy watching Sanvaunt make a tit of himself on a stage.'

'Of course,' Esher said. She linked her fingers with mine, and I was all too aware of the contact of our skin. How it made me tingle all over, raising gooseflesh up my arms. I still didn't know what to make of it. Neither of us did, I thought. I'd never had a friend like Esher before. I couldn't tell her everything about me. I had secrets born from the grave that needed to stay there. But I could be myself so easily around her. I could let her see the damaged little edges that needed shoring up, and she was always there plugging the gaps and holding me up when I felt like I was about to fall down. Maybe I was mistaking it all for something else entirely. At times the guilt rose up and I felt that it was going to bury me. At others, I wanted to just sink beneath it, to the warm waters where it didn't trouble me at all.

It wasn't like with Sanvaunt. Not at all. With him, I wanted to be one of the heroines in those ridiculous stories he wrote. *Romances*, they were called. I wanted him to kick my door in, tell me it was high time I stopped spinning him in circles. It was all fantasy, of course, but that's what fantasy is for. Confusing, rude, destructive, rapacious fantasy. But no more than that. Thoughts are free, after all. But when I really thought of him, I thought of that quiet, relaxed calm of complete control. I thought of him making a dunce of himself trying to run up a wall to impress me. I thought of him bodily throwing himself in the way of a Mawleth, sword bared as he told me to run. I thought of that quiet anger that sometimes spiked, and how he owned it and didn't let it carry him away. He wasn't perfect. Nobody is. But at times he felt close.

Esher did too, sometimes. Moments like now, when her soft closeness, her easy touch, her bright outlook and the way she never seemed to judge me filled me with a sense of being at home. I'd never felt home before, not really, but if I'd had one, it was here with her. We talked about life, and training, and gossip and when we talked about the boys who'd flirted with her I laughed and joked along even as the jealousy spat hot little sparks inside me. I wasn't without attention of my own, and it wasn't fair of me—it wasn't even realistic of me—to imagine that she didn't have it too. But somehow she felt like we belonged to each other.

We entered the playhouse. The light was low inside, and as I'd feared, the open doors had failed to dispel the thick, cloying heat. Sweat began to drip from me the moment I stepped inside. Esher and I uncoupled our hands. They were already sticky, but physical contact of any kind in that theatre became downright messy. High windows were thrown open but offered no breeze. What had promised to be an enjoyable diversion from the seriousness of the world now loomed like an ordeal.

'I feel like I've heard this whole thing recited out of order in drips and drabs already,' Jathan said as he sat on a bench alongside Esher. The seating ringed the raised stage on three sides.

'I feel like I've tried not to hear it,' I said.

'I'm excited,' Esher said.

'So am I,' Ovitus said, as he found a space beside me. I hadn't expected him to come, as overwhelmed as the greathouse was with his Brannish guests. His wolfhound, Waldy, snuffled at my fingers and decided to lick the perspiration from my palms. His doggy smell was intensified in the warmth. 'This is such a good way to bring culture to the masses. Maybe even deliver messages, to teach the people.'

'I think it's just supposed to be funny,' I said.

'Maybe, maybe,' Ovitus said. 'But think of the opportunities. A forum to raise public awareness. Perhaps even to show the benefits of our new labour homes. We've secured backing. Investment! The smaller clans are eager to be involved, and most of the north wants to get on board. Not LacAud, of course. They were hardly going to throw in with us, not when they have their own candidate for the throne, and that's keeping a lot of the north-western clans from giving us full support. But our charitable endeavours could reach people through this type of thing, couldn't they?'

'I'm just not sure that's the point of it,' I said.

'How does it work, exactly?' Esher asked. 'The charitable endeavours, I mean.'

'We provide the work, and the people have something to take away with them,' Ovitus said. 'It's simple economics, really.'

I didn't know anything about economics. I understood that money changed hands and people got rich or got poor. It just sounded like work, though.

'It's not that complicated,' Ovitus said as he scratched his dog between the ears. Waldy panted in the warmth, nuzzling his head against Ovitus's fingers appreciatively. 'It's a tried-and-tested system. Mathilde's the one who started making it work. You take a man in need, give him clothes, food, a bed, and an honest day's work. Everyone benefits.'

'I thought that's how it worked already,' I said.

'How's a man on the street to find a bed before he has work? And how can he work before he has a bed? A man can't work while he's hungry, and he can't feed himself while he can't work. Our new beneficial enterprise will lift up the poor and dispossessed, give them purpose again. They'll be fed and clothed, warm and fulfilled, a living, functioning part of the workforce. No more wasting all their money on drink and Olatte leaf. It really is just simple economics.'

Enthusiasm emanated from him in waves. He stared right at me as he spoke, and I realised that what he wanted from me was approval.

'There are a lot of poor people these days,' I said. 'A lot on the streets.' It wasn't what he wanted to hear from me. He'd expected me to applaud the idea, but maybe I just didn't grasp how it was different to a normal busi-ness. 'It's a noble cause,' I said, and fortunately, that was enough for him. He beamed at me. Beamed so hard I thought his face might expand and take up another seat. Perhaps there was some part of him that needed my approval, maybe to undo the shame he'd felt when his lies were exposed. He thought of himself as kind, sensitive—but it was important to him that others thought of him that way.

I was saved from further economic discourse by the opening of a door at the back of the stage, and Liara emerged. She was dressed in a robe of tattered red and black stripes, her red curls hidden beneath a demonic mask, long-horned and leering. She rang a hand bell loud enough to quiet the sweating audience. When she had everyone's attention, her voice rang out clear and strong.

'Hear ye, one and all, friends and foes alike. Tonight we bring to you a most terrible tale. A household that lived in fear of the past, but could not face the future. A tale of two great lovers, their passion forbidden but uncontrollable. A tale of jealousy, and of bitter betrayal. A tale of I, Lord Croak, the wicked Faded Lord who sought to break them apart. Hear now, the footsteps of noble Dadorus, first of his house, a man of noble birth, cursed by an unlucky star. Hark, he approaches . . .'

Sanvaunt came out onto the stage, his face painted white, his lips absurdly red.

'How are you feeling about the Testing?' Ovitus whispered.

'Shush,' I muttered.

'I'm not worried,' Ovitus went on. I could feel his sheepish smile. 'And if I'm honest, since I—you know—since I made the Second Gate, I think it's more of a formality than anything. Redwinter can hardly deny me now.'

'Let's listen,' I said again, and thankfully Ovitus did as he was told. The play began. As it progressed, I came to realise it followed a standard kind of formula, filled with tropes that the audience recognised but that I was unfamiliar with. A kind of Hidden Folk spirit oversaw the proceedings in the house and needed to be appeased, boys played girls and girls played boys, and much of it was narrated by Liara, whose arcane robe denoted her as the namesake Faded Lord Croak. I didn't get a lot of the jokes, but the audience seemed to, and most of the laughs landed.

Sanvaunt seemed nervous. He was usually so confident, so self-assured, that it felt odd to see him needing to clear his throat before delivering a line here and there. He kept his eyes away from the audience. Liara smashed through her lines with the power of a charging bull, and most of the laughs belonged to her. She made a very convincing Faded Lord. I was happy for her—she was getting her recognition.

The basic story was that one of the lovers asked the help of the Faded Lord to demonstrate his love for his paramour, but the creature sought only to enter the house and steal away a baby. The house, being a place of refuge, was protected by powerful spells preventing him from crossing its threshold.

Eventually the lovers realised his plans and tricked him into transporting himself into the house's confines, whereupon the wards paralysed him and they were able to contain him in a little box. It all seemed highly implausible to me.

By the time the final act was done and the small cast took a bow, I was dying for a cold drink and a dunk in the river. The smell of sweating bodies thickened the air. We applauded the actors before escaping into the marginally cooler evening.

'That was *amazing*,' Esher exclaimed when we finally escaped. 'I've never laughed so hard. That bit about the merchants was so funny.'

I wished that I'd enjoyed it as much as she had. It had seemed beyond me in some ways. Perhaps there was some amount of this stuff that one had to see before it could be fully understood. It was another reminder that even after all this time, I was still something of a stranger down in the southern lands, and a greater stranger to the wealth needed to attend this kind of thing. No matter what I did, I always found myself feeling like an outsider.

. . . . . .

Testing preparation began in earnest the following day. Palanost began walking with her assigned apprentices in the gardens, or taking them to the dusty stacks in the library. Esher packed a bag, and she was gone with Eiden, as was his way. I watched her riding out beneath Redwinter's gates, gone for days, or weeks, who knew? The house mourned her in its empty spaces.

I waited nervously for a summons. The grandmaster was a busy woman. I couldn't envisage us going out rambling as Eiden did, or following Palanost's quiet lead. But a day passed, and then another, and another, and I received no message to call me to her. The LacNaithe greathouse remained overrun with Brannish guests.

The days ground by like millstones, crushing time to powder as I waited and waited for the grandmaster to summon me. A week, then another. Everyone was so busy, myself as much as any of them. I received a note from Sanvaunt, who was staying down in the city for a few days while he tried to resolve trade deals between north and south that had defaulted when Gilmundy was taken, although I thought he might have felt reluctant to see the rest of us after we'd seen his performance. Men could be funny like that. It sounded extremely legal and technical, and it seemed like a lot to put on the shoulders of someone so young. It was easy to forget that Sanvaunt was only in his early twenties. Ovitus had a good legal mind, but he was too wrapped up in all things Mathilde to be of help, and I couldn't really blame him for that. I might have offered my own help if I'd thought I'd have understood anything at all about it, which from the first mentions of *appellation* and *inculpatory* my mind wriggled away to other things. I'd resolved Ulovar's trial by throwing a severed head on the floor but that probably wouldn't work so well in this case.

But those things didn't matter, and they weren't why he'd sent the letter anyway. At the end of the letter, he'd written:

> *Brown's Inn (a stuffy, boring place where many lawyers have their chambers) is holding its summer ball in three days' time in the early evening. It will be full of stuffy things and boring lawyers, but there will be wine and even lawyers can dance. It might be nice to get out from Redwinter and relax a little. Join me?*

Tingle, tingle.

But what about Grandmaster Robilar, and training, and the book, and Ulovar's failing health, and . . .

Better not to think on it too hard. Write and be damned. It was time I committed myself. Time to have what I wanted, for once. I wrote back that I would meet him at the LacNaithe business premises in Harranir, late afternoon three days hence, and sealed the letter with wax before I could bring up any more excuses. My mind was incessant with chatter these days. Too many thoughts are bad for you. Think too long on anything and you'll find a way to see all the problems in the world, and inside you, reflecting back from it. I despatched it to be sent down to the city with the afternoon's messages.

I retired to bed, and I thought of Esher, gone, and Sanvaunt, waiting, and Castus having kissed them both when they were so much younger, and burning eyes in the dark that sought to extinguish life, and the lies that had been told about me, and Ulovar, sleeping deeper every day, and Colban, his ghost screaming in the night.

Midnight had passed when I was finally summoned to see my mentor.

17

Vedira Robilar had held the position of grandmaster in Redwinter for ninety-five years, but she had lived a lot longer than that. I met her in the study where I had sat with her once before, the day she had refused my training as Draoihn. Everything had been different then, I had been different then, but I appeared before her now dressed in the simple clothes I had thrown on, the day's weight still upon me, feeling like dough that hadn't yet had time to prove. Grandmaster Robilar could not have been more ready for me if she'd had an army of servants to straighten her out. Thick, lustrous brown hair twirled into winter blonde as it passed her shoulders, resting in spirals across a green gown fit for parties grander than the one Ovitus had thrown. The colour matched the shading above her eyes. I was glad that it was this form that she was greeting me in. The crone meant business, the young woman meant secrets, and secrets I was better ready to handle.

'Apprentice Raine. You were sleeping,' she said without rising from her desk. She held a pen in one hand, tracing pencil lines that depicted an open human chest, ribs cracked outwards and organs on display. She didn't offer me a glove to kiss.

'No, Grandmaster,' I said dutifully. A little rose-thistle bristled in my mind. It wanted me to say something more, but I'd only taken a nip. Just enough to knock the weariness off. The room was well-lit with oil lamps, driving shadows back from the gruesome anatomical drawings framed on the walls. It seemed even the grandmaster was cutting back on cadanum globes with the prices rising higher by the day, a result of disrupted northern trade.

'I do not have a great deal of time. But I asked to mentor you specifically. It is a great honour. Agreed?'

It didn't feel an honour as much as it was generally terrifying.

'Yes, Grandmaster.'

'Good. It is important that you understand your place in things. We begin now,' Robilar said. She gestured to a smaller desk to one side of the room.

'I have prepared a list. Simply mark the column that best describes each of
your fellow apprentices. Write a few lines beside each name explaining the
reason behind your decision.'

She returned to her drawing.

I took a seat and drew it in close to the desk. This wasn't what I'd expected. The list named every apprentice currently training in Redwinter.
I wasn't sure what I'd imagined, but the late night summons had made it
all seem more mysterious and mystical than clerical work. The clean white
sheet of paper lay on the table, names staring back at me in flamboyant
script. Alongside them lay a number of columns.

Archivist. Cartographer. Artificer. Diplomat. Teacher. Poet. Warrior.

I felt a little queasy, a swell of acid burning at the base of my throat.
Maybe it was just the rose-thistle. I was being asked what position I felt each
of the others would be best suited to if they were successful in their Testing.
It was a test in itself, but there was something here to learn, unless Grandmaster Robilar had felt like she needed someone to do her job for her in the
middle of the night, which seemed unlikely. I took up a pen.

Adanost of Murr, one of my cohort in the greathouse. He was well-liked,
easy-natured. Didn't say much, but perceptive. I couldn't see him as a diplomat or teacher, and certainly not a poet. Cartography was something that
Draoihn excelled at: the command of the First Gate enhanced depth perception, judging distances and angles. Redwinter's mapmakers provided a
lucrative income. He wasn't bad with a pen. I ticked *cartographer* and wrote
that it played to his strengths.

Beatrand of Dalwinny had no aptitude for anything that involved sitting down. I didn't like her very much but she stood up for herself when
criticised by Draoihn Roth. In fact, she'd once told him outright that his
method of teaching wasn't helping her. I ticked *diplomat* and wrote that she
had a strong character.

As I worked my way down the list, I began to feel nervous. What *was* this
for? Was this what they pulled together for Testing us, summations from
other apprentices about where our skills lay? If it was, I didn't want to be a
part of it. Some of them I didn't know that well. Danforth was a strong lad,
I ticked *warrior* for him. Dynae was rude and often got into fist-fights down
in the city seemingly for fun, and so she got the *warrior* tick as well. It was
the name that came next, eighth on the list, that I was dreading.

Esher. My darling, beautiful, impulsive, fearful Esher. Archivist? No, she belonged outside. Cartographer? She hadn't the patience. That ruled out artificer and diplomat as well. The options were growing smaller. Teacher? She was strong in her trance, had been strong in it from the first time I met her on Tor Marduul, but she drew on it instinctively, and being good at something does not make someone a teacher. But she knew her stuff, she was bright, she liked to communicate ideas, but she didn't have Palanost's confidence, her self-assured manner of coaxing us along towards discovery. Poet? She liked to ride. She liked wind in her hair. I didn't even know what *poet* meant, since Redwinter didn't keep a bench of orators or writers. If I ticked poet, did that mean confining her to the waste pile? I stared at the last word in the row. I remembered her on the tor, her first words to me.

'Don't interfere, *Fiahd,* or I'll cut you in half!'

I thought of her gift to me. A sword.

I thought of her waiting with me in the dark, asking to go with me into danger.

She didn't know it about herself. Didn't realise it maybe, but Esher was a warrior at her core. She wasn't like Dynae, brash and ready for violence. True warriors seldom are. They know when to bide their time, have nothing to prove to the world about their capacity for harm. But they're ready for it. My pen teetered over the column, poised to condemn.

A tick for warrior was a statement that she would best serve in the Winterra. That my friend would serve Redwinter best far, far away, riding and fighting and serving another land's king. Nobody retired from the Winterra. Nobody came home.

And then I remembered, that same dark night when I'd gone to find Hess, gone to find answers, Esher guiding me. Helping my trance along. Pushing me towards understanding.

'You can do it with me,' she'd said.

But I hadn't. I hadn't been able to follow her that night, and I'd failed. She'd tried to teach me and it hadn't worked.

I ticked the box for *teacher* anyway, wrote that she'd helped me to learn when I needed it. It wasn't true, but I didn't know the point of this exercise anyway.

When I was finished, I'd listed Gelis as a librarian, and Jathan as a diplomat. I'd consigned seventeen others to the Winterra, but they weren't LacNaithe.

I took it to Robilar and put it down beside her gruesome drawing when

I was done. She pushed the paper aside without looking at it and bid me sit in front of her.

'Questions?'

'What was it for?' I asked straight away. Rose-thistle bluntness at work. My edges were all sharp and dull at the same time, like glass washed up by the sea.

'You are to be Tested as Draoihn,' Robilar said easily. She laid her pen alongside her artwork then shifted it slightly on the desk so that it lined up precisely alongside the paper. 'Do you think your opinions should be worth more after you have been Tested?'

'I suppose so,' I said.

'Then how would we ever be able to tell who should, or should not, become Draoihn?' Robilar asked. 'If we only started listening to you after we'd given you the power, what would be the point?'

'I suppose so,' I said again.

'Some excellent supposing.' Robilar gave me a lazy-eyed, arched eyebrow to pass comment on my lacklustre responses. She only looked ten years older than me, late twenties, early thirties. What she thought had been her best years perhaps, and she'd had a lot of them. 'Let us get on with some actual learning. I'm sure you don't want to be here all night.'

'I'm happy to be here all day and all night if I learn what I need to, Grandmaster,' I said quickly. A fawning response, but no less true for it. Robilar peered towards me, staring deep into my eyes.

'Well, all zapped up on rose-thistle, you'll last a few days at it, anyway. Come now. It's rude not to share.'

'I haven't . . .' I started, but that eyebrow rose higher still on her face.

'Apprentice Raine. I was partaking of things you've not even heard of centuries before you were born. Do you think that the activities of the young are somehow unknown to the rest of us? Or that we stop when we get older? You're a bright girl. You should know better than that. Come now. Don't be rude.'

I had to wonder whether this was a trap. Adults weren't like that, were they?

'I didn't bring it with me,' I said. I'd left the hip flask on my dressing table. It had seemed an error to bring it. This was not panning out at all as I'd imagined. Robilar made a bothered expression, then shrugged. She opened a desk drawer, took out a small pellet of something dry and brown, and held it over the flame of an hour-counting candle. The candle was burned down to a 3, the old, melted numbers no more than bloody rivulets in the melt. She held the pellet over the flame for a few seconds, then broke half of it off and tucked it beneath her tongue. She settled back with no discernible difference.

'It is deeply frustrating to converse with someone who has intoxicated themselves without doing the same. It doesn't have the same effect on me that it used to, but that is the way of it. We have a long way to go tonight. But first, I want to know how you are managing after your shock at Gilmundy.'

'People would be surprised what I find shocking these days, Grandmaster.' She waited for me to go on. 'I've done what I've been asked to do, or that I had to do,' I said.

'Indeed. Which is nothing to say with shame or dismissal. There is much honour in serving. But those who serve the Crown must learn to act on their own initiative, and we are shaped by our responses to experience. So I ask you again, how are you managing?'

I didn't have much else to say about that.

'I've been given tasks. I've done them.'

'And how did it feel, doing those things?'

Those things. Was she referring to the bottles she'd laid out on the drinks trolley? Did she know which bottle I'd poured from?

'I try not to feel,' I said. 'I try just to be.'

'I remember the scar that lay across you mind. I remember how deeply it had been cut, how much of a wound Ulovar had inflicted upon you. Does it linger still, I wonder?'

Robilar's pupils had grown wide, turning her eyes to orbs of black with the barest pale halo at their rim.

'I don't think so,' I said. 'It burned away in the end.'

'And yet you have killed, and you did so at Gilmundy. You will kill again. And you didn't feel, you just were?'

'There were reasons to do it. The situation called for it. So I did it,' I said. 'The choice wasn't really mine to make. I've sworn myself to Redwinter. I'll do what's asked of me.'

'Spoken like every apprentice about to face her Testing,' Robilar said. She smiled broadly, sitting back in her chair and touched her fingers together, pressed them to her lips. 'But is it the truth? We shall see.'

'I've killed for Redwinter,' I said. 'I know it. Everyone knows it.'

'But how does it *feel*?' Robilar demanded again. A dog with a bone, just a very powerful, ancient dog, and my mental wellbeing was the bone.

'It's work,' I said at last.

My answer didn't seem to satisfy her, but she was hard to read. She donned expressions plainly, but I didn't know how much I believed any of them represented something real. This was a woman who didn't just put on a face of glamours, but one who put on an entirely different body. She'd had centuries to practise showing only what she wanted. She was, I thought, the most dangerous person I'd ever met. The thought was oddly comforting.

'I am not without awareness that this meeting must be strange for you,' Robilar said. 'When first you came to Redwinter, I thought you too damaged to be trained. I do not always dislike discovering that I have made an error. To learn is always valuable. I have lived a very long time, Raine, and I have learned many things in that time. I have learned things that nobody living would ever have thought possible.'

She sat back, staring at me. Waiting for something. I had never imagined that the grandmaster didn't hold arcane secrets close to her chest. Was it even possible that a creature of her great age and power wanted to impress someone like me? I had to appear as little more than a puppy to her.

When I first came to Redwinter, I had been required to let the grandmaster inspect the scar across my mind. Ulovar had assured me she couldn't pluck thoughts out of me at will, but she hadn't been looking. What would happen if she did? Grandmaster Robilar would have been intimidating—or, more honestly, frightening—even if I wasn't engaged in seeking forbidden magic. It wouldn't matter to her that I was only doing it to try to cleanse myself of it. That was definitely what I was doing.

Definitely.

'We all have secrets, I guess,' I said. My throat had tightened up, a blocked pipe. 'Some,' she said, inflection rising, 'more than others. I am very old, and I know many things. Not all of the secrets I hold belong to me. But I am going to share one that is. It is a dangerous secret; I will be very clear with you now, Apprentice Raine. If you were to tell anybody this secret, you would die. The one that you told would die. And any that they told, and so on, and so on, until Harranir lay buried with the bodies of unwitting listeners. Every woman whose ears heard it, every husband whom she told it to, every child and dog who crouched listening at the door. I would bring down such fire from the sky to wipe all of Harranir from the earth if it meant that there was only silence after.' For a moment I glimpsed her other self, ancient and wizened, head banded with iron flickering as she spoke, molten light behind her eyes. I felt myself forced back into my chair by the strength of her words and my heels pushing against the floor. And then gone. 'Do we have a perfect understanding of this?'

'I don't know that I want to know it,' I said. I carried too much hidden truth inside me already. I didn't want hers.

'No,' she said. 'I don't suppose that you would. A secret is a dangerous thing. Two can share it. That is the limit of all secrets. But I have decided that you, you of all people, shall be the one with whom I share it after all these months.'

'Why would you give this to me?' I asked.

'Because I will be the one to Test you when the time comes. And if I cannot trust you with this, then there is no purpose in Testing you at all.'

I breathed in slowly through my nose, out slowly through my mouth. Again. My blood thumped hard in my neck. The grandmaster leaned forwards across her desk, young eyes staring hard into mine.

'I know what caused the colour storm. I've known since the day it happened.'

The colour storm lay long months ago now. It had caused panic at the time, uproar. There had been rioting in the city. I had spent countless hours poring through old books, looking for any kind of reference to a similar event before. The colours of the world had flashed and shimmered, flickering one to the other until with a rush a vast wind howled and it all disappeared. The world was left in shades of grey. Its effect had lasted days. Every Draoihn, even apprentices, was handed heaps of books from the archives, to pore through to try to understand what was happening.

'Then why did we look for an answer for so long?' I asked.

'Interesting,' Robilar said. 'You don't want to know what caused it?'

'I do,' I said. I did. 'But you'll get to that, and by the time we get there I might forget to ask.'

'Everyone searched, because that was what everyone should do if nobody knows the reason,' she said. 'To do otherwise would have indicated that I knew what caused it, and the Council of Night and Day would never have stood for that. I had to let them do what they would.'

'But you couldn't tell them,' I said. I thought about it for a few moments. 'Because . . .'

'Think it through. You have time.'

Robilar's eyes were dark holes, her pupils wide as saucers. The pellet she'd taken was pure rose-thistle. It wasn't a rose, nor a thistle. It didn't grow in our land. I wondered just what her body could take if she could deal with that much concentrate. I'd have diluted a pinch that big in a whole flask of water. Sips would have kept me awake for days on end. Her hair didn't move, I noticed. Not even a bit. Like its straightness and its spirals were formed from wood. Robilar snapped her fingers.

'Your mind is wandering,' she said. 'Keep to the path. Why could I not tell them?'

'It mattered to you personally,' I said. 'It's dangerous to you. And you didn't trust them. You thought one of them might be behind it.'

Robilar looked pleased.

'I would like to show you something, using Fier. The Fourth Gate,' she said. 'As I did once before, when I showed you the Crown beneath Harranir. I need nothing from you, will take nothing from you. I will only show you things. You will still be in control of your own thoughts, we will merely share space. Will you permit me to do so?'

I'd survived this once before. There were secrets in my head, but she had not been able to pry them out. That wasn't how the trance of mind beyond the Fourth Gate worked. And she was asking my consent. Nicely. If she wanted my secrets, she had other ways to force them out. Maybe it was the overconfidence of rose-thistle that brought my answer so swiftly, recklessly even.

'Yes. Show me.'

Grandmaster Robilar raised one hand, and showed me a finger. The nail was well-manicured, painted green to match her dress, her eyes.

'All you need do is touch my finger. The Fourth Gate requires contact.'

'I thought that everything is one.'

'Be that as it is,' Robilar said, 'it's still easier to eat your dinner with a knife and fork than to float it up into your mouth. Make contact with me.'

I took a breath, reached out and put my finger against hers. It was cold to the touch.

And then everything different, and I was somewhere else.

18

Two women stood opposite one another, one dark-haired, one fair. Moorland wind rushed around them, harrying, setting long cloaks to flapping. They were dressed all in black, a great fallon stone towering thirty feet above them on one side of the hill. Four sides of yellow-grey hardness, not stone, not exactly. Something else. Something hard, and enduring, and out of place in the world.

The dark-haired woman was Robilar, older than the form she chose to show me in her office. Her office body also stood beside me, but the two of us were just spectators. The wind didn't touch us, held no cold. There was something blurred about the whole scene before us, as though I looked at an impressionist painting, not everything quite formed and whole. I turned to look across the moorland, and beyond the purple heather, the yellows and greens and browns of its wildness, moor and sky together faded into a grey haze.

'This is a memory?' I asked.

'It is more construct than truth, as all memories are,' Robilar said. 'It is what I believe I remember. I know that I do not remember it truthfully. That is not how any memory works. We take an impression and fill in the gaps, or supplant them with what we wish them to be, or what suits our view of the world. But I have tried to show you what I think it was like.'

'When are we?'

'It is the year 661 of the Succession Age,' she said. 'I am fifty-one years old.'

The conjuration on the hilltop seemed to glance towards us as if she knew that we were talking about her, but it was only the grandmaster turning memory's face towards us. Her hair billowed out, dragged on the wind. There was something different about her. Something that was familiar and yet not of the woman I knew now. Gentle crow's feet dabbed the corners of her eyes, and she was sleek and magnificent. It wasn't just her age. *Something* was different.

'You were beautiful,' I said. Robilar smiled.

'You sound surprised. We only get better with age, you know.'

'You look younger now.'

'It unnerves men to be told what to do by a younger woman, and I enjoy that,' she said. 'There is a balance to be struck. But I have probably just imagined myself that way. I have learned not to dwell too hard on the unpleasant. We shall see it soon enough.'

In the scene before us, the second woman began to chant, reading from the kind of book that could never have held anything but spells and incantations. The book's cover was cut from the gnarled bark of a tree, the pages glimmering like silver. The second woman was younger than Robilar-of-Then, fair haired, the woman from the painting outside her reception room. The second woman's voice joined Robilar's, but I couldn't quite make out the words.

'What are you saying?'

'Magic of the Faded. The lords of the Hidden Folk,' Robilar said. 'But they were not words for sharing, so I am not giving them to you here. We were guided to a tome, buried deep beneath Harranir in the ruins of ancient Delatmar. It took us half a year to excavate it, but what we found—well. It was a path to immortality. I had come into my Fifth Gate early in life. There were more of us who had, then.'

'And your sister?'

'Her name was Alianna,' Robilar said.

'Did she have five Gates too?'

Robilar smiled a little as she gazed at her sister's face. Perhaps there was no room for her careful control, her delicate pantomime of emotion here. She was an actor in the real world. But in our minds, she was just herself. Or maybe that's what she wanted me to see.

'No. But she was strong in a different way.'

The two figures chanted together, and the wind intensified. They stepped closer together, bowing their heads until they touched. Shining silver symbols gleamed into being around them. Those around Alianna seemed familiar, but misshaped. I felt like I recognised some of them, but they were lacking something. Incomplete, like a portrait with the face scrubbed out. A noise kicked up all around, as though a thousand voices were suddenly raised in a song of praise, but they were kicking, scratching at the edges of it as though the song itself contained them. Clouds rushed by overhead, dashing in grey and purple as rain began to fall, then stopped. Around the two figures, a silver circle appeared across the grass, a metallic, glowing intensity. And then another, and another, and more as another circle of circles emerged within the rings.

'Six circles within six circles,' I said.

'The circle that is everything. I know that you've seen it before,' Robilar said. 'You saw it the day of the colour storm. And you said nothing of it.'

My dream head turned sharply to look at her as the magic powered on within the circle.

'I—I never saw anything,' I lied. Robilar ignored me.

'There was a lot more chanting. But I'll skip to the important part.'

A colour storm struck. It rippled within the silver circle, shaking the sky and turning the blades of grass to a flashing, rainbow-hued light show. But this one was contained to the confines of the circle. The women's clothes pulsed from purple to green, to orange to yellow, blue and red and every imaginable combination between them. But it was them, and only them.

'What were you doing?' I asked.

'We were making ourselves unbeatable,' Robilar said. 'Redwinter was not as stable as it is now, even with the clans at each other's throats. It was only six years since the first Harranese rebellion had been defeated. There were those who sought to replace the grandmaster of the time and drive the Brannish from the land. But we had already lost many in the conquest. It would have been disaster. Those fools forgot that Redwinter serves the Crown, not the king that wears it. There were those that suspected my sister of practising forbidden arts. But it was hard to prove.'

'Forbidden arts?'

'Sarathi arts.'

'They would have killed her, then?'

'They would have set her the unbeatable trial. She would be bound to a pyre, and those that believed her innocent would be challenged to try to save her. If by dawn none had done so, she would have been burned alive. Of course, by coming to her aid, those who tried it would have been declared in league with the Night Below, and treated no differently.'

'Then this . . .'

'My sister and I sought to give ourselves the power we needed to see her take the grandmaster's seat. To become invincible. So that they would burn her, and she would walk clean and free from the flames.'

The colours faded. Robilar-of-Then looked down at her hands.

'I don't feel different,' she said. Her sister nodded gravely.

'We started again. It was Alianna's turn next,' Robilar-Now said. Her face had turned solemn. 'But the backwash in the colours of the world showed our enemies where we were. I do not remember what comes next in strong detail. You've fought, so you know how that goes. But I will show you the aftermath.'

The hillside changed instantly.

Robilar lay on her back. Three arrows jutted from her torso, two in the chest and another in the belly. One leg had been torn away, the stump that protruded was scorched and blackened by fire. She was gasping, and then I saw the chunk of rock lodged in her throat, the dark blood welling and draining around it. For a moment I felt fingers clench hard around mine, but Robilar-of-Now had her hands clasped tight together. Her face was set like stone.

Alianna had been torn in half. Her head, one arm and shoulder lay up against the pale grey-yellow fallon, blood streaking it. The rest of her was nowhere to be seen. The silver circle was gone, the wind had fallen. The sun was setting in the west, throwing waves of gold and peach across the sky. The grass was wet with blood. People and horses lay scattered around, at the base of the hill, all the way up the hill, their oxblood coats wet and scorched. Great tracts of earth had been torn away, the bracken burning. A pair of bent trees glistened with frost. Shards of glass lay scattered through the heather, puzzling until I saw a man's face among them.

'They could not kill me,' Robilar said. 'There were thirty of them, and they were strong. But nothing would stick. They turned me to stone, they tore me open, they filled me with arrows and lightning and the spell Alianna and I had wrought brought me back, and back, and back. You will have heard that I have been killed before, but that is not true. I could not be killed. I could not die. My soul was bound too tightly to the world, and to the flesh that housed it.'

I felt cold tears running down my face. They were not my tears. They belonged to Grandmaster Vedira Robilar. This was her construction, drawn from memories two hundred years old. She was bleeding into me, the weight of her emotion pushing at my edges. It was a scene of utter horror, but to me it was like looking into a moving painting.

Robilar-of-Then struggled to her feet, tearing arrows from her body, the wounds closing as soon as they were removed. She looked to her sister and howled.

'I should have died again, many years later, in the year 681. Sul, a Faded Lord, burned me from the inside out and shattered my skull. That was harder to undo, even for the magic we had enacted from the book. But by then I was grandmaster, I had stabilised the nation. I ensured that no mention of the colours that had betrayed us to our enemies ever made it into a book, and I turned my Fourth Gate on those few who had seen it from a distance. I purged it from their minds, and from history.'

Everything changed.

The crone form of Grandmaster Vedira Robilar bathed in a claw-footed marble tub in a windowless, underground room. The cadanum light was low. Her head was held together by iron bands. Her skin was warped, wrinkled, burned in places. Her body seemed almost hollow in the cloudy water. Her eyes were closed to the silence. The room looked cold, the water gave no steam.

'Which is the truth?' I asked. 'Is this the real you?'

'It's all me,' she said. 'However I choose to shape myself. We are all what we choose to be, and what we choose changes in every moment of our lives. Some things we can control more than others. Fat, thin, scruffy, smart, clean, dirty, awake, asleep. We are not just one thing that stays immobile. We move and change and are remade in every passing moment. Though time does not exist. It is only a concept we use to describe that things are, or are not. A way to explain to one another how we came to be as we are.' She nodded towards the withered body in the tub. Small cracks in her skull glowed with inner fire, a fire that her body had contained but never been able to expel. 'Sometimes I am this. Sometimes I am other. It's all one, in the end.'

A glow surrounded the tub. The old woman's eyes flickered open, dragging up as if from the depths of sleep. The light grew, emerging as a column around her, and then the colours began to rage. The old woman howled, thrashed gaunt, bone-and-skin limbs, clouded water flying.

'This goes on a while,' Robilar said wearily. 'The colours disappear at the end of it.'

'The colour storm—it was you?'

'No,' Robilar said as her other self dipped beneath the bath water and then emerged again. 'It hurt. A great deal. They took it from me. The spell that had been cast all those years ago on that hillside. The spell that kept me from death. That made me so powerful that few imagined it could be done. Nobody living knew that I had cast that spell. Or should not have. But the colour storm was the reversal, the undoing of what Alianna and I had done together. I destroyed the book, after it was done, though it would have been priceless. Hallenae's own magic.'

'The Riven Queen?' I said. 'You used the Riven Queen's own spells to become immortal?'

'I tried,' Robilar said, a wry smile on her lips as she watched her other self thrashing in the grey water. The colours faded. Everything fell into greyness, and with it the broken-headed woman sucked in great gasps of air. 'But immortality is hard to reach.'

Another change. From underground, to up high. We stood atop a tower, and the air here was different. I couldn't smell it, but I felt it around me. A great castle spread out all around us, and beyond it a city of rooftops. There was Redwinter, beyond the river, beyond the great cathedral, beyond the city walls, perched like a city of its own on a mountain plateau, looking down over everyone below. We stood on the King's Tower, the highest point within the city, surrounded on all sides by the valley and the rearing mountains.

A bed had been erected up here, in the cool air. A bed with posts and drapes, wide enough for ten people side by side though it had only one occupant. An ancient, tired man, his eyes half closed and gossamer threads of hair fanned out around him on a pillow. He murmured quiet words to a solitary listener. The second man stood over him, nursing him, dabbing a gathering of spit from the corner of his mouth. He was just as old, and just as thin, his soft oxblood woollen robe hanging loose over a chest which displayed ribs like the keys of a harpsichord. I looked from one to the other. They looked so alike they had to be brothers. The man in bed was distant, unfocused. Unaware of his surroundings. The one who nursed him was resolved, but aching with sadness even in the brush strokes of Robilar's mind.

'Who is this?' I asked. 'When is this?'

'When, is now. Or close enough. In the bed, King Quinlan LacDaine, lord of Harranir and bearer of the Crown's burden. Beside him, Draoihn Kelsen, a member of the Council of Night and Day and the king's personal healer.'

'They're brothers?'

'No. Not by blood, anyway. Kelsen was born to be nobody. His mother and father served meals to miners, I believe. And yet, he is the most powerful Draoihn I have ever met in all my long life. In all the world, only he and I command the Fifth Gate. And, once, he summoned magic beyond even my abilities.'

I found it hard to believe that this old man, so frail and thin that the flesh seemed to have escaped from his body, was more powerful than the grandmaster. I had seen her appear in a flash of fire, and even now walked the dreamscape of her mind.

'Is this accurate?'

'It's close enough.'

'They say Kelsen killed his own wife when she lost her mind.'

'Indeed. Poor man. After she died, he sought a path to peace and dedicated himself to the Crown. He has not left the king's side for forty-five years. Neither day or night,' Robilar said. 'It was an easy succession. His father, Rhoubert, was a strong king but lasted only five years under the Crown's influence. Quinlan has borne the burden much better. But his time is at an end. Soon, the conflict for the succession will begin.'

'Prince Caelan is the rightful heir,' I said.

'He has the support of parliament to try for the Crown, for now. But the Crown is fickle. Many who try to bear its power are driven mad, or destroyed by it. The Crown is a burden. To enter it, to take on the mantle, is to look into the Night Below and see everything that lies beneath our world.'

'Why does anyone do it?' I asked.

'Someone must bear it. And honestly, people are very good at telling themselves that they are different to everyone else. Better, perhaps.'

'But we don't take it ourselves,' I said.

'The Night Below can drive a man mad, or it can destroy him. But without an open Gate, it cannot pour through. It must ever be tied to a man.'

'Or a woman,' I said.

'Women have their place in the ruling of the world. But the Crown was made for a man, by a man, and so it has always been. Do not think us hard done by: to bear the Crown is to be plagued by its torments for the rest of your life.'

Across by the bed, Draoihn Kelsen leaned forwards and gently laid a kiss on King Quinlan's brow. There was such tenderness in that moment that I

Ed McDonald

felt suddenly like an intruder. It was not a brotherly kiss. There was more than sibling affection in that gesture.

'Why do they look so alike?'

'For forty-five years, Kelsen has kept the king whole, and sane,' Robilar said. 'Using the Fifth Gate, he has poured vitality into the man and given him a life worth living. He has driven out every sickness, mended broken bones, prevented an attempted poisoning on one occasion. The more he has given of himself, the more he poured his own self into the king, the more they have become one. They are tied so closely now that when Kelsen can no longer keep Quinlan's heart beating, his own will fail him. They have lived together, and are doomed to pass on to Anavia in the same golden ship.'

'Why do I need to know this?'

'Because the colour storm and the king's failing health have arrived too closely together for them to be a coincidence. By stripping me of my protections, somebody has begun to lay a road that will lead them to the gates of power. The king will die. They will attempt to destroy me, and they may succeed this time.'

'Who would dare it?'

'The world never lacks for men of ambition. Henrith the Second, the King of Brannlant may claim our Crown alongside his own. Merovech Lac-Clune, Onostus LacAud, these men of the Council of Night and Day have long been possessed of towering ambition.'

'Ulovar LacNaithe does not,' I said defensively.

'Ulovar knows his place in the world,' Robilar said. 'But he weakens daily. I have tried my own healing art on him. But the Fifth Gate cannot undo whatever it is that has brought him low. He is fading, Raine. And that can be no coincidence either.'

'He's just resting. After he exerted himself,' I said quietly. But I didn't believe it.

'He is fading,' Robilar said. 'It all comes together in conspiracy. Our enemies are many, both those that stand in the mortal world and those that plot beyond it. It is for this reason that I tell you these things. The preparation for your Testing is not just to face a trial. It is to bring you to the side of right—to my side—so that we may weather whatever storm is coming.' She looked fondly at Kelsen, and the king in his bed. 'They were a wonderful partnership. In so many ways. I shall be sad to see them go. But this journey is done, and we have another to take in the real world.'

And I was back to myself. My fingertip rested against Robilar's, her skin cold to the touch. I shivered. The world seemed sharp, hard-lined and bright. I gasped, sucking in a breath of air. I looked too hard into the candle, my eyes not yet adjusted back to this world, and filled my vision with its bright imprint. The number 3 on the candle had barely been touched. The journey through Robilar's dreams had lasted only a few seconds.

'I understand why it's so dangerous for anyone to know,' I said. 'I won't tell anyone.'

'You will not,' Robilar said. 'Or you will die, and everyone who knew you will forget that you ever came here. I believe I was very clear on that.'

'You were. Completely clear.' I didn't want to ask, but my mouth went ahead without me. 'Why me, Grandmaster? I'm not the best at anything. I don't hold any power.'

'Everything I have told you in this room is true. I have exposed to you a great secret. I would not lie to you about these things, Raine. Why you? Because I need your help, and you are the only one I can call on to give it to me.'

'Me?'

'All will become clear. But for now, I just need you to acknowledge that you understand that everything I have told you so far is the truth.'

'All right,' I said. 'I acknowledge it.'

'Marvellous.'

Robilar stood, and in concert I rose at the same time. She walked to a coat stand and took down a luxurious fur mantle and wrapped it around her shoulders. Red fur around her shoulders, white reaching down to the floor. Like her hair, I thought. She took down a second cloak, this one black fox fur, considered me, then put it back. She sorted through various extraordinarily expensive furs until she found one she felt would fit me. Black and white, though this one was largely black fur, studded with patches of white in diamond shapes.

'Perfect for you,' she said. 'It's cold where we're going.'

I wrapped it around myself, and the sudden warmth enclosed me. Too hot for this room. Robilar went back to the table, picked up the second half of the rose-thistle pellet and warmed it over the candle for several seconds. A thin wisp of smoke rose from it. She broke it in half and crossed the room to me. The pellet had become sticky on the end of her finger.

'It will be several hours' travel. We will not arrive until dawn. I have much to tell you, and I'd rather you be alert on the journey. And nobody enjoys being sunshined on their own.' She nipped half of the pellet from her finger and tucked it beneath her tongue. No sign that it had impacted her at all. Even a small swig from my flask usually caused me to shudder and grimace. Robilar held her finger out before me. 'Open your mouth,' she said.

'That's a lot,' I said. 'I'm not sure I can take that much.'

'You'll be fine,' she said. 'Do not think that because we've shared a little dream that we are girls together on some moon-horse night. I'm giving you a command, as both mentor and your grandmaster. Open.'

I didn't really want to, but I couldn't very well refuse either. But one of the things about rose-thistle was that you always wanted more. Always wishing. Never wanted to stop, never wanted to sleep and let the sunshine fade away. The least wise part of me wanted to try it in this way. Sometimes it was better not to think. I opened my mouth and raised my tongue. Robilar's finger slipped into my mouth and I felt the warmth of the rose-thistle pellet wiped below my tongue, and then it was fizzing there, a mild burning sensation as it worked its way into my blood.

'I have a carriage arranged,' Robilar said. I felt a little woozy on my feet. I staggered a little. 'Are you all right?'

I had to stay upright. It was important not to show how much the instant hit of rose-thistle was affecting me. I wanted the grandmaster to see that I was strong, that I was old enough to get sunshined with a woman of her stature. I wasn't some lightweight about to pass out from a dab under the tongue.

The world lurched around me and I steadied myself on a counter. I felt nausea. Lights, lights all around me in fairy-tale colours, winking and sparkling and then I knew my legs wouldn't hold me anymore, and there was nothing I could do about it.

19

There were broken stars, and rainbows that lacked beginning or end. There were memories of places I hadn't been to, and hungers for things I couldn't name. I don't know how long it lasted. Hours, maybe. Weeks. A century. No time at all. My head was resting on something soft. I knew that before I knew anything else.

'Well, I am sorry about that,' a matter-of-fact voice, filtered through the rushing haze. 'I may have misjudged the potency somewhat. But all seems to be better now.'

I opened my eyes. The grandmaster's face, pale and flat-planed, looked down at me. She waved a hand in front of my face and I blinked at it a few times. We were in a dark, wood-panelled box of some kind. Windows. Seats. A carriage? My head was in her lap.

'What happened?' I asked. My lower lip was a little numb and my teeth ached. I could still feel the light pressure of a finger, where she had pressed it below my tongue, and the burn of the pellet it had left.

'I overtaxed you. But don't worry. The intoxicant has passed now. We've arrived. Can you sit?'

I did it slowly. Beyond the windows, the night still claimed the world.

'Where are we?'

'We have travelled, a brief journey. Ten miles or so from Harranir.'

'Where . . .'

'Let us alight and see. Careful now. I need you in one piece.'

Robilar helped me down from the carriage. I felt a moment of dizziness as I put my feet down on the hilltop. The barest discolouration of dawn, a faint dark blue, gathered across the eastern horizon. The grandmaster allowed me to rest a hand on her arm as I found my walking legs. My head felt foggy. It was hard to get my thoughts in order.

A great old house towered above us at the top of the hill. Three storeys tall, with wooden boards, crooked and all leaning at uncomfortable angles. The windows were shuttered, no light beyond. I heard the rattle and clack of wood, and saw the carriage had already set off again, the team of black horses pulling it away into the night along a road that saw little use. Before a minute had passed we stood alone on the hilltop, the moors dark as pitch around us.

Robilar shook a cadanum globe to life, and passed it to me to hold. The sphere was fully loaded with best, purest quality shavings and the light spilled out across the hill and the house, ghostly pale, ghostly blue. The house was old, in poor repair. One wall was stone, the roof shingled.

'It seems almost familiar,' I said as I looked around. Robilar said nothing. Familiar, but like looking at a portrait of a child when you've met the adult, only in reverse. A tell-tale hummock here, the gradient of the slope there. I raised the globe higher. A small picket fence ringed what might have been a vegetable garden before it was overrun by tall grass and invading heather. A thin, square stone stood upright amidst the overgrowth. I looked to Robilar.

'Can I?'

'If your feet are steady.' She nodded. I walked over. The rose-thistle seemed to have left me completely. Shadows made smudges of detail, the ghost-light of the cadanum sphere washing the world around me into wax and shadow. The stone was a grave marker. It was unadorned by writing, but a sun and moon had been carved into its face. I took a step away from it, not wanting to stand atop whoever's bones lay beneath. I looked around again, back to the grandmaster, who stood silent and unmoving, swathed in heavy fur.

'I know where we are,' I said. 'It's the hilltop. The one where you cast the spell with your sister.' I looked around at the house, the gravestone. 'Is this her?'

'This is Alianna's last resting place,' Robilar said. She walked towards me, gliding with quiet dignity. 'I buried her after the battle. Raised this old house here so that I could visit. And to cover the fallon. People are less inclined to bother a creaking old house than they are a standing stone.'

'It doesn't look like it gets used much.'

'I have not been here for many years,' Robilar said. 'Not since before you were born. Not since Ulovar was born, perhaps.'

'What am I to learn here?' I asked. I looked towards the house, tall enough to hide even one of the huge standing stones that pierced Harran far and wide.

'You have learned enough for one night,' Robilar said. She walked away from the house to a clear a patch of ground. The same ground where the silver circle of six-in-six had appeared beneath her feet, all those years ago. The moor had swallowed any sign of that conflict, growing and covering as it did all around it. When man stops changing things, the land takes it back. If everything was one then it didn't make so much difference anyway. Everything is as it ever was. 'I have gifted you with secrets. And it is only fitting that you gift them to me in return.'

Secrets?

Oh no.

'What do you mean?'

Robilar's eyes were bright in the cadanum light.

'I *know*, Raine.'

Everything locked up tight. My whole body turned to planks of badly nailed wood. Robilar's hair stirred in the night wind.

'What do you mean, Grandmaster?' I didn't sound convincing, even to myself.

'You're a clever girl,' Robilar said. 'Very clever, in fact. You know exactly what I mean. I will confess, it took me a little time to work it out. You left many things unsaid after you destroyed Kaldhoone LacShale. Ulovar is a man who prefers to allow his charges to keep their secrets. That does not work so well for me.'

I looked around. Harranir's early lights were tiny points of fire, far across the moor. The darkness swallowed the rest of the world.

'I only did what I had to,' I said, and my voice was a brittle, paper-thin shred.

'Oh, and I applaud it fully,' Robilar said. 'But there were things that did not add up terribly well. How did you defeat a pair of Mawleths? I have dealt with worse, but for you? You are an apprentice. You have studied no incantations, no spells to my knowledge. One Gate only. It shouldn't have been possible.'

'I don't know how I did it,' I said.

'Oh, you do, Raine. I thought to myself, "How does one defeat a demon of the Night Below without the Third Gate?" And I thought of how you helped defeat Ciuthach, and I thought of the Blackwell, and so I checked. You ventured inside and took your bow. There's no need to deny it. I had your room searched.'

I swallowed the hardness in my throat. I didn't want to look away from her, didn't want to reveal how hard my heart was pounding in my chest. I had thought myself so clever, hiding my stolen treasure. I had accepted the idea that people were oblivious. Oh, what arrogance I'd held.

'I was under attack,' I whispered. 'I had no choice.'

'The bow? You can keep the bow. Those tools were made to be used. I am not angry. Do not be afraid, Raine. I am not angry, not at all. I did not spend half the night dragging you through dreams in order to berate you now. But the question that then came to mind was of course only logical. How could a girl like you enter the Blackwell? The Fourth Gate protects the minds of those that try it. But you haven't even the Second. Strange that you should be able to go where so few can, even in an hour of need.'

Was now the time to run? I could throw the light away. I could dash into the darkness, hope not to break my ankles, hope not to run into dark-covered banks of gorse and heather. But I'd seen what the grandmaster was capable of, what she had done on this very hillside to those with vastly more power than I. She would put fire into the sky, and she would turn me to glass if I ran. So I carried on the vain, pointless hope that she was going to put three and three together and somehow the answer she reached was not going to be six.

I had nothing to say that would not damn me, so I kept my mouth shut. The rose-thistle—if it had even been rose-thistle at all—had been a ruse. A way to bring me here quietly in the night. There was no sign nor sound of the carriage at all. Not that it would have been any help had it been.

'I prefer to be direct tonight,' Robilar said. 'I shall make this easy. You have passed the Sixth Gate.'

The words echoed around the hillside, naked for all to hear. I could have taken the criminal's defence, arguing blindly that the insurmountable evidence was wrong. But the truth is, there's only evidence when wrongdoing has been done, and the grandmaster was right. She'd brought me out here to this lonely hilltop, far from friends and allies. I wouldn't shed my dignity by denying who I was, not when it was revealed so entirely.

'Are you going to kill me now?' I asked. 'Or have me hobbled and thrown into the harbour?'

'That is the punishment for possessing the grave-sight,' Robilar said. 'But we both know that your abilities stretch beyond that. Many have taken the time to ask how you overcame Kaldhoone LacShale, four Gates against your one, but none found the answer. You are Sarathi, Apprentice Raine. Spirit-sighted, grave-speaker, nightcrafter, witch, all those things and more. You have looked beyond life, and called on the spirit world, and you have kept your tongue still all the while. It is time you shared that knowledge. With me.'

'No,' I said immediately. 'You don't want it. Trust me, you don't want it.'

'You are wrong,' Robilar said. She seemed to swell larger in the night. 'I omitted a detail earlier. I told you that my sister, Arianna, was named Sarathi. They were *right*. She was cursed, and blessed, with the Sixth Gate. It was only through combining Vie, the Gate of Life, and Skal, Gate of Death, that we could master Hallenae's magic. The spell that should have made us both invulnerable was one that can only be woven through twinning those two sides of the world. To create such constancy, everything must be one and there is no oneness in life without death by its side. Do you see, Raine? Do you see what we must do now?'

The young Vedira Robilar was melting away. Pieces of skin flaked in ragged, paper-thin strips on the wind as her hair fell from her head. I saw the gleam of iron bands, the glow of fire from within the wizened scalp beneath.

'I am not Sarathi,' I said. 'I am not a traitor to Redwinter. I can't open the Sixth Gate, I just see things. Things I don't want to see. It's not my fault.'

'I am not asking for *apologies*,' Robilar roared. Her voice reached up and out across the night sky, crashing into the distant dawn. She seemed to grow taller, stretching higher. 'A grandmaster of the Fifth Gate. A loyal vassal commanding the Sixth. I can still bring forth Hallenae's magic, and undo what the colour storm did to me. I will give you this power as well, a gift so that we may work in perfect unity. Together, forever, we will rule the Draoihn, rule Redwinter, rule the whole world when we so choose. They will not defeat me. They will not defeat us! Teach me the power over death and I will learn to command it. We need not die, Raine of Redwinter. We can be *forever*.'

She loomed tall and vast, flames licking around her heels from cracks in her broken skin. She flung out her arms, fur billowing in sudden wind.

'You will tell me!' she thundered. The house behind her shook, the timbers flexing.

'No!' I yelled back, like spitting into a rain storm. 'I've seen what they become. The Sarathi who served Hallenae—they become things of the Night Below. Like Ciuthach, a blight against all life. You have made a killer of me, but I won't become that. Not now. Not ever!'

'You already are!' Robilar roared again. The wind buffeted me and I staggered against the wall of the house. 'Teach me now, Raine, and I will show you wonders you have never even supposed could exist. I will teach you to ascend through the Second, Third and Fourth Gates. Those who seek to depose me will find themselves facing not just a grandmaster, but a new Riven Queen, with all the powers of life and death, all the wrath of Skuttis and Anavia at her command. Together we shall take the Crown, and bring all five under my dominion, with you at my side.'

'You want the Crown?' I gasped. My whole body was shaking. 'You can't take the Crown. No Draoihn, no wielder of magic can ever touch the Crown. You told me that yourself.'

'A pretty lie I concocted many years ago to keep its power from the wrong hands,' Robilar spat derisively. 'In the wrong hands? Grasping the wrong mind? The Crown would do untold damage. But I am one hundred and forty-five years old. I have been preparing my mind for centuries to take it. But I need your help, not your fear. Hallenae's ritual requires life and death to work in unison.' The ancient, shattered creature glowered at me from a sunken, skull-like face held together with bands and rivets. 'I chose you, Raine, because you are the one to bring me forwards. There was a prophecy that I would find you. Its words have echoed in my ears, and here you are, presented right at my hour of need. Teach me what I need to know so that we can end this bickering over Crowns, so we can free Harran from the Brannish imposition, so that you can rise to stand proud and true and unveiled before them. Draoihn and Sarathi will work in unison again.' She reached out an oversized hand. 'Join me.'

The offer was not without temptation. I felt it, as all do when offered great power. Morality flexes and bends, so much more uncertain when immense personal gain lies in its abandonment. We tell ourselves we have beliefs because they suit our needs, but in the end, everyone betrays themselves.

The offer of power was thunderous, massive beyond reckoning. But I could not take it. I would not take it.

I turned and ran. Ran for the house, for cover, for anything that would put the terrifying creature behind me. Robilar's howl of rage shook the ground. I flowed into Eio, felt it respond sluggishly against the after-sludge of the rose-thistle, but it rose up and my night vision intensified. I heard the rush in the air and flung myself down into the grass as the night lit up behind me. A wave of fire howled overhead, dashing against the house and leaving licking flame in its wake.

'If you will not serve, you will be destroyed,' Robilar thundered. 'There is nowhere you can run. Nowhere you can hide from me. You will serve me, one way or another.'

I scrambled across the grass, the cadanum orb hurled away into the night, but the grass itself was ablaze. I heard laughter at my heels as I scrambled around the house's corner. Should I go in? Or down the hill? I didn't have long to think. House or hill? I chose hill. As I began to run again, the clouds overhead boomed and a rip of white-blue lightning blasted the earth two yards in front of me. Bracken and shrubs ignited, fire spilt across the ground like liquid. I batted at the heavy fur where tiny flames began dancing, but it was igniting fast and I threw it off.

'I am offering you an alliance!' Robilar's voice came from everywhere. 'A chance to serve me. To serve Redwinter. To serve the Crown.'

'That's not what we are,' I shouted as I ran towards the house. What a fool I'd been. All these months thinking that I was the clever one, that nobody would work it out, that nobody would put it all together. And here the grandmaster of the Draoihn was a traitor to our very cause. She sought power not to protect the Crown, not to ensure the succession, but to commit the ultimate crime. She sought to become Sarathi, and to take the Crown for herself. She was everything that we fought against, embodied every danger that we trained to combat, to protect the people against.

I reached the house and kicked at a door. It crashed open, rotten boards splintering. I looked around, desperate. Maybe there was something I could use here? She was vulnerable now, she'd told me so herself. The room was dark, stank of mould and wet slithering things. I tripped on something soft, fell onto my hands. I pushed deeper into the first trance, magnifying every little bit of firelight from outside, the tiny rays of dawn through clouded glass. I tried to see what lay beneath Palanost's blanket in my panic and desperation, and on the floor I saw a body. No, bodies. Some long rotten, flesh brown and sunken, eyes eaten by worms. Some were fresher.

'You are making a mistake,' Robilar called. 'I do not wish to hurt you. I only wish to be as you are. Teach me, Raine. I am giving you a command, as your grandmaster, and as the woman who holds your life in the balance.'

It wasn't fair. It wasn't fair and I'd done nothing wrong. Well, that may not have quite been true, but I certainly didn't deserve to be killed on this fecking hilltop. I cast around the room, and there, against the wall lay a forlorn hope. A short-hafted, long-bladed spear. The kind used to hunt boar. I crawled over the corpses, my hand sinking wetly into a decomposed chest, ribs cracking beneath my palm. I retched, but I crawled.

'Have it your way.' Robilar's voice seemed to fall from the sky across the dark building. 'If you will not serve, you will burn.'

There was a hissing, then the smell of smoke as it began to rise from the walls. And then came the fire. Bright illumination filled the room, what had been a kitchen at one time, and now was a tomb. I grasped the spear, yanked it down from its wall mounting. The heat swelled over me as the walls of the house ignited, a rushing, roaring crackle of old dry wood and hissing damp. I saw the open mouths of the bodies staring up at me wide-eyed. The house would be an inferno in moments, burning like the taste of rose-thistle beneath my tongue.

'You are choosing death over ruling this land at my side,' Robilar snarled. 'Is that truly the choice you make?'

I surged towards the front door, kicking it open as I drew back my arm to throw the boar spear. It was a foolish hope, I thought, and I was sad that my last thought was likely to be that I was being a fool. I saw the grandmaster standing before the house, large, unmissable, molten liquid bubbling across her scalp, her yellow-toothed mouth a vicious snarl. The spear was heavy, not intended to be thrown. The grandmaster's First Gate meant she already knew I was coming. Her Second Gate would let her turn her skin hard as stone as it impacted, or change the spearhead to wet clay. Her Third would send it flying with a gust of wind. And her Fourth . . .

The rose-thistle burned beneath my lip as the fire raged around me. She stared at me expectantly. Daring me to try.

I lowered the spear.

'I would have thrown it, Grandmaster,' I said. I dropped it onto the ground. It wasn't a spear. Not really. 'But would you please take your finger out of my mouth?'

20

The world, the true, real world came back into focus. Robilar's finger was indeed in my mouth, below my tongue, the bitter, astringent taste of rose-thistle burning around my gums. She was looking at me with dark, whirling eyes, a hard smile across her painted lips. No more crone. She only showed what she wanted to show.

I took a step back, spitting her finger from me. I was shaking. It wasn't just the intoxicant. *She knew.* She knew, and I was still here trapped with her, and there was no way out for me.

'You tricked me,' I said. 'You lied.'

'Come now,' Robilar said, wiping her finger on a handkerchief. 'Who lied first? Would any of this have been necessary in a world where truth was easy to come by?'

My muscles were tense as taught strings. Five paces to the door and the night, a run to the stables, a wild rush into the dark. I could be gone. I could be out of this place and away and nobody would ever have to know that Raine Wildrose was a girl who possessed the grave-sight. And yet those thoughts sounded like echoes within my own mind. The voice of some other girl, an earlier conception of me. I may have still looked like that girl, though my body might have become harder. I might have still sounded like that girl, though my words have grown jaded. But I didn't kill like that girl, not anymore, and if you brushed away the old dead skin then beneath her lay a different beast.

A beast, indeed. Was that what they'd been making me into all along?

I wasn't going to run. It was a flash-thought of foolishness anyway. The grandmaster had chased me with fire in the constructed fantasy she'd made in my mind. I suspected that when she didn't have a point to prove, she would be far more efficient. Only an amateur lets fire do their killing for them.

'How do I know this part is real?' I asked. 'How do I know you're not in my mind?'

'How do we know anything is real?' Grandmaster Robilar countered. 'None of it is, really. It's all just so much invention in our own minds. Perception is everything. Something is, and isn't, and it's really all one and the same.'

'That's no answer.'

'It's the truth. But, in fairness, people are seldom interested in what is true. Only in what will change their fortune, for better or for worse. Beyond the details of our own lives, we care very little. For a practical answer, whilst I can implant fiction into your head, and take you on a run around a little dream or two, I cannot pry thoughts from your own mind. Ask somebody to tell you something that you already know. Some minor personal detail I could not possibly guess. When they give you the right answer, you can be confident I am not inflicting it on you. But that is for later. You'll want to sit down. The nausea is going to be with you in a few moments.'

Robilar gestured to the sweeping, padded green sofa. I glanced towards the door, but there was more than just rose-thistle in whatever she'd given me. My head was swimming. Everything seemed a little further away than it should have, like I was spectating from behind my own eyes. Dizziness. And then came the nausea.

'What have you done to me?' I staggered to the sofa, where I lowered myself slowly. Sharp movements were not my friend.

'It was rather a lot of Olatte leaf, mixed in with the rose-thistle,' Robilar said. 'For which I apologise. Although given the subject of our most recent conversation, you will understand that I do not wish to have you running around shouting right about now. There was a reason I wanted to have that particular conversation with you within a shared mind. I believe you can probably understand why.'

Here I was. Exposed. Discovered. What I'd feared for so long had finally come to pass in the worst possible way.

But, rather surprisingly, I was still upright and breathing, though the effects of the Olatte leaf were making me question whether that was something I wanted to change. A wet, wretched nausea writhed like a pile of slugs flopping over and over one another inside my gut. I'd seen Olatte smokers, their bowls tucked up against their stained lips as they inhaled, their eyes cloudy, their lives wasting away around them in a haze. But the haze didn't come upon my mind. The rose-thistle kept it at bay. I was sunshined and I was mooned out alongside it. Perhaps the worst of all worlds. But I wasn't dead yet. I hadn't been turned to stone, or burned alive, or had my bones cracked one by one as I lay screaming.

'You were there with me,' I said.

'In a fashion,' Robilar said. 'The simulacrum of me was just that—an avatar in your mind. The same was true of you, of course, only you didn't know it. There wasn't actually anything at all. What you observed was more like the thoughts you hear in your own head. They don't really exist.'

'Sounds like a good way to spend one's time,' I muttered. My gut roiled. I made a dry, retching heave but nothing came out.

'You would be surprised by how good a time one can have with it,' Robilar said, then covered her mouth as a slight giggle escaped her. Intoxicated, just as I was.

'Let's keep to what's relevant to me,' I said. My voice shook, my throat was sore from the heaving. My arms and legs were leaden, another effect of the Olatte leaf. I couldn't have run if I'd tried. 'You know what I am. Why am I still alive?'

Robilar sat back in her chair. She really did take a pellet of rose-thistle this time, dropping it into a glass of whisky the colour of thickest honey and swirling it around with an equal measure of water. She reclined in her chair, legs stretched out before her, the toe of one emerald-studded slipper showing from beneath her gown.

'When I was a girl,' Robilar began. She laughed to herself. 'Which was a very, very long time ago. When I was a girl, my father had this idea about whisky. He said that whisky must be drunk neat, just as the brewer intended. And meat must be served bloody, so that the flavour was just so. And I tried to go along with it. It didn't matter all that much. He was not a kind man, and he didn't share whisky, or meat, often. But he had other ideas too. A child should speak only when permitted to. A young woman must marry where she was told. And he ruled me, and my sisters, and my mother and brothers, because he could. And of course, we feared him. How do you take your whisky, Raine? With water? With a lick of ice? Mixed with something else?'

My head was swimming. It couldn't be a good idea to drink whisky on top of the twin intoxicants revolving around inside my head. But anything had to feel better than the slug-ball in my gut and the dryness at the back of my throat.

'I don't mind,' I said.

'That's an answer at least, and fair.' Robilar poured a new measure—a small one—and brought it to me. My hand was shaking as I tried to take it. I could barely hold it, but I managed to get a sip past my lips.

'Are you going to kill me?'

'Oh, don't be silly. If I'd intended to kill you, would I really have gone to these elaborate lengths of display? I'd have snuffed you out like a candle. But anyway, that's not what we're about right now. I'm telling you why I haven't killed you, I'm just doing it in a long, unnecessarily convoluted way because I don't get to say this very often and I think it's rather clever. Listen along, will you?'

I nodded, and as Robilar returned to her chair, I forced another sip of whisky past my lips. It was likely a very fine single malt from the western islands. Probably the finest. It all just tasted like rose-thistle and burnt herbs and fumes.

'So my father was a man of ill temper and self-aggrandisement, like most people's fathers were in those days, and probably still are today. And we did what he said until I learned a valuable lesson. I came into my Second Gate quite young, and when I wouldn't marry his friend, he punched me in the face. I became as stone, and he shattered his hand. He didn't understand it. Anyway, saving you a long story in which I learned not just to protect myself but to stand up for myself, eventually I killed him, and I killed some of his friends, and one of my brothers who was too eager to become our father. And what happened to me?'

'I don't know.'

'Nothing. Nothing at all. A Draoihn took me and my sister to Redwinter, made me rich, and told me that all those people I'd killed didn't matter. They didn't matter, because I was above them. That's how the world works, Raine. When you're higher up, when you're richer, or hold power whether magical or political, the rules just don't apply. That's the lesson. Although I do enjoy talking about killing my father. I crushed his skull between my hands.'

'That's . . . nice . . .'

Robilar was sunshined, and she was tired. The mental effort she must have gone through to craft that dreamland had drained her. The intoxicant was keeping her awake, though she was rabbiting like one occasionally does when they've had too much of a good thing. Or, as I was beginning to feel about it, possibly a rather bad thing.

'So what I learned,' Robilar went on as she poured herself another whisky, 'is that the world doesn't work the way people think it does. Take the law, for example. If you're Draoihn, the law ceases to matter in ways that would inconvenience us. The reeves tactfully forget that it applies to us. We have our own law. So you understand now?'

'No,' I said. The slugs had grown sleepy down there. The whisky was knocking them out, maybe. I felt wretched. I was struggling to stay focused. 'Why aren't I dead?'

'Because, dear girl, the law does not apply to those above. Not the law of the poor, which says you are born poor and stealing bread is enough to have you mutilated. Not the law of the rich, which says you are born rich, and the poor are yours to use. Not the law of kings, which says that there is no real law but whatever your whims dictate at that moment. Not even the law of the Draoihn. When a poor man steals a loaf of bread, we take a finger. When a rich man steals a thaildom, we call it business. And when a king steals the world, we call him a conqueror, raise statues and make him a legend. So you see, Raine: when I realised what you hold in-side you—when I understood what you are—the likes of you and I do not abide by the rules. By *anybody's* rules. Particularly not the rules of men who were born hundreds of years ago. Men who never knew us, or cared about us, or knew we even existed. Men who might have spat on us had they passed. The truth of all the world is that nobody abides by laws that they do not have to. And who has the power to enforce them upon the likes of you and I?'

'You're saying you're letting me live because you don't care for laws?'

'I'm saying that there was never a question about me hurting you, Raine, because *there are no laws*,' Robilar said. 'Not for us. We were born to be dif-ferent. Ours was a privilege that rises higher than anything. Higher than all. I have been searching for one like you for more than a century. Together, we can do great things.' She laughed then, interrupting herself. 'Oh, not all that nonsense I said on the dream hill. You'll do your side, and I'll do my side. But I would never harm you just for being.'

'But what I am—every Draoihn in Redwinter would turn on me if they knew.'

'Is that really true?' Robilar asked. She arched one fine eyebrow at me. 'There is a difference between being seen to obey the law and actually do-ing so.'

And she was right. Sanvaunt knew what I was. Ulovar had always known what Hazia was, too.

'But without laws—what's right? What's wrong?'

'Right and wrong.' Robilar shrugged. 'Nobody follows the law because it's right. We just insist that others do.' She snuggled down into her chair, swirling her whisky. 'That is the lesson that the rich learn early. The law exists to keep those in power in power, and to keep those without it from gaining it. It is the same with us. Only we answer to nobody. Not even kings.'

'I'm not powerful,' I said.

'Nonsense,' Robilar said. 'You're Draoihn.'

'Not yet,' I said. 'I'm still an apprentice.'

Robilar laughed, snorted the world's best whisky down the world's finest silk.

'It has not occurred to you yet?' she said. 'This was your Testing. You realise that, don't you?'

Oh. *Oh.* Against all that had happened, against everything that Robilar had said about rules not applying, it was still a shock, and it filled me with a light, majestic fulfilment. Treacherous brain.

'Officially I'll have to do something or other for show, but I've Tested you and the council will do what I tell them. Mostly. Between you and I, you are Draoihn now.' She sat up in the chair, put her elbows on the table and laid her chin on the backs of her hands. 'I'm sorry. You probably hoped for more fanfare.'

'No,' I said. 'I just think I'm going to be sick.'

'Oh. Yes. You will be. Use that plant as a bucket.'

I did as she asked as the slugs found their way out. Noisily. It took a long time.

'So I'm Draoihn now. Really?' I asked, wiping a trickle of slime from my mouth. 'And you're not going to kill me because of—'

'Hush,' Robilar snapped at me, both lips and fingers. 'You are not to speak of what passed inside your head. You are not to use it against or around me, or admit it to anyone else. But come now—did you really think that a Testing is some kind of formal exam, the kind they hold in a common school? That we would toss away a useful apprentice over something like their knowledge of astronomy, or their skill at arms? Every Testing is unique, tailored for the individual. Some are simple. Your friend Castus LacClune was never going to fail. How could he? Can you imagine if someone with his power, his wealth and connections—not to mention talent—was denied? Do you think you would have sat in on my conversation with Onostus LacAud if the decision was not already made?'

'I'm young,' I said by way of defence. 'I have a lot to learn.'

Robilar laughed.

'I have much to teach you, given time,' Robilar said. 'But I have put you through enough for one night, I think. Go home, and sleep, and take a long rest tomorrow. Your body will need it. And in the coming days I will have great need of you. The Winterra are coming, here, to Redwinter.'

'They're what?'

'I sent for their recall months ago,' Robilar said. 'It is the first time in many years that the Winterra will be back on Harran's soil. There is a reason that we keep them away, Raine. They do not fight another king's wars because we wish for his endless conquest. It is far safer to keep the nation's strongest fighting force hundreds of miles from home. Men with armies at their backs begin to find that they have ideas. The Winterra are too great a political force to let them sit on our own doorstep.'

'Then why recall them?'

'Because I am no longer immortal. Somebody has changed the world so that I can be killed once again, and whoever they are and whatever they think they can bring against me, I shall build a wall of swords around myself if it means that the Crown remains under my control.'

JUST A DREAM

It is commonplace to me now to dream this way. I do not always remember it, but I know I will remember this one. It comes to me down countless years, or perhaps it is only the invention of my own mind, moulded by the unspeakable darkness within the book. The book exists in this time as well, but it is not a book. It is a staff of great power, and I hold it in my hand as I look across my courtiers.

The finest nobility of the land sit at great tables, but the meals before them lie cold and desiccated. Flies have not touched them, even after more than a century. They do not touch the princes, the queens who sit rigid and grey in their thrones. I have brought every throne here, one from every land that I have ground beneath the might of my legions. These lordlings squabbled and sought my approval once. They resisted me later, when they saw that the right to rule the world was mine.

They move slowly. Little gestures, the slow turn of a head. Dry skin creaks with every motion. It is not life. There is no life here, in this grey land I have created. I have seen to that. There was so much noise when the living roamed these dim halls. All their chatter, all their lying, all their pointless thoughts and emotions cluttering my space like swarming locusts, devouring, using. But it was nothing but noise. I put an end to all that.

She visits me, as she has done from the beginning. She appears through the darkness of an archway which has not seen feet for many decades. I thought she loved me once, in the heady days of exploration. But she, like everyone has come to despise me. She would unmake me, if she could.

'Song,' she says. 'I have made a mistake.'

Behind her, crow-like wings flex and furl. I have gazed into the darkness of the tunnel, I have brought forth the Night Below to consume countless lands, but still I have never understood her. It is as if she does not belong anywhere. Not even my power can touch her.

'No. Mistakes,' I say. It is difficult to make words. Everything is so dry.

My body failed long ago. It moves only through the force of the spirits bound around my limbs.

'I had such hopes for you,' my teacher says. 'But I am forced to admit that I was wrong. It was not you.'

'Three. Hundred. Years,' I say. 'And. Now. You. Think. This.'

'I had to be sure,' she says, and her wings furl away into her back. 'It is time for you to go. You are empress no longer.'

'You. Have. No. Power.' My voice is just a wheezing croak.

'It is not I who unseats you,' she says. 'They are coming. An alliance of the eldritch kin, the Hexen, the Tharada Taan. It is over.'

'I. Shall. Smite. Them,' I say, but even to me, the words feel empty. None have dared challenge me in a century. But the world has moved on as I languished here.

I utter Serranis's words. I see them then, demon souls inhabiting the bones of the dead at my great table. A table where nothing is eaten, nothing is spoken. They stare back at me, accusing, filled with hate. My power is spent. I can only await the end.

21

I would have to kill her. It was the only solution.

The rose-thistle and the Olatte vied for which could taste the worst in my mouth. A dizzying, dream-distorted period of sleep had fled, leaving me exhausted but awake after less than an hour. I sat at the top of the LacNaithe greathouse's high tower, where the wind was cold even in summer. Seclusion, solitude. Time to think, though my mind was worn so thin it felt hard to trust what I saw.

Harranir's valley spread out below me, nothing but blank white mist until hills and mountains broke cover. The cloud came down during the night. Nothing to see, just blank whiteness. The purples and browns of the moorland, the yellow-baked grass, were lost to the all-swallowing fog. The pine forest that covered the mountain slopes around Redwinter poked witch-hat stems through the obscuring blanket, but I could see nothing of the city, or the great silver river that cut through it like a slash of slate. In the early morning, the mist across Redwinter's vast grounds muted all sound, leaving me alone atop the tower in the cold and damp.

It felt a shame to have to kill the grandmaster. She hadn't done me in after she realised what I was. But how could I go on here when someone like her knew what I was? She had such power over me I could feel it pressing against the back of my head.

I rubbed my hands together against the chill. How would I kill the grandmaster? She could never see it coming, that was for sure. Poison wouldn't drop her instantly, and her Fifth Gate would open and she'd burn it right out of herself. Torgan had taught me that there were only three ways to instantly kill. Massive damage to the brain. Decapitation of the head from the body. Massive damage direct to the heart, so that the blood no longer flowed. An arrow from Midnight, straight to the head or the heart would do the job. But only if she didn't sense it coming, and given how old she was, she probably would.

It was a dilemma and no mistake. Probably safer to let her live and see what would come out of it. Maybe I wouldn't kill her after all.

'This does not usually happen until much later.'

I shouldn't have been surprised that the Queen of Feathers would visit me now. I had grown used to her whispers, most often as I studied the book. They no longer surprised me. She came to sit beside me, as ephemeral as the fog that filled the world.

'I don't want people to know,' I said.

'Because it endangers you?'

'Not exactly,' I said. 'Maybe because it makes me dangerous to other people.'

'A person who cannot be dangerous is a useless person,' the Queen of Feathers said, and though her words had all their usual hardness, her tone was soft. 'Strength lies in knowing how to hold your capacity back, and to exploit it at the right moments.'

'But it's dangerous to those around me too,' I said.

'Hallenae said the same, as did damned Unthayla, and Song Seondeok, and Serranis. But they all rose to greatness.'

'They were all great queens,' I said. 'But they were destroyers. Were they all Sarathi?'

'They were great,' the Queen of Feathers said. 'And they all expressed the same doubts that you do. But they learned that ultimately, it was standing alone that brought them the greatest power. You are an island, Raine, and an island will weather any storm. But it stands apart in a turbulent ocean. It does not draw land around it.'

'Is this what you want me to become?' I said. 'Another queen rising to power on a mountain of corpses? They were evil. And all of them were destroyed for it.'

'You are seeing the trees and thinking you see the forest. The wars, the power, they were not goals in themselves, only a means to reach higher power. Not even the Faded Lords seek destruction for its own sake. No, what I have sought from each of those great women, what I seek from you, is a gift. I have experienced many failures. Only a few have come close to success,' the Queen of Feathers said. 'Some it slipped from by the breadth of a single hair. I felt it then. I know that eventually I will succeed, because it is the only outcome possible.'

'You're so annoying.' I sighed. 'Do this, do that, help me, humiliate me, comfort me, mock me. Go learn all this dark shit, Raine. Don't destroy the world, Raine. It's just cryptic riddles.'

The Queen of Feathers laughed.

'Maddening, isn't it? The truth is, I don't know what you do to achieve the goal. I have no memories of events that have not taken place yet. But we do it together. I only know that much. My memory is like anyone else's: I only keep the big things with me. Many centuries have passed since I first became. I doubt you even remember what you had for lunch last week.'

There was truth in that.

'You want me to do something?'

'That is correct.'

'But you won't tell me what?'

'I do not know what it is you, or one like you, will do. Only that you will do it, and I could not come to you otherwise. But if I knew what it was, then I would guide you clearly and directly. I tried that before, more than once, but here is the bitter jest: every time I engage with you, the chances of failure increase. But if I do not, failure is certain. And so I stay my hand, as much as I can bear to.'

'I sort of feel like you want to destroy the world.'

She smiled, a gleam of teeth, a darkness of raven feathers.

'Like everyone else, I just want a chance to exist.' She traced strong, delicate fingers across the book's surface, drawing trails of mist. 'This is the key. I know this is the key.'

'I can't penetrate the book's nonsense,' I said. 'I know I need it, or I wouldn't have it. But it's too hard.'

The Queen of Feathers pushed a strand of dark hair back from her face. She was so regal, so controlled. So familiar these days.

'Everything is one,' she said eventually. 'Even the things we can't see. You'll come to understand it. We have to.'

I clutched a blanket around my shoulders, and somehow I fell asleep up on the tower in the morning cool. Sometimes the rose-thistle was like that, supporting from underneath like the sturdiest stage one has ever stood on, and then the next moment it dropped out like a trapdoor. I didn't notice it happening.

I woke to a bright and sunny midday, the mist long since burned away below. The river shimmered silver as it wound quietly through the valley.

The city was alive with people and the smoke of ten thousand chimneys. One moment I'd been looking out across the white mist, the vague purple of the rising peaks looming like sea monsters from the depths, the mist and the sky so close in colour as to be inseparable. The next, I opened my eyes and the world was a riot of summer colour, transformed so richly and so beautifully that it was as if a carnival had sprung into being and consumed the entire world.

I wouldn't kill the grandmaster. I valued my continued existence for one thing, and making that attempt had the lowest chance of success that I could imagine. But she was trusting me with knowledge, too. She had given me secrets of her own. I saw then how she had joined me to her. I didn't know what it meant, or what she would ask of me, but there is a power in trust. Not a strong one, not one that lasts forever, but a power nonetheless.

More than one person told me that I looked like shit that day. I could not disagree with them.

·   ·   ·   ·   ·   ·

Motsommer passed, and it was the fifth day of Somerdhoone. The other apprentices still had a few weeks before their Testing, and Redwinter seemed to have entered a strange lull. Ordinary classes were temporarily suspended as the mentors worked with their charges. Not me, of course. Robilar did not call me back to her immediately, and as she had told me, I had passed my Testing already. When I heard Jathan and Gelis talking nervously about what they might expect from it all over the dinner table, I had to fight down the urge to tell them that it was all a bit of a lie. Predetermined for some—maybe for all. Those that mattered would not make their decisions on some kind of impartial test. Like most things in life, those matters had been determined long ago. Maybe when we were born. Who would tell Castus LacClune or Ovitus LacNaithe that they had no place in Redwinter?

I wondered what would have happened to Colban if he'd lived. For a while he had been toasted nightly at the dining table, but his name had faded from our lives.

I received a summons from Ulovar, down in what he referred to as the Other Library, beneath the greathouse. I traipsed down, past the false shelves hiding the door behind them, into the cadanum lit cold. I didn't see him at first. Instead I thought that someone had stacked a huge pile of furs together in a chair, and it was only as I approached that I saw their slight, steady rise and fall. Ulovar's face appeared like a bole in a tree, an oddity among the vast stack of bear, beaver, fox and elk furs that swathed him. He was asleep. He looked tired, as bad as I'd seen him when he bore the page down from the north. Hazia had stolen that demon-bound page, and it had consumed her utterly. Ciuthach fell, but Ulovar had been forced to battle that dark influence on the long ride south. Perhaps he had never truly recovered. The hardships this aging man had endured on our behalf couldn't be repaid. I wondered whether that long journey, the cursed, stolen page in its lead box sapping his vitality at every step, had opened him up to this new affliction. He was weakening day by day.

Quietly I backtracked my steps to the chamber entrance, then made a show of slamming the door open. The fur pile rustled.

'Go easy on the door,' Ulovar grumbled as he shrugged off a rich fox-fur stole.

'You asked me to attend you, Master Ulovar?'

'Come. Sit.' I walked back across the room and took the chair opposite him. 'How are you coping?'

'With what?'

'With everything,' he said. 'Don't make me point out the hardships in your life, Raine. I may be confined here, but don't think I've forgotten the world outside.'

I could have hugged him then. I could have buried my head in his shoulder and burst into tears and just thanked him for caring. But it was Ulovar, and he would have been embarrassed, so instead I decided to give him honesty. It was the best reward I could offer.

'Nothing is easy,' I said. 'Everyone is worried. I drink too much. I don't sleep.'

'The same dreams?'

'The same,' I said.

'When you sleep at all.'

'When I sleep.'

'I understand,' he said. 'I was like you once. Back when I was young, and . . . all this . . . seemed so new.'

'You're saying they'll go away when I get older?'

'No,' Ulovar said. 'But they come less frequently to me now. I could not tell you why.'

He seemed to have more to say, but he fell silent. He pushed his hands out of the furs, and used his left hand to pull at the fingers of the right, popping the joints. His left hand seemed almost dead, the fingers barely moving.

'Why are you down here in the cold?' I asked.

'I have been searching,' he said. 'Searching for a remedy for this malady that has afflicted me since before Gilmundy. But it grows worse.' He stopped again. Whatever he was trying to tell me was hard for him. Ulovar LacNaithe was built of duty, honour and pride in equal measure. I could tell that whatever it was he wanted, this was hard for him. 'There are books down here you'll find in few other places. After the Glass Library burned, the greathouses began keeping their knowledge separately. But I have exhausted this place. I can find nothing to tell me why my body fails me the way it does now.'

'You endured a lot over the last year,' I said. And I didn't just mean physically. The Queen of Feathers had dumped him into a whitewater river. Ciuthach had filled his eyes with blood. The page from that cursed book had drained his strength, and few emerge from a prison in robust health. But he'd also lost Hazia, a girl he'd fostered since she was ten. He'd scarred my mind, and that he'd done so haunted him. He'd nearly lost his nephew, Sanvaunt, to a demon's sickle. I was not the only one who'd suffered. 'It's rest you need,' I said.

'You think me simply sick?' Ulovar rumbled. 'That I am old and my time has come, that my body fails me?' His eyes, their red legacy gleaming darkly in the blue light, dared me to agree.

'I just want you to get better,' I said.

'It is not just my body that fails me,' he said. 'Though I barely feel my left hand anymore, and my right weakens by the day. You know the feeling, after you've caught a finger in a door, when the pain dies away but the throbbing continues? It is like that. Only then comes numbness, and now I cannot move them at all. I feel my chest growing weak, and it has started in my feet. I can no longer stand without assistance.'

I had not known it had grown so bad. Like a dying cat, Ulovar had hidden away from us, hiding the truth of his failing body. Once I had thought him invincible. The Queen of Feathers had dropped him into a broiling river. He had caught my arrow from the air. It seemed inconceivable that he be so undone.

'But I've seen you stand. I've seen you walk,' I said, confused.

'I used the Second Gate. To strengthen what little power my muscles had left,' Ulovar said. And there was more. I could see there was more coming, and it hurt him so badly to say it. I didn't want him to. Things had always been so complicated between us, what with me starting out trying to shoot him, and him breaking down the gates of Dalnesse, the slaughter that followed, but fighting beside him against Ciuthach, him scarring my mind, bringing me to Redwinter, training me . . . But he was the rock on which our household rested. It was his surety of leadership, his steadfast devotion to those who served him that made us what we were: a clan, even if I didn't have the name.

'You've lost your Gates,' I said, whispered it so that none other could know the awful truth.

Ulovar could not bring himself to say the words.

'When?'

'As my body fades, so too have they,' he said finally. 'I follow the paths, but the spark is not there anymore. I lost the fourth, then the third when I extinguished the fire. The Second Gate I can force myself to, barely. But it will be gone soon. What will be left of me when all is done?'

I reached out and placed a hand over his right one, the one that could still feel.

'You'll be Ulovar LacNaithe. Our lord, and the van of your clan.'

'I no longer believe I will survive this,' he said. 'This is no natural illness to strip me of my Gates. Someone has worked a great evil against me. Unfit to face me in battle, they snipe at me from the shadows with dark sorcery.'

The grandmaster's invincibility, taken. Ulovar's Gates, broken. A move to take the Crown.

'Do you think it was LacAud?' I asked. 'Onostus LacAud is an expert in incantations, could he have worked that against you? He has this . . . creature of some kind, a blood drinker. I know it sounds mad but—could she be one of the Faded Lords?'

I had seen her only that time in Gilmundy, and only briefly, but the woman called Akail was still an unpleasant image to bring to mind. The unnatural paleness, the clatter of bones, the spurs thrust through her skin.

'The Faded Lords are fell and terrible,' Ulovar said. 'But we destroyed them long ago, and few have ever found the power to return. I cannot believe even Onostus would be so vain as to think he could control one of them.'

'She was white as snow,' I said. 'Even her eyes. And she had bones all over her, and thrust through her skin. She looked like a monster. This affliction isn't of mortal making, it can't be. It just can't.'

'If a Faded Lord has been summoned then it would desire to enter the Crown over all else,' Ulovar said. 'But to enter the Crown requires the Keystone, and the Keystone is locked away in the Blackwell, warded against more than just men. The ancient Draoihn who protected it ensured that the Faded cannot even approach it, let alone enter it. But do not entertain this thought too strongly, Raine. Appearances can be deceiving. Just because one looks like a monster does not mean that they are. I wish I knew more. I see so little, trapped in this failing body.'

'But weakening you weakens Redwinter . . .'

'Then why not kill me and have done?' Ulovar said, anger flashing in his eyes. 'Why consign me to this fading demise? No, despite recent events I have always considered Onostus to be a friend, and whatever else he is, he would not bring the Faded to Redwinter. He denies attacking you at Gilmundy.'

'I know. But he's lying,' I said.

'I will not accept that he did not attack us. But to risk the Crown to the Faded would be to risk unleashing the entirety of the Night Below on the world. Onostus is paranoid. He weaves so many wards around himself because he is a man who has always been afraid. He fears for himself, and for his people. I do not think this is his work.'

'Then whose?'

'Perhaps someone who fears an alliance between LacNaithe and the House of Wendlan. As a clan, our power will increase tremendously when Ovitus marries Mathilde. We will no longer merely be a great clan, but will have enormous support backing us if one day we were to make a bid for the throne. Neither Ovitus nor Sanvaunt, nor I especially, could be a candidate, but we have other kin who have no Gates to their name. We could raise one up with the backing of our Brannish friends.'

'That would all but make Harran part of Brannlant,' I said. 'Brannish heirs on the throne. You think they would have had time to do that, even if they were present when Ovitus and Mathilde's betrothal formed?'

Ulovar's lips quirked in the slightest of smiles. He smiled most often when he was pleased with himself.

'It would be nice to think that this match came about because two young people met, and Ovitus was charming and fell in love, and his story about saving her from a boar was all the truth of it. But the truth is I have been working towards making this union happen for seven years. Why do you think LacNaithe so unflinchingly supports the Brannish levies? Yes, it's good to keep our neighbour happy. But I have wanted this for our house for a long time.'

Ulovar coughed. It was a weak sound, as though his chest wasn't strong enough to expel whatever gathered within it.

'You need rest,' I said.

'Never mind all that. I've jobs for you.' He fell into coughing. It was so wet, so feeble. My heart ached to hear it. 'You've become friends with Castus LacClune despite my best efforts. I want you to see if you can get access to the LacClune library in Redwinter. See if they have anything that our books don't, anything that might stall this cursed affliction long enough to learn who my enemies are and put them in the ground.'

I thought that I probably could, if I could avoid Haronus LacClune and get in there when he was down in the city. I hated him anyway, remembered watching him dispense the order to stone Nairna LacMuaid to death for having the grave-sight. It was best to avoid him all round. Haronus was taking his newly assigned apprentices, including Jathan, out to do some roaming around, and once he was gone, Castus would be in charge there. I didn't think he'd overrule his uncle otherwise, since I couldn't tell him about Ulovar's worsening condition.

'I'll do it,' I said. Ulovar nodded a little as he bent the fingers of his numb left hand back until they formed a right angle to his palm. Trying to feel something. I couldn't imagine what it would be like to be unable to feel my own body. To see it failing, piece by treacherous piece. I stood up without looking at him.

'And one other thing,' Ulovar said as I turned to get on with it. 'It is a hard thing to admit, but I am not fool enough to pretend. I cannot lead the clan in this condition. Ovitus is now acting as van. I know there was bad blood between the two of you. He made a foolish error. You must forgive him now, and ensure he sees your value as a part of the clan. His friends cannot all be Brannish. We must not lose that part of ourselves.'

'I can act like I forgive him,' I said. 'But he never apologised.'

Even a man who has known the power that Ulovar has is able to make that parental face, where one of their charges has done wrong, and they know it, but it doesn't suit them. A kind of guilt in knowing that they can't take sides.

'Forgiving him would ease your own burden,' he said.

'No,' I said. 'I won't forgive when it's not asked for.'

Ulovar's grey brows creased together.

'Then act as if you have. It's all the same in the end.'

* * * * * *

I sat on my bed with my knees tucked up to my chin, wrapped in a winter cloak that had seen better days. It was cold down there. Cold, dark, and the right kind of place to be alone with my thoughts. Except I wasn't alone. I never knew if I was alone or not those days.

'You're troubled.'

The Queen of Feathers. Somehow I'd known that she'd find me that night. That she'd come to me and give me her maddening, cryptic, less-help-than-nothing advice. She had a faint bluish glow to her in the darkness, wisps of vapor coiling from her shoulders and the train of her dress like steam. Her face was narrow, her eyes deep set. Her hair fell like a violent waterfall over a fox-fur collar. She was not always the same. Not in appearance, at least.

'The times are troubling,' I said.

'They always are. It is time you tested what you have learned from the book.'

'Why do you do this to me?' I asked resignedly. 'You appear, you disappear, you give advice, you get mad at me. You help, you berate me. I don't understand the point of you.'

'Haven't you just described everyone in your life?' the Queen of Feathers said with a smile. 'People are people. They come, they go. The ones who have any value are seldom constant in that regard.'

'It's all just philosophy and riddles,' I said angrily. I pressed my forehead against my knees. I had been reading the book. And something had clicked that night. It was a memory of what I had seen on Robilar's hilltop. The symbols had floated around Alianna, and I'd forgotten them quickly—just a little of Robilar's memory, some ninety years ago. But then that night I'd been poring over the page the book had wished to show me and it had fallen into place. The symbols I'd seen in that dreamscape hadn't been accurate, Robilar had remembered them incorrectly because they were missing certain threads. Robilar had no grave-sight; she saw only the physical manifestation

of the power, she didn't see the strands of souls woven together like rope
that formed the interweaving links.

I had begun to understand now. The missing parts, the parts that had
been blocking me from grasping what the book was trying to show me.
Only half of the diagrams existed in our world, the rest of them were spun
from gossamer threads of spirit.

The new knowledge ran around the inside of my skull like a mouse
trapped in a bowl, because I understood the incantation I had been reading. It wasn't just curiosity anymore. By taking in the knowledge, by understanding what was written there, I had made it a part of me.

The spell was called Soul Reaper. It was brutal, and it was awful. I wished
that I didn't know.

'Can you take it away?' I asked quietly.

'Take what away?'

'The book,' I said. 'I don't want it anymore. I don't want to learn anything
more from it. What it teaches—it's an abomination.'

'You have not understood it yet as you think you have, but you will,'
the Queen of Feathers said. She was closer to me now. I could almost feel
her ghostly form pressing in on me again. The thought was unnerving.
A dead thing talking to me, probing at my life. And yet it was unnerving
in other ways. I was very aware of her closeness, and her wild, statuesque
beauty.

'This thing the book speaks of,' I said. 'It shouldn't be done. It shouldn't
be known.'

'Is a sword a good thing?' she asked. 'Does it have any function but
killing?'

'It's different,' I said.

'Do you not train to kill?' she said.

'This goes beyond that, and you know it. Some of these things in the
book—they don't just kill a person. They use their souls. They take *everything*. I can't do it.'

'Perhaps you will use this knowledge to do what you feel is good. Would
that make a difference?'

'I don't know that any of it makes a difference,' I said. 'I just need to think
about it. And there's no time. Before I adjust to one thing I'm hurled into
the next.'

'Such is the nature of an exceptional life,' the Queen said. 'You remember our bargain, don't you, Raine? That you will provide me with one favour, whatever it is that I ask of you, large or small, when I ask you for it?'

I shivered.

'I haven't forgotten. Although it feels like you tricked me into it. You weren't much help at all.'

'I was all the help you needed.' She smiled, and there was something cat-like in the way she reached up to stroke a lazy finger along the line of my jaw. 'I know I am a confusing creature at times. But I do not exist purely for your benefit. I am not your spiritual guardian. I have plans of my own.'

'And I'm a part of them?'

'Do not be too flattered,' the Queen of Feathers said. 'There have been many like you, over the long, long years of my existence and my non-existence. You are merely another attempt on my part.'

The Queen of Feathers was a deeply annoying part of my life. She appeared when she wanted to, not when I needed her: I'd had to summon her for that in the Blackwell, and it had not ended well for me. I'd wondered whether the Ashtai Grimoire might provide the knowledge to get rid of her. Whatever she wanted of me, I didn't need it. But—and it was hard to phrase this to myself so I seldom tried—she was mine. I'd never had a real father and I'd abandoned my mother. Ulovar was slowly slipping from the world. I didn't want her to go. She was the only one I could be truly honest with.

'An attempt at what?' I asked.

'At everything,' she said. 'I came close with Hallenae. Very close. But I turned away at the last. I balked, if you will. She was good, and she drew power like I never suspected, but she was rotten at the core. She thought herself invincible. I put an end to that.'

'The Sarathi were the ones who cracked open her defences,' I said.

'And who do you think guided them to do so?' the Queen of Feathers said. 'That drunk, eyeless child, Maldouen?'

Oh. That was new.

'You knew the Riven Queen—you guided her—and you betrayed her in the end.'

'That depends on your perspective. Hallenae was like you to begin with. Confused. Doubting. Unsure what she wanted to be in the world. The girl she began as—did I betray that girl by ending her reign of destruction and domination? Or did I betray the thing that she became? Would it have wanted me to stop her, if it remembered who that girl had been?'

I rolled onto my side and closed my eyes. Better not to have to look at her.

'Is that what you'd make of me? You'd have me embrace this power—this command of death and spirits—and raise me to be a new Riven Queen?'

'Not at all. And not tonight. Tonight I came merely because we need a friend, one who understands. But sleep now. I will watch over you.'

The promised day came. The day when the lawyers would hold their party, and I would walk in on Sanvaunt's arm. I was not as frightened of it as I'd been when people had tried to kill me, that is a different kind of fear. More immediate, less internal. But there was a kind of fear, nonetheless. I'd been trying to build a bulwark against it in the lead-up, with all the pressures, all the worry over Ulovar, and Grandmaster Robilar, but I had to allow myself something. I couldn't go on, drained, afraid, empty. I'd known this day would come, and it would try to eat me if I let it. But no. This time I was going. This time I would get what I wanted.

Sanvaunt had chosen a venue where I'd know nobody else, and I doubted he knew how much easier that made everything for me. The stuffy lawyers wouldn't know the sordid rumours that clung to me, even after all these months. Maybe everyone else had forgotten, but I remembered. I was always waiting for another to arise, for another lie to puncture the stillness of the surface. He was taking me somewhere that was public enough that there was no pressure, but that provided the privacy of anonymity. Nobody need know who or what I was. I didn't enjoy my Redwinter fame. I just wanted to be invisible.

I picked my outfit like I was going before the king. Nothing too hot, nothing too shaped. I feared looking frumpy, I feared looking loose. What would result in me being judged the least? But also judged pretty. And sophisticated, but not like I wasn't trying too hard. I went through all of my wardrobe, and halfway through Esher's before I settled on a light summer dress of pale rose, with full sleeves and a modest neckline, but tall boots in the Murrish style.

I wished that I had Esher's help as I got ready, and I was glad that she wasn't there to see. Confusing. I wished she was there to tell me that I looked pretty, or not to wear that shirt, so that we could laugh and start drinking earlier than was sensible, and think up dumb and charming and lewd things to say. Liara was around, but it hadn't been the same between us since I'd killed her father and I could respect that. So my friends weren't able to be on hand to help me, and I was guessing.

I put on my glamours. Party Face, we called it. As I added a blush to my cheeks, my eyes fell to the scar that crossed one half of my face. Hazia's knife had marked me for life on that terrible night in Dalnesse. I'd been collecting scars for years, but none so visible as this. The cut across my face loudly proclaimed who I was, what I'd endured. Hazia had not cut cleanly: as I'd pulled away, the blade had veered up from my jaw, across my cheek, then sliced up across one side of my nose. The scar wasn't far off forming what Palanost called a right angle. Felt more like a wrong angle—an inch higher and I'd have lost an eye. I tried to soften the scar's definition, as though if I covered up these little errors with creams and paints and powders then I could leave that part of me behind, just for a night. It was Esher who'd taught me to do all this, and as I applied the powder and paint it felt a little like she was with me.

I was doing the right thing: I was going to go and meet a handsome boy, a boy who had proved himself time and again, a boy who could tolerate what I was. But when I thought of Esher, and how she would have helped me, and how I found myself looking at her on the practice court, and in the bath house, and just anytime I was around her, somehow this all felt like a betrayal. Maybe the universe saw it fitting that I was betrayed in turn.

I don't know how Princess Mathilde heard that I was going down to the city to meet Sanvaunt, but she had, and she appeared in my room with her young cousin Dauphine, her bowl-hair-cut protector, the stern dowager, and a trio of interchangeable ladies-in-waiting.

'Forgive the intrusion,' Mathilde said, and I had to. 'A little sparrow tells me you're off to a social occasion, and it ill befits any young woman not to have the support of other women before she embarks.' She was all radiant smiles and polished grace, and I had to allow that too. 'Now tell me,' she said, 'what are you planning to wear?'

I looked down at my favourite pale rose dress, my lovely tall Murrish boots.

'I don't know,' I said.

Mathilde was pleasant, and excited for me. It all took much longer than it should have. She and her ladies tried things out up against me, while Dauphine sat sullenly at my dresser as if this was all a personal affront to her ambitions towards a man ten years her senior. I wondered whether this whole show was for her benefit, to remind her she was just a child. It seemed like too much activity over too small a thing for it to be about me.

'Do you like this?' Mathilde said, passing me one of my own dresses. Full length, a high collar, bright red and patterned all over with darker brocade. It was much too stark, and I'd never worn it. Before I had a chance to argue, her smile erupted. 'It's perfect!' she said. And that was that. The pale rose was forgotten.

It was not a comfortable ride down to Harranir. I had to use a side-saddle on account of the dress, and I drew eye after eye, a young woman in scarlet with loose white hair. I felt mortified before I'd even begun.

I had fled Mathilde's ministrations as soon as I was able, so I had time to kill, and I wandered. I headed into the western part of town where the houses were run down, the thatch rotted or sagging, where children played naked in the street and the gutters were thick with refuse nobody had any intention of clearing. They called it Poorside, which was blunt but honest. The town had spilled out well beyond the old stone walls, and in the alleys between buildings I saw the consequences of the sheep sickness in the north. Canvases had been thrown up between buildings to provide shelter for entire families. Their roughspun woollens had once been much the same as I'd worn most of my life, but they were tattered now, fraying at neck and hem. A begging woman had four grubby children clustered in the dark alley behind her. The alley stank of sewage. They all looked sick.

An old man, missing an arm at the elbow and a leg at the knee, begged me for coins. He told me that he'd fought for the Brannish in distant Garenthia, but that the king had refused him a pension after he'd lost his papers of service. It was probably true. I had started to reach for my purse but I saw the others further along the road, watching and waiting. They weren't threatening, but they were hungry. Hungry people can do bad things.

I stood out in my absurdly bright red dress. I'd not gone unarmed; Esher's sword, slung from the saddle horn, kept anyone from bothering me more than calling out to ask my pity. I thought of her as I gripped the sheathed sword's hilt in my left hand. Wondered where she was, off with Draoihn Eiden. Wondered what she'd know when she came back, and if it would be enough. Even if it was, what did it mean? I cared deeply for Esher, but I knew that just as Robilar had picked me for a killer, her skills made her a strong candidate to join the Winterra. She hated the idea of it, and yet, that would be her life if Redwinter willed it.

Apprentices who failed their Testing were sent home. I couldn't imagine what they would do if they were sent from Redwinter. Perhaps she'd find peace working at her mother's kitchen, but it was hard to imagine.

A large building on Foxglove Street had received a fresh roof of shingled bark. There were no foxgloves to be seen, and I doubted that any had grown here for a long time. The street was cleaner, swept free of rubbish, and there were fewer people out and about, no naked children and not even the wild pigs that infested Harranir's streets had ventured along this particular lane. The large building even had a sign painted across wooden boards over its broad central doors.

LacNaithe & Wendlan Labour Houses

There were two tough-looking men on the door wearing clean white shirts and LacNaithe breacan kilts. They weren't especially big or muscular, if anything they had the look of footpads who'd been dunked in a bath three times and wrapped up in a richer man's clothes. They had cudgels on their belts, as if their surly faces and air of menace might not be enough to drive off unwelcome guests.

The first, a swarthy, greasy-skinned man hitting thirty, looked me up and down with that offensive, invasive leer that men who admire themselves try to unnerve you with.

'Think you got the wrong address here, sweetmeat,' he said. He lounged against the door post, letting his eyes do their wandering.

'I'm here to visit the proprietor,' I said. 'I'm from Redwinter.'

'Sure y'are,' swarthy grunted. The second man, bigger, a little older, with flopping sandy hair, got up from his stool.

'Northern accent?' he said. 'Down from the High Pastures, is it?'

'Once upon a time,' I said. 'Redwinter now.' The second man didn't leer at me like I was a red raw steak waiting for a doggish tongue to spread drool all over me.

'I think the boss is inside. I'll go see if he's available if you can wait.'

'I'll wait.'

The sandy man opened a smaller door within the large doors and disappeared into the labour house. From within I could hear the sounds of industry—a rarity in Poorside. Sounds of hammers and saws, voices calling one to the other.

'So what might the master be doing for you?' the swarthy doorman asked. 'Pretty young thing like yourself. How much is your time worth, eh?'

He knew I wasn't a Silk Street girl. I didn't know why men behaved that way. He'd call me a whore while complimenting my looks, one to lift me up, the other to break me down. Both to remind me that the only thing he saw when he looked at me was a body to bed. It was incredibly tedious to have to deal with. Tedious and draining. It was most draining of all because he could only say those things on the understanding that I was going to be too dispirited, shocked or embarrassed to do anything in return. And all of it because he wanted me, knew he couldn't have me, and that made him feel small.

The likes of you and I do not abide by the rules.

Grandmaster Robilar's words. Castus LacClune had shown me the truth of it once. My own grandmaster had nailed the words into place. I didn't have to abide by the smirking, unshaven thug's understanding of how the world worked and what my place in it was.

I could kill him, I thought. *I wouldn't even need to draw my sword.* Torgan had shown me how to do it, had drilled me in it over and over. A bladed hand driven into the right part of the neck. Crush the windpipe. Leave him choking and dying on the ground. Or I could try the Mind Chill, see how he liked it when his own spirit was cutting off his airway. He wouldn't be making those smartmouthed comments then.

I blinked at the sudden surge of violence that had rippled through me. Was I really thinking that? This man was just some Poorsider, picked up off the street, given a job and dressed in another man's clothes. He was talking the way his father had shown him how to talk. Didn't excuse it, but he didn't deserve to die for it. And what would I accomplish? Prove that I'd been given expensive training, and that my position gave me the choice of right and wrong?

That's how the world works, Raine. When you're higher up, when you're richer, or hold power whether magical or political, the rules just don't apply.

Maybe there were no rules. Or maybe I just needed to apply some of my own.

So I just smiled at the unshaven man. It was a novel thing, to realise that if I wanted to I would be able to end him in moments, but this was kind of

Ovitus's doorstep. He'd probably have to clear it up. It wouldn't be a good idea, but if I wanted to, I could. The power this grubby man thought he had over me didn't exist at all. He didn't know what to do with a smile.

'Boss is in,' the sandy-haired man said as he returned. 'I'll show you through.'

I stepped past the swarthy doorman, trying not to breathe his sweat, and onto the work floor. The building was open plan, with stairs and railings leading to galleries above. Men and women laboured at simple tasks. Huge piles of old wood—beams and boards, not sticks and branches—sat heaped in huge bins on one side of the room. On the other, boxes and barrows held shaped stones and bricks. The noise was terrific on the inside, the constant grating of the saws and the *chip-chip-chip* of hammers against chisels. Women and men worked side by side, children of all ages scurried underfoot gathering chips of stone, or sat using tongs to pry old nails from broken planks. Every man, woman and child was dressed the same in pale blue with a stained white apron and a white head scarf.

'What is all this?' I asked.

'This is where we start making things better,' Ovitus said, stepping across the floor to meet me. 'Raine! I'm so glad you found the time to come see it.'

Ovitus was wearing a fine green frock coat with thick ruffs of lace at the sleeves, the shoulders slashed to expose the black silk lining within. He took off his eye glasses and wiped them on a handkerchief. It was hot on the work floor. All that bodily motion, sweat and grime made the air feel damp. I waited for him to say something about how I was dressed, but he didn't. He didn't even notice my garish attire at all.

'It's noisy,' I said.

'It's the sound of change,' Ovitus said. He had a walking cane with an elaborate head in the form of a dragon's snarling mouth—a new fashion in Harranir, one that had arrived with our Brannish visitors. He was much too young to need a cane to walk, but it was useful for him to gesture with around his work floor. 'See that man over there?' He pointed at a man seated on a chair who was lathing down short planks of wood. It took me a moment to realise the man was missing both his legs beneath the knees. 'Crippled in the Kwendish civil war. But we picked him up off the street, gave him a bed, and now he has work again. Putting bread in his own mouth. It's good work we're doing here.'

'That is good,' I said. And it was. 'This is what Mathilde does in Brannlant?'

'Somewhat,' Ovitus said. He was smiling, causing the end of the scar on his face to twist sideways. 'She's a marvellous, wonderful woman, Raine. She had the idea. I just helped with the details. This is all her, really.'

He led me up one of the staircases to where an office lay behind windows panelled with diamonds of glass. It had a desk, a few chairs, a map of LacNaithe lands and another of Brannlant on the wall. From up here, the foreman could oversee the toil of humanity going on down below.

'What are they making?' I asked.

'Nothing,' Ovitus said. 'It's repurposing. There are plenty of old houses that have fallen into such disrepair that they're of no use to anyone. We buy them up, tear them apart, then the workers here turn those parts back into something that we can sell on. They take a share of the profit, we take a share and everyone wins.'

'Rotten old wood and broken stone?' I said sceptically. 'That sells?'

'The riverboats always need wood for patching, and scavenged wood is cheaper than importing firewood from the surrounding country. The good bricks I buy back from the workers and use to build houses on the plots of the old, and those I will rent out when they're done. But these are just details. There's no real profit in it—but that isn't the point. It's a work we do for the people.'

Ovitus poured amber liquid from a decanter into an elaborate cut glass with stem shaped like a leaping fish.

'Whisky?' he asked. I shook my head.

'It's still early for me. So there's no profit. You're losing money doing this?'

'No venture starts out making money,' Ovitus said. He waved it away. 'My pockets are deep. We are all one country, Raine. The south must provide for our northern countrymen now that they have fallen on hard times.'

'And the workers—they sleep here?'

'They do indeed. Beds for hard working heads. That's a slogan I've been playing with. It's not quite right though, is it? Beds for good heads? Is that better?' Ovitus pointed down into the pit below. 'See that woman there? An Ashium-leaf addict. She'd been kicked out of a tavern, found lying in the street mewling. We cleaned her up, gave her work and now look at her.'

I did look at her. She looked like an addict, sunken and sallow, fumbling fingers trying to pry nails from boards. Her fingertips bled.

'She looks sunshined,' I said.

'Impossible,' Ovitus said. 'We don't pay them money.'

'No?'

'Mathilde thought of that too. We pay them in tokens, and the tokens are redeemed for clothing, food and their board. If they don't work, they don't get a token for the day. The bread gets made at another labour house, on Northway Street. So we keep it all together, for the common good. These people have made some poor decisions. Honest work puts them on the right track.'

I stared down at the busy work floor below. It would be fair to say that I would not have favoured any of the work that they were doing, but I would not have favoured shepherding, or sailing, or butchering pigs either. Most work is considered work because nobody would actually want to do it. But at least those other things resulted in money. In choice. But maybe Ovitus was right. These people had been rounded up from the streets and given a second chance. Maybe he wasn't paying them money, but at least they weren't drooling in Ashium dens, filled with wine with the sun only half risen, or begging half-limbed in the gutters.

The Ashium addict had stopped prying nails from the planks and was sucking on one of her fingers. I didn't think that any amount of hard work was going to right whatever problems had driven her to her despair.

'I hope you like it, Raine,' Ovitus said. He stood beside me, his arms crossed over his chest like a general. 'Thank you for coming. I wanted you to see it for yourself. To understand how I'm trying to help your northern kin in these troubled times.'

'You and Princess Mathilde seem very happy,' I said. Ovitus swirled his whisky in the fish-stemmed glass and took a sip of it. He grimaced.

'I still can't drink this without retching,' he said. 'Horrible stuff.'

'How is she finding Harranir?'

'The princess finds it all a little rustic. What we consider fine, she thinks of as quaint, I fear. Harranir is hardly a match for the sights and sounds of Loridine. It's a magnificent city. You think that people are varied here? There's hardly a Brannish person in sight in some of Loridine's districts! So much trade, so much culture crossing over back and forth.'

'You certainly seem to have worked some magic on her to get her to leave Brannlant for you.'

For a moment Ovitus looked hollowed out, offended, and I didn't understand why.

'I would never, ever, *ever* attempt to coerce somebody by magic. We've both been on the receiving end of that kind of badness, haven't we?'

'It was just a figure of speech. I was trying to congratulate you on finding the perfect wife.'

'Few people are perfect,' Ovitus said. 'We all have our flaws, don't we?' He raised the cane and tapped a few times on the glass pane until he had the attention of a floor manager, then gestured towards the Ashium addict who was sitting with her knees tucked up to her chest, rocking gently back and forth. The manager nodded and headed across to get her back to work again.

'Ovitus,' I said. I turned to face him directly. 'Do you think there's such a thing as right and wrong in the world? Real right, real wrong? Good and evil. Like the priests say. Is it real or just something we make up to justify what we want to do?'

Ovitus put his cane down on the table. He came to stand closer to me, then reached out a hand to rest it on my shoulder. He had soft eyes behind the eye glasses. Light Above, but we were so young, and we had such responsibilities resting on us.

'Yes. Of course it's real,' he said. 'Right and wrong are as real as love and hate, or day and night.'

'But one person's right is another's wrong,' I said. 'Don't you think that it all gets muddied somehow?'

'I can't speak for other people,' Ovitus said. He sighed. 'I can only speak for me. Ultimately, I think we know whether what we do is good or bad. What is says about us, what it makes of us. Did I tell you how I got this?' He indicated the scar running down his face.

'A boar hunt,' I said.

'Yes,' Ovitus said. 'The boar came right towards us. I wasn't with the hunt. I'd not gone out with the spearmen. The flushers chased it, and instead of going into the line of hunters it veered away to the meadow where Princess Mathilde was taking luncheon with her ladies. I happened to be with them, pure chance really.'

'You don't really like hunting,' I said.

'Quite so. Anyway, I don't know what got into that boar. It saw the picnic all laid out and charged up the slope towards them. Have you ever seen how fast a boar can move? Like lightning, just a streak of orange hair flashing up the incline towards us. And I threw myself in its way.'

'That was very heroic,' I said. 'Ridiculous. And foolish. But very dashing.'

'I didn't really consider it,' Ovitus said. He sighed. 'It's hard to tell this story without sounding like I want praise. And believe me, I was praised enough. I suspect that my ridiculous, foolish behaviour that day may well have been part of what won Mathilde's father over. But there was no doubt in my mind about what was right or wrong. There were vulnerable women and children behind me. It wasn't even bravery, it all happened without a thought. So I tackled the boar, and it tore my face. The pain was—oh, it was quite something. And then I desperately wished I was covered in armour, and my Second Gate opened right there and then. I made my skin like steel. And then Waldy charged in and tackled it, bit its throat open. He doesn't have that many teeth, but the ones he has are still sharp.'

'I guess you're a hunter after all then.' I breathed onto the window pane, misted it as the people began to head towards a food station where something wet and brown was being ladled into bowls. 'So it's that simple for you? You know it in the moment?'

'Autolocus wrote that we all know how to react in the moment,' Ovitus said. 'But it's how we get to those moments that defines us.'

'Helpful,' I said. I breathed in heavily. I hadn't just come here to be shown Ovitus's work. There was more that I needed from him. 'Your uncle is fading, Ovitus,' I said. 'Something has to be done to help him.'

'I wish there was more I could do,' Ovitus said. 'We've hired the best physicians, the best spiritual healers, even the grandmaster has tried to help him. Nothing works.'

'I don't think it's natural,' I said. 'I think it's a spell.'

Ovitus paled for a moment.

'A spell? Why? How?'

'There was a woman with Onostus LacAud. She was dressed all in bones. She looked like a corpse, or a person made of corpses. I don't think she's of our world. I think Onostus has had her put a curse on your uncle. He won't believe it—he can't bring himself to think that another Draoihn would turn on him that way. Thinks they're still friends. But I don't think that. I think it's her, doing it to him.'

'My uncle is a formidable enemy,' he said. He nodded slowly. 'You could be right. Does the grandmaster know?'

'It must have crossed her mind.'

'Then what do you propose?'

'Perhaps there's a way to break it. Or at least find out what it is. I was thinking you could have the scholars in the library research it—Hexen magic, the hidden-folk's curses, Faded magic, that kind of thing. They like you there. The kind of books we'd need are probably off-limits.'

'I'll do it at once,' Ovitus said. And he sat down at his desk, drew out paper and ink, and was about to set to. 'If there's anything in the library that can help Ulovar, we'll have it.'

'Thank you,' I said. 'And thank you for showing me what you're doing here. And the talk.'

He looked up from the page that he was rapidly beginning to fill. There was still some of his old softness around the edges of his face. There was pain there, too. Talk of his uncle couldn't have been easy for him.

'Any time, day or night,' Ovitus said. 'In fact, the night shift will be starting soon. We're rich on hands wanting to work, low on premises. But we'll help everyone in the end. One day I'll make it all right.'

The time of Sanvaunt's party was approaching, and it was time to go. Ovitus seemed happy that I'd come. It was important to him that I see it, I realised that as he was thanking me for coming by. He had a princess to wed, lands to inherit, and a Second Gate even before he was full Draoihn, and he still wanted my approval.

My path through Harranir's streets had to lead to Brown's Inn, but there were different routes that I could take. The one I chose took me past Nelda's Corn Exchange, a place I knew all too well. It was not a corn exchange by any stretch of anyone's imagination. It was big enough, being a series of three parallel long halls connected by short external corridors, but it was more than apparent that no agricultural trading had gone on there for years, if it ever had. Ulovar had told me to speak to Castus, but he hadn't been home for three days. That wasn't abnormal. His wild gambling sprees could go as long as a week before he either ran out of rose-thistle, or his uncle Haronus sent retainers to bring him home. It was on the off-chance that he might be at Nelda's, one of his favourite, that I went by there. It had been on the off chance that I'd visited two others on my way. I still had half an hour to get to Brown's Inn, and it had to be better to be late than early.

There were more doormen to navigate, but unlike those from Ovitus's labour house, these men were lifetime professionals. Mashed noses, ears that had once been ear-shaped, lips that had been swollen so many times they'd forgotten their original shapes.

'Been a li'l while,' one of them said to me, stepping aside to let me pass on by. I didn't like being recognised.

'Is he here?'

'Been here two days,' he said.

The usual combination of shrill, drunk laughter, desperate fingers clutching at table edges, people with their heads in their hands, and pretty young things on the arms of those with the wealth to lose and lose again and still keep on smiling filled the first hall. A deep incense odour filled the air, covering the scents of a thousand bad mistakes. It was noisy, shouts of frustration and victory crossing like swords over the clatter of hard thrown dice and noisily slapped down game tiles.

'Rivers of Skuttis,' I murmured to myself as I saw Castus across the room in a booth with three other young men. He'd been hitting it hard, and by 'hard' I meant as hard as the grandmaster had. His pupils were gaping voids, one hand drummed against the table, tapping an irregular rhythm his feet didn't match. Bottles of whisky and wine sat half empty, and the laughter was shrill.

He saw me, and it didn't make him happy. He looked a mess, his collar stained, his blue-and-white coat scuffed with days of continuous wear. He wasn't just sipping rose-thistle and drunk, he was on Olatte leaf, Ashium leaf, maybe other things as well. He was, to put it bluntly, absolutely fucked.

'Thought I'd find you here.'

The three young men sharing Castus's table were similarly sunshined, though perhaps they'd headed out today on their mission, while Castus had been at it for days. I could tell he'd barely eaten in that time, if at all; his face had gone all thin. If he hadn't been so stained, he'd have looked fantastic.

'Joining us?' he said. 'Budge up, lads. Raine's a good one.'

'The big fight's up soon,' one of his boys said.

I followed Castus's glance down a door to the second hall. The atmosphere was altogether different there. The old sweat and animal stink oozed out, the shouts and jeers of the audience weren't simply cut between victory and defeat. They were somehow in the middle, a different kind of elation and despair. Patrons were gathered in a ring, watching two women fighting with their fists. Hard, wiry bodies, black eyes and missing teeth. Professional fighters. They danced back and forth around one another, one hand well out in front of them to ward off blows, the other back a little to deflect anything that got through. One of the women was bleeding from a cut to the forehead.

'Kill her!' one of the patrons yelled enthusiastically.

Castus averted his eyes from the battling women, focusing instead on the first hall and its gathered chancers. He wiped at his eyes with the back of his sleeve.

'You all right?' I asked.

'Of course. Just smoky in here.'

'It's not that smoky.' As if in support of my statement, Castus sniffed.

'You look like you drowned and washed up and got thrown back in,' I said.

'It doesn't matter,' he said. He sounded suddenly weary. 'Join us. Have a drink.'

I took one from a passing tray. It was honeyed wine, overly sweet and horribly viscous. One of the young men tried to put an arm around his shoulder. Castus shrugged him off and defused things with something witty enough to cause the man to laugh good-naturedly and laugh at the air. Castus was a beautiful young man. A fine, straight nose, stark cheekbones, and a rush of thick golden hair and he was half a dream for any young woman, let alone the men who turned their sheets that way. When you're beautiful, people go out of their way to do things for you. They give you things they shouldn't, they let you in where you don't belong. But they also flock around you, causing commotion like cooing pigeons, not to mention the burst of disgruntled feathers when they're turned aside.

'Love the dress,' Castus said without looking at me. 'Fancy night out, is it?'

'I guess.'

It didn't feel right to start asking him about his clan library, here in the thick, sweat-rich air. *I should go.* I was going to be late if I tarried. But I drank my drink, and I reached for another when the tray came round again. Seemed like we didn't have to pay for it.

'What's your tab at?' I asked.

'Someone will take care of it,' he said, waving it off. 'Not enough to matter.' There was no good humour in the black zone of his eyes. 'Where were you off to?'

'Nowhere important,' I said. I finished my drink, reached for another. 'I'll head there soon. I just . . . I just need to sit for a bit. I just need time to clear my head. Of everything, you know? Of everyone.'

'Cheers to that,' Castus said, though his drink lay untouched on the table. He just stared off into space, towards one seat in particular, an empty chair beside a gaming table nobody was using. His eyes were fixed to it. I wondered what it had done to offend him.

I sat in silence. The buoyant lads competed to speak over one another, a gabble of meaningless words. One of them was sort-of handsome. I looked at the water clock, saw that time was moving quickly. I would be late when I arrived. *Poor Sanvaunt.* He'd worked this out so well. He'd understood me, understood what I needed in order to free myself from all of Redwinter's constraints. He was such a good man at heart. He'd thrown himself in front of a demon for me, and been terribly wounded in the process. I'd never really thanked him for it. Now was my chance. But I'd need some courage to say that out loud.

Ghost's Claw. Soul Reaper. Banshee's Wail. Spirit Knot. The Dance Macabre.

'Top you up?' Castus asked. He didn't fill my glass, just pushed the bottle across to me as he stared and stared at that chair.

'One more drink,' I said. And I meant it.

It was two days later when Haronus LacClune turned up at Nelda's Corn Exchange, cleared Castus's tab and dragged us both home because a large part of Harranir was on fire.

23

I should have been in a lot of trouble for disappearing the way that I had, but the longer I'd stayed, the harder it had been to go. I imbibed, and I drank, and I laughed, and danced and cried and argued with Castus and ran down the street with him, and together we wasted those hours into a void scarcely remembered.

The fires started somewhere on the east side of the city, thankfully far away from Nelda's Corn Exchange. It ravaged Northbank, bringing down whole streets until its advance stalled when it ran into the river to the south, and the cathedral grounds west and north, whose tall, stone perimeter walls were having none of it. Redwinter only had two Draoihn of the Third Gate in residence at the time, and they were sent down to assist as best they could, but there was a lot of fire and a lot of panic. Rows of houses were demolished to form fire breaks, and eventually, it was done.

I felt the heat beating against the curtains of a LacClune guest room when I woke, and whenever I did I just buried my head beneath my pillows and went back to sleep again. I slept for most of two days. My body had given up on anything else. That's the thing about rose-thistle; it doesn't give you more time, your body always needs to take it back later, and more. Physically, I felt wretched, but that wasn't the claw that curled around my heart and crushed down on it. I couldn't even face thinking about Sanvaunt, and what I'd say to him the next time I saw him.

I'd stood him up. At the time it had felt so easy, one drink had drifted into another and I was half aware that I was making a choice and half so intent on not thinking about it that there was nothing there at all. Then once I'd started, I couldn't stop, and then when it was too late I couldn't face the apology. No, I had blown it, well and truly and the worst part was, it wasn't even the first time. I'd failed to show up the last time, and he'd still made an effort. I didn't think that he would again, and truth be told, I didn't deserve another shot. If he simply didn't speak to me at all I couldn't have blamed him. And lying abed, my head pounding, mouth dry, stomach knotted and weariness so deep it smothered like a weighted blanket, I couldn't have borne it.

I would apologise to him. I knew I had to make it up to him somehow. Maybe he'd invent a reason to be out of town for longer, or he'd take meals in his rooms, or—something. But I was as wrong about that as I seemed to be wrong about everything else these days.

I missed dawnsong and took the opportunity to take a long bath when everyone else was off chanting to the Light Above. I lay in the steaming water and stared at the tiled mosaic on the ceiling, thinking of all the mistakes I had made, all the follies and errors. There seemed to be so many of them now I couldn't even count them. Sanvaunt had offered something good, and easy, and safe, so I'd taken an axe and chopped through the ropes that bore the bridge that connected us.

I had wanted so much for him to see me and think I looked pretty. I had wanted to dance with him, and feel his warmth pressed up against me. I wanted to kiss him. I wanted to sleep with him. I wanted him to playfully pin me down on the bed and nip at my neck, to taste his mouth, to breathe his sweat. I wanted him to touch me, soft, and teasing, and cruel, until I had to beg him to start, and then beg him not to stop.

It was easy to imagine him, but even in those fantasies, there was me. Broken, haunted, murdering me. I couldn't let him touch me. He'd feel the rot inside me. He'd taste it in my sweat. He'd know.

My hair was still damp when I headed back towards the LacNaithe greathouse, and by the worst possible chance, Sanvaunt had just started crossing the Osprey Lawn as he headed towards the baths. He gave me a quiet smile.

'Morning,' he said, and then continued on.

Morning, like it was just a normal morning. *Morning*, like nothing had happened between us. *Morning*, like I hadn't hurt him. *Morning*, like I hadn't dreaded this moment. *Morning*, like he didn't care at all.

He looked worn and smelled like woodsmoke. There was fatigue in every line that made him.

'Wait,' I called after him. Sanvaunt stopped. There was a moment of tension in his shoulders—maybe, I wasn't sure, perhaps just wishful thinking— but he turned easily. He had his Draoihn coat slung over one shoulder, his hair was tousled and sweaty. He'd been up early, training, and I could smell it on him.

'What can I help with?' he said.

'Should—should we talk? About what happened?'

He kept the smile up. It wasn't a real smile.

'I don't really have anything to say,' he said. 'But if you'd like to say something then we're here now. I'll listen.'

The sky was covered by a pall of angry clouds. Spits of rain ticked cold against my skin, and a small wind nudged at Sanvaunt's curls.

'I messed up,' I said. Sanvaunt didn't say anything. He was unnaturally calm. So calm that I knew that I'd hurt him, oh, I'd hurt him as badly as if I'd thrust a spear into his chest.

'I know,' he said.

'I'm sorry,' I said.

Sanvaunt gave me a smile that said he'd predicted this, and he knew I'd be sorry. And that this apology was worthless.

'Can we start over?' I asked. 'I know I messed it all up, but I can do better. I can be better.'

'You don't have to be anything,' Sanvaunt said with a sigh. And rather than hate me, or feel anger towards me, I realised something much worse: he felt sorry for me. 'But I'm a person, Raine, and people are worthy of respect. If you spend your time chasing around after someone who doesn't respect you, then that makes you a fool. And I'm not a fool. So I'm not going to chase you anymore.'

'I do respect you,' I said, my voice breaking. Tears burned across my eyes. 'I respect you so, so much.'

Sanvaunt held his arms out wide.

'Those are just words,' he said. 'Don't feel bad. I like you, Raine. I've always liked you. But I'm not disposable. If you wanted to be with me, then my feelings should matter to you as much as your own. But they don't. Maybe I got it wrong. But I believe in love. I want to be in love, and be loved in return, and no great romance starts with someone who doesn't bother to show up. So let's just forget it happened, and let's be friends and move on.'

'It feels like so much more than that,' I said. 'Like a cliff falling away into the sea.'

Sanvaunt's eyes, those sleepy eyes, turned away from me then.

'I know,' he said. 'But I'm done.'

And he walked away from me.

I made it back to the baths and threw myself into the water where nobody would see the tears streaming down my face. I kept my head down in the hot water, where the crying and the snot wouldn't show. I'd done this to myself. I didn't deserve Sanvaunt. I didn't deserve to be happy. I'd let him down, yet again.

But I'd protected myself, too. Because if I let myself get any closer to him, at some point I'd have to show him what lay beneath the skin. He'd hear me screaming in the night, and he'd see the blank deadness in my eyes when I killed someone new, and he'd see me tear souls apart and silence even the dead. I was a grey-souled, dead thing on the inside. I was poison. And I hungered for it, all the time, I wanted to know more, to see more, to do more. I wanted to learn what Hallenae the Riven Queen had known, and I wanted to stand beside the grandmaster and be her right-hand woman. I wanted to be strong, and I didn't care who stood in my way. The rules didn't apply to someone like me.

Kind Sanvaunt. Good-hearted Sanvaunt. Noble Sanvaunt. He was the opposite of Grandmaster Robilar's philosophy. But he was strong too. Perhaps I could convince him. If I could show him that there were no rules for him and I then couldn't we just do what we wanted?

I didn't feel that I was in any position to convince anyone of anything just then. So I cried instead, and did nothing, and the emptiness grew.

· · · · · ·

'We will rebuild,' Ovitus said. 'Northside will rise from its ashes. We will build fast, and stable, and strong.'

The fresh timber used to form his speaking platform had come from his labour home in Poorside. His voice was magnified by the Second Gate, reaching across the assembled throng of people who had lost everything in the fire. Waldy lay at his feet, unbothered by the sound, content.

'We have nothing left!' someone shouted from the crowd. 'The fire took it all!'

'I hear you,' Ovitus said, sounding as much like a statesman as ever I'd heard. 'This morning I addressed parliament. They will release funds to further the Better Works project that I and my wife-to-be have devised. You were all working people. You will all be aided to continue your work as we clear what has fallen, and raise what we need.'

Princess Mathilde stood a way back from the podium, giving Ovitus the space to stand alone. Her cousin Dauphine was with her, as well as the usual collection of bodyguard, dowager-virtue-insurance, ladies-in-waiting and servants. Ovitus had brought the LacNaithe apprentices with him as well. Everyone had dressed down to watch him make this address, clothing that could look humble at a distance.

'What do you know about what we need?' a woman called from the crowd. 'Your blood's half silver. Everything I had burned!' Angry murmuring. I wasn't sure why anyone would think the fire was Ovitus's fault, but it's easy to cast stones upwards.

'Do we not all need the same thing?' Ovitus asked. 'Shelter, food, water, security? These will be provided. I have brought my people here to ensure that nobody misses out.'

And, credit to him, he had. A large team, thirty or more retainers with ledgers, ready to redistribute the people of Northside as best as could be managed.

'There must be a thousand people,' I muttered.

'Probably double that,' Princess Mathilde said. I hadn't realised she would hear me. She missed nothing, that one. Princess Mathilde seemed to know everything that was going on around her at all times. 'This morning we bought nine warehouses. Two of them we were already looking at, to house the northern refugees. The rest will all be new labour-homes for the dispossessed here.'

'So they'll move into labour-homes too? A lot of these people were tradesmen.'

'It will help them get back up onto their feet,' Mathilde said. 'And when they're ready, they'll move on. Others in your parliament have seen the opportunity for what it is—to build new houses where the old once stayed. There is much work and much profit to be had.'

'I thought it wasn't about profit.'

'There must be profit or there can be no expansion. The money trickles down from the top,' she said. Ovitus continued to tell the assembled crowd about his plans to raise a new crafting centre along the scorched riverbank. The plan seemed very detailed for one thrown together over a couple of days. The crowd's attention waned as a wagon loaded with boxes drew into the square. Food; many of them hadn't eaten since their homes were destroyed. Harranir was mostly wood, and the fire had been savage.

'Where is Dauphine?' Mathilde asked, glancing back over her shoulder.

The ladies-in-waiting didn't know. The big man with the bowl-cut hair suddenly began scanning around, his body tense. I couldn't see her either.

A sudden surge of panic swept the little group. The young noblewoman was gone, but she'd been there just a moment ago.

'Split up and find her,' Liara said, taking charge. 'She can't have gone far.'

I climbed up onto the edge of the platform, hanging from a beam by one arm to look out across the crowd, but I couldn't have imagined her pushing her way in among the commoners. The smell of dirty woodsmoke hung over the square, almost visible in its density. I expected her to be found within a few moments, but the unease was growing as she wasn't found immediately.

Ovitus finished up his speech and headed towards the stairs.

'Getting a better view?' he asked me, cheerful at having come off well. Waldy roused himself to follow his master from the dais, panting in the summer's glare.

'I was trying to find . . .'

'It went well, didn't it? I thought it went well enough. All those poor souls. I wish I could make it right for them, here and now. But you think this is good work?'

'I hope things work out for them,' I said cagily. If the labour-homes ran as the one in Poorside did, I couldn't see how the workers could rebuild their lives as they had been. There was something in the system's design that felt like a cage.

'I need to know I have your support, Raine,' Ovitus said. He looked earnest.

'Of course, lord van,' I said.

'Not just that. But as someone I care about, too.'

'Lady Dauphine has run off somewhere,' I said, switching the subject back to the more urgent matter at hand. 'We're trying to find her.'

'She's over there.'

He pointed, and I saw Dauphine being escorted back towards the stage by one of the ladies-in-waiting, who had her by the arm as an angry mother might. Dauphine was spitting poison, her face heated, but the young woman who had her was brooking none of it. A few steps behind, a chastened looking Jathan followed in their wake, and I had a very bad feeling. He looked less the handsome rogue and more like a child whose hand had been knocked away from the biscuit jar.

'Tell me this is not what I think it is,' Ovitus said, and all his good humour vanished. The scar on his face seemed to settle deeper. I had only ever once seen him with this expression before, the night he had Castus

LacClune abducted and beat him beneath the greathouse. He took the stairs down from the stage two at a time, his wolfhound following along wagging its tail, unaware of what was transpiring.

'I was just showing her the view from the bridge,' Jathan said defensively. He didn't sound convincing. He'd turned red as sunset. Mathilde was speaking to her cousin in hushed, stabbing words.

'Jathan,' Ovitus said, and it was the first time I'd heard him use that voice. It wasn't his; it was Ulovar's tone, commanding, filled with a depth of presence that imposed his authority with a single word. 'Why did you take Dauphine away? Even you could not have mistaken her bloodline.'

'She was perfectly safe,' Jathan said. 'What?'

'I didn't ask if she were safe,' Ovitus said. 'I asked why you took her away.'

'To show her the view from the bridge!' Jathan said. I could see he wanted to bluster, to protest and declare the injustice of it all. Ovitus was as good as his lord now, but the princess's cousin was under no such need to hold her tongue.

'He was just showing me the view, Light Above!' Dauphine exclaimed. 'Can't I do anything? Jathan is one of your Draoihn, and it's broad daylight in the middle of the day. I wasn't in any danger. And I'll go where I want.'

Mathilde was about to say something to that, but Ovitus spoke over her. 'You will not. While you're in Harran, you're my responsibility. I promised King Henrith you would be well taken care of.' He gestured to Mathilde's entourage. 'Take her back to Redwinter. We live in dangerous times.'

I wondered what it had taken for Ovitus to find this change in himself. The love of a princess? Maybe finding the Second Gate had given him the confidence. Or perhaps it was the knowledge that sooner rather than later, he would be the van of his clan. But no, he'd started this journey before he'd left Redwinter for the south. He'd begun to treat himself differently, and now he treated others differently too. He glared at Jathan.

'As for you, you'll learn your place. You bloody Kwends are all the same, snapping at what's not yours.'

Jathan's face had turned bleak. He bit back his defence, I could see it in his face.

'I'm sorry, my lord. I meant no harm. Lady Dauphine asked me to go with her. I had not thought it unsafe.'

The apology did nothing to mollify Ovitus.

'You've always been a brat, Jathan,' he said. 'Get out of my sight. I'll deal with you later.' He thrust a finger in front of Jathan's face, held it there a few moments and then stalked away to his princess. Waldy snuffled around at Jathan's feet for a few moments, barked once and then followed him away.

Lady Dauphine was being taken away, shamed like a child. A cruel glimmer of spite tinkled inside me. I remembered her fawning over Sanvaunt, the same Sanvaunt who no longer cared to see me. That was my fault, deep down I knew it. But we rarely get to control how we feel.

'I was just being friendly,' Jathan said quietly to me. 'I didn't do anything.'

I looked at him sidelong. It doesn't matter what people say sometimes, it's their actions that count, and there was no way he and Dauphine could have easily slipped away together without making an effort. Obviously, they should have told someone where they were going. Obviously, they should have been accompanied.

'Use your brain,' I said, and that was all I was going to give him.

It was three weeks before the apprentices would be Tested. The atmosphere that night around the dinner table was cold and formal, and I wondered how long it would last. But then news arrived that Onostus LacAud had taken the port of Penreet on the Black Isle, and all we could talk of was war.

It must have been unthinkable for the people of Penreet. The port had changed hands many times, but not in my lifetime. They called it the Black Isle because of the soil, dark and heavy with peat. The island didn't boast a large population; it didn't boast much of anything. It had been governed by LacSpurrun, a minor clan, but Onostus LacAud saw some kind of strategic advantage in it. Seventeen days ago, the people would have seen the high-masted ships closing in flying friendly banners, and now they knelt to LacAud. As with Gilmundy, Penreet had been taken without violence.

'Penreet lies off the western coast of LacAud lands. If LacClune were to seek to sail up the coast, it's a natural staging point if there was an intention to invade,' Ovitus told me the morning after we heard the news.

'So it's to deter LacClune from getting involved?'

'It seems likely,' he said. 'Good grief. It's strange isn't it how everything can go from normal to chaotic in the blink of an eye.'

'You think LacAud is making a play for the throne?'

'It seems hard to imagine anything else at this point,' Ovitus said. 'Only LacClune would be in a position to challenge them on the western coast, and Merovech LacClune has stayed largely silent. Your friend Castus hasn't let anything slip, has he?'

'He doesn't seem to care,' I said. It was true, and it also avoided having to choose whose trust to be in. The truth was, Ovitus was not Ulovar. To me, Ulovar *was* the clan. If Ulovar succumbed to the illness that weakened him daily and Ovitus took over, the clan would be a different thing. Different values, different policies. Those who lived on its fringes like me would find the world changed with it.

The days were quiet. There were no more morning seminars on Eio, or history. Lady Datsuun was greatly displeased with me for having missed two of my sessions because of my excursion with Castus, and she worked me greatly. It was a quiet time, and Sanvaunt's measured cordiality was worse than if he'd shown that he was angry with me. I was lonely.

Castus had sunk into a bleak depression. That long week of excess and imbibing had been a signal fire, but nobody knew how to handle him. I used that to my own ends. Haronus LacClune was usually out with the unfortunate apprentices who'd been assigned to his tutelage, and so I took advantage of his absence and used Castus to gain access to the LacClune library. I spent hours among their banks of musty, yellow-paged books. What plagued Ulovar couldn't be Draoihn magic, and nothing in the Ashtai Grimoire indicated it was Sarathi born either. A dark certainty began to grow within me. I had met a woman who held to some dark power that reflected nothing of Draoihn magic; a bone-witch; an eater of flesh. Onostus LacAud kept her close by—and why else would he want such a foul and wretched creature as Akail at his side? She stank of the cruellest magic. In my desperation, perhaps I hoped it was her. She was something that breathed, something that could be fought, an obvious enemy. But I had no proof, only a hunch that wouldn't go away.

But day after day I found nothing. One night I returned back to our own greathouse with a book beneath my coat. Ovitus had been as good as his word, and the scholars of Redwinter's library had scoured the annals for any indication that might help Ulovar against a curse from the Night Below. Mostly he came back empty-handed and apologetic, but finally his scholarly friends located one that I thought might possibly give some indication of what was happening to his uncle. I sat with Ulovar through the night as I read a translation aloud to him. His eyesight had weakened, and no amount of candles lit the room enough that he didn't have to strain.

'You're pronouncing it wrong,' he said as I read to him in the dead, declension-rife language of Elgin, which our ancestors had written in. It was a treatise on magic used against the Draoihn by the Faded Lords and their Sarathi allies, long ago, before they were banished beyond the veil, using the bones of their enemies as talismans of power. It was fascinating. Like I'd found a missing link from what I could read in the Ashtai Grimoire. Like seeing something that has been described to you as a dream suddenly painted on canvas. 'Kiss your teeth at the end of the word. Like this.'

He looked so old now. So weak.

'You're still trying to tutor me,' I said, and my heart cracked a little.

'When I'm gone, you will remain,' he said. 'Life will continue. We cannot hope that our death has meaning, only that we had meaning to others in our lifetime. Now kiss your teeth.'

I laughed even as I wiped a tear from my eye.

'It won't come to that,' I said.

'We both know that it will,' he said. 'I am not bitter, but I am resigned. Had I acted sooner—had I not denied the signs as long as I did—perhaps there might have been time. But if a remedy even exists, we will not find it. You did well to find this text. I've been searching for a copy for twenty years, more probably. But this is not what I need.'

'There are still more pages—'

'No, Raine. This book is rich with detail of what the Faded could do, but they are long dead. They have no answers for us.'

I fell silent and for a moment I felt very young, like I was new and the man I was sitting beside was nearing the end of a long, rich life. There was a gulf between us, but somehow it made us closer.

'My van,' I said, and in that word I felt it so much. Felt it so deep and so true that I knew that Ulovar truly was my van. He was my leader. There were times I wished he'd been my father. 'How far would you go to be cured?'

'Far enough, and not,' he said. Tugged at his numb, dead fingers. 'There are lines that one should never cross. Perhaps there is more to dying than I thought. Perhaps in death we need to be the best we can be.' His bloody eyes were still as he watched me, breaths wheezing with a phlegmy gurgle. He could no longer clear his chest easily.

'What would you have given to save your sons?'

He blinked slowly.

'Anything, and everything.'

I could not do this alone. Ulovar had asked this of me in a last ditch wave of the flag. What he needed didn't exist. The Glass Library had burned in the year 172, and the Draoihn had lost so much of their most guarded knowledge, and if Ulovar was right and he lay under some kind of curse, then those that practised such magic had been purged from our ranks a long time ago.

And that made the decision easy for me. It wasn't permission. He didn't know what I intended, what mad plan had come to me. But it was all I needed to hear to remind myself that there were no rules for people like me.

. . . . . .

I returned when Ulovar was sleeping. He left his door unlocked now, and that was new. Despite his attempts to carry on as normal, he might need help and he knew it. That made him sad. I was going to try to give it. I was the only one who could.

I crept through the dimly lit room, a case in one hand, a canvas on a frame tucked beneath my arm, and slowly sank down into a plush chair beside one of the few candles. The room had a sweet, dried-sweat odour, the smell of sickrooms everywhere. It's an indignity that our bodies turn against us in so many ways when our time approaches. Maybe there was nothing I could do, but I was going to try. I owed him too much not to.

I wasn't good at this. Palanost had only managed to get me so far along, but anything was worth a shot. I'd asked the book for something specific. Something I needed so badly its edge could have drawn blood. And there, deep in the night as I lay reading on my bed as I'd done so many nights before, it had opened up for me. I'd turned a page, and it was all laid out. Not unreadable, not indecipherable, but so clear and obvious to me that its meaning was abundantly clear to me. Clear as if I'd written it myself.

I laid out my inks, gold, green, red and blue, and pens for each. I didn't need the ruler or the rest of it. It wasn't to be that kind of incantation. The geometric tools were helpful if I wanted to make a change in the world, but this—this was all about me. I took a deep breath, watching Ulovar's once bulky form rise and fall with his slow, wheezing breaths. And I began to draw.

I started with the world. Abstract patterns and shapes, and not the things I saw, but the way the world existed around me. Not the goose-feather-plumped bed, not the walls, or the tables or armchairs. I drew being. Symbols for existing, for knowing, for belonging, for feeling. I formed them into a ring around the edge of the page. I drew life in gold and death in blue. I marked amusement in red, and fear in red, and time in red. I recreated my universe in ways that only I could have understood it, in the ways that only the book could understand it. The tethers, the collapses, the absences of anything and the discovery of the new. I lost track of time. The candle dripped and pooled.

I didn't notice when she arrived. I was lost in the page, in a world of ink and canvas.

'What are you doing?'

The Queen of Feathers stood over me, her dress long and blue, a wreath of raven feathers about her temples and dripping black war paint smeared across her cheeks. She looked at what I'd drawn across the page. Trying to decipher the chaos I'd constructed. Lines overlay others, concepts blurring together where ink had smeared.

Something was wrong with it. It wasn't quite right. I thought back to the Ashtai Grimoire, which I'd left hidden beneath the floorboards in my room as I always did. Why wasn't it working? I tried adding depth to the world, to the borders of my feelings, to the sense of loss that permeated the whole greathouse. I recoloured the sickness at our heart. It still wasn't right.

'Why are you here?' I asked. I rested my pen.

'I'm always here,' she said. 'Even when you don't acknowledge me. I've always been here.'

'Babble, babble, babble,' I muttered.

'This will not be easy to explain if you're caught,' the Queen of Feathers said. 'And you still owe me that favour.'

'You'll get it, whenever you care to ask,' I said.

'How can I help?' she asked.

'I can do it alone,' I said. 'I think I can, anyway.'

'Can I watch?'

It felt different somehow. I realised that it was the first time she'd asked my permission for something.

'I guess so. Just let me concentrate, all right?' The Queen of Feathers said nothing, but moved away behind me, outside of my view.

I returned to my work, trying to blot out her presence. I hadn't tried to work myself through it, but I couldn't. I knew that it wasn't going to work. Something was absent. Something wasn't right. I dipped gold ink, then set the pen back. I was only going to ruin it if I kept changing it without direction. The new candles went about melting, their light fragrance thickening the air.

'What am I missing?' I muttered aloud.

'It's us,' the Queen said. 'We're missing from it.'

'No,' I said. 'I'm here.' I indicated the central sigil, annoyed that she'd been watching me work over my shoulder. Intent on the incantation's designs, I'd forgotten she was there for a time. Now I felt like my work was being checked by a teacher.

'You're there,' the Queen of Feathers said, though how she could tell that I'd written myself into the incantation I didn't know. My symbols weren't like anyone else's. 'But you're not connected to any of the rest of it. Here's Ulovar.' She pointed at a writhing squiggle, and she was right. 'But you haven't crafted the connections. You're supposed to be a part of it, aren't you?'

'How do you know that?'

'Because I've used it before,' she said. 'The Eyes of Serranis. That's what you're trying for, isn't it?'

'Did you make it work?'

'Of course. I gave her the idea.'

It was the tunnel that was missing. The reason I wasn't connected to anything around me, the thing that kept me apart from them all when all I wanted was to draw closer. The tunnel was my isolation. It was my exile. It was my fear, and it was my great love, and I was part of it and it owned me in return. That's what I'd read in the Ashtai Grimoire. But the book was too disconnected from the world. It lacked substance, somehow. It didn't follow the rules that an ordinary book should have. So it couldn't tell me everything I needed, because it belonged to another time, the thoughts and ideas of another person, or people. The incantation I had written was for me, it was me. I had to become it.

Only the black ink was necessary. Now that I'd realised what was missing, it was easy to fill in the gaps.

'Your penmanship leaves a lot to be desired,' the Queen of Feathers said when I finished the last stroke.

'Yes,' I said. 'Yes, it's horrible. But it's right. I'm going to try now. Give me some space.'

We call them Gates because we can pass through them, but they are not gates. None of them were, really. They were openings, but more in the sense that one opens a box than a hole in the wall. I reached out for the tunnel. With the incantation as a focus, it came easily. As easily as breathing. The droning, metal-tearing sound filled me. The world tremored and shook, but just for me. Death, death, it was there and it was ever present, lingering so close we nearly touched it in every moment. I poured myself through the Sixth Gate and through the focus before me as I spoke words that were formed from the images I'd crafted. They had names, but names known only to me. I chanted in a low, dry-throated voice. And then the spell took hold and I knew the world in different shades.

I had always seen things that others couldn't. The spirits of the recent dead, or those that wouldn't pass on, had been a plague in my mind since childhood. But there are more things that lie between worlds than the souls of the dead. Serranis's eyes became mine. She'd been a tyrant once, blessed or cursed with the same power that lay within me. I saw the world as she had learned to see it. The world was patterned all over in the dappled shadow of something else. A world that lay beyond our world, beyond the simple visions of the dead, to a place where the fell things were born, and slithered and thirsted.

Around Ulovar's sleeping body, a great worm was coiled, its body dry as a snake's, but smooth as old leather. It wound around his legs, his torso, coiling around his arms and every finger, at points thick and bulbous, at others thin as a wand. Its body had no substance; it passed through the heavy blankets, through the bed itself, wrapping around Ulovar's neck, and finally coming to stop at his head. I could have choked on sudden tears. The demon-worm's head was latched onto Ulovar's skull like a leech. A little ripple ran through its body, starting at the leeching maw, as it took something more from him, digesting it.

The worm had no physical form. It wasn't spirit either. I could feel it, filling the space between us, its presence bearing a weight that carried out all around it. It saw me. But it remained where it was. Feeding.

'It's killing him,' I said. 'Someone did this to him. It's killing him.'

'I see it now,' she said. 'And yes. It's killing him.'

'What is it?'

'I've never seen this before, but I have known of things like it. It is something from the Night Below. Something that has been called to take from him. It isn't his life force that it consumes. It's draining his Gates. And when the last of them goes, he'll be empty. A husk.'

'How do I stop it?'

'That, I do not know. It could be Sarathi magic, or there are other magics in this world, Raine. The Draoihn destroyed the Hexen and the Tharada Taan, but magic is buried deep through the bones of creation. '

The page on the desk began to smoulder, the lines of ink sizzling like boiling tar. I punched through the canvas, tore it from its frame and dropped it into a basin of water. The water boiled, bubbling and churning before foul-smelling steam drifted away leaving little ash-like fragments of the canvas floating in an opaque grey pool. Ulovar didn't stir.

'This is what Sanvaunt was trying to do,' I said quietly. 'So it attacked him in the corridor, and burned the book. It knew that it could be seen. Sensed the book, maybe.'

'But it didn't stop you,' the Queen of Feathers said.

'No,' I said. 'It thinks I'm an ally.'

'It would not have worked for him,' she said. 'It is an incantation for your kind, not his.'

'Can we kill it?'

'There were those in times gone by who could have undone this,' the Queen of Feathers said. 'I don't think anyone living knows how to defeat something like this.'

'No,' I agreed. 'Nobody living.'

I rode by daylight. I had consulted old maps in the archives, drawn by Draoihn cartographers and showing where the fallons were dotted around the
land. I drew a ten-mile radius around Redwinter, and checked them against
more recent maps. One of the standing stones was missing. It was that stone
I made for, a stone that seemed lost to time. But it wasn't lost, it was merely
out of sight.

The hilltop was cold, the wind hard, and the midges were implacable as
they bit at me. Summer is midge season, and clouds of vicious bloodsuckers
made for my skin. I rode South hard, but there were more midges waiting
for me atop the hill where an old, tumbledown house still stood.

I felt a pressure as I approached it, a desire to turn away from the place
and go back. Three storeys tall, the roof had collapsed inward and nobody
had come to occupy it in all the long years it had stood here. I could smell
the old rot, but there was more than that to the deterrence. The closer I drew,
the more I felt fear welling up inside me. This was a dangerous place. Who
knew what lurked within the rotten walls? I had best get on with it.

I should have known that the grandmaster would have warded this place
with some kind of incantation, but it was difficult to bear. It wasn't a command that emanated out from this dead hilltop, but a suggestion to all the
little anxieties that lay inside me. I ignored them, took my hands from the
reins and let South plod up the hill. She didn't seem to notice, this ward
wasn't meant for her. I tried to turn my mind to anything—anything else
that would stop me thinking about what lay at the top of the hill. The intrusive thoughts were hard, dominating. I tried to count through Torgan's nine
principles of battle and couldn't keep track of it. I tried to recite liturgical
verse in Elgin to myself, and that was doomed from the beginning. I put my
hands on the reins to turn the horse around.

I snapped them away and balled my fists. I had to go deeper, deeper
into something that could occupy my mind totally as the pressure grew

unbearable. I needed something spectacular. I needed something that could absorb me totally.

I imagined Sanvaunt ripping open the buttons of my dress, tossing me onto a bed. I imagined him smiling at me, hungrily, sweetly, cruelly. I pictured his body, his hard muscles and his leather-and-ink scent. I let myself think those things about him, and I pictured myself under him, atop him, biting at his neck, dragging my nails across his back. I had so much anger around him, angry at him for dismissing me, anger at myself for forcing him to do it. In my imagination it was a powerful, shuddering lust. I let him in. I let him conquer me. And then an intruder arrived in the scene, Esher, golden-haired, and Sanvaunt was replaced and she worshipped me like a queen. Her touch was delicate but persuasive, her grin ready, her self-doubt abandoned. We ground together, bodies sweat-slicked, hands searching, tasting her kisses. And then I thought 'Why in Skuttis not?' and I put them both in there together and I had no idea how that would work but it all felt pretty amazing, and I found myself laughing. Sex should be funny, I thought. Exciting and intense and funny and a bit twisted all at the same time.

I thanked my horny brain as I opened my eyes and found that we'd reached the summit. The press of aversion dissipated here, existing in a ring around the hill. The grass grew tall right up to the collapsing house and I noticed that there were no midges here. It was a spot of serenity. Even the wind seemed not to want to disturb it.

I let South crop the grass, and fished in my pack for the Ashtai Grimoire. It was so light, much lighter than a book this thick should have been. I flattened out some of the grass and opened the weathered pages, somehow knowing that I'd find what I wanted this time. The book admired purpose; it wanted to be used. But it was fickle. *How* it wanted to be used didn't necessarily meet what I wanted. I wanted to check back what I had read before, many weeks ago now: the memory of bone. But the book had other ideas.

The nineteenth attempt was made by Raine, at that time an apprentice of Redwinter.

I slammed it shut on instinct. What had I just read? What in all the freezing rivers of Skuttis had I just read? I opened it again, and this time it was just diagrams. I flipped pages, searching for the page I had just read but no, it wasn't there. I had to have been mistaken. I had to have read that wrong.

I was not stupid. I knew that there was something wrong with the book, and that I had been meddling with things I couldn't understand. But to see my own name written there was like one of Torgan's fists to the head. My mind searched for reasons that I could have read what I'd read. Someone else had found the book and written it in. The book was writing itself. It was just coincidence. The Queen of Feathers had done it.

I looked for her. She'd brought me this book. She had to understand it. But she was nowhere to be seen just then.

I wrapped the book with one of my scarfs, bound its pages tightly shut as I shivered in the fading afternoon. The book knew who I was. It contained *me*, somehow. Dear Light Above, I was part of it. I felt tears form, and I wondered at who I had become, at what I was choosing to become. I was abhorrent. I could spin my mind a fantasy but how could I turn to Sanvaunt's arms, or Esher's, when I was going to do what I was about to do? I was everything the Draoihn fought against. I was the enemy. I was making myself the enemy.

I'd told myself that I was seeking a way out of all this. That I would unlearn this power by learning it. But that night, I couldn't lie to myself anymore.

It was *my* power. Others were born with wealth, or were handsome, or tall. Life wasn't fair. But I'd earned this power through death and death again and why shouldn't I use it?

Did they all begin like this? The Riven Queen Hallenae, Grandmaster Unthayla the Damned, Empress Song Seondeok, Serranis Lady of Deserts? Those great and terrible women of the past who had raised empires, who had fought wars, who became the most dreadful forms of enemy to the people of our world, had they felt a moment like this upon them? At first I had seen the dead, and then I'd spoken to them, and then commanded them. I didn't know where this road would lead me. I had to do this for Ulovar, though he would have told me not to if he'd known what I planned to do. Might have sentenced me to die for it. But I would do it all the same, because it was the last thing I could think of and the hourglass was about to run out of sand.

I had brought a shovel with me. I found the place, used my sword to cut down the grass, and then I dug. It is hard work to dig a grave, even a shallow one. The sun fell against the horizon like an explosion, spreading gold and peach fire across the sky. Our country is always most beautiful before the darkness.

The digging took hours. I found small bones first, and what had to have been cloth a hundred years ago. I went more carefully then. I didn't know how this would work exactly, but I felt the skull would be best. I didn't want to smash it. When I finally unearthed it, the dome was already cracked and broken, but the teeth and face were all in one piece. I found the jawbone and attached it too. I didn't know if that mattered or not. I had intended to climb back out of the hole I'd dug, but somehow it seemed more fitting to do it here, hidden from the world of the living by walls of earth. Worms wriggled around me, a silently squirming audience.

Power, from bone. I had memorised the incantation at one point or another. I had never tried it, but I'd worked great magic once before when I summoned the Queen of Feathers to me under the Blackwell. I cut a symbol in the dirt with the edge of the shovel, six circles within six circles, then sat at its centre with the skull in my hands. There were words as well, meaningless to me, but memorised from the Ashtai Grimoire's pages. I hoped that would be enough.

The skull was cold, and dry. I shook the dirt out, polished it with the hem of my sleeve. It is a weird thing, holding another person's skull. Once upon a time this held their brain, and their eyes, and everything that made them what they were was bound up in it. It had function. But as a skull it's barely anything. I was going to change that.

I chanted the words, and then, as I had done before on the day I killed Kaldhoone LacShale, I poured myself into the skull. I felt the cold come across me at once, and there was a feeling like the moment of climax, a release of something inside me that had been pent up, pushing at the seams, waiting to be let out. I expanded, and I tranced into Eio as I did so, and the skull grew warmer in my hands as I gave myself into it. I let it know me, let it take from me. The bone still recalled what it was, and I reached out into a different place. A place that lay beyond the tunnel that opened around me, its dark walls leading to greater darkness beyond. A place where there was no temperature, where there was no sound or sight, and existence is utterly alien to anything we experience through our short lives.

There were things there. Inhuman things, and some were malicious and some were gentle. Most didn't notice me at all, I was invisible to them just as the shades of the dead are invisible to most of human kind. I sensed the presence of a Faded Lord, long banished from the world, and I drew myself small to avoid its slowly sweeping eye. There were things of tentacles, and things of mouths, and things with wings and things of fire and pain. They were all jumbled together. Space had no meaning. But as my chant concluded I whispered a name.

'Alianna Robilar.'

Something deep in my chest latched onto it, binding us together with rainbow-hued thread, and I pulled on that thread and I drew on it. The weight at the end of that cord resisted, and the hungry things sniffed at me, but I drew harder. I felt my pulse in the flicked-cat-tail scar on my face, as though my broken parts might allow me to spill out into the world. But I contained it. The tunnel, the Sixth Gate groaned and made its metal-on-stone squealing as I dragged Alianna's spirit into it, pulling hard and drawing her forth, through that terrifying, shrieking void.

I fell backwards against the wall of the pit, and there she was before me.

Spectral, green and white and smoking vapor. She towered over me, her feet within my feet, a woman of fifty years, a kink to her nose.

'How long has it been?' she asked, her voice hissing in the stillness of her grave.

'A hundred years,' I said. 'Give or take a few.'

She looked around, head and shoulders above the side of the pit.

I had done it. I'd only just gone and fecking done it. I hadn't known it would work. I felt a wild, surging elation at the sense of my own power.

'It looks the same,' she said. 'Apart from the house.'

'I need to know things,' I said. Not very articulate. 'I need your help.'

'It is too late to help me,' Alianna said.

'I'm not trying to help you,' I said. 'I'm trying to help someone else. You might know the answer I need. I serve your sister.'

'Vedira is still alive?'

'She is. She showed me this place. Showed me how you died. Please, I need to know the things you knew when you were alive.'

Alianna's shade drifted up from the pit, her lower legs passing through the soil. I jumped up and pulled myself free, smeared with dirt. The spirit was looking around, taking in the night. There was a light glow around her, a ghostly beacon in the night.

'Did she ask this of you?'

'No,' I said. I had not planned for a recalcitrant or uncooperative ghost. I'd just assumed she'd answer my questions.

'Then by what right do you have to ask this of me? There are laws against such things.'

I steeled myself. I was going to have to be firm with her. I could feel the tunnel's pull, its desire to return Alianna back from where she came. My mind was open with it.

'The rules don't apply to people like me,' I said. I made her laugh.

'Spoken just like Vedira,' she said. 'You truly are her pupil.'

'Maybe I'm the master,' I said. She laughed again.

'You're just a slip of a girl. What could I possibly tell you?'

'I've never met a Sarathi before,' I said. 'I might be the last one. The others were all purged away. And you might know the magic that can save my—' What was appropriate? Not friend. Mentor? It sounded too distant. Alianna smiled, and it was made of the sound of knives on whetstones.

'Shall we make a deal?'

This was the problem with summoning the dead, or feathered queens. Once you got them there, they didn't seem obliged to do what you wanted them to do.

'What kind of deal?'

'You can ask your questions, and I'll tell you the answers truthfully. In exchange, I get to . . . live a week in your body.'

I had not been prepared for that.

'In my body?'

'Yes. You'll still be there. You'll see and hear everything, smell it, touch it too. But I will be in control.'

That sounded like a really bad deal. A really, really bad deal. Because if it were me, then I'd use that time to glue myself to the body and not go back. Or would I? The glimpse I'd caught of whatever lay beyond the tunnel had been too alien to understand what was really there. Senses didn't exist, and maybe neither did space itself. Everything was just *there,* but there were no physics, no width or depth. Maybe she wouldn't want to stay.

But deals with the dead, and with creatures like the Queen of Feathers *did* have rules, whatever the grandmaster said. A deal made between the living and the things beyond the veil somehow had greater solidity.

'One hour,' I said. 'And you tell me what I want to know first.'

'Three days,' she countered. 'And I answer your questions at the end.'

I needed to ask her about Ulovar. I had to know if there was a way to counter his affliction. But did it matter if I asked first or last, if I had to give up my own body anyway?

'Half a day,' I bartered. 'And you don't control me, you can just . . . ride along with me. And we won't kill anyone, hurt anyone, or do anything that goes against my goals or ruins my life. But I'll try to do what you ask me to do within those terms.'

'One day. You can do all the actions, but I'll tell you what I want. And I answer you at the end.'

I might have been able to bring her demands down further, but was the deal all that bad? Moreover, I was fighting down a huge sense of excitement at the prospect. Firstly, I wanted to feel what it was like to have a passenger along for a ride, but a day—a whole day—where I got to relinquish control? Someone else would be responsible for whatever I did. It was a free pass to be someone else, even if just for a day.

'Deal,' I said.

'Deal,' she agreed. 'Bring my skull with you. I don't want the connection to break until we're done. We're going to have some fun.'

I should probably have thought harder about it, but standing atop a dark hilltop, talking to a ghost whose skull was in my hands, and with the prospect of learning what I needed from one of the actual Sarathi, exultation coursed through me.

She disappeared and there was a feeling like plunging into a warm summer lake. It wasn't unpleasant.

'First, let's lower the noise, shall we?' she said. And she did something to my Sixth Gate, like she'd ringed my mind with stones, and the droning of the tunnel rescinded. 'That's better. You're very new at this, aren't you?'

'I don't know much,' I conceded. We shared a mind and a body now. I felt I had to trust her. It would all come out when I had to ask her later on anyway.

'What was your first death?' she asked inside my head.

'Strangled at birth,' I said aloud.

'And the second?'

'Did I have to have a second to find the Gate?' I asked.

'Yes, of course,' Alianna told me. 'Is this what you wanted to ask about?'

'No,' I said. 'I need to know how to help someone.'

'You should engineer a third death,' Alianna said with a hint of mischief in her voice. She sounded just like the grandmaster. 'That's when things get really exciting.'

'I don't want to die again,' I said.

'There is no more self-defeating goal than living forever,' she said. 'We all die again sometime.'

I breathed out.

'What do you want to do first?'

*   *   *   *   *   *

There were a number of things that Alianna wanted to do. We walked bare-
foot a little on the hill, and then she had me do some springs and cartwheels.
I could feel her laughter inside me, a girlish glee at being able to do all the
things that don't exist in the spirit world. I made a little fire and warmed
my hands for her. We sang together. It was silly and I only then began to
understand exactly how much joy there is to be had in moving your arms
and legs around, just being a physical thing in the world. We don't realise
how important that all is until we can't do it, I suppose. Getting old, feeling
your body fade must be frightening. I drank some of the wine I'd brought
so she could taste it—it wasn't very strong, and she didn't want to waste our
time together on getting drunk. There were better things to do.

Some details are best skipped over, but I'd thrown myself into this, and I
wasn't against them. She had a particular way to guide me in how I touched,
and where, and I had never known I could do that to myself. It was in-
tensely personal, and it was beautiful, it made me feel beautiful in a way I
never had before. I shouted, was left gasping, and then howling with laughter, rolling over in the grass at having just done that. And Alianna laughed
along with me, and I thought, 'Well this is the weirdest use of the Gate of
Death I could ever have imagined,' and she howled with me and asked me
to do it again.

When the sun rose we basked in its beauty and warmth. I rode us to
Harranir and we visited places she used to know, and she told me how everything had changed. I ate the things she'd once loved. The more I went along
with whatever she wanted, the more I enjoyed it, and the more I came to see
how I'd limited myself. I'd worked so hard to become what others wanted
me to be—retainer, Draoihn, warrior—that I'd let this raw joy of life slip
away behind a curtain. My eyes were opening now. It wasn't like when I
indulged myself with Castus, imbibing rose-thistle and booze to drown out
the world around me. It was welcoming it in, and seeing how much fun we
could have. And fun we had.

'Redwinter,' Alianna said. 'I want to see it again. We only have a few
hours left.'

So we saw Redwinter, and much inside its walls had changed too. I waved hello to a handful of people, but our route was inevitably taking us towards the grandmaster's residence.

'No,' Alianna said as it came into view. 'No, I don't think so.'

'You don't want to see her?'

'It wouldn't be the same,' she said. 'I'm not you, and you're not me. It wouldn't be the same at all. And I think I'd rather remember her the way she was. She might be different now, and I don't know if I'd like it.' There was sadness there.

'What's it like, after you die?' I asked.

'It's not really possible to describe it. When I'm there, I don't have thoughts, or a body. There are different things, but there are no words to describe them. There's no place and no time. There's existence, but it would be like trying to describe colour to someone who has never seen. At best I could give you allegory, and it would be too flawed and take too long to be worth trying.' I felt something like a grin open up inside. It was an odd thing, feeling someone else's emotions atop your own. 'Do you have a young man?'

'No,' I said. I thought of Sanvaunt and I felt an unfair surge of anger towards him. I knew I'd been the one to ruin everything, but that didn't stop me feeling something unjust had been done to me.

'Shame,' she said. 'That would have been fun. I quite enjoy riding along. Maybe someone else will summon me up in another hundred years' time.'

'I have an idea,' I said. 'It's a really bad idea and it might not work.'

'Was raising me from the dead a good idea?' Alianna said with gentle mockery. But it had been good. It made no sense but I hadn't felt myself so much as I had with Alianna calling the shots in a long, long time. No responsibility. No doubt or pressure. Liberty.

I found Castus in the LacClune greathouse, fortunately in his own chambers, wearing his nightrobe. He'd been painting, just a lot of dark and miserable colours swirling around together, but the painting lay abandoned and he was just staring out the window when I arrived. Maybe this wouldn't be good for him. Maybe the depression that had crashed down on him was something I should have left well alone. But he was all I had.

'What are you doing?' I asked.

'Brooding,' he said in a melancholic tone. 'Want to brood with me?'

'No,' I said. 'Let's have sex.'

He turned his face towards me with a puzzled, but amused expression.

'You want to sleep with me?'

'It's a long story, and I probably won't ever tell you it. But today, just now, yes. And that means sex and nothing else, no promise of anything in the future, nothing cloying or messy, just a one-time deal. You've done it with women before.'

Castus stood up, and let his robe fall open as he opened out his arms. I'd never been attracted to him, but he was an exceptional physical specimen.

'Very nice,' Alianna purred. 'Ask him if he minds me being here!'

'I can't tell him I have a passenger,' I thought back. But then I thought about it again.

'Two things,' I said. 'You can't tell anyone about this, ever. And secondly, you have to not mind if someone you don't know is watching.'

Castus grinned at that.

'Oh, now you have my interest,' he said. 'Is someone watching?'

'Only in a very non-conventional sense, and I can't tell you who,' I said. 'Also, you have to be fecking good at it. I'm on a schedule.'

Castus chuckled to himself.

'Darling Raine, you have no idea.'

He was, it turned out, immensely good at it. He read me better than I'd read a book.

Sex with Braithe had, I discovered then, been absolutely terrible. It had been one-sided, perfunctory, a race to his finish line. Castus was a different animal altogether. Maybe it was because there was nothing to care about, no emotional investment for either of us. Everything was boiled down, nothing but bodies smooshing together. He didn't like girls, but he liked himself a lot, and he and I shared that need to be the best. I had no reserve, no fear. I flung myself into seeking pleasure, and he rewarded me and I gave it back as best I could. Castus had all the practice, but I hoped that I made up for it in exuberance. Some of the things he taught me that night I'd never even heard about. All of them I wanted to do again.

I had seldom been that sweaty. We took breaks for wine and sat looking out of the window, talking like nothing bizarre had just been happening in the rumpled bed across the room. Then Alianna would suggest something, and Castus would shrug and was game for anything. I went around the mountain more times that night than I ever had with Braithe.

It was freeing, and maybe something inside me began to heal that night. I'd been afraid of this, I realised. Afraid of letting myself loose, because it had ended so badly in the past. But it was just bodies, and those are all we really have in the end.

'I have to go,' I said. Our time was done. I got up and tried to fix the madness my hair had become.

'Was anyone actually watching?' Castus asked. He appraised the closed door, as if he might find an eye at a crack.

'Isn't it more fun not to know?'

'Well, I hope they enjoyed the show,' he said. 'My father would be thrilled if he thought I'd gone back to women.'

'Well he won't find out,' I said. 'Will he?'

'You have my absolute word on that,' Castus said. 'Thanks. You brightened up an otherwise miserable day.'

'You're the best!' I called as I snuck out.

'Bravo,' Alianna said. 'You're sure you don't want to keep me around a little longer?'

Honestly, it was tempting. I hadn't enjoyed myself this much in a long time. Maybe never.

'Sorry,' I said. 'That wasn't the deal.'

I took us over towards the Blackwell. It felt like a suitable place to go. Alianna's skull was in my satchel. It would be exposed out there, but it was distant from most of the well-used buildings and nobody ever went there. The stone bridge stretched between the plateau and the spire of rock on which, and within which, the Blackwell lay.

'This is it then,' she said. 'It's been a good day.'

'If I'm honest, it's been the best day I've had in a while,' I said as I sat cross-legged on the expanse of stone. 'You have to be honest with me.'

'I think you're owed that.'

I could hardly bring myself to explain what I had seen in Ulovar's chamber. The leeching worm that was coiled around him, and the slow loss of feeling in his fingers and toes that had progressed through his body. After the joyous abandon of a day without feeling guilty about what I did, it felt a hard and dark thing to have to remember. But summer doesn't last forever, and winter was about to reassert itself whether I wanted it to or not.

'It is a curse of blood and bone,' Alianna said. 'The drawing of a person's Gates is no small thing. I never knew of it happening in my lifetime. There was a book I once had that detailed it.'

'The Ashtai Grimoire,' I said. 'It's in there?'

'Sometimes,' Alianna said. 'Then you know it. And you've met Her too, haven't you.'

'The Queen of Feathers?'

'I called her something different. I knew her as Ravilaine, and I do not think she has ever been a queen, though I see why you call her that.'

'Then she knows?'

'Ravilaine . . . was a confused source of information at the best of times. She often wasn't sure of where or when things were happening. I made a deal with her once.'

'She asked for a favour.'

'I died before I could fulfil it,' she said. 'Yes. She asked me for an undeniable favour. In exchange she gifted us with a different book from the ruins beneath Harranir, one which we used to bend the world.'

'And became invincible.'

'I came close,' Alianna said. 'But didn't finish my ritual in time. I have wondered what it was that Ravilaine would have asked me.'

'Don't we all?' I said. 'But it's a spell of blood and bone?'

'Whoever has worked it must possess some of the victim's,' she said. 'But the knowledge for it was lost even before my time. If I remember it right, the Ashtai Grimoire described it being used by the Faded Lords, to strip power from their most powerful enemies. With the blood and bone of their enemy, they turned the person's body against them. It is your master's own body that is doing the damage, trying to fight what it perceives as an invasion.'

'How do I reverse it?'

'How are these things ever reversed? A curse is an ongoing, living magic. Kill the one who cast it, and your master may recover. Or it may be too late already. I'm sorry I can't offer better tidings.'

'So I need to find out whether Ulovar is missing a toe?' I said.

'That would be my most likely guess,' Alianna said.

And my worst fears were confirmed. There was one woman I knew who, through a dead man's eyes, I'd seen tearing blood from throats with her teeth. I'd seen her body pierced with little spurs of bone. Her name was Akail, and she belonged to Onostus LacAud. What was it he'd said about her?

She is something we all forgot. And honestly, had I not needed her rather unique services, I'd rather things had stayed that way. But I'm a man who pays his debts.

It had only been a hunch, but sometimes your gut knows the truth.

I needed to kill her. But she was far away, and no doubt surrounded by LacAud's forces, and even if I had some unique skills, I couldn't take on the world by myself. So my worst fears were confirmed, and the one thing I needed to do more than anything was still far beyond my reach.

'You're strong, Raine. You can be stronger still. I feel a great wash of grief inside you, that you've suffered greatly. But even after a wildfire, flowers will grow again and bloom.'

I was crying again. I seemed to do that too often these days.

'Hush now,' Alianna said. 'There is balance in all things within the spheres of the world. After darkness comes light. Each action has an equal and opposite reaction, and the greater the magic, the greater the exchange.'

'Look at me,' I said through messy tears. 'I've embraced it now, but—this road, it hurts so much. Alianna, I'm so lonely. I have no choice but to hide myself, what I am, from even my closest friends.'

'All lives are lonely,' Alianna said. 'But that just means you're getting older. But we exist as one whole, one entire thing that is both separate, and together. It is love that binds us, in the end.'

'I'm sorry you have to go,' I said.

'Don't be,' she said. 'There's a whole different existence waiting for us after we die. It's nothing to look forward to; it's just different.'

'Are the rivers of Skuttis real? Is Anavia?'

'We make them ourselves,' she said. 'It's hard to explain. But our deal was made, and now I have to go.'

'Wait,' I said. 'The book—why won't it help me? Why won't it show me what I need?'

'There is no book, Raine. The book Vedira and I used was burned to nothing.'

'Then what is the Ashtai Grimoire?'

I felt her shrug mentally.

'I don't think it's anything.'

She was drifting from me, turning to insubstantial nothing.

'I'll miss you, I think. What should I do with your skull?'

But there was nothing there anymore.

26

I'd found half the answer, but I had no solutions. I tried to find an audience with the grandmaster, but she'd thrown herself into politics, a rare move on her part. The strife between the three great clans threatened the stability of the Crown. I learned from her staff that she was spending more and more time with the king, using her healing Gate to keep his body functioning as we awaited Prince Caelan's return. He and the Winterra could be here any day, and only then would King Quinlan's reign be allowed to end.

I tried leaving messages for her, but I saw her servant place my vague note in a stack of paperwork half as tall as I was. There was already a retainer bringing up a stack of ledgers behind me.

'It's urgent,' I said. 'She needs to get this today.'

'I'll see she gets it,' the retainer said, with a smile that said that there was absolutely no chance of that at all.

Fourteen days is a long time when you're waiting for something life-changing. The Testing loomed closer, and so I busied myself with work. I didn't want to think about what it would mean for my friends who failed. And I didn't want to think about what happened if Esher passed and found herself banished to a life in the Winterra.

I trained with Torgan, I trained with those who'd train alongside me in Redwinter. I spent mornings and evenings practising my trance, reading history and philosophy, and studying magic. I ignored languages; I had no gift for them. Keeping busy worked to keep me from excesses; I even managed to stay off the rose-thistle, most of the time. It was too hard to study if I was sunshined. I avoided Castus; I did not think my resistance would hold out around him. With Alianna's departure, I was mortified about what I'd done. He didn't seek me out, and I was glad for that.

Each day I left another message at Grandmaster Robilar's residence, and every day that stack of papers grew higher. On the fifth day I practically snarled at the retainer. He added the note to the pile and closed the door, and I knew it was futile.

I saw Ulovar each night. He helped me prepare from the bed that he could no longer leave, and I brought him whatever interesting reading material I could find. His bedroom was lit by lamps and candles rather than cadanum globes, a strain on the eyes. Onostus LacAud had strangled the cadanum trade at Gilmundy and the north no longer supplied it to the south. Both Harranir and Redwinter had been unprepared for that, and the blue-light glow that often suffused the city had dwindled away.

My heart ached for Ulovar. He didn't deserve this fate, drained and hollowed by Arrowhead's blood-witch. We needed him now more than ever. By taking Penreet, Arrowhead had opened new hostilities with Clan Lac-Clune and faced enemies on two fronts. Perhaps he'd thought deposing Ulovar would leave his soft, weak nephew to lead the clan, but Ovitus was a changed man. They'd find his uncle's iron had grown up into him. Ovitus sat with us often at those times, and part of me wished I could entrust what I'd learned to him so that we might have the power of the clan to apply to the problem, but I couldn't reveal what I knew without explaining how, and my need for secrecy had not diminished.

I awoke to the smell of burning. I jerked awake, my mind rushing back to the awful night that Sanvaunt had been caught among the flames. I scanned around for the source, but there was only a neat little hearth banked high and putting out a powerful heat. Firstly I saw that I was not alone, and only then realised that I wasn't in my bedroom anymore. I wasn't even in bed.

'I got your note,' Grandmaster Robilar said from a comfortable chair. She was all crone today, head strapped together with metal bands, fingers wrinkled with ill-fitting skin as she held them to the fire, the only source of light, the room in shadow. 'This had better be worth bringing you here.'

We were not alone. In the grand four-poster bed, an old man drew wheezing breaths. His skin was flaky, almost grey. Tiny green-black veins threaded beneath it, crossing and breaking through his cheeks. He was thin, and the blankets and fox furs were piled up over him. This was our king, Quinlan LacDaine. Beside the bed another man sat in a high-backed chair, similar in appearance to the first, fleshless and spent, but not so worn. He had a wood-framed canvas beside him, covered in row after row of neat golden runes and broad strokes of black and red that smeared the paint and left it in chaos. Draoihn Kelsen of the Fifth Gate, personal healer to the king, looked different in person. I had glimpsed him in Robilar's dream. I didn't feel right, and the smell of burning was not just in my nose, I could taste it. I could feel it against my skin.

I looked down at myself. I was made of oily smoke that coiled from a brazier and melded into a smooth, coal-dark body.

'What's happening?'

'You're dreaming,' Draoihn Kelsen said. His voice had a rasping, gummy lisp to it. 'Or close enough. We brought you here in the fire. A little of you, anyway, and it took us a long time. But we have a lot of time on our hands here, and hopefully this is enough to stop Vedira from fretting.' He gave a soft, somewhat mean chuckle, but Robilar looked at him as though he were just a funny old man, and she tolerated his silliness.

'Oh,' I said, as though any of that made sense. 'So I'm still back in Redwinter?'

'You've been barraging me with these notes,' Robilar said, not bothering to answer my question. I guess her retainers had done more than I'd been giving them credit for. 'This had better be worth it.'

'I know who cursed Ulovar. I know how they did it. Kind of,' I said. I'd finally got here and I wasn't about to squander my chance even if I was made of smoke. I tried to step forwards, away from the oily brazier that was connected to me by smoke, like a tail, but I couldn't go anywhere.

'Don't jiggle it, girl,' Kelsen said. 'It was hard enough to get you here.'

A low moan came from King Quinlan. Kelsen reached out a bony old hand and placed it on the king's sleeping chest, and I felt myself waver as the Fifth Gate opened. I'd never had the training to sense it before. It was soundless, more like a rush of air, as if we were contained within a box and the lid had been thrown open. Nausea battered me, but it was nausea in every part of the form, not contained to the gut. The Gate gusted for a few moments and the king's moan subsided.

'I told you she was good,' Robilar said calmly. She looked tired. 'Who was it?'

I got everything I could out. I couldn't say where this knowledge had come from, but I'd earned it, and now—now they could do something, these mighty people. But I could name Akail. For once I had a clear target. I never wanted to be an assassin, but now that the task presented itself I found myself prepared.

'Good,' Robilar said. 'I knew I picked wisely when I took you as my apprentice. Find her, and kill her.'

'Oh, Vedira,' Kelsen said chidingly. 'After all this time, all the things we've seen and done, that's still your answer?'

'It tends to work when time is of the essence,' Robilar said. 'You should let me take over for a while.'

'Not yet,' Kelsen said. He looked to the king. 'Another hour. I still have some more to give.'

'You give too much as it is,' Robilar said, and her tone was kindly. The gentlest I'd ever heard her speak. They'd known one another for a long, long time, I thought. Probably longer than anyone else had known anyone. Kelsen looked to be close to ninety, and Robilar was much older. It seemed easier to believe it when she let the façade drop. Beside the fire, flexing creaking finger joints, a knitted blanket across her legs, she looked every year her age.

'I'll do it,' I said. 'If I can find her, I'll kill her.'

'A blood-witch is no easy thing to dispose of,' Kelsen said. 'This is a woman who has consorted with the foulest dark intellect. What's left of her is half demon.'

'There are weapons in the Blackwell that can do the job,' Robilar said. 'Unless you want to summon the Anam Teine and do the job for us.'

Kelsen took a deep breath in through his nose and then exhaled slowly and noisily. I heard the gurgle in his chest. There were little black-green lines along the veins of his hands, rising up from his robe to caress his neck. It was the corruption of the Crown, and the healing bond he'd formed with the dying king over decades of service, reflecting back into him. Then he laughed, the staccato chuckling of a body that should have lain down and fallen silent years ago.

'The Anam Teine only answered me once, Vedira, as you well know.'

'And you never told me how you did it.'

'What's Anam Teine?' I asked.

'The fire of the soul,' Robilar said. She reached up to press a finger against the molten cracks within her head. 'The manifestation of life energy that flows from the Fifth Gate in its purest form. I've held it within me, but I never managed to call it forth it as Kelsen did.'

'That was a dark day,' Kelsen said. 'And one I have sought atonement for all these long years.'

'But the Fifth Gate brings life,' I said.

'Life?' Kelsen muttered. 'It brings life, but even those who create a life force the inevitability of a death into the world. Do not believe things are so clear and plain as all that, young apprentice. You're young. You think everything is clear, crisp and clean. Take it from a man who had to end his own wife's madness, you'll see everything through clouded glass if you make it to my age.'

I certainly didn't think anything was crisp and clear. The old like to believe we don't know anything. But even I had to admit there were things I didn't understand. Like being made of smoke.

'I can see the path forward clearly enough for now,' I said, trailing a smoky hand across the room. 'Arm me. Give me what I need. I'll destroy Akail, and free Ulovar.'

'Yes, that's fine,' Robilar said. 'But you'll need to find the opportunity. You can't go marching into Arrowhead's territory. At least, not until you've done your Testing.'

'But this can't wait—' I began, but Robilar interrupted me.

'Off with you now,' she said, 'you're making the room smoky.'

I didn't remember any of it until I awoke the next morning in bed, as if I'd never left it in the first place. I'd hoped for more help, but at the least, I'd have the weapons I needed.

.   .   .   .   .   .

Everyone began to return home.

I saw Esher at the foot of the stairs, her saddlebags in the arms of a servant. I hurtled down the stairs three at a time and flung myself into her arms. She grabbed me back and spun me around.

'How did it go?' I asked.

'It was tough!' Esher said as she deposited me back on the ground, a little breathless. She'd put her hair into many small braids. It made her look older somehow.

'Where did you go?'

'All over. We covered so much ground. Eiden was brilliant, though. Maybe getting out of this place for a while was what I needed. I feel confident in a way I haven't for months.'

'You feel ready?'

Esher's smile was a powerful thing.

'Yes, Fiahd. I feel ready.'

We alighted to one of the comfortable sitting rooms where we could talk in private while Esher ate, and Liara joined us. Little Maran was sitting reading at the other end of the room, but they wouldn't interrupt us. Maran kept to themselves most of the time, not yet acclimatised to life in Redwinter and a few years our junior. They didn't have a Testing tomorrow either, and read the room well.

Esher talked about her travels with Draoihn Eiden and the other apprentices who had been assigned to him. They'd been gone for nearly forty days, and it felt like a lifetime.

'So let's get to the real news,' she said enthusiastically. 'How did it go?'

'How did what go?' I said.

'I'm sure there are better things to talk about,' Liara interjected, her face blanking through it. 'I'd like to hear more about those powises.' Esher didn't pick it up.

'Didn't you walk out with Sanvaunt? The party?'

'Oh,' I said. 'That.'

'It didn't go well?' Esher looked crestfallen, like she'd been expecting much better news.

'Not well,' I said.

'It didn't happen,' Liara said. 'Things got in the way.' She didn't look at me. I'd known she and Sanvaunt were close. He must have told her. Confided in her. It occurred to me that perhaps this was why she'd been avoiding me. Torn between different allegiances. For some reason I'd believed Sanvaunt would have kept it to himself.

'What things?' Esher said.

'I don't need another lecture about it,' I said with a sigh. My joy at seeing Esher again fell tumbling down a bank, hitting all the rocks on the way. 'The timing just didn't work out.'

'That's not true, Raine,' Liara said. She seemed older than us lately, fully Draoihn and working at her responsibilities. I had seen how much Sanvaunt and Ulovar had come to rely on her. 'It didn't happen because Raine got obliterated with Castus LacClune instead.'

'That's a cold way of putting it,' I said, feeling anger rise.

'Isn't it just fact?' Liara said.

'You don't understand,' I said. 'Nobody can understand. I just can't do it, all right?'

'Nobody's saying you have to,' Esher said. She reached out to take my hand.

'You told him you'd go, and then you didn't show up,' Liara said. 'I don't think you even realise how hurt he was.'

'I'll make it up to him somehow,' I said.

'Don't,' Liara said. 'No. Don't go trying to make it up to him. It's one time too many, Raine. I've spent the last few weeks trying to persuade him to put it behind him and find someone who actually appreciates him. He nearly died fighting to protect you from a demon, and you didn't bother to show up.' I was fuming, and Liara saw it. She held my gaze for a few moments, unforgiving. 'Give him the time and space he needs to get on with his life. You've gone through a lot, but so did he. Let him forget you, if you don't have time to spare for him.'

'Nobody understands!' I said, standing up and coming close to knocking over the drinks table. I didn't want to be chastised like this, least of all in front of Esher.

'Nobody has to,' Liara said. 'It's not their problem.'

It was not what I needed the night before my Testing. Esher looked mortified and embarrassed.

'I don't want him,' I said. Which wasn't true. 'It's best if everyone just accepts that and moves on the way I have.' Which was also untrue.

I stormed out hard enough that even Little Maran looked up from their reading.

. . . . . .

I started the morning of my Testing with two duck's eggs, milk and a slice of ham. I'd need the energy, but I didn't want to feel heavy. The previous night's argument had to be put to the back of my mind. Didn't people understand that there were much bigger, more important things to worry about?

Of the thirty-eight Redwinter apprentices, Fisha, Helastus, Maran and Perdia had not been in Redwinter six months, leaving thirty-four of us to take the Testing. Usually it all happened behind closed doors, and the methods by which apprentices were Tested were kept a closely guarded secret, but on this strange and unusual day, with the sun raging overhead, everything was to happen on the Wyvern Lawn. The wyvern was the symbol of Clan LacNaithe, which we'd all taken to be a good omen.

There were to be three stages. The three healthy members of the Council of Night and Day currently residing in Redwinter would question us to reveal our knowledge of history, of the Draoihn's work, and of magic. They would test our ability to enter and maintain Eio. When—if—they were satisfied, we entered the physical test of our martial abilities. We would face off against one man untrained in war, one man who was well skilled, and lastly a drunk. It was a common way for the defence schools in Harranir to test their trainees; a drunk man fights very differently to a cautious swordsman, and we had to show ourselves capable against each. It was all very good natured for the men and women who'd been asked to attend from the city. There were a lot of them, three men or women for each of us, and those who were tasked with drinking had already started. They were expected to lose, but rumour had it they'd been offered five hundred pel if they could take one of us down, or a thousand if they could do it drunk—more than a month's wages for a farmhand. The competition wouldn't go easy on us. Lastly we would each swear to serve the Crown before the council members, and five Draoihn would have to vouch for each of us. The council members then decided whether or not we had succeeded, but by that point it was all so much formality.

The councillors in attendance were Grandmaster Robilar, in her younger form, the master of artifice Suanach LacNarrun and Kyrand of Murr. Ulovar was unable to leave his bed, Merovech LacClune had not travelled from his clan seat of Clunwinny. Onostus LacAud was obviously absent, as was Kelsen, who could not leave the king's side. Lassaine LacDaine was the commander of the Winterra and was returning with them, but had not made it in time, and it seemed that Hanaqin Clanless still had not turned up and it was so long since anyone had heard from him that people had begun to suggest that he might be dead. So we had only three councillors of the nine who could have sat in judgement, and that made the chances of a veto a lot smaller. Neither Suanach nor Kyrand had reason to dislike me, and so if I could make it through, I didn't think I had to worry about that.

Five Draoihn needed to vouch for me, though. It didn't matter that the grandmaster had told me I'd passed, I still expected something to go horribly wrong. We were about to be on display, and despite being told it was a foregone conclusion, part of me didn't quite believe it.

'Don't worry about it,' Ovitus told me as we began to assemble to watch each apprentice undergo their ordeal of words and battle. He gestured towards an array of Draoihn wearing LacNaithe black and green among the spectators, of which a crowd had formed. Every Draoihn in Redwinter had turned out in their best, sweating in formal oxblood coats and clan colours in the rising summer heat. The Brannish contingent had set up wide parasols for Princess Mathilde, Lady Dauphine and their attendants.

'Hard not to worry,' I said, but Ovitus smiled broadly and leaned in rather close to whisper into my ear.

'I brought in our most loyal people and instructed them to give the necessary nominations. It's a formality only.'

I had been counting on Sanvaunt, Liara and Ulovar, and had hoped for two more, but now I saw that other clans had done the same. LacAud's people stood away from the blue-and-white Clan LacClune Draoihn, Castus and his vile uncle Haronus among them, and our LacNaithe and subsidiary clansmen formed little knots alongside their overlords. I just had to get through this one day.

It hadn't really hit me before, not with everything that had been occupying my mind. Me, Raine Wildrose, Raine Clanless, raised to the rank of Draoihn. It hardly seemed real, but then, a lot hadn't seemed real of late. That morning, gathering with the other apprentices, I thought of Mama, and what she would have said about me. Would she have approved? Or would this have just earned another slash from her razored tongue? Probably she would only have resented me all the more. I found myself wishing that Ulovar could have been there to see me take the Testing, and wiped a tear away and turned my mind to the task at hand. There was no time for me now.

'How are you feeling?' Esher asked, stood beside me. 'My stomach is all butterflies. I threw up twice already.'

'I'm ready,' I said, and for all the worry that had led to this point, I found that I was. We held hands as we waited, and there was none of the tension that sometimes passed through contact between us. Our hands were clammy, and we both needed the reassurance.

The first stage of the Testing began with little ceremony, and the unlucky first apprentice went up before the council. I couldn't hear Dynae LacClune's answers, but she did well. They moved her right on to her display of prowess, allowing her a choice of wooden practice weapons. Her reputation for brawling in taverns was well earned, and she knocked the drunk down three times in quick succession. The unskilled man fared no better, his nerves getting the better of him, and the fencer showed good respect for her skills but her First Gate meant he didn't really have much chance. To the Gateless observers, she must have seemed to have lightning-quick reactions and judgement, but I could hear Dynae's trance thumping away in my mind. She proved herself well, and I felt vindicated for having ticked *warrior* for her in Robilar's study. Once she was done she swore her oaths, and then went off to wait on the other side of the Wyvern Lawn. Nominations from the assembly would wait until the end.

Gilden, Janry and Dannforth of Brannlant all followed in quick succession without mishap, and others after. We were a quarter of candidates done before Mendel LacGilfry made the first misstep of the day. He'd been drinking to calm his nerves. He answered his questions slowly, and then I could tell that he couldn't hold his trance as he took the field. His drunken opponent launched straight at him, he fumbled the parry and took a knock to the head that left him reeling. He failed against the unskilled man, and threw up and didn't even compete against the last. That changed the tone of everything. We'd taken to whooping and cheering each other, but now the prospect of failure loomed. Had everything Mendel trained for come to this, just one bad day and some poor alcohol-related decisions?

Ovitus was next.

'Good luck,' Esher said as he prepared to step up.

'Thank you,' he said. 'I'm sure it will be fine.' He was smiling.

He answered his questions with long, convoluted answers, referencing texts I'd never heard of, going on long enough about the kingships of Haddat-Nir that the grandmaster stepped in to bring his answers to a close. That brought a murmur of laughter from our rival greathouses, but Ovitus didn't seem bothered. He was offered the choice of wooden weapons; an arming sword with a round target shield, a basket-hilted sword, a longsword or a pole. His opponent would have the same. Eight months ago he might have seemed ill suited to this, and he had never been a good swordsman, but his newfound dedication to his training had purged that lethargy from him. I found myself hoping he'd put up a good showing. He selected the longsword seemingly at random and walked out to the field.

'Show us some of those legendary LacNaithe fighting skills you've inherited!' Haronus LacClune called. Ovitus was unruffled.

The first man, the drunk, had watched a number of his fellows get clobbered and he had to expect the same was coming his way. He had a padded helmet, a thick gambeson and armoured gloves but even if the goal wasn't to kill anyone, broken fingers weren't uncommon through the protection. We were expected to exercise caution, but the drunks weren't. That was the point. I saw that Ovitus was wearing Princess Mathilde's favour around his arm, like he was a Brannish knight at a tourney. He tipped his head to his betrothed, and she nodded back, her face all serenity.

'Ready for me, my lord?' the drunk man said, hopping about and waving his stick.

'Come at me with all your might,' Ovitus said proudly. The man came towards him, and as he closed the range, Ovitus tossed his wooden sword aside. The drunk couldn't believe his luck and swung at him with reckless abandon. Ovitus raised his arm, stood still and upright, and there was a massive *crack* as the sword smashed into it. The drunk stepped back. Ovitus spread his arms and turned around, grinning.

'He's using the Second Gate,' I muttered.

'Is that allowed?' Esher asked.

'I think the Testing is designed so that you can't fail if you reached the Second Gate already,' I said. Ovitus had hardened his skin, or turned the air around himself solid, or some other trick he'd managed to learn. The drunk seemed astonished. He raised the stick again, then glanced to the assembled councillors. Grandmaster Robilar nodded at him to continue. He looked nervous, but he steeled himself, and brought the sword down on Ovitus's head. The snap rang out as the wooden blade snapped halfway along its length. Nobody seemed to know what to do. Ovitus just stood there smiling. Then he reached out and grabbed the man by the shirt and flung him from the arena.

'Very good, Apprentice LacNaithe,' Councillor Suanach said. 'Shall we omit the following tests of prowess?'

It was agreed that they served no purpose, much to the relief of the two men who'd been warming up to fight him. Ovitus spoke his oaths, then crossed not back to join the rest of us apprentices but over to his bride-to-be. On the way he tossed a broken piece of wood to Haronus LacClune.

'A memento for you,' he declared loudly. Haronus looked like he could have chewed through a table leg, teeth bared in a snarl.

Three more went, and then my name was called.

27

Nerves chewed at me as I stepped out and felt every eye upon me.

'Do us proud, Fiahd,' Esher called after me. 'You've got this!'

I breathed deeply as I approached the stand where the councillors awaited me. Outside the herd of apprentices, I felt exposed. I didn't like the feeling much.

Kyrand of Murr started the questioning. She was a solemn woman, responsible for overseeing Redwinter's library archives. She asked me to explain the rise of the Kingships of the Delac-Mir after the Age of Bronze and the fall of Empress Serranis, which I had some good ideas about, and then the Age of Soot and the Nine Devastations. The questions weren't complicated, and I'd seen plenty of apprentices do this already. Kyrand's questions weren't the ones I was worried about. She finished by asking me to explain the lineage of our current king, Quinlan LacDaine and how a relatively middle-tier clan had won the Crown from Nessia LacClune some fifty-one years ago. I thought my answer weak, but I got through it.

Next came Suanach's questions and tests. He had me open the First Gate, and performed one of those ridiculous cloth tests that Draoihn Palanost had put us through. My stomach had fallen down somewhere around my ankles, I was sweating and nervous, but I opened into Eio easily enough. The object was an apple—they were giving us easy ones. I found my way to it not by its shape, but by its scent. Those mental muscles Palanost had exercised on harder things really had honed my skills. It was far easier than I'd imagined that it would be and I felt my confidence growing. *Look at me now, Mama. See what I've achieved since I left you.* Suanach's following questions were about Draoihn business; artificing, cartography, art, diplomacy, war. I handled them well enough, I thought.

That just left the grandmaster, and unlike the rest of the apprentices, she was the one I was least concerned with. But her questions weren't as simple as I'd imagined. She had to put on a show even if she wanted me to succeed.

'Why must a grandmaster of Redwinter know the Fifth Gate?' she said.

Not the subject matter I wanted to deal with, but I answered honestly.

'Some Draoihn may learn the First, Second, Third, Fourth and Fifth Gates. But no Draoihn can know both the Fifth and Sixth Gate. Those who open the Sixth Gate do not need to know the Second, Third or Fourth. But the Fifth and Sixth Gates are entirely anathema, life and death. By choosing a grandmaster who has proven herself with the Fifth, it becomes impossible for a Sarathi to take control of Redwinter, since they cannot have both.'

Notes of my answers were being made by scribes. That only added to my anxiety; having one's words recorded meant they had to be right, and nothing that could return to bite me later in life.

'How many in Harranir are capable of accessing five gates?' Robilar asked next.

'There are only two,' I said. 'Yourself and Kelsen, the king's healer.'

Who was this for? I began to wonder. Kelsen would expire with the king he had spent his life with. What then would happen to Redwinter's leadership? Robilar would need to accompany Prince Caelan into the Crown, but then would she take Kelsen's role as royal healer? I couldn't imagine it.

'What is the name of the seventeen incantations that breach walls?'

Trick question.

'There are nineteen,' I said, eager to answer correctly and move on. I began to list them. 'There is the Incantation of Shattered Stone. The Incantation of Molten Fire. The Incantation of Broken Pride . . .'

'That is incorrect, Apprentice Raine,' Kyrand of Murr interjected. 'There are but seventeen. Think again.'

I frowned, unsure how Kyrand could be incorrect about this. I began to run through them in my mind, and suddenly my error struck me. I had counted the Voidbreaker Incantation, and the Incantation of Howling Bone. And they were only available to those who could open the Sixth Gate. I swallowed, took a deep breath. No. The day I'd spent with Alianna inside me had done something to my resolve. I was so tired of hiding who and what I was, even if I wasn't about to blurt out that I was Sarathi, I didn't want to bow down and be told I was wrong for knowing the things I knew. I didn't want to pretend to be stupid, or restrained, or hide myself away. Alianna had let me feel free for the first time in years.

'Begging your pardon, Councillor, but there are nineteen,' I said. And I continued to list them. I left Voidbreaker and Howling Bone for last.

'Those are not—' Suanach began, but Robilar cut her off.

'Apprentice Raine is correct,' she said. 'In my tutelage of her, she has had access to my private library. There are indeed rare recollections of two such incantations being employed by our enemies during the Age of Soot. The apprentice has exceeded the question's expected answer.'

'I have never heard of them,' Kyrand muttered quietly. Had I not kept my Gate open, I would not have heard it.

'But she's right,' Robilar said. Then louder, 'Let us move on. Tell me, Apprentice Raine, why did I outlaw the long-held practice of summoning familiars?'

'A familiar must be summoned from beyond the veil,' I said. 'Though a familiar can offer a Draoihn greater power, the familiar itself is not without its own motivations. Too often a familiar seeks to subvert its masters' wishes and the Draoihn instead becomes the servant of whatever she summoned.'

'Very good,' Robilar said. 'And your last question, name the thirty-three known types of demon.'

I did my best. I got to twenty-eight, and then my mind deserted me. I tried reordering them in my mind into categories: shadows, abominations, deathless, energy. I named Scrivers, and got my count to twenty-nine but the last few defeated me.

'That is enough for now,' Grandmaster Robilar said finally. 'Let us continue with the test of prowess. Prepare yourself.'

Esher met me at the table where the weapons had been laid out.

'You've got this, no problem,' she said. She took me by the shoulders and looked me dead in the eye. 'You're a Fiahd. Stay light on your feet and don't go soft on them. You're ready?'

'I'm ready,' I said.

She slapped me in the face. Not hard, but hard enough to get the blood flowing.

'Are you ready?' she asked, harder.

'I'm ready!' I shouted back.

I nodded, saw the intensity in her eyes, and then she put one hand on either side of my head, pulled me to her and kissed me quickly on the mouth.

'That's my girl. Go show them what you're made of.'

For a moment my head was swimming. But if she'd meant to get my adrenaline going, she'd done the right thing. I took a pole from the table and flourished it in a figure eight.

'Each time I down one, it's for you,' I said.

Ovitus appeared at my other elbow.

'Do this for us, Raine,' he said with an intensity that felt out of place. 'Do it for Clan LacNaithe. We all have great faith in you. I have great faith in you. I know you've trained so hard for this and you deserve it so much.'

'Right. Sure.'

And then I stalked out into the centre of the ring.

Everyone went quiet. They knew me, the white-haired girl who'd thrown Kaldhoone LacShale's severed head into the middle of the Round Chamber during a trial. A lot of my battle training had been private, but those who mattered would have known that I trained under Lady Datsuun. It was an expensive education, but they knew the prowess of those that had gone before me. I tried to remember what Torgan had said through Ibaqa and the only thing that came to mind was 'don't overthink it.' That would have to suffice.

My opponents wore padding, but I had none. This was a stage show, a fight in name but really an exhibition of ability. For Mendel LacGilfry to have failed was unexpected. As they padded-up my first opponent, I wondered whether there'd been a requisite amount of drinks to be consumed, or an allotted starting time, or whether by the end of the day they'd be falling over on their own. When he was led over to join me I thought he already looked unsteady on his feet. He had a pole of his own, not as heavy as a quarterstaff, but padded at both ends. He was medium height, medium build. This would all have been much easier if I'd had my bow and could just have shot him down, but it wouldn't have made very good sport.

There was little to be said of the fight that followed. He seemed to have no training at all in the spear or staff, and I put him down three times in swift succession. He was laughing all the way, and he had a story to take home. I didn't hurt him—it was easy enough to find openings to trip or lever him down when his balance went.

The untrained opponent was a robust woman with freckles and an easy smile who wasn't quite prepared for how this was going to go. I found I'd enjoyed the cheers of the audience, and so I began to show off a little. I disarmed my opponent in three different ways, each one ending with her tumbling to the ground. I don't think she'd expected to be victorious. By this point in the day, not many would. We shook hands and she headed off to collect her purse.

My third and final encounter was to be different. I'd been warned about being overly confident against those without a Gate. If you feel your training makes you superior, you can let that overconfidence blind you. Torgan forbade use of a trance during his training sessions, though he had no way to know whether I used it or not; reliance on it was a crutch. I hadn't used it against either of my first opponents, but this last one, I wasn't so sure. I had no illusions about being a master; many of the defence school students had been training a lot longer than I had, and the man who I faced off against now looked to have been training for a long time. He had half a foot on me in height, must have weighed half as much as me again, but there was nothing slow about him. He'd come prepared with a longsword, so I swapped my pole out. Taking advantageous options wasn't the day's purpose.

'I'm Calden LacLoch,' he said, offering me a sportsman-like bow. I returned it.

'Raine Wildrose,' I said. I'd come to rather like using the slur as a name.

'I'm the master of my school of defence down in Harranir,' he said.

'You must be good to be a master at your age,' I said. He couldn't be much more than twenty-five.

'I won't go easy.'

'I don't think you're meant to.'

We settled into guards, each taking the watchtower, swords raised high. Calden was smiling, either a man who enjoyed his sport or maybe looking forward to testing himself against a Draoihn. He moved well, and I took my trance now, the world coming sharply into focus as I flowed through Serenity and Awareness.

He came on fast and hard, powerful strokes flying up and down, linked chains of motion that reminded me of the Dharithian style of assault. I kept my distance, kept light on my feet, chose not to parry and instead kept on moving around, but it wasn't going to work forever. He was fit and powerful, and he didn't relent in his attack. Eventually I had to deflect his wooden sword with my own, and countered. He blocked it and pulled off a technique I'd never seen, coming in fast and only Eio saved me from taking the point in my face. I tried to begin a flurry of my own but he broke my rhythm as I tried to make the second cut and kept our blades together.

There is much to feel along the length of a sword in the bind, when it meets and rests against another. The pressure resonates through it, guided from hand to arm and up into the entire body. We tested each other, wooden swords together, looking to push from one side to another, levering to open up an angle to slide through with the point. Calden went for it first, and I got it aside, twisting and turning it to open my own. But he was really very good—much better than I was, that had become clear to me—and he put it aside easily.

'Come on, Fiahd!' I heard Esher shouting from the sideline.

The fight went on without either of us scoring a hit, always finding the distance, him through experience and me through Eio charging my mind with insight into where everything would come from next. The sweat steamed from us, and my muscles began to weaken. I knew that I'd be the one to tire first. Trancing or not, he did this daily for a living and though my crash course had been intensive, it didn't make up for a decade of daily practice. I began to slow down and his thrusts and cuts began to come closer. One I had to throw myself backwards to avoid, tripped and rolled head over heels but came up on my feet. The crowd cheered me for that, but I was beginning to burn with embarrassment. I was supposed to beat this man, to prove my warrior status.

'That's enough,' Grandmaster Robilar called out from the dais. 'We don't have all day. A good display of measure and patience from both combatants. Raine, you may leave the arena.'

Calden was still smiling. He gave me another bow.

'An absolute pleasure, Apprentice Raine,' he said.

Tingle, tingle. There was something rare and exciting about having just fought and sweated against this man. I wondered if this was a result of carting Alianna around inside me, or whether this was just how I got to feel when I let myself be what came naturally to me. I'd been holding it inside for so long.

I bowed in return, bowed to the councillors up on the dais and then I had to swear oaths about the Crown, and serving it. It all seemed like routine at that point and I was distracted, afraid that having failed to take Calden down I was going to fail the Testing despite what Robilar had told me. Somehow I got through the words I'd prepared. I even swore to root out and destroy Sarathi wherever they may be found, and Robilar did an excellent job of keeping a straight face. But I got through it and thank the Light Above, it was over and I only had to receive my support and be awarded my coat—provided my final draw against Calden had been enough to see me through.

The other apprentices went on through the afternoon. Jathan performed well, though his opponents were not formidable. Adanost did better than I'd expected. When it came to Esher's turn my heart was in my mouth, but she conducted herself brilliantly. She moved fast, committing hard to the attack, and dropped all three of her opponents maybe faster than anyone else. I cheered her on and after we stood with our arms around one another's shoulders as we watched Gelis take her turn. She fumbled two of the questions, and she lost to the drunken man who perhaps had lied about his lack of training or hadn't been drinking quite as much as he was supposed to, then went on to beat the next two opponents without taking a hit. Two apprentices performed worse than Mendel LacGilfry had, losing all three of their bouts to the groans of their onlooking supporters. Not everyone is cut out to be a fighter.

It was a long day. The sun beat down, and I felt my pale northern skin burn, but there was nowhere shady for us to stand. House retainers brought us cups of cold water, but nobody had provided food so I was both burnt and hungry by the time the last of the apprentices finished.

'Can you believe it?' Esher said. 'This was all it was. We're done now, Raine. We get to name ourselves Draoihn now. It's done.'

'Let's hope so,' I said. 'Nearly there.'

'It's all arranged. You two have nothing to worry about,' Ovitus said easily. He looked comfortable despite the reddened skin on his cheeks and nose.

'Not unless they tell us we're all off to the Winterra,' Esher said. I squeezed her hand.

'It won't come to that. I'm sure of it,' I said.

Just one more step, I thought. *Just one more.*

The last business of the day was for our supporters to stand up for us. There seemed to be no corresponding order, and Esher was the first called out to stand before the councillors.

'Oh Light Above! Why me?' she gasped. 'Have I failed? Are they doing the failures first?'

'It will be fine,' I said. 'Just go.'

With quivering steps, Esher made her way to kneel before the dais. Five Draoihn, hot and sweating in their oxbloods, stepped forwards from the audience. They were all much older than us, one of them must have been seventy if not older. I'd seen one or two of them around the LacNaithe greathouse when they visited, but I didn't know even one of them.

'Who can speak of the worth of Apprentice Esher, and her dedication to the Crown?' Grandmaster Robilar called.

'I stand for Esher of the city of Harranir, a worthy apprentice and fit to be called Draoihn,' the oldest woman said.

'I stand for Esher of Harranir, a worthy apprentice and fit to be called Draoihn,' the next man stated. They didn't know her I supposed, but that wasn't the point of all this. It was sponsorship and showing that she had a place in Redwinter. Three more went after, and with five, it was time for Esher to kneel before the council. The three of them bowed heads together, speaking unheard, and then Grandmaster Robilar stood.

'We have observed this apprentice's performance, and her diligence in training. We have heard her First Gate mastered clearly. We have heard her profess knowledge, skill at arms, and the voices of those who stand in her support. And we have heard her swear her undying duty to the Crown. We hereby confer on Esher of Harranir the rank of Draoihn of the First Gate. Your life is to serve the Crown; all else is dust to you from this day onwards. Arise, Draoihn Esher.'

Esher rose slowly. She turned to face the gathered throng. I could see tears in her eyes, and then she punched hard into the air and let forth a high, ripping, ululating sound from her throat that I never knew she could produce. The crowd went wild for her, golden and strong and wonderful, gleaming in the evening's falling light. I'd never heard such a sound within Redwinter before and it rang from the walls.

Liara met her first and they embraced each other for a long time. Then she moved among us, hugging and back slapping and making excited, thrilled noises in place of words.

Nobody was going to top that, but everyone had their supporters. It seemed like it hadn't mattered that much how we'd performed after all, and when Mendel LacGilfry, eighth to stand, was accepted, it was as though an audible sigh of relief passed through the apprentices still gathered. I was called out right after him, and the five assigned Draoihn stepped up to vouch for me and declare me worthy.

'Arise, Draoihn Raine.'

My legs were suddenly weak, but I forced my wobbling frame up. It seemed implausible; unbelievable; impossible. But here I was and I had done it. Calden LacLoch's skill at arms hadn't undone me after all. I couldn't believe what was happening to me. It had to be happening to somebody else.

Ovitus smiled at me.

'I knew you had everything it takes,' he said. 'I knew you were the best of all of them. I'm so happy for you.'

He didn't hug me like the others, and I thought that was appropriate, especially as Princess Mathilde wasn't so very far away beneath a gigantic parasol.

'Your turn,' I said to Jathan when his name was called. He grinned and walked out, waving to those around and blowing kisses. We were all exultant and maybe it wasn't decorous to make a show of it, but it was very Jathan to do so. He grinned out at the audience.

'Let's see how long that grin lasts,' Ovitus said quietly.

'What do you mean?'

He glanced at me.

'Some people are too cocky by half,' he said. I frowned at that, feeling it an ill sentiment on what was proving to be a joyous day.

'Who can speak of the worth of Apprentice Jathan, and his dedication to the Crown?' Grandmaster Robilar called.

Silence.

The five LacNaithe Draoihn who had vouched for me, for Esher, for Adanost—they all remained still. Not one of them stepped forward from the crowd. Jathan looked towards them, and the grin on his face lingered, then changed to puzzlement, and he looked back and forth between them and the grandmaster. Not one of them moved. They didn't meet his eye, instead finding the grass fascinating, or picking at a loose thread.

'But—no,' I said. 'Ovitus . . . You told them not to stand for Jathan?'

'There's no place here for a man who can't restrain himself around things that don't belong to him.'

Jathan continued to stand there and his grin of triumph had faded to one of utter consternation, sliding rapidly towards despair.

'Vouch for him!' I said. 'Tell them they should vouch for him.'

'It's done,' he said. 'I warned him not to go near Dauphine. Now he'll understand the cost of disobedience.'

'You can't be serious. Nothing happened—Ovitus—'

But Ovitus wasn't listening anymore. He was watching Jathan, a mean, satisfied smile on his lips and his arms folded.

The silence stretched out. Seventeen had gone before him, and every time the response had been immediate. He looked over to us, as if there was something we could do.

'Is there nobody who stands for Apprentice Jathan?' the grandmaster called out. There was anger in her voice. Her proceedings were being disrupted.

'I stand for Jathan of Kwend,' a voice called out. It was Liara, shoving her way through the assembled Draoihn. 'A worthy apprentice and fit to be called Draoihn.' She was pulling on her oxblood coat, unprepared to have to step forward.

'As do I.' Sanvaunt, pushing forth beside her. 'A worthy apprentice. Fit to be called Draoihn.' He looked towards Ovitus with abject fury turning his handsome face vicious.

And then silence again. Sanvaunt's shoulders shook with rage. He was a calm man, a controlled man, but when his anger was drawn it was a force to be reckoned with.

Grandmaster Robilar cast her eyes across those gathered. She tapped her fingernail against the tabletop, and the sound magnified and carried across Redwinter's grounds as if it was a sledgehammer cracking bricks.

'There are no others from the LacNaithe household who have forgotten to stand forth?' she asked. Annoyed.

Across the Wyvern Lawn, I caught Castus's eye. He'd won his coat earlier that year. He still counted. I made an imploring look, and he rolled his eyes at me.

'I stand for Jathan of Kwend,' Castus said as he stepped forth. 'I beat him up one time, but the Crown matters; all else is dust.'

'This is still a formal ceremony,' Kyrand of Murr declared loudly. 'Speak the words correctly, by the Light Above!' Castus tried to turn his face blank, did a poor job, but managed to get out the words correctly.

'I'll stand for him.' Of all people, it was Haronus LacClune, the three green furrows in his brow gleaming metallic in the long-shadowing light. 'I mentored him. He has the substance.' Councillor Kyrand gave him a dour look, but Haronus wasn't fazed and stepped back among his followers.

'That bastard,' Ovitus growled. 'He's doing it to spite me!'

'It's not about you, dear Light Above!' I said. 'This is Jathan's future on the line here. How could you be so cruel?'

'What goes around comes around,' he said. 'He still only has four.'

'Feck this,' I said. And I strode forwards into the arena. 'I stand for Jathan of Kwend. He's a worthy apprentice. Fit to be Draoihn.'

This caused some consternation among Kyrand and Suanach.

'Can freshly made Draoihn stand for other apprentices? Surely there's some rule about this,' Suanach said. But Grandmaster Robilar waved it away.

'It's an old custom, and not designed for this number of apprentices to take the field in public view. I trust Draoihn Raine's judgement. Get on your knees, Apprentice Jathan. You're going to rise as Draoihn after all, unless either of my fellow council members sees a reason to veto you.'

Jathan practically collapsed. By the time he returned to us he was shaking. The jubilant mood that had filled the air, the surety of success, had fled. The grandmaster continued as if not a beat had been skipped as one by one the rest of the apprentices had their turn.

Jathan stood away from Ovitus for some time. He was shaking, tears in his eyes. He would talk to nobody until I approached.

'That bastard,' Jathan whispered. 'I've lived alongside him for seven years. We're supposed to be friends. Why would he do that to me?'

'It's all right,' I said. 'Everything's all right.'

'You think I can stay with LacNaithe now?' he said. 'After he humiliated me like that?'

'You're still made Draoihn,' I said. 'You can choose whatever you want.'

But the spear had sunk deep; Jathan was not to be consoled. Nor could he approach his future van and spill his anger. I wondered whether Ovitus had truly thought through what he had just done, the axe-wound he had struck into his own greathouse. We should have been able to depend on each other through storm and magic, life and death.

And then when there were only a few remaining, it was Ovitus's turn. He walked out into the centre of the lawn, straight-backed, and made a formal bow to the councillors. His five pet-Draoihn stood forth and spoke the words for him, but there was a sour hush across the audience. They knew that Jathan's humiliation had been his doing. Ovitus had changed so much since his first Testing, a Testing he'd failed at. But he'd come through this round with the most impressive performance of all. He was well read and his memory excellent. Moreover, his Second Gate had made a mockery of the test of prowess. Maybe it was designed so that apprentices who reached the Second Gate couldn't fail. But all the change I'd seen in him—I'd seen it flake away like dry old skin.

Ovitus looked over to me as the last of his speakers declare his worth, and I thought that he mouthed something to me. I couldn't be sure, but it looked like he'd said *For you*, which made absolutely no sense.

'We have observed this apprentice's performance, and his diligence in training. We have heard his First and Second Gates mastered clearly. We have heard him profess knowledge, skill at arms, and the voices of those who stand in her support. And we have heard him swear his undying duty to the Crown,' Councillor Suanach intoned.

But Grandmaster Robilar interrupted.

'I move to veto Apprentice Ovitus LacNaithe's acceptance into the rank of Draoihn.'

I'd thought that what happened with Jathan had silenced the crowd, but even the breeze seemed to die. The grandmaster's words stilled the birds in the trees, the creak of timbers. Even the other councillors looked shocked.

'*What?*' Ovitus said, his voice a furious lash through clenched teeth.

'Are you sure?' Kyrand asked.

'I confirm my veto again, for any who had not the ears to hear it the first time,' the grandmaster said. 'I deny this Testing, as is my right as a member of the Council of Night and Day.'

'No apprentice has received a veto in centuries,' Ovitus growled. His voice rose to a scream. 'This is an outrage! On what grounds do you deny me my rights? I'm stronger than the rest of them put together!'

'Do not think to speak to me like some common retainer,' the grandmaster roared back at him, rising to her feet, her voice booming around the walls. 'We have one task as Draoihn: we serve the Crown above all else. We put aside our differences as clans, our personal desires, all for the continued security of the Crown, that keeps the Night Below beyond the veil. You showed today that petty spite governs your choices when you tried to deny one of your own a position here. Even Clan LacClune stood for him, and they hate your guts. How then do you understand your duty to the Crown? You are ruled by self-satisfaction, and would have denied the Crown a precious guardian.'

'This is unfair,' Ovitus protested, but it was fury driving the spittle from his lips. 'I have mastered the Second Gate. I am to marry a Brannish princess. I am to be van of Clan LacNaithe, and you would humiliate me here?'

'You have forgotten yourself, apprentice,' the grandmaster boomed. 'You will do penance as I see fit and we shall see whether you receive a third chance.'

Ovitus stared at the grandmaster, his fury boiling from him like waves of heat. Like actual waves of heat. The air around him shimmered like a mirage. Grass beneath his feet began to blacken.

'Are you seeing that?' I whispered.

'It's impossible,' Esher said. Her fingers locked around my hand. 'How can it be possible?'

'It is my *right* to become Draoihn!' Ovitus roared, his face turning redder than his sunburn. Sweat ran in rivers down his face.

'Calm yourself,' Grandmaster Robilar said, and for a moment, for the first time ever, I saw a twitch of concern on her face.

'I. Will. Have. What. I. Am. Owed!'

A sudden noise filled my mind, like the clanking of vast metal gears connecting one to the other, a deep and resonating sound. Then a flash of light, blinding, a blast of hot air, and a bolt of blue-white lightning leapt from Ovitus and flared upwards into the sky. It lasted only a moment, less time than it took to breathe out, and then—gone. The air stilled as Ovitus stared at his hands, as surprised by this occurrence as everybody else.

'The Third Gate,' someone breathed. 'He opened Taine!'

It should have been a moment of great celebration. Of joy. Instead there was nothing but shock and awe and the stench of burning grass. Ovitus looked down at his smoking hand, then back to the grandmaster.

'It is done, then,' he said. 'I will lay my own road.'

And he turned and strode away across the field. Councillor Kyrand made to rise, but the grandmaster stopped her, watching him walk away.

'So be it,' she said, her voice returned to its normal level, but her eyes following Ovitus as he stalked to gather his Brannish princess. Mathilde rose silently and took his arm to accompany him as Waldy fell in alongside at his heels, rubbing his face up against his master's leg. Lady Dauphine was pale faced and wide-eyed, the ladies in waiting scrabbled to find scarves and net hats. Everyone watched them go, and then the grandmaster cleared her throat. 'Who is next?'

28

How to even get one's feelings into order after all that? There was shock, there was confusion, there was joy. Each vied for everyone's attention as the proceedings came to a somewhat anticlimactic end.

'Off with you all for now,' Grandmaster Robilar said the moment the last of us had been given rank, and she turned and walked away.

I'd hoped to get a moment to talk to her alone. I saw it stalk away from me with Robilar, her anger unmasked.

'We did it,' Esher exclaimed, hugging everyone she got near to. 'We did it, we did it!' She was flushed with exultation. I'd always had such faith in her, even when she'd told me her doubts it hadn't really sunk into me just how much she'd feared this day. My own belief in her had dismissed her fears as unimportant. I hadn't been a good enough friend to see it.

Jathan's easy smile was missing. He was shaken, and badly. That Ovitus had turned on him so easily—what did that mean for his future? It would be hard for him to live under the LacNaithe roof now, knowing that his future van had tried to demean him, and it would only be worse for him after Ovitus had been denied the rank of Draoihn. He had become a symbol of Ovitus's humiliation.

I congratulated Gelis and Adanost.

'Well, you made it through,' Liara said. I could see the worry written across her features, her usual cheerful countenance displaced. 'That was a sight easier than mine.'

'Can you tell us what you had to do now?' I asked.

'No,' Liara said. 'It's something I'll never speak of.'

'Does that still apply?'

'It's not just that. I don't want to. You all had a simple test of skills and knowledge. My Testing didn't involve either of those things. It was a lot worse.'

Word spread around: we were all going out on the moor, and everyone was to bring as much alcohol as they could carry and blankets for when the night came down cold. We would put previous parties to shame.

As we returned to the LacNaithe greathouse to put on our most celebratory costumes and party faces, activity had already begun. The Brannish contingent were packing, and Ovitus was outside giving directions. He'd donned the coat of mail he'd worn the day he arrived with Princess Mathilde, sword at his side, dressed for war. Waldy lay on his belly with his paws across his nose, sensing his master's displeasure even if he wore a wooden smile.

'Going on a trip?' Liara asked.

'I find the air not to my liking,' he said. 'I'm moving my household down into Harranir for the time being. I've nothing left to learn here.'

'How did you do it?' I asked him. 'You opened the Third Gate. We all saw it. Did you know?'

'No,' he said. 'But I just felt so much anger, you know? In the moment. It wasn't the first time Vedira snubbed me.'

'You still need to call her by her title, apprentice,' Liara said.

'I don't think so,' Ovitus said. 'Being spurned in my first Testing was enough for one lifetime, and twice—well, it's all so much mulch now, isn't it? I have the Third Gate whether or not that old whore wants to acknowledge me. I don't need a woman's approval to know what I am.'

'These are dangerous words, Ovitus,' Liara said. I could see dismay on her face. 'You'll isolate yourself from Redwinter if you leave.'

I didn't enjoy Ovitus's smile. He took on a regal, pompous tone. The kind I'd heard from Haronus LacClune. The kind I'd heard from Braithe. 'Once upon a time, I was a man of lowly ambitions. But Vedira changed all that. Everyone will see, in the end. I went to Brannlant and brought home a princess. I've given work and life back to the idle, and I've earned this power on my own. I still need to practise it, of course, but if Redwinter doesn't need me, then I don't need it either.'

'What happens to Draoihn who don't serve Redwinter?' I asked. I had a bad feeling about where this could go. I could understand his anger. He had known privilege since birth, and failing his Testing the first time had twisted something inside him. And then he'd put in all the effort to be fitter, to seem strong and now—this story would get out. It would spread across Harranir. Far away in Clunwinny, Van Merovech LacClune would hear the news, and he would laugh. Van Onostus LacAud would smirk. And Ovitus's standing among the Draoihn would never be what he wanted it to be. *The heir who failed twice.*

'All will be well,' Ovitus said. 'In Brannlant, their magical gifts are different. Artists, they call them. Perhaps it's time that we sought out Artists of our own in Harranir now that I've made this new alliance. I have learned not to place my trust in those that seek to abuse it.'

'You need to be careful,' I said. 'The grandmaster is nobody's fool. She won't take it kindly if you challenge her authority.'

'No, Raine,' he said. He reached out and I was too shocked to move as he took my chin in his hand. 'She's the one who needs to respect mine. I know she tutored you, and it must have been awful. But I don't consider you responsible for any of this. I want you to know—your good opinion matters to me. More than you realise.'

He turned then and walked away, leaving Liara and I looking at one another, perplexed.

'I don't like that,' Liara said. 'It's how he used to talk to me. Back when he was obsessing.'

I wiped my face on my sleeve. His hand had been moist with sweat.

'You can put a Third Gate inside Ovitus, but he's still Ovitus,' I said. 'Bloody hell. What a day.'

'I'd better go and see Ulovar now,' Liara said. She offered me a sad smile. 'I'm sorry if things have been strained between us. I want them to go back to what they were.'

'I know,' I said. 'Me too.'

'It's just every time I look at you, I think of my father.'

I nodded. I didn't have anything else to offer her.

Esher and I got ready together. I was dressing warmly. It's fun showing off a bit of leg, but we'd have to survive the midge hour, and it's never fun being cold. Esher showed no such acceptance of reality, although I did persuade her to put some woollen stockings on under a ruthlessly short dress. We started drinking as soon as we began getting ready.

When I was prepared I went to visit Ulovar. I steeled myself to enter. I knew the serpent was there, coiled around him, its leech-like mouth latched onto him. Without the Eyes of Serranis I couldn't see it. But I knew.

'What are you doing here?' he asked from his sick bed. His face had lost flesh lately. He wasn't the man I'd known. 'You have friends to enjoy yourself with.'

'I wanted to see you,' I said, sitting beside the bed. I took one of his hands. His fingers were cold, though the fire was banked high. 'I needed to say thank you. You gave me a place here.'

'You've earned it,' he said. 'And more besides.'

Even his words were diminished now, slurred by lips that had grown numb. There was a rattle in his chest, phlegm he didn't have the strength to clear.

I wished in that moment that I could have told him everything. About who and what I was, about what I could do. How I would use it to help him, if I could only work it all out. How I could turn the Sixth Gate inside me to help him, and Redwinter, and everyone. But it would have broken his heart. I was a liar on so many levels by then.

'Does this help at all?' I said, lifting a dead-weight hand and massaging his stiff, cold fingers.

'I barely feel it,' he said. 'But I'm happy that I've lived to see this day. They call the apprentices who study under my roof 'Ulovar's Army,' did you know that? Because you bond together. I always believed that giving you all a community would help, would allow you to depend on one another. My nephew is in a rage, and I am not without displeasure at what has occurred in my absence. But he will have another Testing, and my heart surges with pride that even as my power has faded, he has found his own.'

'You think he'll come back?'

'He's a LacNaithe. We believe in doing our duty. He just needs time. He always just needs time.'

'I'll do what I can to help him.' It was not a promise I had intended to make, but I made it now. I had tears in my eyes. How many more visitations like this would I get to make? I thought we measured things now in weeks and days rather than months. Ulovar would lose the ability to swallow, or breathe, and that would be his end.

How I resented the world for taking him from me. I didn't know what it was like to be raised by a father, but I would experience what it was like for one to die.

'Go on.' He coughed, a wet, weak sound. 'Go out. Have fun. The day I got my coat we made so much noise we could have brought down Redwinter's walls. Take this night for yourself. You've earned it.'

I squeezed his hand and nodded. I thought I'd cry if I tried to speak.

. . . . . .

The moorland of Harran changed colour across the year. In spring, yellow gorse dominated, spreading like butter across the hillsides. But in late summer it was the heather that dominated, rich and purple and I had always loved it. We rode out and tethered our horses up in a clear stretch of scratchy grass. The boys, having had to make little preparation before they disembarked, were already there. There were two distinct groups; those of the LacAud household, and then everyone else, even LacNaithe and LacClune sitting together. A few had brought retainers with them, but for once the servants were outnumbered. Many of them had chosen to wear their oxblood coats. The whisky had been flowing freely, and Nimman the Younger was already swaying about. His older cousin, Nimman the Older, had brought a set of pipes and was blasting out a jaunty, wailing tune as a call to arms, summoning us faster, faster across the moor. Little Maran was there even if they hadn't been Tested, gazing starry-eyed at a girl who'd just won her coat and was busy demonstrating the manoeuvres she'd employed to win her bouts. Adanost was engaging in a drinking game which thankfully was being played with ale rather than whisky. Everyone had dumped their bottles in one big pile. Esher and I added five more. Things were going to get bleary.

I took a slug of whisky, noting that the label said it came from the Black Isle, and wondered whether the distilleries there suffered from Onostus Lac-Aud's occupation. I had to divert myself away from all that. One night. I got to have *one night* to celebrate this, and then I'd go back to all my worries. Not like when I'd got myself obliterated with Castus, that had been about forgetting. Tonight was about celebrating. I was glad that Ovitus wasn't coming, busy moving his very large number of Brannish friends down to the city. But talk of him was on everyone's lips.

'Who would have believed it?' one of the boys, Gilden, said. 'Fatbucket Ovitus, popping out the Third Gate like it was a playhouse.'

'I think it was all staged,' another lad said. 'He had it figured out with the grandmaster. She wants to open up a new place, bring in Brannish Artists. It's a conspiracy.'

'That is such nonsense,' Gilden said, but I saw that for a moment he considered it. It *was* nonsense, of course it was. Ovitus wasn't a good enough actor to hide his feelings that way. Gilden slapped his neck as a midge bit him.

If there is one way to avoid midges, it's fire. They don't like smoke, and so we were building fires. The largest was in the centre, and being experienced moorland party goers, someone had thought to load up a pair of mules with bushels of dry branches. We put a ring of four smaller ones around it. Fill the air with smoke and you're less likely to be dinner. I helped to get one of them started, somehow finding myself on the outside of everything despite throwing myself at the middle. Jathan came to help me. He was subdued, as well he might be.

'How are you feeling?' I asked.

'Odd,' he said. 'Strange. Like nothing was what it seemed.'

'Life's like that sometimes,' I said, ripping sparks from a flint with a little metal file.

'I just don't know what to do,' he said. 'Do I keep on going like before? Ovitus tried to stop me taking the coat. He actually stood in my way. What's my life now?'

'You're asking the wrong person for advice there,' I said. The bird's nest I was using for tinder took the sparks, and I lifted it up as Jathan blew through it, curling the flames alight. We put it down and started erecting a tent of twigs on top.

'I didn't do anything wrong,' he said. 'Dauphine asked me to walk her to the bridge.'

'Technically, you didn't,' I said. 'But you knew it was stupid at the time. She's still a kid.'

'Dauphine is nearly sixteen,' he said defensively. 'Back home in Kwend, the high houses betroth when we're fifteen and the bride-to-be fosters for three years with her new family to see if she likes it there, and marry at eighteen.'

'And yet, she's a lady, and related to the Brannish king,' I said. 'It's different.'

'You're not much older than she is,' Jathan said. 'Nobody cares who you're bedding down with.'

I wondered for a moment whether he knew something. But I knew that Castus wouldn't have gone bragging about our one-time deal. He had nothing to gain from it, and I knew he'd respect that. It was why I'd chosen him, after all.

'I'm not a lady either,' I said. 'And people did very much once care whether I'd been sleeping with Ovitus, which of course I hadn't. They treated me differently.'

'People see boys and girls differently, I guess,' Jathan said. 'It's not fair. But it's true.'

'So maybe it's Dauphine's reputation you should be thinking about rather than your own,' I said. 'You have your pick, Jathan. All the girls like you. Is that why you thought about going after the one girl who was off-limits?'

'Not really,' he said. He forgot about denial. 'I just thought she was pretty.'

'More brain thinking. Less trouser thinking,' I said. He seemed to find that amusing. We added sticks to the fire and went to find drinks. A drum, a flute and a pair of fiddles had joined the pipes, and the musicians had fallen into an easy, improvised melody. The drums were hardly needed, trances were thumping along as the musicians brought them into line with one another.

'Dance?' Jathan asked.

'I'm no good at it.'

'Me neither!' He grinned and gave me his hand, and we joined the circle of dancers around the fire. Never let it be said that the people of Harran don't know dancing. It was a long time since I'd done any, not since I'd been part of Sister Marthella's colour-singing troupe of followers. Step, step, turn, clap, step, step, turn, clap. There was whooping and laughing, and ale cups thrown high when they were emptied. I found myself laughing.

'Congratulations!' Little Maran said as I took their hands and we spun in a circle.

'Thank youuuu!' I laughed back as I got dizzy. I changed partners and found Adanost next, and though he was Murrish and the dance was foreign to him he didn't care, he threw in steps of his own and was doing just as good a job as anybody else.

Night came down, the whisky level was lowering but there seemed to be ever more in reserve. The first vomit of the night came from Mendel Lac-Gilfry, who after his poor performance in the test of prowess had started putting drinks away the earliest. But he rose, wiping his mouth and calling for more, as perplexed as any of us that he'd made it through, but altogether happy for him. We played stupid games that I'd played before, and more that people invented on the spot. Focus got blurry. More than one newly created couple disappeared off into the heather together.

Others arrived, even through the darkness, with smiles and congratulations. They were welcome additions, younger Draoihn keen to welcome in the new. Liara smiled broadly, and as soon as she dismounted someone began begging her to tell a joke. She ended up with a little audience. I'd heard some of them before, but they were still funny. Sanvaunt had arrived. He seemed out of place here, all straight-backed decorum even when he laughed at something Liara said about perfume vendors. It was a little harsh to judge him, when the rest of us had been hitting the bottles for five hours already. I wondered, maybe foolishly, if now would be the time to make it up to him. Be damned with tomorrow and all the worry, and who I was and what I was.

I tried to get his attention, but he greeted me cordially, shook my hand and congratulated me on my Testing, and then he was pulled away by an apprentice—no, a Draoihn now—that bloody Beatrand and her friend Raddesia, who was prettier than I would have liked and I had to calm myself down and remind myself that I didn't have any claim there. I'd no claim at all, had actually ruined any chance I'd ever had of trying to make one. Sanvaunt's friendly neutrality was more punishing than if he'd been angry with me. Anger I knew how to deal with.

I found myself back in the dance, and after another breathless romp around the flames, the piper took a rest and the fiddles took up a slow, soft tune. It was the *Flower of the Heartland*, almost mournful in its rise and fall, but beautiful, and sad, and filled with longing. Esher appeared, sweaty from the dance, and she put her arms around me.

'I,' she proclaimed proudly, 'am very drunk.'

'I'm amazed there's any bottles left at all,' I said. I put my arms around her, and we swayed in time to the music.

'I was so scared, you know,' she said into my ear. 'Terrified, really.'

'You didn't have to be.'

'Easy to say that now,' she said. 'I feel like I've been keeping it all in for so long. I've been afraid since the first day I came here. I never thought I'd succeed. This little voice inside was always telling me I'd fail.'

Her body was warm up against mine. We swayed together, turning soft circles. I laid my head on her shoulder.

'I never doubted you. Not even once, from the moment I met you. *"Don't interfere Fiahd, or I'll cut you in half!"* That's what you said to me. I'm glad you didn't.'

'So am I,' Esher said. Her fingers were on the back of my hair. Her voice was a delicate thing in my ear.

As I looked out behind her, I felt so calm in that moment. So comfortable, like maybe everything was going to be all right after all.

Beyond the dying central fire, I saw Sanvaunt, sitting with Raddesia. She was pouring a drink for him, her with her tanned Brannish skin, her simple glamours accentuating wide lips and starry eyes. They laughed about something and she tugged at the top buttons of his shirt until he allowed her to undo two of them. I felt she wanted to undo more, but two buttons was about all the relaxing he was prepared to do. A wave of heat passed through me, and I let the sway of the dance move me around and away, the fiddles filling the air.

'I'm glad not to be chopped in half,' I said. Esher smelled so good. Like wildflowers and sandalwood. It was a scent that was all her own.

'Me too,' Esher said. 'That was when I wanted to do it, the first time.'

'Do what?'

Raddesia was laughing too hard. Sanvaunt wasn't that funny.

'To kiss you,' Esher said.

My awareness was pulled back suddenly to where I was, who I was with, how closely and slowly we were dancing.

'You want to kiss me?' I said, and my voice caught in my throat. She dipped her head forwards a little, causing her hair to fall down across her blind eye. It was intentional. Self conscious. She didn't look up at me, her lower lip caught in her teeth.

'Always.'

Raddesia laughed again, and I took my hand from Esher's shoulder and pushed the lock of hair back.

I didn't need to say it. I'd have felt it in the air already if I hadn't been letting myself get distracted. As a child, I'd asked Mama how adults know which way to tilt their heads when they kissed each other. It had seemed like magic. 'You just know,' she said. It *was* a kind of magic, in its own way. But there is never any doubt inside you, when someone wants to kiss you. Not unless you're utterly oblivious.

Esher was beautiful, and the firelight was turning her golden hair to flaming orange. I had quarrelled with myself in silent moments over what I really wanted, whether I wanted to be with her or I just wanted to be her, but I was done lying to myself. I knew what I wanted, I had always known what

I wanted, I just hadn't allowed myself to accept it. It became clear as steel to me now. I leaned forward, and pressed my mouth against hers.

It wasn't like kissing a man. In a way it was almost like a competition. I tasted the whisky on her, and she must have tasted mine. Her tongue quested tentatively towards mine, and I met it and gently dabbed at it. It was nothing like Braithe, powering down on me like he could own me with his body, it was mutual and delicate. Nothing like Castus, whose mirth at the absurdity of our coupling had teased me with every touch, it was serious. It was breathless. Nothing like I'd imagined it would be to kiss Sanvaunt. My whole body seemed to wake up, afire and bright. Esher's hands were solid against my shoulder blades, pulling me to her, and I could feel her love flowing through that kiss and part of me reached for it and asked to be healed.

And another part, the part that lay awake at night, the part that longed to speak forbidden words, the part that feared what everyone knew or whispered . . . That part said *no*.

I opened my eyes, and I saw Sanvaunt across the fire, staring towards us. He looked like someone had run him through the chest with a spear. My eyes locked onto his, and I stared into him, and all that I saw there was my own broken self.

Esher split away, and I heard her breath coming hard but a smile on her lips. Joy in her eye. And too late, she saw where my gaze was directed, and she turned and saw Sanvaunt, and when she spun on her heel and looked back to me there was only destruction.

'Sorry, I—'

'Oh, Light Above and all the rivers of Skuttis.' Her voice cracked. 'Raine . . .'

It all changed in that moment. It all changed to darkness and the night crowded in on me. 'Not like this,' she said. 'Oh, no, not like this.'

'Esher, wait, you don't—'

'You've made a fool of me,' she said. 'I'm a fool. I'm a fool, I'm a fool, I'm a fool.'

'It wasn't.'

'Just *don't*,' she cried, stepping away from me. 'Am I just a plaything to you? Using me to make him jealous? I finally work up the nerve to tell you and— Light Above, I'm such an idiot.'

Tears streamed down her face, from good eye and blind. People were turning to look. Nobody had paid much attention to a kiss. But they looked now.

'I'm sorry,' I said. 'Let's sit down, let's—'

But I had ruined it. A first kiss, and I'd been so tied up and conflicted and full of all the different things at once that everything had been thrown onto the fire. It wasn't fair.

Esher stormed away onto the moor, beyond the ring of fire. I watched her take ten paces, twenty, and then I moved to go after her and Sanvaunt blocked my path.

'No,' he said firmly. 'You've done enough.'

'I didn't mean to do anything,' I said. 'I didn't—I didn't even do anything.'

'Enough,' he said, more gently. 'Enough.'

'You understand? It was just a mistake? All of this has been a mistake.'

'Enough. Liara will go talk to her. Just leave her be.'

For a few moments, the fire was caught so brightly in his eyes it was as if it was held within them, like inside he was burning to ash.

He wasn't angry. He was just so disappointed in me. I fled in floods of tears. I ran to my horse, and saddled her and lit a precious cadanum globe to light the way and fled my new-made Draoihn brothers and sisters.

I couldn't bear it. I couldn't bear any of it, and it was my fault and I'd destroyed everything.

'Queen of Feathers!' I yelled into the night as I rode. 'Come talk to me. Come tell me what to do to put it all right.' But she didn't come to me, and if ever I had felt alone before, I knew it with new meaning.

It was the early hours when I hammered on the door. I didn't even tether South. A retainer admitted me after I was insistent. I stormed into the bedroom.

'Just make me feel something else,' I demanded. 'Just do it. Don't ask questions. I know I look a terrible mess. But just do it, all right?'

'Are you sure that's what you want?' Castus asked, sitting up shirtless in bed. I began stripping off my clothes, my lovely party wear tossed onto the floor.

'This is what I want, today. Just be my friend. Please. I just need you to be my friend.'

'I don't sleep with anyone who's crying,' Castus said. 'Come here.'

I got onto the bed, and he folded me in his arms and we lay there together.

Tears flowed harder then, not a trickle in the cold wind but a shaking, choking torrent. He didn't speak, didn't tell me it would be all right. He just held me and stroked my hair and was there with me. I slept in his arms.

I was woken by the bells of Redwinter's church, calling out a steady, continuous dirge. Castus stood by the window, dressed and facing the glow of dawn as they rang out over, and over, and over.

'What does it mean?' I asked.

'War,' Castus said. 'It means war.'

The news was not good.

Onostus LacAud was marching south with the army of the north. Estimates put his numbers at around six thousand Harranese infantry, backed by contingents of Kwendish heavy cavalry and bowmen. The people of the north had been dragged through the mud by sickness and famine, but their spirit had never been stronger. United. Determined to change their lot in life. The Kwendish civil wars had left battle-hardened regiments of mercenaries looking for work, and they would do it well.

At a time like this, I wished we had Ulovar to lead us. LacClune were too far away to aid Harranir, and there was no standing army to speak of. Perhaps a thousand warriors could be raised quickly from LacDaine's land, and the able-bodied men and women of Harranir could be conscripted—but nobody needed to calculate the odds of putting an earnest man up against a professional. Riders went out to every clan who could put warriors in the field, but LacAud had been bringing men down from the north, to Gilmundy, drip by drip as he amassed his forces. With his new port at Penreet, whatever forces he had there threatened Clunwinny, the seat of Clan LacClune. They could not come to our aid without risking their homes being put to the torch. Arrowhead's strategy was all beginning to make a lot of sense.

The only good news was that armies were slow. Best guess was that we had about six weeks until his army made it from Gilmundy to Harranir, crawling eight to ten miles a day. We had time, but not much.

'Onostus LacAud seeks to take the castle in Harranir, and thereby access to the Great Seal that protects the Crown to secure accession to the throne for one of his lackeys. His actions threaten the stability of the Crown,' Grandmaster Robilar declared angrily as she addressed Redwinter's Draoihn in the Round Chamber that afternoon. Everyone had gathered, veterans and newly made Draoihn alike. She had known this was coming, I realised. Why else rush through our Testing? 'Onostus LacAud is hereby stripped of his seat on the Council of Night and Day, and those lords who ride under his banner will be stripped of rank. The Winterra will arrive at Redwinter within two days. They number seven hundred, and are more than a match for the rabble LacAud has pulled together. We will ride out and meet him.'

I stood apart from LacNaithe on the echoing, tiered stands. Castus was beside me. The previous night's incident seemed far away, but all too close. I knew Esher and Sanvaunt were both there, in the Round Chamber, wearing their oxblood coats, but I couldn't look for them. I was too afraid of what I'd find looking back at me. War was coming, but I found their hatred even harder to bear.

'Surely he must back down against the Winterra?' Haronus LacClune said. His green-furrowed face was a picture of disdain and disgust. 'He will be faced with seven hundred battle-tested Draoihn. The distilled might of Redwinter.'

'Even the Winterra cannot fight an army of nine thousand directly,' the grandmaster said. 'We have all heard the tales of the arrow storms that Kwendish bowmen create. Even were the Winterra to somehow prevail, the casualties would be enormous.'

'LacAud cannot be allowed to take control of Harranir,' Haronus growled.

'And he will not.' The voice came from the Round Chamber's doorway.

'You are not called to speak, Apprentice LacNaithe,' Grandmaster Robilar said from her podium.

Ovitus strode into the chamber. His hair was slicked back with oil, and he wore an iron circlet around his brow. A gold-hilted longsword in a magnificent green scabbard hung from his belt, but it was the look of determination on his young face that stole the show. Waldy padded in behind him, sniffing at Draoihn boots.

'Well feck-a-dee,' Castus murmured. 'Look who showed back up. He barely left.'

'Shush,' I said.

'I feel you'll want to hear what I have to say,' Ovitus said grandly. 'I will be leading the army that opposes LacAud.'

There were unquiet murmurs, and more than one laugh turned into a cough as Ovitus glared, and they recalled that he'd broken through the Third Gate. There were few who could match that power in Redwinter.

'Apprentice Ovitus,' Grandmaster Robilar said coldly. 'You are not recognised in the Round Chamber at this time.'

'But I am recognised by my people in Harranir,' Ovitus said. His disrespect was openly displayed. 'Those in my labour homes will be put to manufacturing weapons at speed, while the dispossessed people of Northbank will be armed and put to service under my care as we oppose the northern dog.'

'A generous offer,' the grandmaster said with derision. 'The craftsmen, labourers and peasants of the slums will surely stand firm against LacAud's vanguard.'

'They will make the numbers,' Ovitus said, and I wondered where the stuttering, confidence-lacking young man I'd first met had gone. His pride had risen with the Gates, perhaps. A few smirks of derision sounded. 'But they are just the spear bearers. At Princess Mathilde's request I have summoned together the Brannish garrisons from across the south. They will number as many as a further thousand, and LacNaithe's warriors another two. I will have more than five thousand.'

'I had hoped yesterday might have brought you some humility,' the grandmaster said coldly. For a moment her anger was so great that her form seemed to shimmer, and a little wisp of smoke trailed up from her head. 'Lassaine LacDaine of the Fourth Gate commands the Winterra. Prince Caelan LacDaine, the heir to the throne, returns with them. We thank you for raising forces. They will take command of the armies of Harran.'

'I eagerly await their arrival,' Ovitus said with mock sincerity. 'I came but to advise you of the aid that I—and I alone—am able to bring to Harranir. Thank you for your time, Grandmaster. Councillors. Draoihn.' He bowed, overly elaborate and mocking. Then he turned and walked from the hall. Waldy looked back apologetically before following him out.

Haronus LacClune was on his feet and about to shout something—probably along the lines of demanding the wretch be apprehended, but the grandmaster waved him down.

'Got to hand it to him, that was certainly bold,' Castus whispered.

'With Ulovar—' and I struggled to find the word I could bear, 'with Ulovar unwell, Ovitus holds a lot of power.'

'May the Light Above help us all.'

* * * * * *

The threat of battle brings a fear like nothing else. Suddenly you know that a day is coming, a day when people are going to die. Many people. Some of them will die through lack of skill, but most of them will just be unlucky. The prospect of trying to endure an arrow storm terrified me: I knew better than most how easy it was for an arrow to end a life.

The LacNaithe greathouse no longer felt like a place in which I was wanted. The exchange between Sanvaunt and Esher and I had been seen publicly. People must have been talking about it. Every time I passed someone on the stairs I feared to be confronted about it, so I avoided being there as much as possible. I spent my days away from home, and some nights I waited until everybody was asleep before I returned. Others I spent with Castus. Most times we just lay there, saying little, breathing, but sometimes we used each other's bodies. That's what it was, and there was no illusion about it. I didn't want him, and he didn't want me, but there was carnality and lust, and for those minutes or hours when we were together I got to turn my mind off from all the fears in the world and just existed in sensation. It was easier, and when I feared that our loveless love making would be discovered and gossiped over, I told myself I didn't care.

What did Castus take from it? The same as me, I thought. There was something missing inside him too, and I was a willing participant when it came to hiding ourselves from the world. He would never struggle for the kind of male company he desired, but for the time being he didn't seem to want it at all. Maybe my body was a safe place, a place without consequence. Sometimes in the night I woke to find him sitting in the chair by the window, staring out at the starlit grounds, his face blank, and dead. I rode out alone to watch the Winterra arrive. I'd heard so much about them, our elite fighting force, but when their column came up the road they weren't what I'd expected. They travelled without their armour, and looked much like anyone else. Weary, I thought. They'd been marching for weeks. I raised a hand and waved to a woman who looked up at me, but she smirked at me and didn't return it. I'd hoped to get a look at Prince Caelan LacDaine, first heir to the throne, but I didn't see him or his banner among them.

I arrived for training with Torgan and Lady Datsuun, but only found Ibaqa there. Furniture was being dragged from the townhouse and roped onto wagons.

'They already left,' Ibaqa told me. 'Gone further south. They do not want to be here if fighting breaks out.'

'So that's it for me? No more training?'

'Training is over for now,' Ibaqa said. As she turned back to the business of packing the Dharithian household away, she hesitated, then turned back. 'Torgan said to his mother he will miss training you. You were a good student. If you see him again, you must not tell him that I said this, or I will be gravely punished.'

'Torgan said that?' It was just about the first praise I had ever had from him. 'What did Lady Datsuun say?'

Ibaqa smiled.

'She said you are a stupid girl who knows nothing. But she hates all Harranese people, so do not think yourself special. This is why they do not speak Harran around you.'

'They speak Harran?' I said, aghast.

'Yes. But you are not Dharithian, so it is beneath them to speak to you.'

'They really do hate us, don't they?'

'Yes,' Ibaqa said. 'But they hate themselves for being in exile more.'

'What about you?'

'I am content here,' Ibaqa said. 'Dharithia was a bad place. Here it is always cold, even in summer, but the people are not so cruel.'

I left her to her packing. I thought people in Harran could be cruel enough when they wanted to be. With a flash of regret I thought of how I'd treated Esher, and Sanvaunt. How careless I'd been with both of them. I'd denied Sanvaunt's affection because I couldn't truly be myself around him. I couldn't let him fall in love with me, not with the things I'd done. The things I was still learning to do. If you love someone, you have to let them know you fully, otherwise there's nothing really there and they love a lie. Just a mask you showed them. And poor Esher, I'd kissed her in a moment of weakness. I hadn't believed anything could happen there. Yes, I was deeply attracted to her, obviously I was. But I hadn't thought of myself that way, and what that meant about me. It had been easy to ignore because nobody else was looking for it.

I had burned them both. They didn't deserve my callousness. I had shown them who I really was, and they were both intelligent people. They would believe it, and they would keep their distance. I was a murderer. I was Sarathi. I was a liar, and a deceiver, and I wouldn't let someone I cared about love me in that way. They deserved better.

With no more lessons to attend to, I took the Ashtai Grimoire with me and rode out onto the moor during the day. There was a difference now. Always before I had read with fear, but that had streamed out of me like the colours had on the day of the colour storm. I had pushed Sanvaunt and Esher away, and Liara would go with them. Ulovar was not long for the world. Once again the home I had found had been torn away from me. Who did I have left? I was not fool enough to believe that the grandmaster was my friend. She would use me for her own ends, as she used everybody. Castus was little different, only we used one another. What did I have left to lose? The only peace I had found was when I let Alianna's spirit drive my actions for a day. My biggest joy had been in letting go. So I let go of it all, and I read, and I learned.

It was a buzzing fly I used it on first. I looked into the grinding, droning tunnel of death, and snuffed it out like it was a candle. It dropped to the ground and lay still.

'Good,' the Queen of Feathers said. She stood alongside me on the hill-side, her royal-blue dress billowing in the harsh moor wind.

'It was just a fly,' I said.

'Other things are harder. The fly's life force is weak. It is made to spawn and die swiftly. The greater the tether to the world, the harder it is to strip it away.'

'It seems wrong,' I said.

'No worse than putting a spear through someone,' the Queen of Feathers said. 'Or an arrow.'

'Do they get to go on? Souls that are taken this way. Do they go to Anavia, Skuttis?'

'Nobody knows what those places are. Not truly,' she said. 'Do not worry over what happens beyond this world. There are still things that nobody knows.'

'Those other women you mentioned. Hallenae, Song Seondeok, Unthayla— was it like this for them?'

'In what way?'

'Were they alone like this?'

'Yes. And no. None of you were the same. I'm trusting you to be different. If you're the same, then I have to start over.'

'What is it you want?'

'What does anyone really want?' she said in her infuriating, evasive manner. 'Just to exist.'

I returned to the book. I turned a page.

In the year 751, Raine of Redwinter embraced her power.

It was true, I thought. I was embracing it.

After she tested her ability against a mere fly, she studied the Banshee's Wail, the mental pathing of which is shown below.

I suppose I did. I studied the diagrams, worked out how they blended with the other trance pathways that I'd studied. Since I'd worked out the missing component, it was all becoming so much easier. And the part that had been missing was me. Only me.

I would use the power I had grown within me to kill Akail. I would save Ulovar. Caution be damned, I had nothing left to lose and they could try to condemn me if they wanted, but I wouldn't be taken alive. I just needed to find her. Find her and tear her soul apart.

*   *   *   *   *   *

Things did not go well when the Winterra took residence across Redwinter and Harranir. They were supposed to be our great warriors, but if you put a person to live a life of warfare, you can't expect them to emerge as holy paladins. They were rough, disrespectful towards the retainers and the city folk. They acted without thought, fearless of punishment. Hostility towards them grew rapidly in the city and two of them were killed in a drunken brawl. Five commoners were hanged in reprisal. The city shuddered.

Each day Ovitus took out his new city-born levies and drilled them with sticks, and then spears and shields ground out from his labour homes. And then word got loose that Prince Caelan had not returned to Harranir with the Winterra. Few who understood the truth of the Crown's inheritance could blame him. He had chosen to abdicate his responsibility to the Crown and remained abroad, and so the succession fell open to those with the power to grab it.

Graffiti and banners emerged across Harranir, proclaiming support for various men of power, or the clans that backed them. With Caelan shirking his duty, Clan LacDaine's claim fell to tatters, and even the most ambitious smaller clans soon gave way to LacNaithe, LacClune and LacAud. Onostus must have had agents in the city orchestrating support for his puppet. Clan LacNaithe had supported LacDaine's claim, but needing to back a candidate, Ovitus put forth Sanvaunt's sister's son, Alfrun LacNaithe. I knew Alfrun to be only fourteen, and he had never spent a day at court, but that mattered little to the parliament who saw only their chance to gather more power. For some, LacNaithe's alliance with Brannlant caused murmurs of disquiet, but others saw the wind rising under LacNaithe's sails. LacClune were rich, but distant. LacAud were strong, but brought war. Enough tongues held back from open support that none of the great clans could raise enough votes for an heir to rise. The politicians were waiting for the battle that would decide the fate of the city before offering a hand. The king's life was an hourglass running out of sand, and we were left without a successor.

* * * * * *

There was only so much that Ulovar could do for us, but he did what he could. He had each of his former apprentices sent to Redwinter's armoury, where Suanach LacNaruun's artificers worked day and night at the forges. I was to be armoured, for when the battle came.

The Draoihn suits of steel were unlike anything I had seen before. A new design, brought from the distant land of Persifa which was somewhere even beyond Murr, worked with Second Gate artifice.

'I am not wearing those,' I said. 'Absolutely not. That's ridiculous.'

The armour itself was a thing of beauty. A bright steel chest piece that could be worn over mail, leaving my arms bare, poleyns—knee protectors—over greaves, and a padded steel cap that would cover my skull and ears. The metal had a bluish hue, with knotted scrollwork around the edges. But it was the armoured boots I objected to.

'What seems to be the problem? I had it made to Councillor Ulovar's specification,' Suanach told me, displeased by my outburst.

'The boots have three-inch-high fecking heels on them,' I said. 'It's ridiculous.'

'Councillor Ulovar requested I outfit you as befits a horse archer,' he said. 'The heels are tall to help keep your feet in the stirrups. The Persifans have been doing it for hundreds of years, and they, as the best archers in the world, should know. I have left your arms free so that you can use a bow effectively. Yours is the most minimal armour we have produced, and it is specific for that one purpose: archery aback a horse.'

'What if I fall off?'

'Draoihn Raine,' he said, and the title sent a little thrill of excitement through me. 'If you wish for a suit of infantry armour, I shall change it. If you wish to fight as heavy cavalry, I shall change it. But as a man who fought Persifans in my youth, I strongly recommend you do as they do. If you fall from your horse in a battle, you will likely do so because you are dying anyway. You have some weeks still to train. I suggest you learn how to use them. I hear that the grandmaster has such faith in your skill that she has entrusted you with an artifact from the Blackwell.'

'She has?'

'Your bow?'

'Oh,' I said. 'Yes. She did.'

Of course, she hadn't, but this at least would allow me to carry Midnight openly. She was a wily one, but I was surprised she had thought of it.

The grandmaster was as good as her word. She gifted me three arrows of the kind I had stolen from the Blackwell before and lost in the under-city. Those arrows could do unusual things, and I was glad to have them. I'd used one to destroy a Mawleth, that terrible corpse-demon from the Night Below. They would do for Akail.

'Haronus LacClune has been given the loan of a most notorious sword. The would-be King LacAud shall find himself met by Redwinter's full force. It almost makes me yearn for my days of battle again.'

'Almost, but not actually?'

'Light Above, no,' Suanach said cheerily. 'A battle is the worst thing in the world. Pray to the lords and ladies of virtue that diplomacy still prevails. Now go and get used to sitting your horse with those on. We have but two weeks until LacAud's war reaches our gates.'

Two weeks would fly by like a diving hawk.

30

'I have to get out of here,' I said to Castus one morning when the late-summer sun was streaming through a window we'd failed to close. Castus rolled over, pressed a hand to his forehead. He'd had a lot to drink the night before, enough that we'd just lain together, bodies pressed tight until breathing deepened and sleep took us over. It had become the norm. The intercourse hadn't really mattered so much as the contact.

'Sneak out the back,' he said, putting a hand over his eyes. 'You were screaming in the night again.'

I ignored the last.

'I don't just mean here. I mean Redwinter. I can't spend another day here, avoiding people. Seeing it all going so wrong. It feels like we're at war on so many different fronts.'

'You want to abscond? I've been dreaming of that my entire life.'

'Liar,' I said. 'You like it when it suits you.'

'Do you have to talk so loud?' Castus groaned. 'Matteo used to talk like this in the morning. It's brutal.'

'Who's Matteo?'

Castus sighed, rolled over and blinked his eyes open. He stared at the ceiling, that blank deadness in his face that stole over it sometimes.

'Nobody that matters, now,' he said wearily. Changed the subject. 'Did you hear the news yesterday?'

'No.'

'Arrowhead's forces have occupied Finglennan. They're only four days march from Harranir.'

'Sounds about right.'

'But there's more. He has outriders ripping the country apart ahead of him, stripping the villages bare. It's not the done thing, given he intends to be set up a king.'

'He's a savage prick,' I said angrily. Four days' march. The growing army in Harranir would march out to meet him in fewer. We teetered on the edge of something horrible. Something that should never have been allowed to happen. And yet, there was a part of me that was waiting for it. The bleak deadness I'd once felt after Dalnesse was creeping back in. My fingers itched for a bowstring, and a shaft to aim at someone. Anything to change things.

'He has his witch doing his dirty work,' Castus said. 'That bone-white creature, the one you met in Gilmundy. They say she eats the dead. Doubtless it's all just a way to spread terror, break down resistance, but—'

I sat bolt upright. I felt the stirring of something that hadn't touched me in all the weeks since the night of the Testing.

Hope.

'Akail? She's leading the raids?'

'Yes, that's the one,' Castus said. 'She's making quite a name for herself.'

'How many in a raiding party? Fifty?'

'Fewer than that, I'd have thought,' Castus said.

'Fewer than fifty,' I said. 'I can work around fifty. Or I can try at least. I'm going to go kill her. Want to come with me?'

Castus grimaced as he sat up.

'This is hardly morning conversation.'

'Tough. Are you in, or out?'

Castus frowned for a moment.

'I've grown sort of fond of you lately, I guess. Riding out to find Arrowhead's terror-witch doesn't seem wise. How many warriors are we taking?'

'None,' I said. 'It's just you and me. We're hunting, not looking for battle, and I only need to get close enough to put an arrow through her head and—and then it's broken. The spell that's destroying Ulovar. Akail's the one that cast it, break her and I heal him. I can still save him.'

Castus was sceptical, but the prospect of doing something reckless and dangerous seemed to interest him, though he tried to hide it behind world-weary lethargy. We geared up, me in my new suit of shiny blue-silver steel, while Castus elected to wear a mail hauberk. I hurried him all the way, new purpose and determination burning through me like the summer's heat. A new mount had been acquired for me at Redwinter's expense, an akhal-teke, trained for war. I'd never seen his like before, much smaller than the destriers, faster than the palfreys, all sleek muscle and agility. His coat shone silver and gold, and he responded to the name Yangyn. A ridiculous name for a horse.

We told nobody where we were going. I thought about telling Robilar, but that ran the risk of her forbidding me. Despite the raiding, our forces weren't permitted to engage Arrowhead directly. They were still hoping that words would prevail. Ridiculous.

We passed through the army of Harranir, which had made a camp north of the city walls, along the road that led between a pair of mountains that looked down across the river valley. The smoke from hundreds of small campfires flavoured the air. Ovitus had been true to his word and employed those who had lost their homes to the fire on Northbank, and more had volunteered. Old veterans whose pensions had never materialised, driven back to the spear by lean times, men and women just down on their luck, and many of them were northerners who'd fled the radish sickness to find a better life elsewhere, and found no welcome. They would be fighting against their countrymen, but the importance of such things can be overstated.

There were plenty of them, but I had to wonder how long they'd stand if Onostus LacAud's tame Draoihn hurled fire into their midst. He had to have Third Gate Draoihn under his command or his challenge was worth nothing. A spear and shield offered little protection against lightning. The only consolation was that the same had to be true of the enemy.

'Where are you two going?'

Inadvertently we had ridden past Ovitus's command tent, a grand pavilion of black and green panels where hard-faced men and women looked at maps and argued strategy. Ovitus cut a fine figure in clan breacan and iron. He was unrecognisable from the young man who'd first watched over me the night of the massacre at Dalnesse, only I could see it more clearly now. In his eyes, he was the same person he'd always been, only the outside had changed. Waldy bounded up to lick at my ridiculous heels, panting affectionately.

'Off to take a look at the enemy,' I said.

'Just the two of you?'

'Just us.'

'I should join you,' Ovitus said. 'Wait there. I'll have my horse brought.'

'You don't need to.'

'No, Raine, no,' he said, and he sounded pained. 'It would be remiss of me not to. I couldn't bear the thought of anything happening to you.'

Princess Mathilde came to his side. She looked as stunning as ever, long hair brushed to an impossible sheen, wearing the glittering jewels she'd worn on her arrival to Redwinter.

'You can send Winterra, my beloved. That's what they're here for,' she said in her not-from-anywhere Brannish accent. 'The commander of the loyalist forces should not place himself in harm's way.' Ovitus shook his head.

'Vedira is their commander, not me. And if I have to fight LacAud, I should get a look at them myself before we do. If a general will not risk himself, he has no business risking anyone else,' Ovitus said. 'That's what Autolocus said in his philosophies.'

Princess Mathilde looked a little exasperated by that.

'Life is not a book of philosophy,' she said. 'Your enemies will not hesitate to take you prisoner.'

Ovitus smiled.

'I'd like to see them try.' He spread his fingers, and a little crackle of power licked between them. 'This is my place, and I'll sit its saddle. You know your place too.'

Mathilde clearly didn't appreciate that. She was a princess of the royal Brannish line. I doubt anyone who didn't share her blood had spoken to her that way and got away with it.

'I know my place, indeed, beloved,' she said gravely and turned to walk away.

'Women!' Ovitus said in a jolly voice. 'Can't do without them but by gosh they drive one crazy at times. Come, my mount is here.'

Castus gave me a sidelong look, and I half expected him to pull out of the idea altogether, which would have been the worst of all possible outcomes by that point. But he was too hungover for the exchange of words that would have ensued, so he just closed his eyes and raised his face to bask in the sun while we waited. It hadn't been the plan, but honestly, Ovitus's newfound ability to open the Third Gate made him a formidable addition to our group, if it were needed. I considered telling him our true purpose, that I was intent on murder. Whatever the politics, he'd have helped if he'd known it would save his uncle. But I had to figure he'd help anyway when the time came. Telling him risked him ordering out a bunch of his warriors with us, and I wanted us to slip up on the raiding party quietly. There was a lot of ground to cover. We'd need to be lucky.

The journey started well enough as I drove a hard pace north. Four days for an army that size was around forty miles. Finglennan was a large village, seeing a lot of the traffic that took the great north road. Many of its people had fled ahead of LacAud's advance. As we rode, my thoughts were on Akail, and the torch of hope that had been lit up in my breast. Finally, I could do something. Finally, I could do what I needed.

'You have to tell me how you did it,' Castus said. 'How you pulled it off.'

'The Third Gate?' Ovitus asked. 'It just opened for me.'

'No, not that,' Castus said. 'The princess. The Third Gate was in your blood all this time anyway. But to make that kind of alliance—well, I have to say I'm impressed. Even if it galls me to say it.'

'Ah, well there's a story there,' Ovitus said. He smiled to himself as we rode over the crest in the pass between the low mountains, heading down to more open country beyond. 'I went to Brannlant to try to negotiate better terms for Harran. I've always thought it was wrong for the levies to take away so many able-bodied people. And I was hoping to find a match for my cousin. Perhaps a wildrose daughter of one of King Henrith's cousins.'

I didn't mind being called wildrose by some people. Sometimes it seemed affectionate, romantic even. But from Ovitus—it just wasn't his word to use. There wasn't any spite in it—it was the way he didn't even realise that it could hurt.

'Did Sanvaunt know that?' I asked.

'He didn't need to know,' Ovitus said with a shrug. For a moment I felt personally affronted. But then I realised that I should always have expected that to be Sanvaunt's future, and I'd hurt him far worse than Ovitus could have. I was glad to be leaving Redwinter and the city behind, even if it was just for a couple of days. I felt like I was hiding there. I wanted to be me, I wanted people to see me for who I was. I'd skulked through my own life for so long, I had to be free of it. Out here in the open air, with a wide sky above me, the sweet scent of summer in the air, without walls to close me in, I breathed out deeply. I could let some of it go, for a time.

'A day of hunting was arranged,' Ovitus went on. He was clearly enjoying telling the story as he watched Waldy bound around, splashing in and out of a stream along the trail. He told Castus the same tale as he'd told me, about the boar coming from the forest and goring his face, his Second Gate opening, Waldy coming to the rescue.

'And just like that—it was arranged?' Castus asked.

'Well, of course not, it wasn't quite as simple as all that,' Ovitus said. 'There were negotiations, and lots of bargaining. But I was prepared for that. I just had to switch Sanvaunt out for myself. The king was very reasonable.'

'And Mathilde wanted to marry you,' I said. 'Because you saved her from a boar?'

'Well, no,' Ovitus said. 'She's more discerning than that, I'm sure.'

'Because she fell in love?'

Ovitus shrugged. He glanced at me and I kept my face pointed away.

'Whatever that means. Our goals are closely aligned. It all worked out well. Are there some days where I wish that I could abandon it all, and find a true soul-match? Of course I do. Who wouldn't? But LacNaithe has ever been a clan who puts its duty first.'

'A soul-match,' Castus said. 'That's a new one on me. I find it's best not to get too attached to people. Nothing but hurt comes from it in the end.'

'Did someone break your heart?' Ovitus said with eager sincerity. 'Is that why you're so sour all the time?'

'Don't make me spank you again, LacNaithe,' Castus said. Ovitus stiffened in the saddle.

'You'll find me a much more formidable opponent these days,' he said. But his attention was dragged away to his dog. 'Waldy! It's just a rabbit—Waldy!' he called as the dog bolted off into the heather. He slapped his heels against his horse's flanks and set off in pursuit.

'Did someone break your heart?' I asked.

'For that, I'd have to have one to break,' Castus said, reclaiming his cocky smile and giving me a wink. 'Thank the Light Above for that dog. Really, I just wanted to know how much dowry she brought him.'

'Good to know for your clan, I suppose.'

Castus cocked his head towards me.

'Do you think it's odd that a woman like Mathilde—so elegant, refined, rich, business-minded, and those who are into that sort of thing would likely say beautiful—would be so charmed by a man wrestling a boar that she'd insist on marrying him?'

'I don't know,' I said. 'Love makes people do crazy things.' I remembered what Ulovar had said, that he'd been working on arranging this match for seven years. I wondered how much Ovitus had known about that, and how he'd have felt if he had. Would it spoil his story? Or was he astute enough to know that it must have been in motion all along?

'You think she fell in love with him over that? A love which, given what he said, he maybe doesn't reciprocate as much as he's been making out?'

'I've no doubt there was advantage in the match on a number of fronts.'

'It hasn't gone down well with the other clans,' Castus said. 'Not at all. Ovitus's forthcoming wedding swings the balance of power far too much in one direction. There's an argument to be made that LacAud's advance is the direct result. The north has been wrecked by the radish disease, and now the south forms a direct alliance with Brannlant.'

'We're already under the sway of the Brannish,' I said. 'Have been for years. What does it matter?'

'Let's assume Ovitus and Mathilde conceive children,' Castus said. 'Either they don't inherit Ovitus's gifts—which have turned out to be pretty spectacular—and they're viable candidates to take the Crown. Or they do, in which case they insert the Brannish royal line directly into Redwinter.'

'I hadn't thought of it like that,' I confessed. 'Makes me wonder whether the grandmaster might have been looking for a reason to keep Ovitus out of Redwinter already.'

'She shamed him. Deliberately,' Castus acknowledged. 'Even if he's been a royal piece of shit to me in the past, it was hard to watch.' But he grinned again. 'All right, maybe not *that* hard.'

Waldy emerged from the heather, drooling happily, having failed to find his rabbit, and that brought Ovitus back to us and shut down that conversation. We pressed on, the horses eating the miles. Yangyn was the most obedient mount I'd ever ridden, and his silver-gold coat was a dream. My horsemanship had improved a lot over the last year, and I'd been practising in my ridiculous archer-heels, standing up in the saddle. I practised as we headed further into the north. My calves would ache tomorrow.

* * * * * *

We passed travellers—refugees in truth—fleeing southward towards Harranir with whatever they could carry. They'd heard the stories of the fanged bone-witch from those who'd fled before her. If her job was to sow fear, then it was working. Once we came upon a troop of our own scouts. They'd seen enemy warbands, but not her. They were under orders not to engage directly.

'They're moving south,' the warriors' leader told us. 'Driving more mouths to feed into the city.'

'A woman who wears white,' I said. 'Have you seen her?'

'Aye. She stands out, even at a distance.'

'Where?'

'You're Draoihn so I won't go telling you your own business,' the warrior said. 'But I'd avoid her if I were you. She rides with twenty men. But if you're intent, we figured she was heading towards the lumber mills west of Piwenny.'

'That's all we needed,' I said. 'Safe travels.'

The scouts were glad to be heading back south, but for us it was west.

Buildings, livelihoods and peace were burned out across what had been LacDaine lands, and now had become contested territory. We rode hard. The relentless, empty summer sky left the land parched and yellow, but we each fell into the First Gate trance that we'd all practiced for so many hours in Palanost's hall, keeping the world in sharp, acid-etched focus. The sun's heat pressed harder against my skin. I felt the tracks of each individual bead of sweat as they serpent-tracked beneath my armour. We saw the smoke eventually.

'Perhaps this is close enough,' Ovitus said. 'We'll not be back before dark as it is.'

'Haven't seen them yet,' I said. 'No. We go on.'

'No,' he disagreed. 'I've decided. We're heading back.'

'Do what you like,' I said. 'I'm going to find Akail, and I'm going to put an end to her before sunset. You can come if you want, or not.'

Ovitus looked uncertain. He had grown used to people taking his orders. But I was Draoihn now, and he wasn't, and I didn't have to do as I was told anymore. I felt it like a fist in my chest. I had power of my own.

'Maybe he's right,' Castus said, eyeing the smoke that rose beyond the ridge.

'Come, or don't,' I said. I didn't wait for them, and instead pressed on over the rolling land.

There weren't many foresters at the lumber mill; those that had possessed the means had fled before Onostus LacAud's advance, or scattered to the hills when they saw the outriders. But there were still twenty or thirty, many of them children. LacAud's outriders moved lazily, unthreatened and unrepentant as they loaded a wagon with the belongings of people they'd never met before.

I peered harder, pushing my Gate to its limit. There were bodies on the ground, two of them. At such a distance, even with Eio thrumming in my head I could make out little about them, but they'd been adults. Nobody had moved them, left them where they had fallen. The warriors wore yellow and grey clan colours, but then, from beside one of the bodies, a figure rose up. Her long white gown was wet and red down the front, the blood running from her jaw. Through my Gate I saw the shards of bone piercing her forearms, her cheeks.

'I'm going down there,' I said.

'At this I draw the line!' Ovitus said hotly. 'There are twenty men down there. Maybe more in the buildings that we haven't seen.'

He was right. The wise thing to do was to do exactly what we'd come to do—stay well back from any sign of the enemy, take a look at what they were doing, and then ride back to the safety of our forces. Yangyn shifted uncomfortably beneath me as if he could read my mood in the twitching of my legs.

'How can anyone accept the deaths of innocents in the name of their own ambition?' I said. 'Look at her. She's a monster. She tore their throats out with her teeth.'

'Man is ever a savage to man,' Ovitus said. 'But innocents in this world are few and far between. It is the whim of man to see innocence in every victim, and a tyrant in every aggressor, but such lines are drawn to suit our own agendas.'

I turned on him angrily.

'What in all the river of Skuttis is that meant to mean? That those people down there deserved to be robbed and murdered because they aren't innocent enough?'

Ovitus looked abashed, and a little annoyed at the same time.

'The writings of the Kwendish philosopher, Maravici—'

'Sounds like horse shit used to justify greed to me,' I said. 'We're not living in a philosophy. We're right here and now. And I'm done sitting back waiting for someone else to fix things.'

It was Akail I wanted. Akail and her curse of blood and bone. If I could kill her, if I brought her down with one well-placed arrow then perhaps Ulovar would be free. Maybe his health would return, maybe his Gates would come back to him. Or perhaps he'd live out a few more years, infirm and abed. It didn't matter if killing Akail would provide a cure: I had to try. I would never have a better opportunity than this.

'There are only three of us,' Ovitus said. 'This mission was to take a look at the enemy. Well, we've seen them. What did you expect to see, Raine? Pleasantries and dandelion cakes?'

My anger was up, and the plight of the foresters dragged on a cork that had been bunging a well of rage, and sorrow, and pain and fear for a long time. Bodies lying in the dirt, just like Dalnesse, where the people I'd begun to see as family had been butchered. The dreams that plagued me through the night, the dead faces, the hopeless, nightmarish existence of trying to live with that at my back, every single day, was bleeding out from the edges.

'I'm a fecking Draoihn,' I said. 'I protect the Crown. And the Crown protects the people. That's what it's for, isn't it? To keep us safe from the Night Below. What's the point of it if we don't protect them when we have to?'

'Three Draoihn against twenty outriders?' Castus mused impishly. 'It's certainly bold.'

'Don't be foolish,' Ovitus said. 'You're good. You're both good. But you're not that good. And they might have renegades among them.'

'Renegades?'

Ovitus nodded. He dropped his Gate and put his eye glasses back on his nose.

'Those who failed their Testing and found themselves without purpose, or those who never came to Redwinter. Onostus must feel he has some kind of counter to the Winterra, and we believe that's it.'

'You found the Third Gate,' I said. 'You're worth twenty on your own.'

'I'm new to it,' Ovitus said. 'I've barely had time to test my capabilities. And nothing can save you from an arrow you don't see coming. I understand. Believe me, I want to ride down there too and teach them a jolly good lesson. But what would it achieve? We might die, and for what?'

I thought of Ulovar, sitting afraid and dying in the dim light of the greathouse. Fading into nothing, his body taken away by that creature. By a curse she'd laid upon him. A thing better left forgotten.

'We die for those we care about,' I said. 'We die because there's something worth dying for. For family. That's Onostus LacAud's blood witch. If I drop her here, then the tables turn. We might end this rebellion in one hard stroke.'

'I want to see it too, darling Raine,' Ovitus said. 'But I still hope that we might resolve this conflict with words. I will make Onostus LacAud see sense. He seeks to press his candidate for the throne. Who knows whether his candidate would survive trying to take the Crown? I must oppose him, but I must also leave the door open for peace. That cannot start with killing his advisors. The sands of power have shifted beneath our feet. LacDaine is done, and when the king dies, a new power will rise. It cannot be any other way.'

'Don't call me darling,' I said angrily. 'You're betrothed, and I've never been your darling.'

'Apologies,' he said. 'Just a turn of phrase they use in Brannlant that has rubbed off on me.'

Akail's raiders were done packing their wagon, and turned it towards the north, about to make their journey back towards LacAud and his forces. The villagers had gathered the fallen. One of them was still alive, I saw, but might not be for long. The pale witch was working a spike of bone through the skin of her arm, blood running red in a stream across ivory skin, mingling with the blood she'd already spilled. People were dead. Homes were burning. The sky lifted them up as smoke, diffusing them until they were as gone as the people below. A lonely ghost stood in the centre of it all, confused, sad.

'They take everything,' I muttered quietly. Images were coming to my mind, diagrams, sigils, words that I had learned to form when I should have been sleeping. 'They take everything from us, and make us into something dark. They make us what we are, these men and women of steel and fire. What's left at the end?'

'We could take them,' Castus said. There was a tense, excited energy in the way he stood in his stirrups. 'Come on, we could do it.'

'No, damnit,' Ovitus snapped. 'I will not risk myself, nor Raine. Not for anything. You may do what you wish. Why are you even here, LacClune? Wouldn't you be better off trying to raise men to support the Crown? Your father dallies, seeking to see where the pieces fall, doesn't he?'

'If I were party to my father's designs I'd probably not tell you anyway,' Castus said. He stared down towards the lumber mill.

'And that is why I alone stand to protect Harranir,' Ovitus said. Gravely, proudly.

But all this began to fall away behind me as I put my stacked-up heels to Yangyn's flanks and started riding high along the hillside above. The raiders may have seen me—Yangyn's shimmering coat was hard to miss against the purple heather and sun-baked grass. But I was only one rider, and they must have seen many of our outriders. Theirs was a large party. They had the numbers not to fear one woman on a horse. They were the terror here, weren't they?

They were fools not to fear me.

Neither Castus nor Ovitus followed me, and that was for the good. I was better alone. Was I ever anything else these days? I thought that I'd found a place where I could belong, people who could be friends, maybe even more than that. But I'd burned that away. I'd taken the bridges that had been formed, and brought them crashing down with hammers of my own making. I held my secrets close to my chest, and even that hadn't let me find a measure of peace. I spent my nights with Castus, a man who could never really want me, I spent my days hiding from those that I'd hurt. I'd been tutored by a legend that I knew I could never really trust, who would use me for her own ends. I was a Draoihn, and I was the Draoihn's enemy, secreted within their number.

I was the enemy of the entire world, they just didn't know it yet.

Yangyn was swift as a hawk. The riders watched me now. Some of them were moving for their horses, taking up spears. I found my place, a jutting rock on the hillside, perhaps a third of a mile from the outriders. They looked up towards me from time to time, measuring what a lone, distant rider was doing, but what was I to them? Hardly a threat. I climbed down from Yangyn's back and looked to my quiver. I had fifteen bodkin-pointed man-killers, but I also had the three arrows Grandmaster Robilar had gifted to me. The long arrows, white shafts inscribed with blood-red runes, gold and blue fletching, heads of stone. Weapons of the past. When I'd loosed them before I'd slain a demon, and I'd blasted Kaldhoone LacShale's followers apart. But I hadn't had time to study them, hadn't understood what they did. But I'd taken the time now.

Midnight felt alive in my hand. She wanted this, wanted to be used. Her silver-moonlight string came alive at my touch, and I fitted one of the long arrows to it, as sure a fit as a hand slipping inside a glove.

I couldn't be the façade anymore. The world was insisting that I be my true self. It was time to step over that threshold. Time to face myself, and whatever my true self had to endure.

I called on the First Gate again, but I did more. I called on the Sixth Gate, and my world was not just the world of the living but the world of souls. I saw them, distant and below me on the road, the green-wisp spirits superimposed across the bodies that housed them. I felt the droning call of the tunnel filling the world around me until I existed in it. I drew back on the bow string, stretching the curved wood of the bow, as the arrow's nock came past my face and all the way back to my ear. I aimed it high, right up into the air. Five hundred yards. Longer than any bow could shoot. Or at least, longer than any normal bow.

I understood the trajectory. In Eio, I understood the wind, I calculated for it—not by performing geometrical equations, but by feel. The same way you throw a ball to hit a moving target, predicting its speed before you release. It was a long arc. It should have been out of range. It was out of range for anyone but me, me with this weapon of the Draoihn, me with my Gate thrumming through me. I wasn't aiming for Akail. I didn't need to be that accurate. The souls below seemed to call to me.

I released, and the arrow sped away into the blue sky, rising higher until it became nothing but a tiny, thin line.

It descended.

A silent fireball blossomed among them, and the clap of thunder reached me a second later. The blast hurled men and horses outwards, the wagon and its plunder detonating, shards of wood and wheel launched in a flaming blast. Men and beasts flew like broken dolls, trailing smoke as their bodies hurtled through the air to bounce and roll across Harran's meadow. Across the moor, birds flocked into the sky in fear of the blast, the cawing of crows and the frightened squeaks of the nesting ground birds filling the world.

I had counted twenty men before. I rode down towards them now, readying an ordinary arrow. Yangyn went fearlessly, trained to battle and the smell of char and blood in the air. The grass around the road had caught fire in several places. The first man I came across was dead. Half of his body had been pulverised by the impact. The second was headless.

When I came to Akail, she was gasping on blood. Whatever foul blood-curse magic she could work, she couldn't do it choking to death. She'd lost her left leg, her left arm. Her pale white skin was burned and blackened. Her eyes were so pale, so cruel, but there was fear there too. I didn't care. I was out of remorse. I was out of feeling for other people. I drew hard on the string, the fletching brushing my ear.

'I am Akail,' she burbled through her own blood. 'I am . . . the drink of . . . blood. I am . . . the chewer of bones.'

'End it,' I said. 'End your curse on Ulovar LacNaithe.'

She stared at me. Even through all the pain I read the confusion in her eyes. She made a choking noise, blood welled from her mouth in a final dark wave, and then she twitched once. Stopped. She was dead.

I had expected something more. A release of power, or a whisper of dark forces banished to the Night Below. But there was nothing, just the death of a woman on a charred and broken road. The bone-witch died just like the rest of them. The Sixth Gate ground and droned, and I sensed her spirit as it began to detach itself from the rest of her.

No.

I reached out, and gripped her soul by the throat. She was vaporous, green and white wisps, but young, seeming barely a teenager. No bones pierced the ghost, and decades of madness were absent from her spectral eyes. What had been done to her, to make her what she was?

'End the curse,' I said. I clenched hard on a throat that she didn't need to speak through. 'Do it! Do it, or you won't go on. I'll claim you. Do you understand?' Spittle flew from my lips.

'I made no curse,' she whispered. Akail's spirit tugged against my hand as if it wanted to go on.

'You cursed him. You did, I've seen it! Arrowhead told me so!'

'No.'

'You understand how it works now?'

The Queen of Feathers sat elegantly on the burning remains of what had once been a wagon, untouched by the fire. She wore a wreath of magpie feathers, her royal-blue dress rippling in a wind I didn't feel.

'I think so,' I said. 'Do you have any advice, or just confusing nonsense as usual?'

'Trust yourself,' she said. 'We like to think our way through things, but most of life is just instinct, and all our experiences are just feeling. So feel, and trust yourself.'

I nodded. It was good advice, of a sort.

I took Akail's spirit into myself, as though I ate her. It wasn't like with Alianna, sharing a body. It wasn't like looking into the bones of a dead man on the road. It was an absorption. I inhaled, and the tunnel squealed and ground its iron, and for a moment I was filled with her.

Akail had been born farther north even than the mountain village of my birth. Out beyond the peaks, where the frozen tundra never thaws, where her people hunted seals and whales and dwelled in the ruins of a lost civilisation. I breezed through her life as if I flipped the pages of a book. A happy childhood. A family who loved her. An adventure down into the dark tunnels where children were forbidden to venture, but she went anyway, looking for a lost dog. A meeting with something old, and dreadful, a dark, wounded creature that whispered the secrets of magic born from corpses. The destruction of her village by a woman who could have been Grandmaster Robilar, but was remembered poorly. Flashing fire. Howling wind. The tunnels were brought low. She'd shared the dark secrets she'd learned.

A ring of bodies around an ancient standing stone. A flickering colour storm across the world.

This was the task to which she'd been put. Whatever strange powers she'd possessed, born of an encounter with something hidden and buried—this was the task. I hadn't saved anyone. Her damage had already been done. She was no Faded Lord. She hadn't even possessed power of her own. She was just a girl, driven from her own mind by things she couldn't hope to understand, used and exploited as men have done to girls like her since time immemorial. My hopes collapsed like a paper tower. I stood amidst the wreckage I'd wrought, the burning bodies around me, and the rage ran through me, through the tunnel in a black torrent.

I screamed. Out of control, out of hope, out of anything but raw seething fury. I'd done this terrible thing, and not even this had been enough.

'How much more do I have to do?' I screamed it into the flames and the emptiness of the world around me. I didn't know who I asked. The Light Above, the Queen of Feathers? Ah, no. It was me. To learn what I had, to have done the things I'd done, only to find myself robbed of victory. It wasn't fair. None of us deserved it.

I'd been holding on to an older version of myself, deep inside. She looked back at me from the darkness, clutching to a single strand of hair that tied us together. And then it snapped, and she was falling away, disappearing into the void.

I finished off three more of the dead. The white shafted arrow had done most of the work. The ancient Draoihn who had wrought these terrible implements of war had known their craft. It was a wonder that the magic had lasted down all these centuries, and standing amid the wreckage I wondered what war must have been like when they carried these by the quiver full. Worse, I thought. Somehow worse. But good for me.

Castus and Ovitus were coming now. They couldn't ignore that blast, but they were still distant, and I still had to do what I had to do.

The tunnel ground like millstones around me, its awful droning screech filling the world. I released Eio, but the First Gate made no difference to that sound within my mind. I could still feel Akail within me as the souls began to rise.

All those weeks ago in Gilmundy, Colban had died, and his spirit had come to me. It had been a puzzle at the time, but it should not have been. The souls of the dead were drawn to the tunnel, and I was the tunnel. I had let that boy down. I had let everyone down, and nobody cared anymore. I'd burned my bridges. I couldn't even have the friends I'd reached for. Onostus LacAud brought death upon us, but no, he didn't get to make that choice. He didn't get to take Ulovar from me.

It was time to rise. The world wanted me to be Sarathi? I would show it just what I was capable of. And I would take the power I needed to change this unhappy world to my design.

I tried to count the dead, but I remembered what Castus had said to me that time: *After twenty, you stop counting.*

It was time to stop counting and accept it. Accept who and what I was. Lean into it, become it, breathe it. And so I breathed it now. I isolated one of the six circles, and the sixth circle within the six, and I worked them in words I hadn't known how to pronounce until they fell from my lips. It was different here, surrounded by the dead, not just studying pictograms in an ancient book that never let me read it clearly. I read the world instead, and the knowledge of the book flowed out of me, and back to me, and I issued my insistence upon the world.

The souls didn't want to come to me, but they were powerless against the Sixth Gate. As they rose over their bodies I drew them in towards me, and I consumed. There was a silent scream of terror as I dragged the first in and I told myself that he was an enemy, and that he'd helped to murder innocents, that he was coming to destroy us and my anger and all the rest of it shielded me from the spirit's terror and its pain. This was no simple fly to snuff and I felt the pull on my body, but I was stronger than these things. Oh, so much stronger. All of the months of reading the Ashtai Grimoire, the deaths I'd suffered, the misery and pain I had endured, they had forged me as a smith folds steel. I was so much more than I had been, and so much emptier, and I could fill that void with other lives.

The next soul streamed into me, and a fourth, as I dragged them to me I felt that space within me beginning to fill. A well, a reservoir, an energy source that only I could wield. Five, six, I took them quicker now. Seven, eight, nine, I dragged them from their bodies before they even left them, no living shell remaining there to tether them to the world. Every one entered me like a wave crashing over my head, cold and momentarily lost for air.

'Yes!' the Queen of Feathers exulted, rising above the burning wreckage, looking down on me with triumph. 'You are made anew! You become! We become!'

Ten, eleven, they were rising faster than I could breathe them in. I didn't want to lose any of them, didn't want to allow them to escape to the After-world and escape me. This was their fate, this was what they deserved for their crime. My body shook. I fell to my knees, but still I reached out to them, stripping them away, inhaling.

I lost count there. But I thought I got them all.

Dizziness swam over me. More powerful than any narcotic-induced high, stronger than a belly full of whisky. I shivered and found the world had grown silent but for the crackling of burning heather.

'I knew you could do it,' the Queen of Feathers said. Her corvid wings were spread behind her. Wings of dark, and light. Within her eyes, I could see stars burning.

I could feel the souls within me. They seemed small, crushed, dormant. They were mine now.

'I shouldn't have done it,' I said, shuddering as cold flowed over me.

'You arise today with truth within you,' the queen said. 'You are Raine, High Sarathi of Redwinter. The power you have begun to draw will reshape the world and you will create that which has always been. I believe in you.'

'What is it you would have me do?' I whispered.

'I would have life,' the Queen of Feathers said.

'I do not bring life,' I said. The rage was leaving me, the wet sheen of sweat cold against my skin the only feeling left to me. 'You made me this. Everyone forced me to this.'

'Nobody escapes the world around them. Those like you least of all,' the Queen of Feathers whispered. 'But you have a chance for greatness only few have dared to dream of, and with that, you can save everyone, and everything. The Riven Queen, Song Seondeok, Serranis, Unthayla—they all started here. But now there is a new chance. A chance to succeed in what-ever our task is that began this, and ends it. I am proud of you, Raine. I am proud of us.'

A cold wind blew across the moor. The stink of smoke was joined by the stink of charred fat and skin. I sat with my eyes close and breathed it in.

A cold wet nose lapped at my face. Waldy, lapping at me. I pushed him away, found Ovitus and Castus looking down at me from their horses.

'What did you do, Raine?' Ovitus said. He looked aghast. Horrified.

'I did what had to be done,' I said. 'I'm winning this war.'

31

We got out of there fast. The sound of that blast might summon others to investigate.

'How did you do it?' Castus wanted to know. He was looking at me in awe, like I was one of the hidden folk revealed. 'Don't tell me everyone has a Third Gate now? Third Gates for everyone!'

'Just an arrow,' I said. 'A Draoihn arrow. A very old one. The grandmaster gave them to me.'

'Don't you see what you've done?' Ovitus said. He wasn't angry, but he was flustered. 'I mean to talk LacAud down—that woman was one of his advisors. We may have lost our chance to work this out.'

'Some people already lost their chance,' I snapped. 'I'm tired of inaction. I'm tired of being told what I can and can't do. I'm Draoihn now. I get to make the rules as I want to. LacAud is bringing an army. This is what happens to invaders.'

'As your van . . .' Ovitus began.

'Redwinter issues my orders,' I said curtly. 'And the grandmaster is Redwinter.'

Ovitus was not happy with that, but he didn't argue further, just wrung his reins through his hands and scowled into the distance.

It was not as simple as it had felt, that drawing of souls. The images, the diagrams and words of the book had flowed together and I understood much of what had been shrouded in shadow before. I had thrown myself into it, had let myself be the Sixth Gate as much as I let it surround me. Everything was one, and our boundaries were thin. But I had not planned for the consequences.

I could hear them. They were deep inside me, crushed together, held, but they muttered and moaned, whispered through me. A score of voices, hissing, angry, or sad, or dour, or lost. I did my best to blot them from my mind and spoke little as we thundered back towards the city.

It was wrong. Of course it was wrong. But I'd been a wrung-out towel, pulled taut with nothing left on the inside. I could have told myself that the ends justified the means. I could have told myself that there were no rules for me. Perhaps I could even have wrangled it in my mind to say that this was no different from any other magic. But I understood now, in a way that I had always denied to myself before, why people feared the Sarathi. Yes, a Draoihn of the Third Gate could break a man's body with wind and fire, but we see our bodies as vessels, we expect them to get damaged eventually. Our spirits, our ghosts, are the one thing that are always ours. But not anymore. Not for those murderous bastards, not for Akail. They were mine now. The doubts I'd felt, the stories I'd told myself had been washed away in a hurricane of desperation and fury and despair. I had given up. Given in. There was too little of me left to give a damn about a few hired killers.

The Winterra were out with the army, armoured in their invincible, sigil-worked armour. Those that practiced together moved in arcs of subtle power and vicious symmetry. Men and women alike had freshly shaved their heads, the better to fit their helmets. Two of them called crudities to me as we passed them by, uncaring that I was Draoihn, uncaring that Ovitus was there. They were a law unto themselves, these warriors who had been stationed for constant war in foreign lands. I ignored those calls in the knowledge that even with my new status, I outranked nobody amidst their force.

Night was already laid over Harranir's valley. My mind was made up on what I had to do. I was going to end the war before it truly got started. Perhaps I had drawn first blood, and perhaps I would draw the last.

Beside a grand command tent I saw Grandmaster Robilar, her youthful form, in heated conversation with a woman with a bare scalp: Lassaine LacDaine, great-niece to King Quinlan LacDaine and commander of the Winterra. They did not raise their voices—in fact, it seemed that a bubble of silence existed around them, holding their words in close. Either of them could have done it. Rumour had it that six months back, Lassaine had passed the Fourth Gate. Soon we would lose the king's healer Kelsen, and Ulovar did not seem long for our world. Ovitus might replace them, if his power continued to grow. But Lassaine held rank as Commander of the Winterra, and a member of the Council of Night and Day besides. She looked a formidable woman.

Whatever their dispute, it ended badly, frustration on both faces. Lassaine stalked away, back towards her warriors, and the grandmaster watched her go through narrowed eyes. It wasn't the best time to approach her, but there never seemed to be a good one. I steeled myself, against the murmurs I heard in the dark recess within me where I'd stowed those souls, and against having to speak to the grandmaster, and approached.

'Draoihn Raine,' she said. 'I heard you'd gone out scouting. With two heirs of the great clans, no less.'

'I did, Grandmaster,' I said, offering her a formal bow.

'I had a mind to send the Winterra out to retrieve you. What would have happened if one of them had been lost to us at this crucial hour?'

There was no rebuke in her tone. The question was not rhetorical. The answer was that someone else would have been placed in charge of the gathered LacNaithe forces, which continued to irk her. Or perhaps if Castus had been taken, his father might have taken more interest in unfolding events. Merovech LacClune had kept his thoughts, and his men, to himself. Waiting to see what would unfold—it is always better to let your enemies do the work for you, or at least, that's what the philosophers claimed.

'I have a private matter of strategy to discuss with you,' I said. The voices inside me itched along my veins and around the inside of my skull.

'Strategy? Very well. Come inside.' She led me into her tent. It was spacious, furnished with pieces each of which would have cost the average tradesman his yearly income. An arc of iron bars held aloft a crystal chandelier, loaded with the cadanum globes that had become so expensive in recent days. A table held stacks of paperwork and volumes bound in soft red leather. But the strangest furnishing was a portrait, an oil painting brought all the way from her residence in Redwinter. Not the great, wall-covering picture of the grandmaster and her sister, but the one of the man in the pheasant-feathered cap: the Faded Lord Sul, who had broken the grandmaster's skull. His black eyes stared from his narrow, nondescript face.

'I am not supposed to be here. In fact, I am not supposed to command any part of these forces. But it does annoy all these up-tight commanders to see me around, so I made a show of moving in. It does them well to remember their place.'

'You don't have a right to be here?'

'Redwinter is supposed to remain neutral in disputes between clans.

Lassaine LacDaine believes that strongly. She is not happy that the Winterra are to be put to such use.'

'She'd rather be back fighting for the king of Brannlant?'

'I doubt it,' the grandmaster said. 'Keeping the Winterra away at war is useful for Redwinter. It gives us somewhere to put all those Draoihn we don't need around. There's no need for quite so many of us, you see. It helps to prevent them getting ideas above their station.'

'Like a punishment,' I said.

'No, not exactly,' the grandmaster said as she settled slowly into a luxuriously padded seat that must have taken four men to carry down. 'The deployment of the Winterra serves several purposes. Nobody sits an army on their doorstep long without that army getting ideas of their own. Additionally, the deployment firms up our alliance with Brannlant, but it also reminds the Brannish king that we have a formidable fighting force available, should we choose to use it. It keeps the focus away from petty squabbles about who rules whom, and lets them focus on taking more land. More land under the control of those who hold the Crowns. You see the benefits.' She waved a lazy hand as if I could have seen nothing else.

'I do, grandmaster,' I said. Right then, I didn't care. 'Will the new-made Draoihn be assigned to the Winterra?'

'Nearly all,' she said. 'They need some fresh blood, but bringing them back to Harran is not without risk. They may find they prefer it here. New blood in their ranks should remind them that they are of Harran, that they have friends and family here. And we were getting rather full on apprentices.'

'Esher of Harranir,' I blurted, feeling a sudden swell of fear for my friend. 'Is she one of them?'

'The name is familiar,' the grandmaster said, squinting as if at a fly. 'But I do not recall. Come now. What is this strategy you wish to speak of?'

I took a deep breath, then settled into Eio as I'd heard many do. I checked the perimeters of the tent for sounds that somebody was listening in, but we were alone. It would have taken a bold spy to try to eavesdrop on the grandmaster.

'I'm going to kill Onostus LacAud,' I said. 'I'm going to end this before it ever reaches a battle. Nobody else needs to die over this. It's just one man's ambition, and I can end it.'

The grandmaster tried to keep her face impassive, but I saw the twitch of her lips. A sly little smile pushed itself forward like a mouse peeking from behind a cupboard.

'I set you the task of killing another,' Robilar said. 'A literal witch hunt, if you will.'

'That's yesterday's news,' I said, and I felt the spirits stir within me. Angry. Afraid. 'I killed her. But it didn't help anything. I was wrong.'

Grandmaster Robilar did not seem disappointed, or surprised. Everything she showed was a performance. I didn't mention that Akail had worked the colour storm that had stripped Robilar of her invincibility. If I had learned anything at all from Vedira Robilar, it was that knowledge was best held close until the time to use it took the stage. It would have distracted her.

'So now you turn to take the dragon's head,' she said.

'To help Ulovar? I'd tear its eyes out with my bare hands.'

She smiled at that. I think she liked to see me acting fierce.

'Onostus LacAud is notoriously hard to kill,' Robilar said. 'Even for the likes of me. Blade, bow, fire, he has even proofed himself against poison. I see you've used one of the arrows I gave you. You think the silver-threaded bow can penetrate those wards, even with those?'

I breathed out slowly. Emptied myself of air. Emptied myself of everything I had to be rid of before I could even say it. Remorse. Self-pity. Self-loathing. Regret. I had to be what I was.

'No,' I said. 'Not with those. With the other thing.'

Grandmaster Robilar leaned forward, resting her elbows on her knees. Goading me to continue.

'And how would that work?'

'Onostus LacAud has woven incantations of protection about himself for every possibility he could conceive. He protected himself against steel, against poison, probably even against your Fourth Gate. He's covered himself in an armour of spells, one by one, to meet every threat he can imagine. But every suit of armour has a vulnerable point, and I don't think he would have covered himself against me.'

The grandmaster stood slowly. She crossed to me and took my hands in her own. Her fingers were cold. They were more delicate than mine, more brittle.

'You could be right.'

'You knew, didn't you?' I said. 'You've been thinking of this all along.'

'The thought had occurred to me,' the grandmaster said, letting me go. She crossed to look at the painting, her back to me. 'Why do you think I brought this here?'

'A reminder to be humble. That's what you told me.'

'Indeed. It is pride and ambition that so commonly bring us to folly, but surety also. Sul was born, much like the creature, Ciuthach, that you defeated in the north. Risen from a black tomb, reclaiming powers better left undisturbed. But he was patient, and he was subtle. He worked his way into Redwinter's trust. I was so young, and as fooled as everyone else. I confronted him as he made a bid to take the Keystone from the Blackwell, to unlock the Great Seal that protects the Crown, and there he would have unmade it if he could.'

'So you remind yourself that nobody is as they seem.'

'He is a reminder not to trust anybody,' she said. 'We were lovers, you see. And love blinded my eyes for the longest time. And yet, even after we fought, even after he shattered me and I shattered him in return, there are moments when I long for him. It is sentimentality, and foolishness. A fancy, I suppose.'

'He was a monster, though,' I said. 'He did terrible things.'

'We have all done terrible things,' Robilar said softly. 'And perhaps we will do them again. What you have suggested is a hard thing to do. It is not the desperate killing of battle. You mean to approach and kill a man in cold blood, and I know what you have to do in order to achieve that. Perhaps you will struggle, after, with what you have done? But we are not merely one thing. Perhaps the portrait reminds me of that, as much as it reminds me not to trust anybody—least of all myself.'

'I need a reason to meet with Onostus,' I said. 'Before it comes to battle. A reason to be close to him.'

'I can arrange it, though he already sees you as a threat.'

'Then do it,' I implored her eagerly. 'It's one life against hundreds, maybe more. The succession has to go smoothly—the Crown matters, and all that.'

Grandmaster Robilar nodded soberly.

'Leaderless, his forces are likely to find themselves without cause. His reputation is built on his invincibility, and if he falls, the resolve of his rabble will fall with them. Onostus does not share power, and his mercenaries will not fight if their payment cannot be guaranteed. One life to avert a war is no cost at all.' She smiled, and for a moment I thought I saw cracks of

flame beneath her hair. 'It shall be so. You shall accompany our next contingent of negotiators.'

And so, like that, I had offered myself as an assassin. The grandmaster
had anticipated it all along, I suspected. She did not play for a short game
after all.

32

I rode back to Redwinter, and the ghosts followed.

The murmuring grew louder, a constant backdrop in my mind. They shimmered at the edges of my perception, growing stronger, welling up from within. I saw the shades of men lining the road, and their dead-eyed stares pierced right through me. I was the world to them; I contained them, and they were mine.

What happened to me? one of them mouthed from fifty yards, but the words brushed into me as if spoken right into my ear.

Where am I? another asked, her voice dry, the shifting of sands.

Murderer, the others chorused.

'Shut up,' I said into the night. 'Shut up, shut up. You're the murderers. You're the killers. I had to do it.'

Is this the Afterworld?

It's so dark.

I'll never see my child again. Never see her . . .

'Shut up shut up shut up shut up.'

I'd told myself I was done with the rose-thistle, but I swigged it now. Make me numb, I thought, make them silent. Make them stop, take them away, end this. End this. But it didn't end it, and only drove my heart to hammer harder.

As I ascended towards Redwinter, the snatterkin were silent, as if they sensed the company within me. As my mind whirled I felt the murdered dead, unclean, on the inside, and now and again a name would come unbidden to my mind. Douglan. Bethswilde. Hal. One of them spoke in a language I didn't understand. One of them just sent images into the back of my mind; an overturned cart, a gooseberry bush, a stable.

'You deserved it,' I said. 'You all deserved it, you pieces of shit.'

The anger wasn't enough to drown them out. The rose-thistle blocked nothing. I set my heels to Yangyn and rode harder.

Murderer.

'Shut up!'

My head was spinning as I reached the greathouse. I stumbled past startled servants, crashed into the newel post at the foot of the stair and hung there, like the worst drunk I'd ever had on me. My eyes were losing focus, my body had grown heavy. In a fit of bitter fury I'd drawn in something that I hadn't understood, I saw that now. Too much, too soon, reckless and stupid stupid stupid. I'd tested this power on insects. Twenty people clamoured inside me like a squawking chorus of gulls. My mind kept trying to ask me, *what have you done?* I bit down on it, clamped it between my teeth. I had done what I needed to, hadn't I? I sought breath. I could barely find it.

I hadn't known what I intended to do with this power. I'd just needed to feel like I could change something, do something, do anything to be on the winning side for once. When I took it, I hadn't been thinking clearly, already grieving Ulovar, and I'd done something terrible. Something that I could never take back. I was just what it was feared I would become. An unstable vessel filled with other people's souls.

The Ashtai Grimoire would know the answer. It had to be the answer. I'd never understood how it worked, why it showed me what it did, or why it had chosen to come to me. But it responded to need, and I had need of it now. I couldn't live like this. The broiling, anguished souls would drive me from my own mind.

'Draoihn Raine, do you need assistance?' Tarquus asked. The First Retainer reached out to support me but I surged away from him. I couldn't let him touch me, couldn't let anyone touch me. What if it bled out, into him? What if he could feel the nightmare I'd drawn into myself? What if I tore his soul out by accident? I didn't know what I was doing. I'd never known.

'Get away from me!' I snapped. Face the stairs. One foot after another.

'I shall summon—' Tarquus began, but I snarled, a high, whipping sound, and forced my unsteady feet onto the stairs.

'No!' I barked. 'I don't need help. Go away.'

I didn't look back, taking deep breaths as I moved one stair to the next. Up the huge staircase, to the landing, down the corridors, until I found my room and slipped into its silent, manicured interior. Two ghosts were waiting for me, a dead man and a dead woman. They were with me, inside my eyes. They stared at me, ire and despair on their ethereal faces.

I got low and rolled back the carpet. There was a loose board here, beneath which I kept the book hidden, safe. It was here somewhere, but—which board was it? I dug my nails between the planks. Had someone fixed it? None of them gave. I heaved upwards, iron nails protesting as I drove down with my legs, up with my arms and tore it free.

Murderer.

I looked into the hole. There was nothing but darkness; wooden beams; dust; mouse droppings.

It wasn't here.

It wasn't here.

Someone had taken it.

I went to the bookshelf. Could I have been so stupid as to put it away? The alternative was too terrible to contemplate. If I was discovered—if anyone had found me out—oh no, Light Above, not like this. Not like this. I checked each of the books like I'd gone blind, or as if the Ashtai Grimoire could somehow be hidden within. Was I making a mistake? Was it possible? Red cover, green cover, white, beige—which was it? I couldn't even remember. What did it *look* like? Did—did I not even know what it looked like? It wasn't any of them. They were just normal books, none of them cold beneath my fingers. I let out a low wail. I had to be making a mistake.

I ripped books from the shelf, one after another, leaving them scattered across the room like broken birds. The shelf empty, I turned to my clothes' chest and began pulling out garments. The ghosts watched me. More of them accumulated, accusing eyes on me as I let out little gasps of exertion. Not there. The bed? Maybe it was in the bed? Panic roared in my ears as I ripped off the sheets and hurled them at ghosts as I felt the hot and cold waves of absolute fear wash over me.

I threw myself back down beside the ripped-up floorboard. I reached down into the hole, into the blackness, fumbling left and right in case some rat had dragged at it. Nothing. Nothing. But as my hand scraped back across the dust—I felt something on the cold wood. I brushed the dust and scat aside and there it was. An incision, cut deep into the wood. A line with a flicked end. A line like a cat's back with its tail stood on end. Not far off a right angle. A wrong angle.

No no no no no no no no.

The churning of ghosts grew louder, building to a tumultuous roar. I buried my face in my hands, then raised my face and let out a shriek that caused even the ghosts to flinch. They stilled for a moment, and when I opened my eyes I was staring into the mirror.

Who was the girl I saw there now? Hair scarred white, face scarred with a knife's blade. Too thin, too afraid, too broken. But in my hands I held the book. Mirror-Raine held it between her hands. It didn't have a cover. It had never had a cover. I knew it so well, had spent so many hours trying to discern its meanings.

I don't think it's anything, the Queen of Feathers had said. And as if thinking of her had changed my reflection, I saw the wreath of black crow's feathers sitting above my ears in my reflection. I saw the lights of the distant universe in my eyes. My hand trembled as I slowly raised my hand to the scar on my face. I closed my eyes. Cold fingers touched the line that marked me from jaw to nose, with its cat-tail, wrong-angle flick, and I felt it beneath my fingertips: dry, delicate paper. It was my skin. *It was under my skin.*

'Oh no,' I whispered. And then a great, mournful cry escaped my throat, and I screamed my terror into the devastation I had wrought.

'Shhh.'

Strong arms wrapped me, the smell of horse and old leather breaking through. I struggled against the binding grasp, my eyes held fast shut. This was it, this was them coming for me. To denounce me, to bind me to a pyre, to lay forth an unmeetable challenge and that would be it. I could fight them, but I couldn't prevail. Not against Redwinter. Not against the truth.

'Raine,' Sanvaunt said into my ear. 'You're going to cause another fire.'

I struggled against him, but he was strong and my efforts had only half my strength. I gasped.

'I can't take it,' I said. 'It's killing me.'

'Listen to my voice. Listen to my trance. Fall into the rhythm with me.'

'It's not Eio,' I said. I could hear his First Gate pulsing, open and deft in its steady beats. But I couldn't tell him the truth, that it was Skal that lay within me, the sixth trance beyond the Gate of Death. It was Skal that was going to tear me apart. They were all around me now, all twenty of the souls I'd drawn into myself. Akail stood at their centre, leading the way. Getting closer. Coming for me.

'It's not Eio,' Sanvaunt said. 'But it's easier if I use it to guide you to me. Listen. Hear the trance behind the First Gate.'

'It's all lost,' I said. 'I'm lost.'

'Trust me, Raine,' he said. 'Just trust me, for one damned moment. Just trust somebody.'

His First Gate was there, *dhum-dhum-dhum, dhum-dhum-dhum*, but behind it there was something else. Something deep. Something that pulsed with heat. Another trance, something bigger, stronger, like vast rocks being dragged over one another, growling in the heat of a forge.

'I know you can hear it,' he said. 'Because I can hear the tunnel inside you too. I've heard it since the night we fought the Mawleths together. The night you awoke this inside me.'

'What is it?'

'I've spent most of a year trying to figure it out,' he said. 'I almost burned down the greathouse because I couldn't control it. I set fire to the North-bank. It's a Gate. One I shouldn't have.'

'Then what is it?'

'Balance,' he said gently. He held me tight. 'Open your eyes. Look.'

The great boulders were grinding against one another, the First Gate was beating away, and the shades of death clustered closer, their voices a dirge. I didn't want to see them anymore. Didn't want to see any of it anymore. But I couldn't go on like this. I couldn't be so very alone. I opened my eyes.

When I saw the mirror, I wanted to scream. Sanvaunt stood behind me, his arms wrapping me, but he was not the Sanvaunt I had fallen in love with. His eyes were forge-bright voids of fire. His skin was cracked, and within him glowing lava set bright tracks across him, like the grandmaster's broken skull. No crow-feather wreath for him—a coronet of fire played around his head. Within his grip I was ghostly, a pale white thing with pits of stars for eyes.

'What does it mean?' I stuttered.

'It means we are what we are,' he said. 'That's all. It's hard to control it. But we can do it. Trust yourself. Find it within. Don't think too hard, it's just like moving another limb. Just breathe yourself in. Be what you need to be.'

'But I've made so many mistakes,' I said. 'I've ruined everything. If I let myself be what I'm meant to be, I'll destroy everything. And I don't know if I can stop myself.'

'There are no mistakes, only lessons,' Sanvaunt said. 'Everything is one, anyway. I'm you, and you're me. We're not really divided by anything. That night when you entered the Blackwell, you worked something there. Something that opened you up truly to who and what you are. You called to yourself. And when you did, you opened this in me too.'

The flames played around his brow, a burning crown.

'It's Vie,' I said. 'The Fifth Gate. The Gate of Life.'

'It's Vie,' Sanvaunt said. He was still holding me, his warm, hard body pressed against my back. 'I couldn't control it until I accepted it. I know it shouldn't be possible, but this is what happened. This is who I am. Whatever you've done, whatever you are, this power you hold is part of you. You can't deny it or drive it away. Swallow it down. Hold it in.' He gripped me tight. 'The soul-fire is a manifestation of life itself. I've struggled to command it, but it can be done.'

'It's different,' I whispered. 'You haven't seen what I've seen.'

'No, Raine,' Sanvaunt said. 'We're joined somehow. You gave me this, and as the fire grew inside me, I've glimpsed its reflection in your eyes. But the tunnel you stare into doesn't own you, or control you, any more than the fire forces me to burn.'

And I realised, on that terrible night when I kissed Esher and broke everyone to pieces, I'd seen the fire in his eyes too.

'You hold life in your hands,' I said. Tears ran down my face, dripping onto his arms. 'I can only ever hold death.' I let out a sob. 'I'm so lonely.'

'I understand what you're going through. And you're not alone. Just breathe, and be. Let it in, and let it go. They're the same.'

It was quiet now.

The spirits were gone. I could feel them, somewhere inside me. They were still there, but muted now. Gone from vision, repressed into something else. Part of me, maybe.

'What are we?' I asked.

'We're whatever we always were,' Sanvaunt said. He let go of me, and turned me to face him, taking my hands in his. My palms were so sweaty. 'I'm so sorry this happened to you. To us both. Neither of us wanted it, or deserved it.'

'But I was guided here,' I said quietly. 'I had a book.'

'However we find our way to ourselves is exactly what we needed,' he said.

'Did you have a book?'

'I had Master Firean. Only I didn't. I've spent weeks looking for him. But he was never really there at all. It's the power, Raine. It's Creation. Some aspect of the Seventh Gate.'

'The Seventh Gate is only theoretical,' I said.

'Or maybe it's everywhere, all at once,' Sanvaunt said. 'I don't have all the answers, only what I've been able to figure out. And I barely grasp most of that. I just know that you won't find the answers out there. They're inside you. They've always been inside you.'

'I'm so sorry I hurt you,' I said. Silly, to be thinking of that at a time like this. On a day like this, when my head was spinning, with everything reeling around me.

'And I'm sorry I didn't come to you with this sooner,' he said. 'I should have. I just didn't know what to say. I was causing so much harm, I didn't want it all to be true.'

A silence dropped between us. He knew what he'd just said.

'It's easy to accept the power of life inside you,' I said.

'We call it life, but it's more than that,' Sanvaunt said. 'It's healing, but it's renewal. That's why it manifests as fire, a force of change. I set the greathouse ablaze and I didn't know why. And then—I burned the Northbank. Every strong emotion threatened to unleash this force within me. I didn't mean to do it, but I became a danger to everyone around me. Until I let it in.'

The Northbank had burned because I'd stood him up. Even in inaction I'd caused harm.

'It's not the same, is it? You know what I am.'

'I won't say it,' he said. 'I don't know what to think of it. But I know you're not an enemy.'

'You're wrong,' I said. 'I'm everybody's enemy.' I let go of his hands and took a step back. 'You're not going to turn me in, for what I am?'

'I know that I should,' he said. 'But I haven't, have I?'

How that conflicted him. I could see it in his face, the way he couldn't look at me. I was Sarathi, every Draoihn's sworn enemy. I didn't just see the dead, I manipulated them. I summoned them. I was halfway into the tunnel myself. At Sanvaunt's heart there was honour, and duty, words cut into the stone of his being. By allowing me to go on, he was betraying his very core. I was dangerous, and that he knew meant he was endangered just by my existence.

'You haven't told anyone else? About the Fifth Gate? You should tell them. They'll be happy for you.'

'No,' Sanvaunt said.

'Why not?'

'Because nobody has the Fifth without someone close to them being open to the Sixth. They don't teach us that, but I know it. I feel it. Creation balances itself. And if I let them know, powerful people will ask those questions.

They'll ask them in ways that mean we can't refuse to answer. And I won't betray you. Not ever.'

I thought of Grandmaster Robilar and her sister. *There were those that suspected my sister of practising forbidden arts.* When I'd opened myself up to the Sixth Gate, I'd awakened this power in Sanvaunt. And two centuries past, when those Draoihn had learned of Robilar's Fifth Gate, they must have known it had brought forth the Sixth Gate in Alianna.

Take it from a man who had to end his own wife's madness.

Draoihn Kelsen, the king's healer, had killed his own wife. Which meant the Fifth had opened within him when she opened the Sixth. And he'd known, and he'd killed her for it.

'The grandmaster knows what I am,' I said. And though my mind was reeling, I wondered whether there was an accident awaiting me too. 'She's using me. As a weapon.'

Sanvaunt bristled. He took the information in, then breathed out slowly. 'That's what they'll make of us, if we let them.'

'I'm sorry,' I said. 'I'm sorry for all of it.'

Sanvaunt took a step back. He looked at his feet.

'So am I. Maybe when the battle comes none of this will matter, one way or another. I have to focus on that now. Protecting the Crown. That's what we swore to do. We can figure out a path through this when the succession is confirmed.'

He looked up to me, then around at the destruction I'd wrought across the room.

'I know, I know,' I said. 'I'll tidy it up.'

'Best not to leave it to the servants.'

'I know!'

He gave me a sad smile. It was all different now, I knew that. The secret we trusted each other with was too big for things to ever go back to normal.

'Will you be all right?'

'It's quiet now,' I said. 'It's all so quiet.'

Sanvaunt nodded solemnly. And then he left.

I was alone again. The world felt oddly silent. Perhaps that was better.

33

It was quiet, inside. There were no dreams, and I slept a night alone, without screaming.

I was what I was. That was all there could be to it. Now that I knew it, it was all there inside me. There had never been an Ashtai Grimoire at all. I was the magic, and the magic was me. The Queen of Feathers was a part of it too: she was a part of me. She had existed before me, but maybe I'd existed before me as well. Everything was one. Wasn't that what we believed? And somehow it was bound to Sanvaunt as well, and that was oddly comforting.

Two days until it would come to a head. It wasn't much, but it was something. I knew I had to make amends, I just didn't know how. So I did what I always did when I could finally accept that I'd been in the wrong. I took the hurt in as part of me, and I cleaned it and polished it and looked at what was left beneath the dirt my own mind clogged around it. And what I saw was me, and Esher, and Sanvaunt, and the tangle that I'd made of everything between us.

I'd covered myself in distance, and in anger. I'd let the easy feelings rule me: anger and fear are the same when you look at them closely. One acknowledges that you're weak, makes you feel small and tells you to hide. The other fills you out, refuses to acknowledge the truth of how you feel, covering it in bluster and indignation. It was all fear, in the end, and I was ready to let it go.

Two days, until everything would change. But I was changed already.

I visited Ulovar the next morning. I didn't know what to expect. Part of me wanted to see him sitting up in bed, recovering, stronger and getting back to ordering everyone about. I already knew that killing Akail had made no difference. He was worse. I would need the Eyes again if I was to see the worm that wrapped him, draining him, but somehow I knew it was still there. Perhaps it was the souls that bubbled and writhed within me, keeping me closer to the in-between world. Alianna had been wrong. I'd brought back the spirit of a woman who'd been dead for a hundred years,

I'd destroyed my enemies, and it still hadn't brought back the man who'd taken me in when nobody else had wanted me. It seemed like death wasn't the answer I'd been hoping for. It seldom is.

I needed more time to figure out who'd done this to him. But I'd had time, and it had all run out. We don't get to solve every mystery. People rarely know who looses the arrow that kills them. Perhaps I'd find a way to take revenge, but Ulovar would still be gone. The hourglass was all but done.

Ulovar slept most of the day now, his laboured breathing and bed-sweat smell filling the room with the decay of a life he'd lived hard, but proudly. I sat with him and held his hand, though I knew he wouldn't be able to feel it.

'I've let you down,' I said. 'I should have done more. Should have worked all this out, or found some way through it. But I couldn't. I thought I'd done it. Thought I'd understood, but I was wrong. And for that, I'll always be sorry.'

I talked openly, quietly. I told him who and what I was. And maybe there was a little part of me that hoped he would hear me. That I could convince him, resting in this dormant state, that I hadn't done wrong. That there'd been no choice but to be what I was. I knew it now. I'd accepted it. I wanted the world to accept it with me, even though it never could. Ulovar didn't stir, and in the end I left him there just as he'd been as I entered, wondering whether this was the last time I'd see him alive. I didn't say goodbye. I'd only just found him, and this place, and the friends I'd made and lost, and I wasn't ready to give it up completely. Not just yet.

· · · · · ·

I'd made a promise to the grandmaster. On the morrow I'd ride out, and I'd get close to Onostus LacAud and I would kill him. He deserved it well enough. If it hadn't been Akail's curse, maybe it had been Onostus's all along. But I didn't think so. Still, I'd do it because nobody else was going to, and I was able to do it. That was all I had left to offer.

I couldn't find Castus, and nobody could tell me where he was. Probably for the best; I needed an early start, and would be riding out by dawn's first light. A delegation would be waiting for me. They wouldn't know what I was all about, in truth. They wouldn't even be able to see what I was doing, if I worked things right. There was no book to guide me now. I'd just have to work it out myself. I'd been doing it all along.

Killer Raine. Raine the Killer. Raine the Assassin. Raine the Sarathi.

It wasn't anything new, but it felt different. There'd always been circumstances directing my hand, one way or another. I sat up on the high tower of the LacNaithe greathouse, sloshing a half-empty bottle of whisky around, sloshing some of it inside me when the feeling took me. It tasted bitter that night, like the promise of fun had been sucked out of it somewhere during the passage of days.

'What are you doing up here all alone?'

It was Ovitus, dressed in a doublet and puffed sleeves more fit for a ballroom than the night air.

'Thinking,' I said. 'Trying not to think. Where's your dog?'

'Sleeping,' he said. He came across and sat down beside me. Our legs hung out into the nothing, and I remembered a time I'd sat here with Ulovar doing much the same once before. The young heir was coming to replace the dying old man in every walk of life, like he'd taken his wardrobe and begun altering every garment. That was the way of inheritance, I supposed. You stepped up into someone else's old shoes and walked them along a different road. 'Did you speak to Esher?'

'What's it to you?'

'Because we're friends. Because she looked like she'd been crying.'

'I don't think she has any tears to shed over me,' I said.

'Maybe not anymore. But it's for the best, really. She might turn her sheets that way, but I know you don't.'

I coughed on a swig of whisky.

'What makes you think you know anything about how I turn my sheets?' I asked.

'Because we're the same,' he said. 'We've always been the same, right from our first meeting.'

'I don't see how you can possibly come to that conclusion,' I said. 'Ridiculous.'

'We both know what it's like to be outsiders,' Ovitus said. 'And I know what you're thinking. That I was born to wealth, and you weren't. That I have titles and you don't. And yes, our lives have been immeasurably different. But I wasn't made for all this. You know that, deep down. I've had to adapt to it, to be someone different, just as you've had to be someone different. And we've both had to make hard choices when they were needed. The choices that keep everyone else going. Choices that lead to a righteous path, even if they aren't what we wanted.'

I shifted uneasily.

'What hard choice have you ever had to make?'

He shrugged and held out his hand for the whisky bottle. I let him have it. It tasted bad anyway.

'I was happy as I was,' he said. 'And I know, I was fat, and people mocked me for it. And I wasn't good at holding the First Gate, I wasn't under any illusion about that. But I didn't want to have to make myself into someone else to be accepted. I know you understand that, because it's the same for you.'

Maybe I'd swigged on the bottle more than I'd thought, maybe it was stronger than I was used to, but that made my head swim a little.

'You have everything now,' I said. I gestured out at the lights of the city, down in the river valley below. 'Respect. Control. You're marrying a beautiful, intelligent woman whom you love.'

'Was I respected when the grandmaster humiliated me?' Ovitus said, and there was a hot edge of bitterness in his voice. 'Would they respect me if I'd kept to quiet pursuits? Why should I value respect thrown at me for having run laps of the practice court and living on boiled fish? People are worth more than their appearance, and yet it's what I'm judged on, just like anyone else.'

'I guess there's truth in that at least,' I said, holding out my hand for the bottle. He took another swig and passed it back.

'You of all people mustn't think I'm a fool, Raine,' he said. 'Love? It's a romantic story, and my uncle thought me fool enough to be deep in the dark about it all, but Mathilde was going to "love" me no matter who I was when I turned up, and I was always going to claim the same. The alliance had been in the works for years, Ulovar just thought that it was better I didn't know. He thought I'd be too weak to accept it if I did. Respect born out of nothing isn't respect at all. It's a trick. Just a terrible, stupid trick played on us. I know what love is, and I've felt it more strongly than most. I just do a better job of hiding it, because I do what I must for everyone else.'

I felt like I was having my own thoughts cast back at me, stolen from my mind and turned into something far less grand than they'd felt as I stirred them around in my own tangle. They felt fouled.

'I thought you were residing down in the city,' I said. Change the subject. Ovitus had always been one to wax lyrical about his great capacity for love. It just reminded me of the nasty little lie he'd told about me, and the lack of apology. I'd thought him much changed, but now he was saying he'd not done it all out of a desire to do better. He just wanted the world to see him as having done it. I thought about all the times he'd professed his love for Princess Mathilde. So earnestly, so deeply, it had been running from his pores. But it wasn't true. It wasn't real. How casually he lied about something so very, very important.

'I came to see my uncle,' he said. 'One last time.'

'He might hold out a while longer.'

'No,' Ovitus said. 'No, I don't think he will. A day, two at the most. I can feel it in my bones. He'll be gone soon.'

It was an ugly thought on an ugly night, with ugly business to attend to in the morning.

'So you didn't want the position,' I said. 'You didn't want the respect, and you didn't fall in love. Why do it then? Why go through all this, for something you never wanted in the first place?'

'I never said I didn't want those things,' he said. 'Just not in the way you're thinking of them.' He took a breath, steadying himself, and rose to his feet. Took a few paces back towards the stairs. But he lingered there, not with me, not quite gone. I could feel his eyes on me.

'What?' I said.

'I'd give it all up. If you asked me to.'

'Give up what?'

'All of it,' he said. 'Mathilde. The battle to come. You despised me because I wasn't honest with you. I know you did, you don't need to deny it. But I'm being honest with you now. I can make it all stop. I can back Onostus LacAud down. I can call off the marriage. I can change this country for the better. I only need you to ask.'

I felt a deep cold, rising from the night air below, reaching for my feet. Flowing up my ankles, into my shins.

'Don't say that,' I said. A great weight heaved in my gut, trying to topple me off and away into the darkness. 'It's not my decision. And you can't ask that of me.'

'We've all made sacrifices,' he said. 'It's you, Raine. Of course it's you. It's always been you.'

I pulled myself back from the ledge before I fell, and faced him beneath the dark, starlit columns.

'That's just not true,' I said. 'You don't even know what you're saying. What are you trying to say?'

'I'm speaking my heart,' he said. Looked down, coyly, like he'd brought me a string of summer flowers and was suddenly embarrassed.

'You don't love me, Ovitus,' I said. 'You don't even know me. Please, tell me it's not Liara all over again. Tell me that you aren't thrusting this—this bullshit onto me now. You're marrying a fecking Brannish princess. Your alliance has brought half the country to war. And you're saying you'd just drop it if—if what? If I ran away with you?'

'Don't be cruel, Raine,' he said. 'I'm just a man.'

I laughed. It was a cold sound. Cruel, even. But this was what he offered in place of apology.

'I thought you'd changed,' I barked at him. 'Despite everything, I thought you'd grown up. What you're saying—it's fantasy. Nonsense, unfair, mean fantasy, where you're playing the lovelorn hero. You don't even expect me to say yes! You're just . . . just doing it because it makes you feel dramatic. The things you've put in motion—you couldn't even stop them if you tried. Don't for one moment—not even one fecking moment—try to tell me that it's down to *me* to change this.'

Ovitus stood straight-backed, and I saw him then. Deep in his eyes, bright points of distant stars caught in them. The real Ovitus. Not the dandy, sim-pering young romantic he'd seemed when we first met. Not the cool-headed businessman, not the mail-clad warrior lord he'd presented with a princess on his arm. He masked it all so well. He hid it from everyone beneath a guise of soft gentility, but there it was, stark as nails and hard as the hammer beneath. Pure, manipulative self-obsession. It was his core. It was what he was.

'I'll do it,' he said. There was a different timbre in his tone. He wasn't pleading, or lost in wisps of dreamlike romance. He was punishing me. Punishing me, for revealing who and what he was. His humiliation drove him. 'I'll make it all stop. I'll be Van LacNaithe soon enough. I'll be Drao-ihn, and a councillor as well. I'll marry into the Brannish royal family, I'll see my heirs in Redwinter and have my candidate on the throne. But there'll be blood. Many people will die. But it doesn't have to be. Just speak the word. I'll send Mathilde away. I'll give Onostus a deal so good he'll head back to the north thanking me. No battle. No war. All you have to do is admit it.'

'Admit. What?' I bit each word off like it was a snake between my teeth. But he wouldn't say it. *Love me. Love me, and show everyone that* you *were the liar. That we were lovers on the road.* And in his self-adoring delusion, he may even have believed it to be true.

He wouldn't do it, of course. He wouldn't truly discard everything he'd worked for. Not with so much power on the table. He just wanted me to say it.

I wanted to call him a hateful, weaselling shit pile. I wanted to rip the lies from his tongue and hold them out like a spine torn from the serpent he'd always been. But I was suddenly so very aware, in a way that perhaps I never had been before, that he had the power to blast me from the tower if he so chose. A wave of fire. A strike of lightning. Maybe just a strong gust of wind.

'What's done is done,' I said. I strode towards the stairs, and he stood at their head, blocking the path. 'Let me down.'

Ovitus regarded me coldly. Had he got what he wanted from this after all? What had he really imagined would have happened? The truth, I thought, was that he didn't really think about it that way. It wasn't important to him what happened; only how I was made to feel.

'As you wish,' he said. But he lingered three heartbeats too long before moving out of my path.

I loved Sanvaunt, and I loved Esher, and I'd hurt them both. Ovitus loved only himself, and he didn't fear hurting everyone around him to make us bow down before it.

I would ask myself one day why it took me so long to see it in him. He'd revealed his colours long ago, had shown me who he was. We like to believe that people can change, because it lets us believe that we can change as well. But whatever the colour of his exterior, his core had always been rotten, and I was Sarathi, and on the morrow, I'd break a man's soul.

34

It seemed the first time in months that clouds gathered at the horizon, but the sun was unrelenting.

The delegation formed up early. A show of power, set to persuade a fool that he faced more than he could possibly hope to defeat. And Onostus was a fool. He may have had the numbers, but the grim-faced Winterra watched us ride out, and I thought anyone who went up against that mass of strength was asking for their head to adorn a pike along Onebridge before long.

Ovitus rode at the fore, warriors who'd served his uncle behind him. Alongside him, the commander of the Winterra, Lassaine LacDaine, with ten of her best. And then there were the Draoihn of LacNaithe, and none of us looked happy to be there.

Sanvaunt. Esher. Liara. Jathan, Gelis, Adanost. Only Little Maran had been left behind. Most of us had been apprentices only a few weeks before, and now we rode with the delegation that would find the words to prevent bloodshed within a few miles of Harranir's walls, or fail, and see them sullied. Princess Mathilde had wanted to come; I'd heard her arguing the point with Ovitus even as we prepared to ride out. But even if he was a self-serving, manipulating sack of shit, Ovitus was right about one thing: her presence would only inflame the situation. She marked out everything that Onostus, fool though he may have been, sought to oppose.

Esher's new Winterra-stamped armour looked majestic. It suited her. My heart couldn't crack any more, or it would have fallen apart entirely.

The sun turned my armour hot to the touch and I dripped and steamed within. I rode hooded, Midnight stowed securely beside me. Worms had uncoiled in my stomach, long and slow, rising up to grip me around the shoulders. We were riding into the enemy. This was not safe. But I had sworn an oath, and it was my duty to Redwinter to put an end to this. If I could.

The grandmaster had anticipated it, I'd come to realise. Tutoring me, building me up. Showing me her tragic past. She'd looked for a way that she could dispose of Onostus LacAud, to bypass his wards and his guile, to find a chink in the armour of spells he'd spent a lifetime weaving around himself. And in me, she'd found an arrow she could launch into his chest. She'd found the answer to her problem. I was the unspeakable enemy of the Draoihn, Sarathi, the most damned of the damned, and yet she was wielding me as if I were a scalpel with which she could cut out a disease.

I knew I was being used, but in the end, it didn't really matter. Our ends were the same, but I'd watch my back when all was done. She'd told me herself, there were no rules for her. Would she allow another to exist alongside her who was as unfettered as she was? I found it hard to believe these days. Her purposes were her own. I had trusted too many, too easily, too eagerly. I wouldn't make that mistake again. What had it got me? I was no happier now. The family I thought I'd found had collapsed around me, a spun-sugar castle melting beneath the sun.

Nobody spoke to me on that long ride. I'd burned too many bridges. I had thought I knew loneliness, once. Had thought I knew what it meant to be numb. I wished for that scar Ulovar had placed in me now. Wished it would slice down into my mind and take away all the pain I'd brought down on myself. Because in the end, for everything that had happened, it had been me that did it. I would have to stand alone. I was always alone.

The sun, the wretched sun, gave us no respite, even as the clouds inched across the blue.

The parley point had been well chosen for symbolic value. A thin grove of trees atop a hill some miles from the waiting northern army, a place that great duels had once been fought, their trunks still bearing old runic marks. No duel of swords today, but a clash of words. Despite everything that had happened, I still had to hope that Ovitus would succeed. My goal was easy enough: Ulovar's former apprentices would be exchanged as hostages. The others weren't really needed, but to send me alone would be too blatant. A deal would be made, and we would return to the north with Onostus. That was why they had brought us. I didn't know if the others realised it yet, but Esher's fear of joining the Winterra had been misplaced. Ulovar's wards would be the bargaining tool to secure the peace. Exchanging hostages was common enough and we'd be treated well, but living in an enemy's lands was no reward for their success in the Testing.

And when the time was right, I would send Onostus LacAud down the tunnel. He'd pay for what he'd done.

And then—then I thought, it would be time for me to disappear. I couldn't return to Redwinter after that. The grandmaster had her use for me now, but I was a constant risk for her. If I revealed that she'd known all along she'd be as damned as I was, and I didn't think she'd take that risk. And so this would be it for me. I'd do my part. I'd take my revenge. And I'd find some quiet life somewhere else, somewhere I could make a better kind of difference. Somewhere that I wouldn't hurt anybody.

Onostus had arrived before us. We numbered twenty-five, and his people the same. I half-recognised some of them; some of them were Draoihn I'd seen about Redwinter, those with strong ties to the north. Onostus was not without support. The man himself, Arrowhead, had come wearing his namesake coat of bent and broken iron points. He sat beneath an awning that spanned the clearing, the sun beating down on it. Onostus looked like a man ready for a fight, though he wore no sword. He seemed ready.

We dismounted and tethered our horses. I could feel Sanvaunt and Liara drumming away in Eio, feeling around us, looking for hidden threats. A surprise attack here, taking us captive or killing the leaders, could have been enough to swing things in Onostus's favour. But the ground was well chosen, the trees thin, and unlike back at Gilmundy, we could see down the slopes around us. If any force of men approached, they wouldn't reach us until the violence was done. Arrowhead must have known that too, and frankly, must have suspected that his men would lose. The Winterra's reputation was well earned, and Lassaine LacDaine had four Gates to her name.

'Welcome,' Onostus LacAud called as he scanned our party. 'Let us talk in peace of the days to come.'

As I dismounted, I wanted to bring Midnight with me, but a strung bow was hardly to be tolerated. The souls I'd taken whispered down in some dark void inside me. I just had to feel it, I thought. But not here, and not now.

Or maybe now was the time? Maybe I should destroy Onostus LacAud and leave them leaderless. But even as I thought it, the idea was lost. Lord Braman, the warrior in the silvered face plate was there, that blank, dead face watching from the sideline. I had enough in me to kill one man. Perhaps it ought to be him.

Ovitus took the lead. He advanced towards Onostus.

'Well, Van LacAud,' he said. 'This is it then. Here we are.'

'Here we are indeed, Van LacNaithe.'

'Not quite yet,' he said. 'But soon.'

'For all our purposes, and all it matters,' Onostus said. He was smiling. I didn't like his smile. He shouldn't have been smiling. 'Who else do we have here? Lassaine, always a pleasure.' He nodded at her. She returned it, face grave. 'Your wildrose cousin, I know. And is that Liara LacShale? Ah, and the white-haired Draoihn-slayer. How she keeps popping up.'

I set my gaze to steel and tried to drill it into him. He wasn't any more fazed by it than he'd been the day the grandmaster had offered me the chance to poison him. He had to know that his blood-witch was dead by now, but what he wanted was within his grasp. Men of war are willing to accept casualties. I'd tell him that it was me, before I finished things. I wanted him to know.

'I see a number of familiar faces in your retinue too,' Ovitus said. 'But we're not here to ogle one another's allies, are we?'

'You didn't bring your lovely wife-to-be,' Arrowhead said.

'I thought it prudent she stayed at home,' Ovitus said.

'It matters not,' Onostus said. 'I've no interest in your princess, beyond the opportunity she presents.'

I knew what Ovitus had said about her. The sham of his declarations of love, his knowledge of her duty-bound obligation to marry him, all of that. But I expected him to take umbrage. I expected him to be offended on her behalf. An insult to her was surely an insult to him. But he'd always been good at this kind of thing—negotiating, thinking it through. It was what made him such an effective liar. 'I don't want to stand around in the sun all day,' Ovitus said. 'State your demands.'

Arrowhead nodded soberly.

'To business then. And quite fair. You know what I want, and you know what I'm prepared to do to get it. Firstly, all Brannish garrisons are to be removed from the north. The tithes can be paid, but my clan shall oversee them. Secondly, there shall be no more levies of our young to fight in King Henrith's endless wars.'

Ovitus nodded. He didn't say anything but he nodded. I looked to Lassaine LacDaine, who had fought in those wars for decades. But she was nodding as well.

'Thirdly, the endless nonsense of parliamentary voting for a succession shall come to an end. Harranir will have a true king, one whose heir takes his seat at the throne without nonsensical preamble and risking death for the Crown. And by doing so, power will be shared. The great clans will be united, and we shall have prosperity for all.'

'And who would that king be?' Ovitus asked.

'I do not find the southern climate to my liking,' Arrowhead said. 'But I have a granddaughter who is of age with you. Our houses can ally, and create a true royal lineage. The Crown will be taken by one who desires only to help the people. My faithful vassal, Lord Braman, shall take its burden.'

I felt the former apprentices tense around me. Onostus's demands rewrote the very nature of what Harranir was.

'The grandmaster will never stand for that,' Sanvaunt interrupted. He strode forwards. 'And neither will the loyal Draoihn of Redwinter.'

'Does the bastard speak for you, Van LacNaithe?' Onostus asked, cocking an eyebrow.

'The Crown is a burden. Those that would be king take it, to fully understand their duty,' Sanvaunt continued, but Ovitus raised one hand and then clenched his fingers hard. A call for silence.

'Who can say what lies beneath the great seal?' he asked. 'Who has ever seen it, but the grandmaster in this age?'

'This is an outrage,' Liara growled. 'Ovitus?'

'Be silent, all of you. Am I the lord of the clan, or are you?' He had a black look on his face. 'I'll hear you out, LacAud.'

'Princess Mathilde will remain in my protection as hostage against King Henrith's retribution,' Onostus said. 'Grandmaster Robilar, who has long outlived her time and who rules Redwinter as her personal playground, will be sent into exile.'

So. It was war, then. Onostus LacAud's demands were extravagant, impossible, and would be met with a curtain of defiance. Ovitus was feigning concentration, as though he considered them carefully. He would list his counter proposals, and I'd heard them before. Onostus would be offered money for the north, subsidies to keep his people through the times of hardship and famine that plagued them. He would give up his seat on the Council of Night and Day, but would keep his Draoihn title. He would receive more seats on the bench in parliament, and rich estates to add to his own. Money, and power. That's what it all came down to in the end, whether swords or words ruled the day.

But Ovitus said nothing.

'And what of the Winterra?' Lassaine LacDaine asked.

'The Winterra are tired,' Onostus said. 'They live in permanent exile, their blood dirtying the sands of deserts that mean nothing to them. The

Winterra will remain in Harranir, and they will enforce the peace, with you as their commander. With the grandmaster removed, the world can be whatever we make it. Together we will march into Harranir—north and south united, a place for all at the table. LacAud and LacNaithe to rule together, LacDaine to be given our highest honour.'

And we waited for Ovitus to say "no."

We waited for his counter-proposals to emerge. We waited for the carefully planned out words, the deals that had been thought through and discussed over and over.

Sanvaunt took my hand in his and leaned close.

'We need to get out of here,' he whispered in my ear.

Sometimes, when I have looked back across my life, I have thought myself an idiot. I just didn't learn. Time and time and time again, I made the same mistake. The same wretched, pointless mistake. I believed people, even after they'd shown me who they were. I still believed them.

Ovitus and Lassaine shared a look. It was brief. A foregone conclusion.

'Then it is agreed,' Ovitus said, and she nodded alongside him.

I felt Sanvaunt trying to draw me back, but I was rooted to the spot. Even after everything. Even after the lies about me, even the challenge placed before me the night past, despite all I had come to understand, I just hadn't seen it.

Ovitus LacNaithe. The traitor of Redwinter.

The grandmaster had been too sure of her position, of her power, of her mighty Winterra. I remembered Ovitus shouting at me not to attack LacAud's men, that I didn't know what I was doing. He'd gone to Brannlant, and brought back a bride he didn't truly want. Maybe he still harboured those dreams of true love. He didn't see himself for what he was.

'We have to go,' Sanvaunt hissed.

'Ovitus, no!'

Liara stepped forward. Her face was flushed with anger. She couldn't quite believe what she was hearing. Not quite.

'You stay out of this,' Ovitus said with nary a backward glance.

'I declare this discussion over,' Liara said, fury in her voice. 'This is not right. This is not legal. You have no right. The Crown is our sacred duty, and the sacred duty of the king. We swore oaths.'

'I didn't swear anything,' Ovitus said. His face twisted into something I'd never seen before. Something dark, and cruel. Something that had always been lurking beneath the surface.

'Cousin, she's right,' Sanvaunt said, releasing me and starting towards Liara. 'You're relieved of command.'

Onostus LacAud chuckled dryly to himself as the silver-masked warrior moved to stand closer to him. Ovitus wore a face like thunder.

'You think you can say that to me?' he snapped. 'You *belong* to me. Don't you see this is better for everyone?'

'Better for you, perhaps,' Liara growled. 'You and Arrowhead divide the country up between you. And LacClune? You think they'll stand for this? You think the Brannish ire will be assuaged because you hold his daughter hostage? You're going to plunge the whole country into bloody war. You think the grandmaster will go down without a fight, now, on the eve of the succession?' She looked around helplessly. Looked to Lassaine LacDaine, her rough, hard features and heavy-lidded eyes impassive as she watched her freedom unfurling before her.

'No great change was ever brought about without sacrifice,' Ovitus said. He heaved a great, heavy sigh. 'And I should know. I've sacrificed more than most.'

'What can you possibly think you've sacrificed?' Liara's voice had risen high, a desperate cry against the madness.

'More than you could possibly imagine,' he said sadly.

'Stand down, Ovitus LacNaithe. I arrest you in the name of Redwinter.'

The look Ovitus gave her had no anger within it. It was pitying. It degraded her. It told her that whatever she had once meant to him, she was nothing now.

'Silence her, LacNaithe,' Onostus said. 'I tire of the prattling of a traitor's daughter. Kaldhoone LacShale was a madman and a traitor. His daughter has not fallen far from the family tree. Why did you even bring them?'

Ovitus looked embarrassed for a moment, and in it, there was that same boyish embarrassment. That same failure to understand the people around him.

'I thought they'd come around,' he said. 'They're my friends.'

'You are banished from Redwinter, Ovitus LacNaithe,' Liara declared hotly. 'You speak for the people of Harranir no longer. Stay with your new friends. You—'

'Light Above, I demeaned myself believing I ever had any affection for you,' Ovitus said. 'You silly, fat bitch.'

And he reached out, and I felt him fling his Third Gate open wide. So sure, so deft. And it wasn't his trance. It was a trance I'd heard before. I'd heard it first back in Dalnesse, the thumping rhythm that brought down the monastery gates. I'd heard it again in the crypt when we fought side by side against Ciuthach, and again the night of the fire in the greathouse.

It wasn't his. It didn't belong to him. The months of slow decay, the loss of each trance, one by one as Ulovar weakened and Ovitus's newfound power erupted inside of him. The power he wielded belonged to his uncle. Power he'd stolen, slowly, siphoning it away month after darkening month.

A curse of blood and bone. A curse of kin.

I've sacrificed more than most.

Ulovar's Third Gate boomed deep and hollow, like thunder all around us. A blinding light flared, and I staggered back, felt the heat in the air, tasted the hot-metal scent. And then I was blinking, and my vision was swimming and the gate roared all around us. And then as it came back, everything was just as it had been. Nothing had changed. People were reaching for weapons, but LacAud's voice cut out through everything.

'Hold, hold, all is well. All is well.'

Ovitus's outstretched hand smoked, grey-white streamers rising in the hot air. He looked surprised at what he'd conjured.

And then Liara toppled sideways to the ground in a clatter of scorched metal.

Esher and I ran forwards, slipping in the mud, skidding down to our knees as we reached her and turned her over. Her eyes were unfocused. Unseeing. Staring. Her skin was scorched in lightning whirls and patterns, up through her armour and across her face.

'No, no, no, no,' Esher cried. 'No, no no no no no no.' I had no words. No words at all, just a terrible pain inside me where someone else should have been.

'Flashy, LacNaithe,' Arrowhead said as he waved his people to calmness. 'Showing me a touch of your new strength, is it? You didn't need to. We're friends now.'

'I—' Ovitus said. He rubbed at his eyes. 'That wasn't—I didn't mean to.'

'What's done is done,' Arrowhead said, as if the whole affair tired him.

Esher threw back her head and howled. I felt my own scream building inside me. I felt it rising, jagged and pitted, a scream I'd been holding in so long it had strained me at every seam. Liara was dead. Ovitus had murdered her. Ovitus had betrayed us all. Sanvaunt fell to his knees in the mud beside us and cradled Liara's head. For a moment I thought I saw wings of fire behind him, imprinted on my vision for just a heartbeat.

'Don't be dead,' he gasped over the rain. 'Please don't be dead. I can fix this. Don't be dead.' But he pressed his eyes tight and nothing was the same as it had been before.

Liara's ghost rose. The sob escaped my lips. But this ghost knew what had happened. It was Esher she looked to. Esher's grief that she saw, as she reached for her with insubstantial, ghostly hands. Even now she tried to comfort her.

'May the Light Above cast you down to the rivers of Skuttis,' Sanvaunt said. 'For what you've done today. That it comes to this. That it all had to come to this. I treated you like a brother, Ovitus. I served you.'

He rose to his feet, and reached for the hilt of his sword.

'Those three at the corpse,' Arrowhead said. He pointed at us. 'Kill them. Start with the white-haired girl.'

The long-held scream welled up, tearing at my insides, and with it came the spirits of those I'd taken, the lives I'd stolen and gathered into me. And with it my rage, my fury, my spite and my grief, whirling and twisting around each other like dust devils, binding and forming into a sixth circle and the tunnel roared and yawned wide. I staggered to my feet as Liara's spirit dissolved into the wind.

'You don't fear me, Onostus, you fecking spellbound coward?' I screamed. My voice pierced into the clouds. 'You've lived your entire life in fear. You're nothing but fear. But you weren't terrified enough.' The souls rose up into me, writhing, desperate to be free of me.

'I'm protected against every weapon you could bring against me, you little savage. I know every weapon in the Draoihn arsenal, and none can hurt me,' Arrowhead said. With Liara's body broken and burned on the floor, he still managed to smirk. I drank it in. It fed my fury.

'Maybe not,' I hissed, and the clearing lit up in front of me wherever I looked, white pouring from my eyes. 'But you didn't know about this.'

I threw my head back, and I screamed.

I let it all out. Released everything I'd brought into me, and I hurled it through the tunnel straight towards him along the lines of that scream.

All my fear, all my self-loathing, all the doubt over who and what I was I abandoned as I drove every drop of my Sixth Gate against him, and against Ovitus. People collapsed clutching their heads. Onostus staggered. His arrowhead tailcoat billowed behind him as he gripped his head in a terror he'd long thought he'd put to rest.

It was called the Banshee's Wail. It had not been unleashed in this land for more than seven hundred years, but I unleashed it against him now. It filled the world.

Onostus LacAud's body buckled from the inside. Panes of skin sucked inwards, bones cracked and bent at impossible angles. One of his eyes burst, and still I screamed. The souls I'd taken flowed out of me, into the tunnel of death, down it and into him and where I forced them they made voids within his body. His hands reached out for a terrible moment, and then his jaw cracked and twisted at a right angle. A wrong angle. His own scream was dwarfed by my own, as it shredded the grass around him, tore the arrows from his coat, bones splintering loud as falling trees.

And then it ran out. Onostus, twisted and broken beyond any kind of repair, teetered on one riven foot for a moment longer, before collapsing, just a sack of broken bone and flesh. There would be no rising soul for Onostus LacAud. I had destroyed that too.

As for Ovitus . . . The warrior in the silver face plate huddled over him, protecting him with his body. He rose stiffly, and beneath him, Ovitus had collapsed, bleary, no ghost rising from him and I knew I hadn't killed him with my power. I'd have felt it. Perhaps he was wondering if he was next. Wondering why he hadn't died. He would be next, I'd kill him too if I could just . . . But I choked on my own breath. I could hardly get air into me. I had emptied myself.

The man in the silver face plate creaked to his feet. His impenetrable armour was dented and twisted. But he'd stood in the way of everything I had to unleash, and he'd taken it.

'Haven't heard that in a while,' he said calmly. The faceplate had cracked through, twisted, and he reached up to pull the helm from his head. As he pulled it off, a wealth of dark hair fell free. He had a short beard, a slender face. I'd seen him before somewhere. But he'd been wearing a pheasant feather in his cap, and if I'd had any breath left to give, I'd have lost it then.

Lord Braman. Their candidate to take the Crown.

'Sul,' I breathed. 'A Faded Lord.'

35

'Hold,' Sul stated, raising a hand to still Arrowhead's followers as they picked themselves up and dragged weapons from sheaths and holsters. His tone mimicked that of a bored aristocrat.

Nobody else understood, yet. Deep and isolating horror flowed around me like a winter river. I'd killed the wrong target.

'They killed our lord!' one of them cried, starting forwards. 'Treachery!'

'Didn't I tell you to hold?' He didn't need to glare at them. There it was, that weightlessness to his posture, an ease of being that carried more threat than any of the withheld aggression of Onostus LacAud's failed bodyguards.

'But Lord Braman,' a grizzle-bearded veteran said, gripping the haft of his axe tight. 'They have—'

'Do not question me,' Sul said. 'The LacNaithe heir is injured. Take him to the camp. The deal he made with your liege lord will stand. Let his death not be in vain.'

'But their deaths will be!'

Sul regarded me with cool, pit-black eyes. It was too big a thing to have one of the Faded stand before us. He looked so ordinary, despite his gleaming armour. He'd played his immortal, long game. But now he was coming for the Crown. My companions, my friends, all save Esher had scattered back from me. Esher knelt over Liara's body, hugging her, wails of grief rising among the steel. Everyone was armed now, and swords would rise and swords would fall and the tunnel waited hungrily for them all.

'She comes with us,' Sul said. 'The girl. We take her too.'

I was drained. I'd thrown everything I had at them, had called on a well that lay deep inside me and emptied it in a flood. Onostus LacAud's twisted, shattered body lay where it had fallen, testament to the eruption of violence and death that made me who I was. I forced myself up from hands and knees, but my legs wobbled beneath me. I could barely stand. I tried to say something threatening and dramatic, but my throat was closed and I barely made any sound at all. Staggering, I fell back to a knee in the dirt. My fingers pressed against sun-baked soil, and I shuddered. I reached out to Esher, but she just quaked and shook, howling as tears poured down to matt her hair, pattering against the armour that had done nothing to save Liara from Ovitus's spite.

A riding boot thumped down in front of me.

'I disagree,' Sanvaunt said. 'You'll have to go through me.' He'd drawn his sword. He always looked so graceful when he held it.

'Noble and courageous,' Sul said. 'I do not mind obliging you.'

The Remnant, this Faded Lord who did not belong in our world and who had played everyone like fiddles, drew his own sword. It was a beautiful thing, masterwork craftmanship turning the guard and pommel into braids of tarnished gold. The blade was rune-worked, and as he held it out to his side, a ripple passed along it, leaving a blue-white sheen of frost along the steel.

'Don't you see what he is?' Sanvaunt barked. He alone understood. At least someone else, someone able to stand, understood the threat before us. 'All of you? You don't see this thing for what it is? He's no lord of the north. He's one of the Faded. He doesn't belong here. He wants the Crown. He'll destroy you all.' He bared his teeth. 'I'm taking my cousin. Whatever influence you've placed him under, I will break it.'

'A compulsion?' Sul smirked. 'How droll.'

Everyone had heard of the Faded. Banished. Contained by the power of the Crown. We had no greater enemy. And yet he wore this simple, human face, and he'd brought us to war. This was what we Draoihn lived to defy, and yet, here they were, unknowingly side by side with a creature of unspeakable malice.

'I will end you,' Sanvaunt said. He took the guard of wrath, sword back behind his shoulder.

'You will certainly try. But you're just a man.'

'You have no conception of what I am.'

Sanvaunt began to circle around, moving towards Ovitus, but Sul stepped lightly in his way. Within the duelling runes, the two men prowled, wolves measuring one another, treading lightly, ready for the pounce.

Esher raised her face, wet and ragged with grief.

'She's dead,' she wept, her voice breaking. 'He killed her, she's dead.'

'Esher,' I said, trying to pull her up. 'We need you. I need you.'

'A Sarathi in our midst,' Lassaine LacDaine said. Her eyes were locked on me, her face pale, but she'd seen what I'd done and was reluctant to approach. 'The grandmaster's own apprentice. What more proof of Robilar's corruption did we need? Take her. She'll be tried on the pyre, as they did of old.'

And then there were more swords pointing to the sky, all of them waiting to fall. But the Winterra, for all their fabled deadliness, were as reluctant as their commander to approach me. I was emptied out. That power I'd drawn and unleashed was spent. But they didn't know that.

'She belongs to me!' Sul said. 'If you want to be spared, you'll move.'

'I do not offer you that courtesy,' Sanvaunt said. And he attacked.

I had always known he was good. He'd fought the Mawleth and lived, and now he showed us how. He tore towards Sul, an air-scorching series of cuts, reverse cuts, double thwarts thrown high, each one melding seamlessly into the next. He was fast. So damn fast and as meaningless as it was now, for half a heartbeat my heart asked me how I could ever have denied him anything. His sword clove the air before him, sending it whistling away before his onslaught.

Sul was better.

He didn't deflect, he just moved, small, tight, controlled steps carrying him backwards. And then he surged in and there was a clash of steel as the rime-coated blade parried Sanvaunt's sword aside and the thrust surged forward in the bind of blades. Sanvaunt forced it aside but the tip caught him high in the left shoulder, and he fell back. He hit the ground in a break fall, rolled back over his head and up onto his feet.

Sul smiled at him and lowered his weapon. Where the tip brushed the grass it shrivelled from the cold.

'I believe, young Draoihn, that I have your measure.'

'Not yet,' Sanvaunt said.

'Your cousin is paving the way for the future. You would do well to join him,' Sul said, though he sounded bored. Ovitus lay unconscious on the ground behind him. Nobody had moved to help him. Sanvaunt was breathing hard already.

'I'm ready to go again if you are.'

Sul's thin lips cracked a smile. A smile that said we were nothing to him. He'd lived a thousand years and more, had seen our lives flicker past him like moths fluttering to the light. He held no anger, no hatred for mortals: we were too far beneath his notice for that. He wanted the Crown. He wanted to take its power and shred the veil between our world and the Night Below, to bring back the Faded in their glorious, nightmarish power.

'As you wish,' Sul said.

I tried to pull at Esher, but she just shuddered and wept. For her, there was no world beyond Liara's body. She hadn't faced this grief before, not as I had. She hadn't made herself hard as stone, encasing her gentleness in a ring-wall of granite. I loved her for that. Esher, Sanvaunt, I loved them both and it seemed that maybe whatever love existed between us would all be ending here, within this thin place of trees, and sorrow and death.

If someone was going to save us, it had to be me. I pushed up, and began to back towards the horses.

'You're going nowhere,' Lassaine LacDaine snarled. She had an axe in her left hand, a war hammer in the right. The men under her command outnumbered the former apprentices of Clan LacNaithe two to one, and they were older, they were battle-hardened, and they looked like they gave no shits about killing any of us.

'I don't know what's happening, but Raine's a good person,' Jathan said, moving to cut Lassaine off. Adanost and Gelis closed ranks beside him as I backed away.

'You're fools,' Lassaine said. 'Don't you see what she is?'

Jathan pushed back that thick, dark swathe of curls that had turned the heads of so many ladies. He tried to put forward his best cocksure charm, made pale by the horrors already unleashed. It was his only real weapon here.

'Come on, it can't be all that bad?' he said. His voice faltered.

Lassaine LacDaine's hard brows drew in tight across her skull.

'Traitors all, then,' she said. And whatever fear she had of me was forced back behind that deadly stare.

Jathan blocked her path, sword held out before him, menacing her with the point. And so she launched forwards. Even in his First Gate trance, Jathan didn't see it coming and the axe cut down into his neck. His parry, thrown so late, batted once against her battle-worn steel with a tinny ring, and then came the blood, a wash of life that flowed out of him and over the axe head. A blankness took him, and he went down.

I ran for the horses, my legs threatening to betray me with each step. The poor beasts were terrified, hurting themselves as they sought to tear their reins free of their bindings. I had to risk a kick, getting up close to draw Midnight from her oilcloth bag, plucked the silver-moonlight string into being and my bow thrummed with welcome. Battle was well and truly joined.

Lassaine LacDaine came on like a cresting wave, swallowing everything in her path. Adanost tried to oppose her, and he died for it. Gelis howled and threw herself forward. Lassaine blocked the overhead strike, flung it aside and her counterstroke smashed into Gelis's helmet and her head snapped to an impossible angle.

Sanvaunt flowed like a stream cascading over rocks, dipping and feinting, slicing left and right. His left arm flopped away from the sword uselessly as the bluish frost crept down it, slowing him as he began to make desperate, sweeping strikes. He grew slower, flailing more with each attempt as the cold pushed down his torso. And then Sul caught his sword against his own and drove it down, the questing point biting into the mud. He reached out and gripped Sanvaunt by the throat.

'Nothing more to say?' Sul asked.

Sanvaunt spat in his face.

'Enough insults for one day,' the Faded Lord said, and his fist clenched. I heard the sound of breaking cartilage. Heard Sanvaunt's throat cracking and then he was cast backwards, sword falling limp from his hand. He made a strangled gurgling sound, trying to force anything through his ruined windpipe. It was a mortal wound. My heart, battered and bruised as it was, clenched just as hard, as if a fist had punched into my chest and crushed the love that had been growing there. I sank to my knees as Sul turned his gaze on me. I screamed my fury as I drew back on Midnight, sighting down and beyond the white-shafted, stone headed arrow. But before I could release it, a wave of oppression billowed out from Sul. The air grew dense and my strength failed. I felt the rhythmic thudding of the world all around me, even if I was too drained to open even the First Gate.

I was not the only one. Lassaine's advance faltered and her weapons clattered to the ground. LacAud's remaining men and the Winterra sagged against trees or clutched their heads. Pulses of weight filled the air, the same oppression that Ciuthach had used against us all those months ago. It had taken everything I had, everything Ulovar had, to resist it. I didn't have it in me this time.

'You're not my enemy, Raine Draoihn Slayer,' Sul said. His voice flowed through the space. 'Come. Speak with me. Let us trust one another.'

'She's Sarathi,' Lassaine gasped. 'She'll kill the world.'

'She is what she is,' Sul said. 'Just as we all are.'

'She is,' a broken voice rasped. 'But she can be more than one thing.'

Sul turned. Lassaine turned. Sanvaunt had risen. His throat glowed with a molten inner fire, the same fire I'd seen burning within the grandmaster. It flowed down from his crushed throat in arcs of burning aether, forcing the frost from his body.

'So,' Sul said as he dropped the oppression field and I could suck in a breath again. 'Fifth Gate. A heart bond. I haven't seen one of those in some time. The day is full of surprises.'

'If you think that's impressive,' Sanvaunt said, 'then you're going to love this.'

And he began to roar. His arms pulled in tight to his chest, eyes closed, as four of LacAud's men came towards him. And then he unleashed. His eyes blazed with flame, and bright eagle's wings of fire erupted from his back as his hair became a bonfire around his head. The blast washed out, and LacAud's men screamed and writhed, shadows within the flame as they howled and died. Sul was taken in the blast. For a moment he became a dark shadow, straining against a beam of blazing spirit that erupted from Sanvaunt's chest and consumed him. The oppression field fell away, and breath entered my lungs as Sul took the full brunt of the blast.

But when the fire abated and the trees' branches crackled with it, he was still standing. His clothing smoked. His sword hung loose in his grip.

Sanvaunt uncurled, his eyes pits of blazing magma, and his sword was sheathed in shimmering, pulsing golden light.

'The Anam Teine?' Lassaine said, her jaw hanging loose. 'There's no way—this boy? Impossible! Unless . . .' Her eyes switched to me, to Sanvaunt, back to me.

So she understood, at least.

'Get out of here,' Sanvaunt growled, his voice so deep it should have been bound in a pit, a guttural, demonic sound. 'I'll not be far behind.'

'No,' I said. 'I won't leave you behind. Not this time.'

He glanced over at me. His blazing eyes were full of pain, but he managed a satisfied smile.

'Then show them who you are.'

Sul came at him now in earnest. Gone, the nonchalance. Gone, the lack of respect. His blade met Sanvaunt's with a flaring clash of light and sparks showered out around them as their swords scythed the air between them.

Lassaine scrambled to her feet, grabbing her axe and hammer, and came towards me, and my first arrow was for her. I wasn't just Sarathi. I saw that now. I was also Draoihn. I was a woman. I was a person who loved, and hurt, and cried and made bad choices and good. I'd only seen the side of myself I feared. But this was who I'd been since the beginning, no matter what new understandings came to me. I was an archer.

I never knew what I was going to get with those arrows, only that they answered my call. The moonlight bow string snapped against my bracer, and the arrow spat out. Lassaine was good. Probably the best. Her Third Gate roared, and she threw up some kind of defence, but the arrow didn't care. It was made to kill other Draoihn, made to break the defences of the most savage monsters of a bygone age, and as it struck the shield there was a hard thump in the air and Lassaine LacDaine detonated. Shards of hot steel flung out in all directions, a piece of breastplate shearing into one of LacAud's men. Branches were torn from the trees, the air alive with debris.

I hobbled to Esher, and dragged at her.

'Up!' I urged, lifting her foot to Yangyn's stirrup, and with the strength left to me I pushed her up onto the saddle. Esher's whole body shook in the shock of seeing her friend die. She'd gone to some other place, a place she didn't even see me. 'Hear my voice,' I said. 'Hear it and do as I say. Hold on!'

Sanvaunt and Sul traded blows, sometimes parrying, sometimes avoiding, and sometimes they got through. No earnest sword fight lasts long. Sul's blade slashed across Sanvaunt's shoulder. A return blow clove the burning sword into the Faded Lord's chest. They each staggered back. The soul-fire was bleeding from half a dozen wounds across Sanvaunt's body, and he breathed raggedly. Sul was on the ropes too.

I had just one of the white-shafted arrows left. I looked to the Winterra, taking cover behind trees. No, it had to be Sul. He struck out and Sanvaunt reeled, liquid fire spraying from another gash. A small fern stood between me and the target, not the easiest shot, but I was done waiting for the world to give me more opportunities. Some you have to make for yourself.

The arrow launched Sul from his feet in a roar. Sanvaunt was flung towards me by the blast, rolling over and over, his body burning from wound after wound. Smoke clouded the air. As it cleared, I thought Sul was still standing—but no. He was upright, impaled on a broken branch that jutted through his midriff. His sword lay some feet away. And now, maybe for the first time in centuries, he was angry.

'Get the girl!' he barked. LacAud's followers, the Winterra, none of them moved. 'She's spent her stone arrows! Do your duty, and kill them!'

Sanvaunt could barely rise. I dragged him to the calmest looking of the wild-eyed horses, stumbling and weeping flames. The fire in his eyes had died. He was spent, and his teeth were clenched together as blood slithered through the stubble on his jaw. The horse shied, but at least it didn't kick.

'Come on,' I said to it, trying to be soothing though my voice came out like it was being dragged across gravel. 'Come on, come on, come on.' It was not easy to get him up, and Sanvaunt gasped in pain. It was no easier getting myself up behind him.

'Take them,' Sul roared, and for a moment, just a flickering moment, I saw the creature that lay beyond that short neat beard, the slim, pale face. It was an alien thing, its grey skin moist and clammy, its eyes too deep set, its ears flaring away to sharp points. And, by the Light Above, how it hated us all.

'Yah!' I lashed at Yangyn with one hand on Sanvaunt's reins and he lurched forward to the speed he had been bred for. It was all any of us could do to hang on. We rode like the hounds of hell were at our heels, and perhaps they were. For all our training, none of us could open a Gate, not First, not Fifth, nor the tunnel and the terror that lay beyond.

Fear of Sul must have been worse than fear of any more arrows. The Winterra followed for a time. I didn't think we could outpace them, but they didn't come into my bow's range. They'd seen what I'd done, what Sanvaunt had done. They gave chase, but their hearts weren't in it.

We rode, and we rode. When the Winterra had dropped back out of sight over the moor, I transferred over to Esher's horse to spare Yangyn's strength. Esher said nothing. Sanvaunt said nothing. I changed horses again. Riding behind Sanvaunt, he began to topple from the saddle and I had to hold him up. We were ten or more miles from the burning grove before we entered a dense forest where I hoped we'd lose any last vestige of pursuit.

Miles from Harranir, miles from Redwinter, and enemies everywhere.

36

The horses began to refuse my heeling. I'd well and truly blown them making our escape. Horses bred for war are not meant for hours of hard riding, they're built for explosive bursts of power. I'd pushed them well beyond their limits, though that was true of all of us.

Sanvaunt was only upright in the saddle through the strength in my arms and a careful act of balancing. He was hurt. He was really badly hurt.

Esher had said nothing. She no longer wept, but her silence was worse. Everything about everything seemed worse.

Midday was long past by the time we hit the trees, but the clouds had retreated and gave us nothing. At the least we were shielded from the sun's glare by the thick, leafy canopy. We rode in shade. The sweat that had slicked me turned cold against my skin. When I saw the hint of ruins ahead of us, I almost cried out in relief. The buildings that had stood here had been broken down long before I'd been born. They were formed of that slick dark stone that ancient Junath had been cut from. They were places of shelter, back during the rule of the Nine Devastations in the Age of Soot when acid and ash fell from the sky to drive mankind to cower below the ground for four hundred years. As I looked on those ruins, I wondered whether the wizards of the Haddat-Nir who'd mistakenly unleashed those powers upon the world had felt as I did as I let the horses come to rest. At what point had they seen the calamity that was about to unfold? Had they seen it unfurling before them as I did now?

'Esher, help me get him down,' I said.

'There's blood on you,' she said. First coherent thing she'd said since Liara went down, burned and ruined. Esher's eyes were cool and blank. She moved like someone who'd cried out every part of herself, emptied, nothing left on the inside.

I got Sanvaunt down.

'It's his blood,' I said. 'Let's get him inside.'

One of the old ruins was a dome of black rock with arched portals at either end to allow access. Sanvaunt wasn't terribly heavy, but a dead weight is no easy thing to move. We carried him into the dark. Animals had made dens here. The dirt floor was littered with scat, gathered vegetation and rubbish blown in from outside. But it was quiet. The rustle of the canopy, the calls of nesting birds were muted here. It wouldn't have been much of a place to live, but whatever sense of safety those ancient people had felt remained. I breathed out, letting some of the fear go. There was still so much inside, but even a little was an improvement.

'Do you have anything to make fire with?' I asked.

'No,' Esher said. 'Of course not.'

'Me neither. Let's just try to get him comfortable.' She nodded.

We worked Sanvaunt out of his armour. It was rent and broken in several places. By the time we'd stripped him of steel, we'd piled what had once been a suit of armour that would have bankrupted many a merchant into a heap of useless metal. Steel shouldn't have opened like that, not Draoihn steel, and not to a sword. It hadn't been an ordinary sword that had inflicted those wounds. I checked Sanvaunt's neck; the flesh looked raw, but it was full and whole and he was breathing. Other wounds across his body were similarly healed, but one had broken open on the ride, hence the blood on me.

'We should wash his wounds,' I said, but neither of us had anything to do that with.

'Look at his hair,' Esher said. She took a lock of it and drew it out. 'He has a white streak now. Like you.'

'At least it didn't all go white,' I said.

'Why does it happen?'

'Too much power too soon, maybe,' I said. 'Or maybe it's proximity to something like that thing he fought. I got mine fighting Ciuthach.'

Esher got up and rubbed at her thighs. It had been a long ride.

'I'll see to the horses. You don't have any feed for them?'

'No. I'll look for water too.'

She went out into the falling day and I was left alone beside Sanvaunt.

'Please don't die,' I said. 'Please.' He didn't answer. He was gone from us, for that time.

I'd had no time to make sense of anything yet, but now it was all flowing through me as I felt my body stiffening in the aftermath of a day. The murmuring souls inside me were gone, and I was so glad to be rid of them.

It had never felt right, or clean. I'd taken them in a moment of consuming rage, and that's never a good thing to hold onto. Sometimes we don't realise what's been eating at us inside until we're able to let it go.

Ovitus. Ovitus, you damn, broken piece of shit. I'd never thought he'd go so far. Had always believed that people fit into the society and the world around them. We do that, I thought. We imagine that everyone else is playing by the rules, no matter what we're told, no matter whether we do or not. Here I was, Raine the Sarathi, infiltrating the Draoihn, eating souls, agreeing to murder, spending days fecked out of my head on rose-thistle, digging wounds into the people around me, making plots with the grandmaster, talking to ghosts, reading books that weren't there—and I'd still somehow believed that it was just me. I was the special one. Chosen by fate, or the Light Above, or just special in some way. I was different, but I wasn't special. I looked down at Sanvaunt in the gloom. He'd been going through his own journey, quietly and secretly, as a fire had grown within him. It had manifested first when he fought the Mawleth, had burned out of him and twisted his sword into ruin while I was making my pact with the Queen of Feathers down in the Blackwell. Was that me? Had I given him this, somehow? A heart-bond, Sul had called it. I'd immersed myself into death; Sanvaunt had been given the Fifth Gate, life. And he'd struggled to control it, to learn it. He'd caused the fire in the greathouse when the mind-worm tried to turn him away. And I thought then of the day I'd failed to meet him, and the Northbank I'd been heading to had burned as well. It had been building in him all this time, and nobody had known about that either.

We all had our secrets. Some are just weirder than others.

Eventually Esher returned, and the light was fading. We had nothing to eat, and I hadn't the energy to attempt a hunt. Eio would have sharpened my eyesight up in the dark, but I didn't think I could maintain it very long. Light Above, I was tired. I rested my head back against the wall of the ruin and dared to close my eyes.

I woke in the night. Esher sat out by the entrance, her back towards me. I could hear Sanvaunt breathing. He was strong, and I hoped that soul-fire inside him was worth something even when he was sleeping. It kept the grandmaster going, so I had to hope it could do the same for him. I rose quietly, though I doubt I could have woken him, and crossed to the entrance. Esher had discarded her Winterra-imprinted armour while I slept. The night was cold.

'I was right, in the end,' she said as I sat down beside her.

'In what way?'

'I was useless,' she said. 'I froze when it mattered most. I didn't do anything.'

'There was nothing anybody could have done,' I said. 'I can't believe she's gone.'

'I don't want to talk about Liara,' Esher said. Her voice snapped like breaking stone. 'I can't think about it anymore. I just can't. It's too much.'

'Esher, I'm so sorry,' I said.

'What are you sorry for?'

'For everything.' I tried to reach out and take her hand but she took it away.

'The memory of it all feels like a blur,' Esher said. 'I was sort of aware of what was going on. Sort of not. Like the things happening all around me were a dream.'

'I'll tell you all of it,' I said. 'If that's what you want.'

'Yes,' Esher said. 'But don't start there. I want to know it all. From the start.'

I saw the Queen of Feathers then, watching us, standing apart and away among the trees. A nimbus of blue light appeared around her, but only when I put my eyes directly towards her. She shook her head as slowly as a millstone grinding. Warning me. But I didn't care anymore.

'The very start? It's a long story.'

'I don't think we're going anywhere tonight, and we've eight, nine hours before dawn. If we even have anything to go back to when it rises. So start now.'

'It started the day I was born, I think.'

'I didn't think we were going back that far.'

'But maybe you deserve to be told everything,' I said. 'I want you to know everything.'

'Fine. Start there, then.'

So I did. I told her about my birth-cord strangling me as I emerged into the world. I told her about falling, bouncing from the cliff and drowning. I told her about the ghosts I'd been able to see since that day. I told her about Dalnesse, and the Queen of Feathers, and Ciuthach, and Kaldhoone LacShale and his cult of Those Who See. Esher didn't say anything, she just listened and looked off into the dark. The Queen of Feathers didn't want me to share it. I told the truth about the Blackwell, and the bargain I'd made there: a single favour, to be redeemed at a time of her choosing, to which I was bound to agree. I told her about the Ashtai Grimoire, which hadn't been a book at all, and what the grandmaster had shown me, and about her sister, Alianna. I told her about stealing twenty souls and funnelling them into a Banshee's Wail against Onostus LacAud. I told her that I was Sarathi. And I told her other things, things that weren't part of that story but which I wanted to be free of anyway. I told her about Ulovar, and how it had felt watching his slow decline. And I told her about Castus, and finally, that drew a response from her.

'I didn't think he liked women,' she said blankly.

'He doesn't,' I said. 'And I don't feel that way about him either.'

'Then why? Why do it at all?'

'Because we didn't need each other,' I said. 'And we did. I don't understand why he needed me, or why he tries to destroy himself the way he does. He hates himself.'

'It was Matteo that broke him,' Esher said with a sigh. 'He loved Matteo so much.'

'He never talked about him.'

'No,' Esher said. 'It was before your time in Redwinter. Do you remember how Liara used to go to the LacClune greathouse to get away from Ovitus's mooning? It was around then. She told me about it. Matteo was a retainer, and he and Castus were mad for each other. They used to go out gambling, drinking, hitting that awful stuff you and Sanvaunt use. Living like there was no tomorrow. They just kind of ... existed for each other, even though Matteo was a retainer. Merovech LacClune learned of it, told Castus to stop so he could marry him off for some alliance—Onostus's granddaughter, I think. Castus just carried on, and his father cut off his money. And then the debtors came calling, because people who gamble while they're off their heads on wine and rose-thistle don't think about tomorrow, and the debts were vast. They couldn't touch Castus, so they went for Matteo.'

'What happened to him?'

'The loan sharks cut his throat, and had the body sent to Redwinter.'

'Light Above. Poor man. Poor Castus.'

'Oh, he took his vengeance on them,' Esher said. 'Castus killed sixteen people that night. Just went down to Harranir on his own, walked into their office and wiped them out. Didn't make him feel any better, but he had his revenge.'

'No,' I said. 'I don't think it made him feel any better at all.' I sighed. 'It was just easy for both of us, you know? At first it was just sleeping together. Getting to let go of it all. To blot out all the pain, and the terrifying dreams, and the need to be something to anyone else. He didn't need anything from me. I'm sorry. I know this can't be easy to hear.'

'I'm not the jealous type,' Esher said. She shrugged. 'I never wanted to put a claim on you, Raine. Not like that. I wanted you to be happy.'

'It's funny,' I said. 'I don't know that I've thought about being happy in a long while. Like it's something that skipped away from me and got forgotten. I don't think saying any of this helps. But it's true nonetheless.'

'I thought a lot about what I'd say to you,' Esher said. Like she was tired of it all. Tired of everything, now. 'I ran these conversations through my head, over and over. And then I realised they weren't conversations, it was just me ranting at you in my own head. I thought when you finally grew the nerve to speak to me I'd let it all fly out. Like somehow that would make me feel different. But now we're here, and I don't think I have the energy.'

I felt a burning at my eyes. Felt the hot push welling up behind them, that emptiness in my chest.

'Can I talk, then?' I asked, though it felt like I'd been talking for hours.

'I won't stop you,' she said. 'None of it will matter much anyway.'

'Don't say that,' I said. 'Please. Don't say it doesn't matter. Because it does, it matters now more than it ever did before, maybe.' I expected her to push back, but she didn't. She just sat with her hands in her lap, away from me, looking out into the dark. I'd come to talk, so I would, only now I found I barely knew where or how to start. So I took the direct approach. 'I didn't mean to hurt you,' I said. 'I'm not asking you to forgive me. But I want you to understand that even if I was careless, and reckless, and I wasn't thinking of anyone but myself—it wasn't about hurting you.'

She looked at me finally, one eye blue, one milk-white. She seemed so much older than me in that moment. The depth of her calm absorbed the sky around her, took control of the world.

'And yet, here we are.'

'I didn't know that you'd kiss me,' I said. 'I was confused. I was hurting, and I wasn't thinking.'

'Those can all be true,' she said. 'But that doesn't mean I deserved what I got.'

'You're so angry with me,' I said.

'Shouldn't I be?' Esher asked. 'You don't even know how much courage it took me to get to that point. I wasn't sure, you know? About you. About me. About what that meant and who we might be. And there was Sanvaunt, and I talked to you about him, tried to help you to be with him, and you rejected everything there, and I allowed myself to think that maybe—maybe—now was my time. But it wasn't. I gave you my time, and you used it to hurt him instead. For me, it was a moment where I got to realise myself. Openly, and proudly, and I allowed myself to dare. For you, it was just another way to get back at a boy.'

'That wasn't it,' I said. I couldn't look her in the eye anymore. I'd seen too much for any day, so instead I shut my eyes. 'I told myself nothing could happen. Not with Sanvaunt, and not with anyone. But that didn't mean I didn't have those feelings.'

'For him, or for me?'

'Can't it be both?' I said, blurting it out as I put my head back to the sky. I looked up into its empty dark. Nothing there was going to help me. 'I can't choose how I feel about people. And I—I—I *care* for both of you.'

'You *care* for me,' Esher said. Resigned. Sad. 'Well, Raine of Dunan, I loved you. Almost since I met you. I never loved anyone before, not like that. But it grew, and the more we did together, the more love there was. I never felt anything like it before. I can't blame you for it. It's not your fault. It's just achingly disappointing.'

'Can't you just be angry with me?' I said hotly. I couldn't bear this weary resignation. What was wrong with her, and Sanvaunt for that matter too, to accept things this coolly? Weren't they meant to call me names, to tell what I'd done wrong, to bite at me with hard words to punish me for my transgressions?

'I could,' she said. 'I was. Oh, don't think there's no anger in me, Raine. But you don't deserve my anger. You took something precious from me. I'll never get to have that moment again, and your kiss left ashes in my mouth.'

'I'm not *right*,' I said, my voice rising as her words rang like hammers against my heart. 'Didn't you hear me? I'm a light-damned Sarathi. I'm a killer. I've eaten people's fecking souls, and turned them into weapons. That's what you don't understand. That nobody understands. I'm not right on the inside, I haven't been right for a long time. I'm broken. Rotten. How can anyone want this?' I put my fingers against my head and dug my nails into my skin. 'All those times we talked about Sanvaunt, you helped me. You told me to go with him. Why would you do all that, if this is how you felt?'

Esher shrugged.

'I was your friend,' she said. 'It's what you said you wanted.'

'And all that time you wanted something else? And you didn't tell me?'

'It would have spoiled what we had,' she said. 'It did spoil what we had, in the end. If I hadn't taken a chance, we'd still have it. Nobody got what they wanted. Why spoil something that didn't need to be spoiled?'

'That's not fair on you,' I said.

'None of it was fair on any of us.'

I made my face stone. I bit down the tears.

'I'm still your friend,' I said. 'If you want that.'

She shrugged.

'We can say that, if you want,' she said. 'But nothing grows in an empty flower pot. I'm glad I got to know you, Raine. At least you made me understand some things about myself. But our story is over. I think I'd rather walk away from it now.'

'Please,' I said, and my voice cracked. 'Please, I can't bear it.'

'But I have to,' she said. 'Maybe you have to as well.' She rose with a grunt, weary limbs heaving herself upright with the weight of a world upon her. 'I'll sit with Sanvaunt a while. You keep watch.'

It is a hard thing to have your heart broken, and it had never happened to me before. Somehow, despite everything else, despite fear and wounds and souls and magic, this felt the worst.

. . . . . .

Dawn came around, as it always does whether you want it to or not. The horses wanted feeding, and we had nothing but fear and worry to offer them. I felt no benefit from having slept. We had nothing to eat, and the last of my reserves had been burned away in our mad-dash flight from Sul and his forces.

Sanvaunt finally woke up, a relief we needed. He was in a lot of pain, which he tried to ride out stoically.

'You can't just heal it all better?' I asked. He looked at me with a worn-out smile and one raised, sleepy-lidded eyebrow.

'I'm worn through,' he said. 'I need time to recover. I feel like I've run fifty laps of the city.'

I could appreciate that. Throwing all that power against Onostus LacAud had drained me dry. But not as badly as it had Sanvaunt. I knew where I could find more power if I needed it, though the thought chilled me. His power didn't come from others; he was burning himself.

'How much time?' I asked. 'Because we could really use you turning into a fiery demon man in the very near future.'

'I don't know,' he said. 'Right now, I doubt I could hold the First Gate open, let alone the Fifth.'

'What does it look like?' I asked. 'Is it a Gate?'

'Not really,' he said. 'It's more like—I don't know. Like the sky.'

'Better than a tunnel, I guess.'

'So what happens now?' Esher asked. 'We have two half-gods sitting here saying they're burned out, and meanwhile Ovitus is planning a grand coup.'

'A coup that will open up the Crown to that thing.'

'Sul,' I said. 'His name is Sul. He's the Faded Lord who nearly destroyed Grandmaster Robilar. I've seen him—only in paintings, but I don't think there's much doubt about who and what he is.'

'They were all being used. All of them,' Sanvaunt said. 'Put Ovitus in control of Redwinter, so he has access to the Blackwell. Braman already set himself up as the LacAud candidate for the throne. He just needs someone to take the Keystone from the Blackwell for him.'

'Let's walk this through,' I said. 'I've seen him close to Redwinter, when LacAud came to negotiate. What stops him just walking into the Blackwell and taking it?'

'The same wards that stop the rest of us doing it, I guess,' Sanvaunt said.

'No,' I said. 'It has to be more than that. I probably shouldn't be telling you this, but the Blackwell is guarded by a soul-web. The spirits of things of the Night Below. I can see them—it's how I got in there the first time, I just stepped around them. I don't think one of the Faded could dismiss them.'

'There are far more wards than just that,' Esher said. 'Think about it. If you were going to put a Keystone that unlocks the seal and gives access to the Crown, and you were a bunch of ancient Draoihn, wouldn't the first thing you erected there be wards against those things of the Night Below?'

'So he can't enter the Blackwell directly,' Sanvaunt said. He groaned, shifted a little. He was in more pain than he was letting on. 'He needs some-one to go do it for him. A Draoihn of the Fourth Gate.'

'And he's lost Onostus, and Lassaine too. Maybe his plan failed already,' I said.

'So that's it?' Esher said. 'When Lassaine and Onostus died—that's the end of whatever he planned. There's nobody left.'

But I knew the answer. It would be painful for Sanvaunt to hear, but there it was.

'It was never Onostus,' I said. 'It's Ovitus he intends to use.'

'Ovitus's rise in ability has been spectacular, but he hasn't reached the Fourth Gate. Maybe he never will,' Esher said.

'He will,' I said. 'When Ulovar dies. Or rather, when he takes Ulovar's last Gate from him, he'll ascend to the Fourth.'

Sanvaunt paled.

'That can't be right,' he said. Despite everything he'd seen from Ovitus, even seeing him kill Liara with a flick of his hand, he didn't want to believe it. But I was done living in denial about who and what people were.

'Ovitus has been planning this for months,' I said. 'Ever since he was hu-miliated. First by me—or by his own actions, truth be told—and then again when he failed his first Testing. He found a way to take Ulovar's power. A curse of blood and bone. I already knew that's what it was, I just didn't know what it meant. Sul went to him, and taught him how to do it. It's a curse that only works on kin. Ovitus decided he was going to make everyone see him for what he's always believed he is.'

'Better than everyone else,' Esher finished for me.

I could see Sanvaunt trying to perform mental gymnastics. Trying to find some way that it wasn't true, some way that his cousin, whom he had loved all his life, could have done that to his uncle. That's the problem with having a belief; it's whatever we want it to be, or need it to be. We hold to it despite truth, against evidence, despite fact. Or we try to, because in ac-cepting what the world is telling us, it breaks what we cherish most about it.

'Ovitus has always seen himself as less,' Sanvaunt said. 'That's—it's the opposite of who he is.'

'No,' I said. 'Even when he was besotted with Liara. The self-pity, the moping about—it's because the world didn't recognise him, or didn't value him for the things *he* thought worthwhile. So in scorn, he's made himself into someone the world will respect, and fear. And he despises us all for not worshipping him for being what he wants to be. I'm right on this, Sanvaunt. And I'm so, so sorry. But if Ulovar loses his final Gate, Ovitus will take it and be able to enter the Blackwell.'

'I don't want it to be true,' Sanvaunt said.

'But it is true,' I said. 'And we're done with lies. We're done with pretending. We are what we are, and Ovitus is what he is.'

'I just can't believe Ovitus would willingly have consorted with one of the Faded like that,' he said. 'Maybe he's under its control somehow. Maybe it took his mind.'

I didn't argue with that. Perhaps he was right. I was doing it again, I thought. Trying to allow excuses for the inexcusable. I shut it down, but there was no point arguing with Sanvaunt about it anymore.

'So what do we do?'

'We take what we've learned to Grandmaster Robilar,' I said. I didn't add what I was thinking: *And I kill Ovitus, before Ulovar expires.*

'What else?' Sanvaunt said. 'We should get moving. We've hours of riding ahead of us.' He began levering himself up, gasped in sudden pain and collapsed onto his back. A few moments of panic passed, but he was all right despite the sudden rapid breathing and the heat that flushed his face.

'You aren't going anywhere,' I said. 'You've done your part.'

'We can't leave him here,' Esher said.

'I need your help,' I said.

'I'm no help to anybody,' Esher said sadly. 'We all saw it. I should have acted. And I didn't.'

'Rubbish,' I said. 'You're the best sword of our generation. I have a feeling I'm going to need your help before this is over.'

'When it came to it, I didn't even draw it,' Esher said. She stated it blankly, like she'd accepted it. Her shine was gone, that life-force that blossomed out of her. 'We can't leave Sanvaunt here alone. He can't even get up by himself. Besides. The horses are done. They won't get us anywhere. And you don't look like you'll get far on foot.'

She was right about that. I was bone-deep weary. Time bore down on us like anvils loaded upon our backs, and I would arrive long after the enemy reached Redwinter, if that was their plan.

'How far do you think we are from Harranir?'

'Forty miles, perhaps,' Esher said. 'Fifty, maybe. There'll be scouts and outriders ahead of the northern forces. If we could bend space and travel through fire like the grandmaster, perhaps we'd make it. But we aren't the grandmaster. There's no way.'

'If I have to go alone, and kill both horses doing it, I'm doing it.'

I'd thought Esher was all out of tears, but it seemed she had two left. They tracked down her face now.

'I'll find more horses. If I have to call the moon horses down from a clear sky to do it, I'll follow you.'

I wiped the tears from her face, leaving smudged-finger trails across her cheeks.

'No,' I said. 'This time it's just me.'

'How do you do it?' she asked. 'How do you keep going, when everything else has turned to blood and death?'

And I thought about it, in the dark gloom of the ruins of a bygone age, and I asked myself the question.

'It's not a "how,"' I said. 'It's a "why." And the answer is that I love you both. And I love the people of this country, and its moors and its wind. I love being alive, and I want to be alive so badly I can't let myself stop.'

'But aren't you afraid?'

'Afraid?' I said. 'I'm the queen of death, aren't I? I'm not the one who should be afraid.'

37

To Redwinter, then.

I wore Esher's Winterra armour. I'd always borrowed her clothes. We were close in height and build, and although her shoulders were broader than mine it wasn't so close fitting as to cause a problem with a little lengthening of the straps. I bid a thankful goodbye to those awful heeled boots. If I encountered any of the northern army's outriders, they'd take me for an ally. Esher's helmet would cover my face and hair if I needed to become invisible.

I unscrewed the cap from Sanvaunt's flask of rose-thistle, and the dank, bitter smell rose to meet me.

'Guess I didn't get that far from you after all,' I said. I swallowed. It was energy of a kind.

The grief found me on the road, braiding itself tight around fury and disgust.

Whatever Ovitus and Sul's plans had been, they lay in tatters now. They'd be improvising, and that would make them sloppy, but they'd know that they had to move fast. Determination rose like a red dawn in my mind. I would not be stopped. I could not be stopped.

There was the Crown, and it mattered, and all else was dust and all that stuff. But Ovitus had killed Liara. Once upon a time he'd professed to love her. It had been a self-serving, self-pitying kind of adoration from afar that he'd never truly wanted to go further than talk. She hadn't been a real person to him, just the idea of a perfect woman to gaze at his own reflection in. I'd never thought of him as dangerous, even as his power and position swelled. Nobody had. We'd all seen that meandering, bookish boy, even though his core had been decaying all along. The truth was, he'd already had everything: magic, position, money. But it hadn't been enough. Maybe nothing would ever have been enough to quell the ego inside him.

What a thing, for a country to be brought to war, and a world to peril, over the fragile ego of one bitter man.

The horses had regained some of their strength, but I needed to ride them hard. I came across a farm, and found they had two decent-looking animals.

'I'll trade you,' I said to the farmer, although it hurt to offer them Yangyn's bridle. I'd only just got him.

'They're almost knackered,' the farmer said, although she could see that they were beasts far beyond the quality of her own horses.

'They'll recover,' I told her. 'I'm sorry. I have to take them. You'll be able to sell these and buy ten others.' She was sceptical despite having a good eye for a workhorse. There had to be some kind of a catch.

'You're one of those Winterra?' she asked. 'Is there fighting yet?'

'I don't know,' I told her. 'I'm sorry, I have to go. Before I do, I need food and water.'

'You can rest here a while,' she offered.

'I can't,' I said. 'But thank you.'

The thing about ordinary people is, mostly they're just trying to get on with their lives. They make mistakes, and they can be petty, or jealous, or mean, but in their hearts, in the main they're good. Those who rose to positions of power were different. To rise high in the world means wanting something more than a home, love, satisfaction with a good day's work. It means wanting something more, something that nobody should really have. They say that power corrupts, but I was starting to believe that it was the corrupt that sought it in the first place.

The Queen of Feathers found me on the ride.

'You shouldn't have told the Esher girl what you are,' she said. She rode beside me on a horse that didn't exist, matching pace. Maybe she could have flown on her black-feathered wings, but they seemed to be mostly for show.

'Are you even real?' I asked. 'Or just a hallucination like the book?'

'I'm different to the book, but a bit the same, maybe?' she said. I rolled my eyes at her infuriating refusal to ever give me a straight answer. I had started to believe that, for all the wisdom she managed to offer from time to time, actually she didn't want to admit that she had no more idea about what she was than I did.

'I saw me as you,' I said. 'In the mirror. Am I you?'

'I don't see how you can be,' the Queen of Feathers said. 'What are you going to do?'

'Not sure,' I said. 'I have to get to Robilar.'

'You trust her that much?'

'No,' I said. 'I'm just a pawn to her, whatever she says. Everyone is a pawn to her. But she's not trying to give the Crown to the Faded, so that's a good start.'

'This is a dangerous time for us,' the Queen of Feathers said. 'Hallenae, Serranis, Song Seondeok—they managed to keep their secret far longer than you did. I fear you've shown your hand too early, and I'll be waiting another two hundred years to try to raise up another girl like you. How will you take power now?'

'That's what you want of me?' I said. I found myself smiling, cracking lines of old sweat on my face. 'You want me to rise up like one of the dark queens of legend? It didn't work so well for them.'

'No, indeed,' the Queen of Feathers said. 'Perhaps this will work out differently.'

'You have power,' I said. 'I might need it soon.'

'Do I really?' she asked. And she laughed, and somehow I laughed as well, and it was all stupid and confusing and I hadn't expected answers from her anyway.

Flight from the battle with Sul had taken us west, so I found myself riding along the northern bank of the river that flowed down and out of Harranir. I didn't know what to expect, but as I crested a rise and looked down on the city, it wasn't what I'd expected.

There was no fighting. No battle ensuing. The armed camp out to the north of the city had doubled in size. The banners that flew there were green-and-black LacNaithe wyverns, yellow-and-grey LacAud sword-and-hammers, as well as the red-and-white flags of the Winterra with Redwinter's crown-and-tower. There was to be no great clash of battle. I'd ridden in from death and blood, but that shocking surge of violence hadn't come to Harranir. Instead, what I found was relief, and celebration.

I needed to cross the river, and Harranir's bridges or river boats were the only option for that. I made my way down into the city.

The people were out in force, the streets filled with laughter and bright eyes. There was drinking and carousing like it was a festival day. Of course there would be. Disaster had been averted. Those who would have faced one another across a blood-slicked field strode arm in arm, filled with relief that the bloody violence all had feared had been cancelled from history. Fathers, wives, sons, nieces, none had to die. North and south were to have peace.

I learned this from the revellers I passed, sitting out in front of shops and homes drinking beer from earthenware jugs. I heard it from town criers in livery of various hues, calling out to all that there was peace and goodwill for all. A great day of celebration for north and south alike. And yet Redwinter still stared down accusing from its mountain plateau.

As I came to one of the major thoroughfares, a great column of warriors were marching past, shields on their backs, spears on their shoulders as they headed towards the major bridges. I rode to the head of the procession and found the commander there, a beast of a man with a long beard. He had none of the joviality of the common folk. I knew a man set on fighting when I saw one.

'What's the order?' I asked. He looked over my borrowed Winterra armour and gave me a respectful nod.

'Heading south of the river to take position at the base of the mountain,' he said. 'Your brigade crossed ahead of us a couple of hours ago.'

'I was riding messages west, seems like I've missed everything,' I said. 'Why's everyone heading south?'

'Not sure that's for me to say.'

'Just say it plain, man,' I said. For all his size, the commander looked nervous about sharing his news.

'The grandmaster of Redwinter had Van LacAud assassinated. Tried to kill young LacNaithe as well. Turns out she's been consorting with the Night Below—sent an assassin to take the leader's heads. Word is she wants to take the kingdom for her own.'

'Grandmaster Robilar? That's what they're saying?'

'Aye, and she's about to see the anger of the people firsthand. Your lot have thrown in with the people, thank the Light Above, and it's the Winterra who're leading the way. Got to know where your real enemy is sometimes,' he said.

'But Ovitus LacNaithe survived?'

'Aye, he did. Brokered peace with the north as well. I'm sorry to be the bearer of bad news, but your commander LacDaine wasn't so lucky though, I'm sorry to say. We lost the greatest warrior of our age.'

She probably had been, in her own way. I had some sympathy with Lassaine LacDaine, exiled to lead her brother and sister Winterra in endless battles of conquest in lands she'd never call home. The grandmaster had kept them out of Harran because keeping them close risked revolt. Ironically, doing so had brought them to do just that. Nobody can foresee all outcomes.

The deaths of Onostus LacAud and Lassaine LacDaine hadn't slowed Sul and Ovitus in their schemes even a step. If anything they'd lit a fire to the sheet music, and now they danced to a burning tune.

'She fought for what she believed in,' I said. Couldn't quite bring myself to praise her, but the warriors seemed to take it as if I did. 'Thanks. And welcome to Harranir.'

The northern warrior gave me a salute, and I gave him a nod and let the column of tramping boots wind its way on and over the river. Time was of the essence, but the rose-thistle was out and I was worn thin. I wished I had some money to spare, but lacking that I traded away my dirk for some ewe's cheese, haggis and ale with a group of women who were singing loudly outside an alehouse. I ate it as I considered my next move. Few of my options felt good.

Sul had control of both the northern army of clan-land warriors and Kwendish mercenaries, the southern army and Ovitus's conscripts as well as the Winterra. How many of them might desert? Lassaine had turned, and my sinking heart told me that she couldn't have attempted to pull that move without substantial support. I imagined those warriors, young and old alike, sitting around their fires in some distant land dreaming of a return to an idealised version of the country they'd left behind as they complained. No, when they'd been recalled they'd not intended on leaving. And why should they when some of their own number had seen what I'd done to their commander? I'd been Grandmaster Robilar's protégé. In my need for vengeance I'd given the enemy a great gift. Perhaps a few would desert rather than turn on Redwinter, but I doubted it.

Liara was dead. I did not regret what I'd done to LacAud. Not even a little.

Redwinter wouldn't withstand a siege, let alone an assault. And once he took root, Sul would have the time he needed to await the release of the Keystone, and he would enter the Crown and the world as we knew it would be riven apart. The veil between our world and the Night Below would be broken, and the unspeakable, nameless things that dwelt beyond would return to claim that which had been taken from them.

Reaching Grandmaster Robilar was the only chance I had. She had fought Sul before, and she could do so again. On my own, I didn't have the power. I'd hit him with everything I had, and it hadn't been enough. I'd hit him with the stone-headed arrow, Sanvaunt had cut him with a sword of fire, and it still hadn't been enough. I had to hope she had something left up her sleeve, and knowing her as I did, she'd been planning for his return for a long, long time. But she couldn't fight him if she didn't know he was coming.

I emptied the last of the haggis into my mouth and tossed away the skin. Not bad, a little more grit than I'd have liked. I swung my borrowed farm horse around and headed over the bridge. A hard-worn, disciplined regiment of Kwendish bowmen stalked across it, armoured in mail and leather, flat-topped iron helmets making them all look alike. I closed the visor of Esher's helmet and tried to look like I was hurrying to catch up with the rest of the Winterra.

The road to Redwinter was thick with warriors. Thousands of them. They poured through Harranir and out along the road, but most had spilled out onto the surrounding heaths. Not so much an organised army but a mass of men and women charging headlong towards one battle out of sheer relief they hadn't had to fight another. I clicked my heels and headed on past them, aiming for the wash of silver that lay at the base of the mountain.

'Lose the horse,' the Queen of Feathers whispered. 'They'll see it's not fit for Winterra.'

'See, you can be useful when you want to be,' I muttered. I swung down, unslung my bow and quiver from the saddle and gave the horse an appreciative pat and let her wander among some Harranese stock, tethered by the roadside while their riders sprawled around in the long grass. How anyone was supposed to order around such a mass of people, all with their own ideas, desires, beliefs, fears and needs, I couldn't begin to imagine.

'Down with the Draoihn!' one group was chanting, lubricated with ale and forgetting that they weren't supposed to be quashing the Draoihn in their entirety. Among another group a boxing match was taking place, men stripped to the waist. Few had any idea what was happening. I hurried on, thighs aching from another long day in the saddle, and headed on towards the back ranks of the Winterra. They had a greater semblance of order, their silver armour polished bright, and I was just another body among them. Nearly seven hundred strong, Draoihn of the First Gate every single one of them. A terrifying prospect for any enemy, and now, they'd turned their insurrection on the place that had made them. Traitors, from the first woman to the last man. Maybe *Down with the Draoihn* was right.

I spotted Ovitus at a distance. He wore the full panoply of war and rode his tall horse. Lord Braman, as they would know him, sat alongside. He'd found a second suit of that gleaming, silvery armour with its closed face-plate. He sat like a statue of steel on a humbler steed. Around them the Draoihn rebels that Onostus LacAud had recruited to serve in his rebellion wore their oxblood coats as if they still had a right to them. The Winterra had pitched up just out of bowshot of the pines that coated the mountain-side and flanked the road. Even if the rest of the army was thinking this some kind of walkover, their commanders knew what would await them when they tried to unseat Grandmaster Vedira Robilar. Just how much did they understand about how powerful she truly was? I'd seen the aftermath of her battle in a dream. I doubted that she'd exaggerated it, and there were those Draoihn who'd remained loyal to contend with as well. But whoever was in Redwinter right now, they were vastly outnumbered.

'Can't say I'm looking forward to the ascent,' a woman of middle years with an upturned nose was saying.

'You think maybe this is all something of a mistake?' a Winterra warrior muttered back. A ring of red hair surrounded a bald patch, tattooed with sea creatures.

'We've had to attack into worse,' Upturn told him, causing his arm to ring as she clattered a gauntlet against his armour. 'Remember that time in Faralant? That city, with the demon priests. The ones who could call down the bird things.'

'I remember,' Redhead grunted. 'But harpies aren't the same as Vedira Robilar.'

'She's just a woman,' Upturn said. 'And we got a few good ones on our side anyway. She doesn't have the men to defend the walls. We'll run right over.'

'Men or not, they have Ulovar LacNaithe too,' Redhead said. 'Not a man I thought I'd ever lift a sword against. That's a man I'd have followed into worse than the harpy city.'

'Nah, the old LacNaithe is sick and dying. It's his son who has all the Gates now.'

'Nephew,' Redhead corrected her. 'There's something off about him.'

'Wouldn't say that too loud, if I were you,' Upturn said, her good spirits entirely undeterred. 'Who do you think's going to take Robilar's chair once she finally vacates it?'

My disguise seemed to be working, but I kept my head down nonetheless.

No reason for anyone here to recognise me. I wondered if Castus was up there in Redwinter too, or whether he'd have found a way out. The place was a death trap now. Going through the Winterra had felt like the best option—a lone rider trying to skirt around them would have been too obvious. But now what? I couldn't wait for them to advance. Surely there'd at least be a pretence at negotiation? Maybe I could tag along with them. Or maybe we'd all go up together, one big marching column. Was there a chance that Robilar might open the gates and accept exile? No. There was absolutely no chance that woman was ever going to cede power to a usurper. Whatever else she was, she'd burn the sky before she gave up her duty to the Crown.

'Ambassador's on his way back,' Redhead said. I followed his gaze towards the road. A rider emerged from the trees at a canter, carrying a branch to which an upside down flag had been tied; it showed both LacNaithe green and black and LacAud's grey and yellow. He tossed the branch to the side of the road, and the Winterra—more interested in the outcome than the idling soldiers along the road had been—pressed close towards their leaders. I was borne with them, but far enough back in the pack that I was hidden by the numbers and the fact we were all dressed more or less the same.

'What news?' Ovitus called out, and his voice strung something inside me, like a hammer clashing against a gong. There was still an edge of boy to him, though he looked serious. Closer up, I saw that his left arm hung in a sling. I'd managed to hurt him a little, at least. Good.

'I delivered your offer, Thail LacNaithe,' the rider said. He didn't sound confident. With a feeling like a punch to the gut I saw that it was Mendel LacGilfry, the apprentice who'd messed up his Testing and been first to throw up as we celebrated our rise to the rank of Draoihn. I realised that among the Winterra around me, they must all have been there—Danforth of Brannlant, Nimman the Younger who'd been first to get drunk, Nimman the Elder who played the pipes, Dynae LacClune, Janry, even Raddesia, who'd flirted with Sanvaunt . . . all of them. The kids I'd shared classes with. That's what they'd been, anyway. Just a bunch of kids with no idea what was coming. It was one thing to trance and figure out what was beneath a cloth in the quiet of the practice hall. They'd never seen the fires and eruptions of power Robilar could bring down. They didn't even know.

'I take it the old bitch didn't want to come down quietly with you, then?' Ovitus asked, his voice augmented by the Second Gate so it rolled out across the gathered warriors. Some of them laughed. Most didn't.

'No, my lord. I was told that the Council of Night and Day still hold Redwinter. They—they want me to deliver an offer to the Winterra.'

'Let me guess,' Ovitus said. 'A pardon for opposing her tyranny if they bring her my head? Is that it?'

Of course, Ovitus, it's all about you, I thought. Though this time he probably wasn't far off the mark.

'Something like that, my lord,' poor Mendel LacGilfry said. I wondered if Ovitus had selected him as a kind of insult. The least capable Draoihn under his command.

'What would Lassaine LacDaine have said to that?' Ovitus shouted. My head rang inside my helmet. They probably heard him all the way in Redwinter.

'No surrender! No retreat!' the Winterra thundered, and came close to matching him in volume. I saw Ovitus smile. Whatever was going on behind Sul's mask, he kept it to himself.

'She has no men,' Ovitus called, letting his Second Gate drop away. He had more to say, but Mendel LacGilfry seemed to be squirming. Embarrassment. 'What?'

'They're flying a banner, sir,' he said. 'Orange and white. And I saw her, up on the wall. The Brannish contingent have allied with Redwinter, along with the withdrawn garrisons. Princess Mathilde holds the walls.'

Ovitus was at a loss for words at that. I could see the quivering in his cheeks. Everything was an insult to him. He saw every little thing as the world taking his dues from him. I grinned behind my visor. I'd always known Princess Mathilde to be a canny woman, but I suppose, like Ovitus, I'd discounted her.

'The Brannish scum will go the same way as the woman who has commanded in the Round Chamber for far too long,' Ovitus declared, ignoring the fact that he'd been due to marry that very same Brannish scum until he received the news a few seconds ago.

'The Council are sending someone down to negotiate,' Mendel said. He looked pale. Afraid. He must have been terrified riding up there. Maybe he'd thought about changing sides. But there were a lot of warriors on the road between Harranir and Redwinter. Whatever forces Mathilde had at her disposal couldn't number more than a few hundred, and Redwinter's walls were far too long to hold against the numbers arrayed against them.

'If we can talk this out, we'll talk it out,' Ovitus said.

'The grandmaster consorts with the Sarathi, and may be one herself.' It was Sul speaking this time. 'She cannot be allowed to live.'

'We are Draoihn, Lord Braman,' Ovitus said. Proudly. He wasn't Draoihn, technically, but that seemed a moot point these days. 'We'll take her to the trees and give her one night to prove her innocence as they did in the days of old.'

'She is too powerful for that,' Sul snapped. Maybe Ovitus didn't get it, or maybe it was just all for show. I doubt he meant what he said anyway. Nothing he said had any real meaning behind it.

Something bumped against my left gauntlet, and I pulled it away. My fingers were wet. It pressed up against me again, insistent. I looked down into warm, dark eyes, and with horror saw Ovitus's wolfhound Waldy looking up at me. His mouth hung open, pink tongue lolling.

'Shush,' I said. 'Shush, dog.'

He barked. Once, then again, and then again, and then again. Happy, excited barks. I knelt down, not easy armoured and amidst all the close-standing Winterra warriors. I tried rustling his ears, and still Waldy just barked away at me.

'Come on, shut up, shut up, back to your master,' I hissed at him. 'Leave me alone, stupid dog.'

He barked again, and again, and then jumped up at me, front paws pushing at me. Panic began to well in me at the noise he was making. I tried to put my hand around his muzzle, but like it was a game he wove his old head around and kept on yapping. His barking became more insistent. I tried to get hold of him by the fur, by the neck. Making so much noise I didn't hear the crowd of warriors parting.

'Hello, Raine,' Ovitus said, as finally, finally, the summer broke.

38

The skies parted, and the rain that had been absent from our land for so long swept over us in a drowning grey torrent, the drops bouncing and pinging from the steel suits all around.

Treacherous bloody dog. I looked up towards Ovitus and he was calm. Calm, and poised, and he wore no outward sign of anger, but half-amused, half-knowing, like he'd been expecting to find me here all along.

'An assassin,' Ovitus said. 'Take her.'

Gates opened up all around me, and they were gates with smooth, weather-worn edges. Like rocks shaped by the wind and rain, each rested in a natural harmony with the others. A fighting unit that over many years had learned to work together as one single, drum-beat entity.

Redhead and Upturn were fast movers, and they had my arms before I could react. Someone else took my sword, Esher's gift, from me. Redhead wrested my beautiful Midnight from my hand, Upturn pulled my arrows from their quiver and tossed them into the mud. Rough hands unbuckled the chin strap and pulled the helmet from my head. There were weapons pointed at me, swords and polearms, ready to strike in a split second if I tried anything. I didn't even dare to enter into Eio, and there was nothing I could have done if I had.

'Came back for another try? Bold of you, but then you were always bold,' Ovitus said. He seemed to clear his throat, as if something had become stuck there. 'It was your boldness that I loved first.'

'You never loved anything but yourself, you whining piece of pig shit.' I spat at him, but it dissolved into the rain. What I wouldn't have given in that moment for an army of souls inside my chest to turn against him, to tear his own from his quivering flesh. But I was out of other people's lives to wield.

'Never did learn proper southern manners, though,' Ovitus lamented. 'I suppose I loved that about you too.' He turned and raised his arms. 'You see what lives among us?' he called out. 'You see our reason, our need to displace Vedira Robilar from a perch she has sat too long? It is the king who must control the country, not the Draoihn. We swore our lives to protect it, and this is how Vedira exerts her control: through assassination. Through subterfuge. Through dishonesty. Through exiling those of you who have the strength to stand against her tyranny.'

'Is this the one?' Redhead asked. 'She's the one who killed Commander Lassaine?' I felt the edge of something sharp up against the back of my neck; Upturn's dirk, I supposed. It could all be over in a moment. A drag back on my hair, an exertion of pressure. The blade would be sharp. Perhaps I wouldn't feel anything. Somehow, I wasn't as frightened as maybe I should have been. Do any of us really believe we're going to die? I didn't want to live forever. I liked having the knowledge that one day it would all be over, and I wouldn't have to worry, or fear anymore. But not yet. I didn't want to go yet.

'Men and women of the Winterra,' I shouted. 'This man is not what he seems. Lord Braman is a demon of the Night Below, a lord of the Faded. He's manipulating you. Using you for his own ends, to grasp for power when he's worthy of none. Redwinter is not the enemy, you're being led by the very thing you swore to fight.'

I didn't expect to get to the end of that speech. I'd expected a blow from a gauntlet to break my face open, or a hand clasped across my mouth. Maybe even the dirk. But Ovitus let my words leak out into the pounding rain as it soaked my hair, dripped into my eyes, drummed a sharp, high rhythm on seven hundred suits of armour. The whole world seemed to have turned cold. This hadn't been a terribly good plan, really. It had barely been a plan at all.

'It's always demons and darkness with you, isn't it?' Ovitus said. But it wasn't all scorn across his face. He was sad as well. Genuinely sad. I just didn't think it was sadness for me. 'Lord Braman, would you be able to show our loyal men and women of the Winterra whether you're a creature of the Night Below?'

The warrior in the silvered armour rode across, the gathered warriors parting before him. He unbuckled his helmet and removed it. Same short, neat beard. Same narrow face. But he bore a livid red scar running from his jaw, up his cheek and stopping just short of his eye. It had been well stitched but looked puffed up hard, inflamed. Self-made, maybe.

'I recognise her,' he said. 'She murdered Onostus LacAud, my beloved master, under a flag of truce. She's the one who killed Lassaine LacDaine and her men, and half a dozen of her fellow Draoihn besides. She's the one who gave me this wound, though I paid the smaller price.'

'Some hero,' Redhead muttered.

'You bunch of idiots,' I shouted. 'Don't you see you're—'

The slap came fast. Not a fist, but an open hand, and still my vision abandoned me as whirls of sparkling dots swam before my eyes. And I was cast back to a moment, many months ago, when another man had struck me that way.

I'm sorry, Braithe had said, and he'd lied.

'It's better you don't speak,' Ovitus said, and that was a lie too. But maybe, like Braithe, he believed it. Men are always able to believe their own narrative when it comes to hurting women, no matter how absurd. 'You'll have a trial, Raine. Just like Grandmaster Robilar will have a trial. I won't have lawlessness or tyranny in the new order of things. I was in love with you, once. I still—' and he choked up like he was trying to handle his own emotions. Which in a way he was. Ovitus was incapable of being honest, especially with himself. I could taste blood inside my mouth where my teeth had cut into my cheek.

'So was it all true then? What happened between you on the road?'

The question came from Mendel LacGilfry. Banner bearing, Testing failure Mendel LacGilfry. I'd just accused someone of being a Faded lord, and all he was interested in was whether Ovitus and I had fucked on the road. Ovitus said nothing, but put his fingers over his eyes as if trying to stop tears.

'I always said where there's smoke, there's fire.' And this time it was Raddesia, that pretty girl that Sanvaunt had talked to at the Testing party.

None of that mattered now, of course. The day was bigger than that, too vital to our survival to worry about whether a bunch of old acquaintances believed Ovitus's falsehoods. And yet, it still mattered. He could have denied it, could have been honest for just once in his life, but that was never going to happen, was it? He sat on the edges, lying and watching, waiting for his chance to strike. Whispering behind closed doors, just as he had with Liara, never confronting anything head on, so that eventually the mountain of lies built, and built, and built until his victims were buried beneath the weight of his shadowed muttering.

I wanted to kill him more than ever. Stupid, that it should still matter after what he'd done to Liara. What he'd done to Jathan, and Gelis and Adanost. How could it possibly matter against so much death?

I looked up at Lord Braman, or Sul, whatever name he rightfully owned. He was no different, but perhaps he was at least honest with himself. He didn't need to deceive himself about what he was, only everyone else.

'There's a horse and trap coming,' he said, turning to look towards the switchback road that led up to Redwinter's plateau. 'The Council of Night and Day's envoy.'

'You're all fools!' I yelled into the driving rain. 'You're all idiots!' Emotion had taken over. Reason had been abandoned.

'Quiet her down, and bring her,' Ovitus said as if doing so was to bear a great weight across his shoulders. 'If they see their nightcrafter assassin has failed, perhaps they'll be more inclined to see reason. I've no wish for blood to be shed today.'

I spat blood on him. That earned me a gag, a screwed up banneret in my mouth and another looped to bind it in place. Struggling would have been useless; my guards were bigger, stronger than I was, and it wasn't like there were just two of them. To the Winterra, I was nobody; they'd never met me before. My word was worth little, and in truth, I had killed Lassaine LacDaine. The best lies contain an element of truth, even if it's twisted until it can no longer be recognised for what it was. The guards weren't gentle, and my arms protested painfully as they dragged me. The long-needed rain filled the world, hard-packed earth turning into mud beneath so many feet.

I got a few puzzled looks from those that had been apprentices alongside me. I realised that some of them may even have looked up to me in those days. I'd been a hero after I saved Ovitus from Kaldhoone LacShale. I'd been poised for great things. That's what they must have thought. I'd never seen myself in that light, and now I saw it cast back at me in shades of be-musement, or disdain, or outright confusion. For those that had only just won their Draoihn coats, things were moving so fast they must have seemed a blur. One day they'd look back and remember the day they were supposed to fight a battle and instead there'd been a revolution.

Ovitus walked to the fore of the group, and Redhead and Upturn dragged me along through the puddles forming in the road. Thunder rolled dis-tantly, a hollow growling in the sky. The air was hazy with rain. Whether the Light Above was seeking to mask what was happening, hiding Redwin-ter's aggressors from sight, or trying to impede their progress was unclear. Most likely, it was just raining.

Ovitus walked out confidently to meet the envoy, who I suspected had to be Councillor Kyrand. Councillor Suanach held sway over the artificers, but he was dithery, and if Grandmaster Robilar had intended to come in person then she wouldn't have been born by horse and trap. She wouldn't bow, scrape and deal. That wasn't, and never could be, her way. The Winterra formed up into something like ranks behind us, but they kept a respectful distance. The trap was flying Redwinter's banner, crown and tower, upside down from a freshly cut branch. They were ready to talk.

It all seemed somewhat futile right then, but this wasn't my first time defying fate. I was beaten, but I took everything in, tried to think through the angles. They didn't have any rope, so I hadn't been tied—that had to be a positive. All right, so there were a whole lot of highly trained, elite soldiers around me, almost all of them good enough that I couldn't have taken them individually, and certainly not seven hundred or so. I was out of souls to burn, and I couldn't just manufacture them—could I? I didn't think I could just tear them out of a person, like snuffing a fly. I wasn't sure I'd do it even if I could.

Surrounded. Outmatched. No resources left to me. I should probably have been more afraid than I was, but in truth I was yet to find a situation I couldn't kill my way out of.

The horse and trap squeaked to a stop. The world was so thick with rain a fish could have swum it.

'How has it come to this, my nephew?'

I looked up from the mud. The trap rested fifteen paces from us. The driver was a young woman, dark skinned, a humble servant riding into the bared teeth of war. Her eyes were wide, and set with fear.

It must have been all the harder for Ulovar. Unbearably so.

'You should be abed, uncle,' Ovitus said. And there was concern there. A catch in his voice. When it suited him, he still believed he was doing right. 'I'm glad you've been able to escape Redwinter.'

My master stared at Ovitus through heavy-lidded eyes. There was a grey pallor to his skin. He had weathered and aged so quickly, as if daily he'd stood before crashing, salt-filled waves and they'd eroded him. The furs were bundled around him, heavy in the rain. He couldn't rise from the trap, just a head sticking out of a pile of bear skins.

My master. The word didn't really sit right. I hadn't known him so very long, but he'd been more of a father to me than any man before, and that had counted for something. He'd helped me. He'd hurt me, cutting the scar across my mind to protect me from grief. It hadn't worked in the long run, but I hadn't killed myself over it, and that counted for something too. He hadn't tried to bed me, as many had before him, and he hadn't thought me lesser. He'd paid for me to be educated. He'd seen potential in me. He'd believed in me.

'My time in a sick bed is over,' Ulovar said. He coughed, but couldn't clear his chest. 'Look around you, you young fool, and see what you've brought us to.'

'I'm just a servant of the people,' Ovitus said. 'I'm brought here by their will, not my own. North and south united. The Winterra back in their rightful homeland. The citizens of Harranir put to gainful employment. Bread on the table. The rain falls around us now, but the sky will clear.'

'And just how much lightning are you prepared to take for your insurrection?' Ulovar growled. 'This was not how you were raised. This is not honourable. This is not right.'

'I believe in what we do here, Uncle,' Ovitus said. Earnestly, like he thought he might convince Ulovar, of all people. 'Sometimes tradition must be overcome for there to be right.'

'And by chance, you are the benefactor,' Ulovar growled. 'Was it not enough to be lord of a great clan? Was it not enough for you to find a marriage that would have bolstered us, and your own power? Not enough that you received the best education, that you even have a Gate to your name? You've been given more than anyone could ask for. And . . . yet.'

The young attendant swept the rainwater from Ulovar's face. He couldn't move his arms to do it himself.

'More than one Gate, Uncle,' Ovitus said sulkily. As though a key point of importance had been missed. His accolades not finely described enough.

'No,' Ulovar growled. 'No. You have only one.'

'I've proven otherwise,' Ovitus said. But I saw the look on his face, and the depth of anger, and horror, and betrayal that Ulovar's accusing, unblinking stare shot across the gap. At Ovitus's feet, Waldy slunk low. And in the depths of horror, I finally understood.

'Did you seek your familiar out after you failed your first Testing, or did it come to you and offer its secrets?' Ulovar asked. Waldy whined, a thin sound against the rain, but his lips were peeled back, his teeth displayed.

'Your illness has clouded your thoughts, Uncle,' Ovitus said. Unconvincing, even to himself this time.

'A bond of blood and bone,' Ulovar said. 'I knew, I think. Deep down, I knew the timing was too neat. As my Gates were taken from me, so too yours emerged. Perhaps I could have deceived myself fully, even today, on the day I die, if you hadn't been so eager to show everyone the Third Gate. But it's not yours, Ovitus. It was mine. And by the Light Above, for the first time in my life, I'm glad my sister is dead. So she cannot see what you've become.'

'Shut your mouth, old man!' Ovitus shouted. He started forward, then thought better of it. Blowing out steaming breath like a bull ready to charge. 'Your time is over. It's my time now. And why not? I'm a better man than you ever were.'

'We both know that's not true.'

'Why not? Because I didn't have meaningless fights like your sons? Because I'm not handsome like Sanvaunt? I have gifts. I have other talents. Why didn't you see me, the way you saw them?'

The rain poured down across the world, across us, through the trees, along the road. Ovitus's tears were masked by it. Ulovar had no words for him. His disgust, his scorn was clear. Ulovar was not a man who could mask his emotions.

'Is Sanvaunt dead?'

'No. Of course not.'

'Then where is he?'

'Why does it matter?' Ovitus screeched into the rain. 'Why is it always about him? I'm right here, Uncle. I'm right here and *still* it's not me you care about.'

The dark young woman wiped the water from Ulovar's cracked skin again. He looked to me for the first time.

'I see you've turned on all your friends,' he said. Coughed again. 'I will speak with her.'

'Raine is a traitor, and a servant of the Night Below,' Ovitus declared. 'She tried to kill me. She spreads lies with every word. She always has.'

'She saved your life. She saved mine.' He looked out towards the gathered Draoihn. 'Where is Liara? Where is my so-called army? I see one gagged and held like a hostage. But my eyes aren't so poor I shouldn't be able to make out one familiar face.' He shivered. Maybe the cold. I didn't think so. 'They're all dead, aren't they? All the time I put into growing them. All dead, because you had to have everything.'

'Sanvaunt is still alive,' Ovitus said. He dropped his head. 'I think. And Esher. I didn't want any of them hurt, Uncle. My heart's broken for them.'

Pretty fecking rich given he'd killed Liara. But lies dripped from him as easily as the downpour.

'The grandmaster has told me everything,' Ulovar said. 'You don't understand what you're contending with. But she has felt the changing in the world. The powers that have been unleashed, and what you'd unleash again.' He looked over to me. 'She has told me *everything*, and I understand it all.'

Everything. There was so much meaning in that one, thin-voiced word.

'Don't you see that your dog didn't just come to you to help you?' Ulovar said. 'Familiars have their own agendas, and you took one on who already had a master. It's not a lord and his familiar calling the shots. It's the familiar, and his vassal. You've been on a dog's leash all along.'

Waldy growled. His hackles raised, and for a moment the old wolfhound seemed to grow in size. Just slightly. Just a little. But he had muscle there where he never had before. Ovitus placed a hand on Waldy's head to quiet him.

'I have sent my terms for Redwinter's surrender,' Ovitus said. 'You have been sent to respond, I believe. Give me the offer, Uncle. I will not waste any more daylight on farce.'

'If you march on Redwinter, hundreds will die. You will suffer immense casualties. Powers the like of which you've never seen will be unleashed upon you. You will not make the summit.'

Ovitus sniffed, licked his lips, and finally stuck out his jaw.

'Change never comes without loss.'

I shook my head, trying to flick sodden white hair from my eyes. The grip on my arms tightened, as though I'd tried to escape. Redhead and Upturn were unmoved by the words before them. Most of it probably didn't make any sense to them anyway, and did it even matter? For the Winterra, it was about changing their lives, but it was also about revenge. They'd been powerless when they were exiled. But together in force, they were something else.

Ulovar looked towards me. He held my gaze with his blood-scarred eyes for several seconds. Finally he looked back towards Ovitus.

'Firstly, Ovitus will never be able to take my final gate. I will never give that to him. He has killed me. But I will die before he takes that. I will cut off the source.'

'I never meant to harm you, Uncle,' Ovitus began but Ulovar just spoke over him.

'Second, take whatever you must. Use it however you need to. I offer this of myself freely, knowing fully what you are.'

'I don't understand,' Ovitus said. But then, he wouldn't. Because Ulovar might have been looking at him, but his words were meant for someone else. *Oh no. Oh, no.*

'Defend Redwinter. Use everything at your disposal. Do not let them win. Protect the Crown.' With immense effort, he turned his head to look fully at me. 'All else is dust.'

'Lord Ulovar,' the young woman said. 'It has been an honour. You will be remembered.' Their eyes met, and Ulovar nodded.

She swung the knife and it slid easily into the side of Ulovar's neck, and then she jerked it free. A jet of blood arced out into the rain, and then another, and then another. Spurt. Spurt. Spurt.

Ovitus roared. The young woman closed her eyes. There was a blinding blue-white flash from Ovitus's hand, and the attendant was hurled from her feet, her body rag-dolling across the ground. The horse yoked to the trap was blasted apart, disintegrating into rain that turned red, for a moment leaving Ulovar wreathed in a bright crimson glow, until the pounding grey rain washed it away.

I sagged between my captors. My legs gave way, and they let me go, to splash in the mud. Ulovar, gone. A void yawned wide in my world. Ovitus was making howling noises as he collapsed down to the ground. Ulovar's blood didn't pump for long. His eyes were already as matte as clouded glass. I heard hooves and looked back to see Lord Braman galloping forwards.

'So it's war then,' he cried. 'We march. We march on Redwinter!' But Ovitus wasn't listening. Instead he bawled on the ground. I hoped it hurt. Perhaps, just perhaps, something might crack through his armour of self-obsession, just briefly. In time he'd come to see himself as the victim. It was just the way he was made.

'Raine.'

Ulovar stood before me. Not as he had been, nor even as I'd ever seen him. He was younger, in his thirties perhaps. He was still bull-broad, stocky, but he had a fuller head of hair, less lines across his face. All of him was greenish-white, insubstantial, and his legs turned to mist before they reached the ground. This was Ulovar as he'd seen himself; the man in his mind, no matter what had happened to his body. His solemnity was there, and his duty, and his love.

'This is *her* doing,' Ovitus cawed. His eyes were red-raw, he'd finally inherited that from his uncle. 'The grandmaster put him up to this. It won't stand. I won't allow it to stand.' He raised his fist. 'Onward! Overthrow the bitch!'

I suppose it was intended as a war cry, but all I heard was the screech of a toddling child.

'Raine,' Ulovar said again. 'Take it.'

I couldn't. I didn't want to. It wasn't like those other men, the ones I'd killed and soaked up like water. This was Ulovar. He held out a hand to me.

'Take it. Use me, before I'm gone.'

'I can't,' I tried to say, but the gag withheld my words.

'In the end, all we can do is gift ourselves to each other,' Ulovar said. 'This is my last gift to you.'

I reached out and took his hand, and my head swam, and thoughts and feelings flashed through me faster than the raindrops could land. There was a child, in the great hall at Uloss, seated beside the fire playing with little wooden animals. There was a boy, crying when a practice sword had smacked into his knuckles. There was the first drink of wine, smuggled from the feast with a pretty girl. There was discovering the First Gate, there was the smell of a dog's mess hidden in his room by his sister after a quarrel. There was blood, first blood, and second and more across his hands. There were demons I'd never known he fought, there was an apprentice who'd shown dark tendencies, gutting animals and starting fires, who'd been disappeared in the night. There was love for a woman, then love for a wife, and children, and the deaths of those children. There were apprentices who filled the void those losses had left behind, and arguments, and compassion, and anger and grief and fear. There was Dalnesse Monastery, and the withering horror at what had been brought to pass. And there was suffering, and there was betrayal, and he'd known—he'd known so early the truth of his affliction—but just couldn't bring himself to admit that it was true. There was a whole life there, spinning into me, filling me, suffusing my own being with someone else's.

And I saw his Gate opening within me. Ulovar's last remaining Fourth Gate. It wasn't an arch, or a tunnel, or a sky, but a web. A billion strands, every one reaching out to the others, and at the intersections of those sparkling white strands lay minds. Ovitus, closed and hardened, the Winterra, eager, cold, afraid, alive. I saw the insects in the air, tiny and questing, the fieldmice cowering in their nests, horses uncertain and alert for danger. And at those intersections I felt Waldy, not a dog but something ancient, alien, wicked. And the Remnant Sul was nothing but a void, but a void still formed and created by each of the other minds, all of them linked together, and the world itself. I threw myself back from the web, my untrained mind breathing in too many existences, and as I soared away from it all I saw the circles, six concentric rings containing a flower's array of six binding circles and all of it together was the entirety of creation. And there was me, just a pin-prick star against the strands of the world.

'I can't do this to you,' I thought. 'I can't. I just can't.'

'Raine,' Ulovar said firmly, his voice warm and calm in my ears. 'I came to give you a chance, to live. My time is over. You fought through Skuttis to save me once. Let me save you now.'

'But then you're gone,' I thought. 'It will all be over. You'll be gone forever.'

'We swore an oath,' Ulovar's spirit said deep within me. 'We serve the Crown, and we protect it with everything we have. I have seen too much for a lifetime. I've no wish to carry it on into another world. Take this chance to escape. Make a difference.'

The web of Ulovar's power thrummed around me, and I couldn't hold it forever and I couldn't cast Ulovar's soul out as power. He deserved to go on into the warm mists of Anavia, or at least I hoped that's where he was going. I couldn't be me and hold onto him, as much as I might have wanted to. But I understood him so well, and so deeply just then, everything that was left of him had poured into me. He wasn't distant and apart as Alianna had been. For that moment, he was with me. And I had his understanding. I had the moment of instant love he'd felt seeing Ovitus for the first time, a tiny babe sleeping peacefully in his crib. I held the pain he'd felt when his name had been driven into the dirt.

Tears choked me.

'I have to do it now, don't I?'

I almost thought I felt a warm, leathered old hand atop mine.

'It's time.'

'Goodbye,' I said. 'I wish you'd been my father.'

'I loved you too, Raine, Daughter of Redwinter.'

Ulovar's Third Gate pulsed from my throat, burning the gag to bitter ash in my mouth.

The Fourth Gate required a touch. Connected or not, a mind could not simply reach to another mind, or so I'd been told. But as the Fourth Gate and Sixth worked together, I saw not just minds but souls, and I reached through the strands, whatever I was, whatever I had become flowing out through each of them, wrapping around them. I was a silent grass snake, weaving between the undergrowth. I caught them one by one, growing thinner and thinner as I flowed out of myself. Memories of the Ashtai Grimoire taught me what to do, which was only me in the end, and words I invented ushered from my throat as I took them from Ulovar's memory, his long life of study and learning.

Sul's head snapped towards me, that grey, otherworldly face flickering against the handsome, neat humanity he wore as a cloak.

'Stop that girl!' he roared. 'Kill her now!'

But it was too late, and I locked eyes with him as I uttered two words of nightmare.

'Soul Reaper.'

39

The Winterra fought me. Gates were thrown open as they sensed danger, but without knowing from whence the threat came. They felt me as I cut into their very being. Mind, life, death, it's all the same thing in the end, each of them one part of a puzzle, and I only needed two pieces to see the whole picture.

Redhead's hands stiffened around my arm as I tore his soul from him, drawing it out, consuming it and swallowing it down. He'd not yet begun to fall as I followed the lines of the web into Upturn and rent her life force from her. *More. More. More!*

I felt black shadow wings erupt from my back, the crown of feathers forming around my head, but I only cared for souls. The tunnel's roar and drone swept over everything, all the world a dark hole through which I ripped and tore people from their lives.

My mind scythed out in an arc across the Winterra. Some got out a choked gurgle, some never felt a thing. It spread in a wave with me at the centre as they fell around me like game pieces, falling, clattering in piles of steel and dead meat. Each life struck into me, ribbons of green spirit energy flying through the rain, and if there was truly a Light Above, for a few moments perhaps I matched her for power. Mendel LacGilfry got in its way, and I wished I could spare him, but I didn't.

The Winterra began to run. They didn't know what was happening, but their comrades were collapsing like string-cut marionettes, dropping dead where they stood. *No! No escape. No life, not for anyone.* I wanted it all. I wanted them all to plummet down the tunnel and into me, feeding me.

Ovitus. I reached for him and as my arc of death reached out the dog threw itself in its path. Like parting water, my dance along the threads of mind were parted, and broke aside as a rush of water splits as it strikes a rock. The familiar Ovitus had summoned to himself wasn't of our world. It stood in the way of my threads, it blocked the tunnel of death. I howled in frustration. Was I not a goddess of death? Was I not the new Riven Queen?

They would bow to me. They would all pay the price for opposing me, for taking what I loved. The world would be mine, it was already mine. I could snap a man's soul like a strand of straw. This was what I was, who I was, and I would hide no more, I would show them, I would eat them one by one—

Something punched into me. I felt it happen, but it was as though it had happened to someone else. Then the pain hit, and I lost my grip on the web of minds, I lost my trance into the tunnel, and I felt suddenly empty as if all of me had been voided. I looked down and saw the rime-crusted sword blade thrusting through my chest. It shouldn't be there. It couldn't be there. It didn't belong. I blinked at it. It didn't make sense.

Everything was cold all of a sudden. Everything seemed dark. I looked up into Sul's black eyes as he drew the sword out. It made a wet, sucking sound as it left my body, and ridiculously my last thought was that it wasn't fair that when you're killed, the last moment is so humiliating.

There is a release when you die. I'd forgotten it, from the last two occasions, but there it was. It's a release of memory that bursts through your mind, calling back things that happened so long ago you've forgotten they ever took place. Mama came first, and she was smiling at me as I played with wooden blocks, even though she was in pain. A thousand flickering memories, images of things I'd done or seen, even just smells.

Oh, I thought. *I remember this. I die.*

I didn't want to go. And it wasn't just a need to kill, or harm. What I felt in that moment as memory after memory washed over me was the great sadness that comes from knowing that there were no more memories to come. Nothing more left in store. I wished I'd kissed Esher properly. I wished I'd gone and danced with Sanvaunt. I wished I'd been kinder, and fairer, and done less harm. I wished that I could have saved Castus from his sadness, lamented that there'd be no more nights of stupid, wasteful excess with him.

I wouldn't go. I wouldn't.

I'd drawn so many souls to me that I couldn't count them. One hundred, two hundred, more. I felt Ulovar leave me. He'd come first, and the last that was left of him drifted away. One by one they began to dissipate, freed now of their constraint. There was nothing but the tunnel now, a tunnel I had to travel down myself, one final time.

No.

I would not go silently into the tunnel. I would *not.*

I wrapped souls around me. I tied them to my own, and I sent them back into the world, a reverse summoning. If things could be brought forth from the Night Below, then I would send myself back using my own power. A captured soul burned, and another, and another, turned into ribbons of spirit-power dragged back from the tunnel and lashed to fingers, elbows. I sent one back into my heart, five more besides, and told it to beat. I sent them into the wound Sul had put in my chest and locked them there to bind it closed. I sent them upward, back to the mortal realm, to open my eyes. I was the puppeteer for my own body, and the dead were the strings that pulled it.

I felt the rain again. Felt the cold of it, the wetness, the life of it. I saw no web of minds stretching across the earth. Ulovar was gone, really and truly gone. There was just me, and the moans and wails of my victims inside me. I shut them out, though they filled my body and held it together. I issued my commands, and the spirits moved my broken form.

Winterra warriors, Redwinter's finest, lay scattered around me, crumpled and empty, lain across one another where they'd fallen. The driving rain chimed across their steel. Others fled across the field, running from magic for which they had, truly, not been prepared. For the first time in their history, the Winterra were routed. What was left of them anyway.

Sul stood some distance away, over a dog and a man who was very likely regretting some of his choices. Ovitus had sagged to the ground, on his knees. Good. An easier target to put an arrow into. I reached for my bow—tried to anyway. My limbs were sluggish, half-responsive. I burrowed more stolen lives into my joints where I seemed to need them the most. I could see the ropes of spirit energy wound around my limbs, holding me closed, propping my neck up. Was I still dead? I thought maybe I was. I was half-alive at best. If I looked behind me, I knew I'd see the tunnel. The Sixth Gate wanted me to pass through it. Time was limited here.

I fumbled for Midnight's oilcloth bag, half buried by Redhead's corpse, but there was too much pain. I packed the wound with spirits, but it wasn't enough. I tried anyway. Articulating my fingers was too difficult. Even if I drew the bow from its bag, that wouldn't be enough.

'What have we done?' Ovitus was muttering, over and over. His cursed familiar nosed at him, lapped at his face with a rough pink tongue, but he didn't seem to notice. 'What have we done? What have we done?'

He'd brought this on himself, a nightmare crashing down on everyone around him. He didn't know. Not truly. Didn't know what Sul was, and what would happen if Sul ascended to the plateau and found someone willing to take the Keystone from the Blackwell for him. But he'd known enough. He knew that he'd caused pain, and suffering. He knew what he'd done to Ulovar, his own flesh and blood. I had no sympathy for him.

Ulovar, dead. Liara, dead. Jathan, Gelis, Adanost, and Lassaine LacDaine, and Mendel LacGilfry and hundreds of others. All dead because he couldn't bear the humiliation his own lies had brought about. He was worse than Sul. The Faded fought for the return of his world, of his ancient banished people. At least he believed in something. I wanted Ovitus to die, but hanging on in this broken body, I didn't think I'd much chance of achieving that.

Movement drew my eye. The young woman who had driven Ulovar down stood beside the broken, blasted wreckage of the trap. She reached across and closed Ulovar's eyes.

'I suppose I didn't foresee it all,' she said. 'It's been a long time, Sul.' And her form shivered and shimmered, and she was not young anymore. She was old, so very old, with bands of iron riveted to her scalp, cracks of fire hissing in the rain.

'It doesn't feel so very long to me,' Sul said. He stepped away from Ovitus.

'It wouldn't, I suppose,' Robilar said. 'Does anything?'

'No,' he said. 'Not really.' He pulled the helmet from his head, and tossed it away into the wet grass. 'How long has it been?'

'Seventy years, give or take. I was really quite enamoured with you back then. Before—well.' She gestured towards her broken skull. 'All this.'

'I never stopped loving you, Vedira,' Sul said. 'Even when I had to kill you.'

'When you tried to kill me.' She sighed. 'It's a fickle thing, is it not? Love, I mean. There's a part of me that will always love you, I think. Or at least a part of me that loves an idea of what you seemed to be. That's probably more appropriate. I don't think I ever knew the real you, but that's the way of all love, isn't it?' She sighed, taking up a slender, broken spar of wood that had been part of the trap, and shook free a piece of charred horse meat. She leaned on it like it was a staff. 'You thought you'd get into the Blackwell and take the Keystone? And you sought to use this child to do it?'

Ovitus looked up from his shaking hands, but he said nothing.

I got more spirits into my knees and ankles. My body didn't respond well. Each motion was an effort of controlled thought. Even as I tried to push up, another soul slipped away from me, drifting away into the next world. I sensed its relief, but I tightened my grip on the remainder. I wasn't ready to go. Not yet. I had to see how it would end. My chest was awash with blood, spilt red smeared across the polished planes of borrowed armour. Slowly I made it to my feet, but nobody really cared about me anymore.

'He came to me,' Sul said. 'Or at least, he took on my familiar as his own. You can't blame him too much. He's a man of ambition. He'll do well in the world to come.'

'Waldy is mine,' Ovitus said. He shivered, unable to look up. 'He's all mine. Not anyone else's. He loves me. He's mine.' And he hugged the dog to himself.

Sul's smile was patronising. Ovitus didn't see it.

'So how will this go now, Vedira?' Sul said. 'We obliterate the land with fire and water, thunder and destruction?' He sheathed his sword. 'Should I begin?'

'We've done that dance before,' Robilar said. 'It took you this long to recover, and I never quite did. Our time is done here, Sul. I've held to this place, held to power for too long, perhaps. It is time we went away. Let the young inherit the mess we've left to them.'

'You have something up your sleeve, then?'

'Did you expect less of me? I'm a grandmaster, don't you know that? I know I can't kill you. You'd only come back again, and again. No, we're going to go away together. For all time.'

'Why would I agree to this?' Sul said. 'I've already won, Vedira. I'll take control of Redwinter, and even if this wretch never finds the Fourth Gate, in time I'll find someone who can, or a Sarathi willing to take my orders. I can wait, Vedira. I can wait another seventy years if I must.'

I had made it to my feet. I took my first step. I faltered slightly, my knee threatening to buckle beneath me. My vision was poor, not just the rain but the rebellious souls I contained, straining against the grinding drone of the Sixth Gate as they sought to be freed.

'You will wait, Sul,' Robilar said. 'You will wait for all eternity. And I shall wait alongside you. We'll be together forever.' Wrinkled lips smiled.

Sul launched towards her, the frost-touched sword rising high, blue runes flaring to life as he surged forward. Robilar spoke a word of power, a word I recalled the Queen of Feathers speaking to tear apart a bridge, and Sul staggered as if he'd run directly into a wall of force. His oppression-field roared out of him, and Robilar staggered, clutching the broken spar for support. Their wills collided in a channel of trance and void, blurring the air between them. The grass withered and died, caught fire, crumpled with frost, shot higher as if life itself channelled through it. Flowers began to bloom all around them, bursting into colour before rotting brown and withering on the stalk. The rain around them hung motionless.

Robilar spoke again. Words of power. Words dredged from the dawn of time. Sul's oppression field lashed out harder, trying to crush her down. Ovitus dropped like a stone clutching his head. But not me. Whatever that dark emanation of power was, it was for the living, and I was not that. I was some undead thing, clinging to a third life. I took another step, and another, slowly gaining ground on the Remnant. Another word from Robilar, and the earth began to smoulder, the cracks in her skull growing wider, the liquid fire within popping and hissing. Strands of her hair burned away, falling in smoking tresses.

Five jets of fire billowed from the earth, and from them snaking trails of flame began to wind around, forming a circle. And then the flames began to close in, five points closing on Sul and Robilar.

'No,' Sul said. And he met her words of power with his own, a counter-chant. The flames sputtered. Robilar staggered. A crack split down from her scalp, through an eye, cutting through her face as life-flame began to drip from it. One of her fingers blackened and turned to ash as it fell away. She redoubled her efforts, her words growing louder, but coming slower, each one breaking away from her to feed the flame even as her lips began to char. She sucked in a breath as her feet began to smoke.

'Come with me, Sul,' she said. 'Let me take you exactly where you've longed to go all this time.'

'I. Will. Not.'

A sheen of ice worked its way up from his feet. But he was stronger than Robilar was, and as one of her knees sloughed away in a gush of molten liquid she caught herself on the broken spar and I saw the defeat in her eyes. Sul's counter-spell intensified. His words grew stronger, louder. His shoulders relaxed as he took control, and his words thundered across the grassy moor like hammer blows against bells.

I threw my marionette arms around him from behind and swung an arm around him. It took him by surprise. I locked him around the neck, just a

Torgan had shown me, choking his throat. Took away his means by which to speak. Sometimes it's the simple things that work.

Robilar's words roared out, and the fire closed in. I sensed Sul's sudden panic as he tried to reach back to grab me. And then with the sound of thunder, the fire closed in and the world spun away.

40

I looked into the tunnel, and for a time there was only blackness.

They were around me, with me rather than inside of me, my precious stolen spirits. Most of them I didn't know. Some of them were familiar. Others, I'd trained with. Nimman the Younger, Radessia, Mendel. I'd killed them by the hundred. I was so far past twenty now I couldn't have counted if I'd wanted to.

They stood silent and still, like they were caught suspended in time. A crowd of motionless beings, existing in a moment in which they shouldn't. It seemed unnatural, but there's nothing more natural than death. Life has no meaning without it. I should have figured that from the start maybe, but I hadn't. I was always so slow to figure these things out.

'I'm sorry for what I did to you,' I said. A ghostly figure raised its head for a moment to look at me. It was afraid of me.

'No,' another of them whispered, the sound behind me. 'You're not.'

'I didn't want you all to die,' I said. My words hit the tunnel wall, bounced back to me, echoing over and over. *Die, die, die.* They had nothing to say back to me. What did I expect? The Soul Reaper had torn them from their bodies. I couldn't stuff them back inside. Could I? Maybe. It was the kind of thing I was getting better at figuring out. As I pondered it, another slipped from my grasp and drifted off down the tunnel. It was oddly peaceful here, just me and the ghosts. But not a place I wanted to stay.

'You need to wake up now,' a rich, throaty woman's voice said. 'It's time to fulfil our deal.'

I wanted to blink, and the ghosts had to do that for me. Above me, walls rose up and up, two dozen of them forming something close to a circle. Every wall was a window, glowing with light, the colours dazzling after the tunnel's darkness. Men and women were frozen in stylised forms of coloured glass, beautiful in reds and blues and greens and amber and all the colours that ever existed and ever would. A woman shining with holy light, a man cloaked in crow's feathers, a formless humanoid shape within whirlwind. Other, stranger figures ascended on and up into the vastness of the tower until they were lost to sight.

I was in the Blackwell.

I pushed myself up onto my elbows. Plinths filled the room with their strange ensemble of artefacts. Ciuthach's page, the frozen clocks, the serpent headed staff, the armour, and all the other strange things that were too terrible to be let out into the world. Hoarded down here by the Draoihn, locked away. It was their prison. And that was the point of it, I supposed. That was why I was here. I was not alone.

Grandmaster Vedira Robilar was broken, her body shattered by the powers she'd called upon. Part of her jaw was missing, the iron bands had torn away, jutting like ribs cracked open from the back of her head. Most of her legs were gone, and one hand. She slumped, leaning against a pedestal that held a huge black scorpion's tail. Breath wheezed slowly into her, and slowly out. She was dazed, and weak. But she saw me.

'I don't know how you're still alive,' she said. 'But I'm glad.'

'I'm not sure I am,' I said. My voice sounded alien to me, a foreign accent. Like the ghost that operated it was forming the shapes in the way that came naturally to her.

'And yet, here we are,' she wheezed. A dribble of orange fire trickled from her lips.

'Where's Sul?' I asked. Robilar moved her head half an inch. The slightest of gestures. My spirits creaked me around to look behind me, and skittered back across the floor in alarm.

Sul sat just a few feet from where I'd fallen. He looked unharmed, but he didn't move towards me. Didn't move at all. He remained completely motionless, not so much as a hair quivering on his head. Like he'd been frozen in time.

'Don't worry,' Robilar said. Her voice was so quiet. 'He's not going anywhere, nor harming anyone. He's just another artefact now.'

'He's dead then?'

'No, not dead. The Faded can't truly be destroyed.' She paused to wipe a drip of flame from her charred lips. 'They aren't like us. But the elder wards that prevented him from entering the Blackwell are as strong inside it as they are around it. He can't move. He's bound here, to remain frozen in time. Forever, I hope.'

I crawled across the jade and cadanum circles that covered the floor to the motionless man and looked into Sul's eyes. Looked to see if I could find some sign of life within them. They say that the eyes are the window to the soul, but maybe he didn't even have one. I found nothing there. Nothing at all. I turned away from him, half expecting to feel a cold hand on my neck, but he'd killed me once already. There was little more he could do to me.

'Can I help you?' I asked Robilar.

'Nobody can help me now,' she croaked. 'I'm held together by threads of will. But my trance is starting to fail. I won't hold it long, now. But there is one more thing you can do. Help me upright.'

It was awkward, and it was clumsy, but I did as she asked. I pushed her away from the pedestal, and let the weight of spirits around me carry some of hers. She was so light, so frail. Another vanished from me, and another, and I had to move them from one place to another. Robilar was not the only woman who would not last much longer.

'No, face me towards him,' Robilar said. 'I want him to see me. I want him to know that I beat him, and to gaze on me for the rest of time.'

'Is there no way to save you?' I said.

'I beat him, in the end,' Robilar said. 'I wondered once what the point of this ongoing existence was. When there was nothing new to experience, nothing I hadn't already done. It was Sul who kept me going. I think that now I would like to rest.'

As I held her, Robilar began to grow heavier. I thought it was my spirit strength failing. I could count those that were left to me now, twenty-five, twenty-four as another left me. I'd lost hold of so many of them as Robilar brought us here through fire. She grew heavier, and heavier, and as I looked down I saw that the ragged, broken stumps of her legs were growing outward, but they grew grey and hard. Stone. Her hair blossomed like an opening flower, covering her shattered head, but all of it was hard, matte stone.

'See me, Sul,' Robilar said. 'See me forever.'

The pulsing of Robilar's Second Gate began to diminish. I no longer had to support her. It only took a few moments, but when it did I no longer held a broken body. My arms were wrapped around the statue of her younger self. Proud, vibrant, beautiful. Her hands rested on freshly grown knees. The trance dimmed further, and then, as the last of her became stone, it stopped altogether.

Grandmaster Vedira Robilar, Draoihn of the Fifth Gate, was gone.

I breathed air that I didn't need. Just a reflex. I rose slowly. There was only silence now. Sul and the statue that had been Robilar stared at each other, and so I had to hope, they would remain. He was powerless here. I thought it best not to touch him at all.

Beyond them, I noticed it for the first time. The Keystone, on a pedestal on the far side of the room. It was just a smooth-edged, triangular piece of stone cut with runic inscriptions. Such a little thing to want to take from this place beneath the earth. A small stone to cast such cosmic ripples. I left it where it was. I supposed that it would have to be Merovech LacClune, or maybe Kelsen, who would come down here and lead the first candidate down into the Crown. *Leave it to them,* I thought. *Everything I touch charred and flaked away like ash.*

It had all come down around me. So many people had been lost. So many beyond these walls were dead. I would be too, unless I replenished the ghosts that worked my body. To find more I'd have to kill, and I was sick and tired of killing. In my grief for Ulovar, I'd let all control go. In a rage, I'd taken things I shouldn't have. Maybe I'd saved us all. But I felt the wrongness of what lay inside me. Could I let it all go? Perhaps I should have done so long ago, back when I first started on this path. It was no wonder people feared the Sarathi. Look what I'd done, touching only the edges of the power I could wield. For a few moments I'd seen myself as Hallenae, the Riven Queen, back to take the world for my own. But I didn't want that. I'd once said to Ulovar that all I really wanted was a bit of sun on my face. I didn't think the sun would touch me now.

I looked down at the rent in my armour. I ought to see it at least. Piece by piece I unbuckled the straps that held the breastplate in place and gingerly pulled it away. Sul had got me pretty good. Just to the left of my sternum, driven sideways so that it had slunk in right between my ribs. It was a mortal wound—had already been a mortal wound, sutured with spirit. But the damage was done.

I had not had a long life. Eighteen years of existence is too short by anyone's standards. But perhaps, with all I'd seen over that brief glimpse into the world, it had been enough. Sometimes it seemed like outside of the fear, and the pain, and preparing for fear and pain, there wasn't much else in the world at all. I'd tried to carve out a little niche of it for myself, secreted among the enemy. For the briefest of times I'd had friends, and a boy had wanted me, and a girl had wanted me. And they'd wanted me for *me*, not just the shell, not just the idea of me, but they'd seen down into who I was and it hadn't frightened them. And in truth I'd wanted them back all along, both of them, as selfish as it seemed to be to admit it. It wasn't a crime to love two people, but it certainly made things hard.

Not that I could have given them what they'd wanted anyway. Look at me now: a bloody incision deep in my chest, driven by ghosts, slowly fading away in the darkness. I'd denied everything I felt because I was afraid of what I was becoming. Of what I was. And I'd been right to, it turned out. I'd killed hundreds, had torn their souls from their bodies. I'd blown men and women apart with arrows. There would be husbands and wives and children and parents who hadn't yet heard the news that their loved ones lay dead in a wet field, and the world would break a little more with every story told. I think I'd known that all this was coming, that once the dam had been breached it was only a matter of time before everything poured through in a torrent. A steady escalation that broke down the walls until suddenly there was nothing left to oppose it, and everything burst through in a flood. My time, brief as it had been, had brought death and destruction in equal measure to the good I'd done.

It was time to die.

Why not here? I didn't want to go outside. Maybe I didn't deserve the sun on my face after all. I'd seen into what came after. There was more beyond our world. Alianna hadn't been able to explain it to me, but there was something.

I lay down on the ground and looked up into that haze, where the light from countless stained-glass images blurred, miles above me. Not a bad view to look into. One by one the spirits would drift away from me, and in a hundred years I'd be nothing but a name, written as a warning in the archives of the Draoihn.

'Raine,' the Queen of Feathers said, and she stood on the far side of the room beyond the circles in the floor. I didn't lift my head to look at her. 'It's time to complete our bargain. You owe me a favour.' Her gown, the blue of day's last light, had a raven feathered mantle. The whisper of wings at her back brushed the walls. She wore her war paint, striped across her cheeks, her nose, her forehead.

This was all I needed. I couldn't even die in peace.

'Honestly, I don't feel like I'm much good for favours right now,' I said.

'We made a bargain in this place. I know you remember.' I sighed heavily. But why had I expected any less? I couldn't even die well.

'What can I do for you now that I couldn't do last time we were here?' I said.

'Technically, quite a lot,' the Queen of Feathers said. 'But you didn't need me then, did you? You asked for help when you had the solution to hand all along.'

'You told me to pick up something from the Blackwell and use it,' I said. 'Thanks for that. Really helpful. I can't say I feel I got much from that deal.'

'You're still here, aren't you?' the Queen of Feathers said.

'I guess,' I said. 'But not for long. Can't I just die in peace?'

'No. That's where our bargain comes in,' the Queen of Feathers said. 'That's what you're going to do for me.'

'What?'

'You're going to live,' she said. 'You want to sink down into nothing and let it all go. But we had a deal, Raine of Redwinter. And you're honour-bound to fulfil it. So you won't sink quietly into the night. You're going to get up and walk out of here. You're going to take all that pain inside of you, all that loss, and you're going to take it with you, and you're going to survive.'

Of all the things she could have asked me, that was perhaps the thing I wanted least right then.

'What's the point?' I said. 'It's all turned to shit. Everyone's dead. I burned every bridge I had.'

'Not everyone,' the Queen of Feathers said. 'Now get up. Get up and walk out of here, across the bridge, and hold on just as long as you possibly can.'

'For what?'

'For everything.'

. . . . . .

The stairs were hard. Seventeen spirits left to me, and they had to work all the harder to power dead limbs upwards. Another evaporated on to the Afterworld as I made the top and looked out onto the dark, wet world.

It had stopped raining, at least. Night had taken the light from the sky. There was freshness in the air, if I gave the command to breathe it in. The stone bridge that spanned out from the Blackwell led across the empty air.

I took a step onto it, and then another, and each movement was awkward, difficult. I had nothing left to me now. But a promise is a promise, even if it was unlikely to be one I could keep for very long.

A dog began barking. Rough, urgent bites at the air.

They were waiting for me at the other end of the Blackwell's bridge, and I wondered how long I'd been down there. I'd been unconscious a while I guessed, or maybe Robilar's travelling spell took longer on the outside than it did inside. But they were prepared. That treacherous dog sat off towards the back, no wagging of his tail now. Ah. He'd led them to me. He wasn't a dog, not really, but he'd sniffed me out. But there was Kyrand of Murr, and a worried-looking Draoihn Palanost, and Suanach, our Master of Artifice, and beyond them a group of surviving Winterra. And right in the centre, Ovitus. Battered and bruised, sporting a dressing on the side of his face, another on his neck. But it was Ovitus nonetheless.

'It's true, then,' Councillor Kyrand said. I stood twenty feet away from them along the bridge. 'Where is the grandmaster?'

'She's down there,' I said in my strange, thin, borrowed accent. 'She won't be coming out. She's gone.'

'Look at her chest,' Suanach muttered. 'Nobody should be able to survive that wound. It's as he said.'

'I told you,' Ovitus said. 'I came to root out those that serve the Night Below. And I have done so. You should see now that I was right.'

'Then it's time to destroy her,' Kyrand said, and she raised her hand. I felt her Third Gate opening, a three-tiered trance rippling over itself.

'Wait,' Ovitus said. He held his hand out to me.

'She's too dangerous!' Kyrand said, and the light around her seemed to darken as the air shimmered around her hand. I considered trying to go against them—perhaps I could muster enough force for another Banshee's Wail. But doing so would have meant the death of me as well, and the only reason I'd come out of here was because the Queen of Feathers had made me. It was all I could do to keep myself moving. I was no danger to anybody.

'No. The rule of law must stand,' Ovitus said. 'She's spent. There's nothing she can do to hurt us here and there are truths she must speak still so that all hear them. She won't hurt us. Not now.' He took a step forward, offering that soft-skinned hand. 'Come, Sarathi Raine. Come to me.'

Come to me. That's all he'd really wanted.

I looked down into the drop that fell away down the bridge, the dizzying fall towards the rocks below. I could jump. Maybe that would be for the best. But I'd made a promise, and it was one that I probably wouldn't have to keep for very long anyway.

I forced my unsteady legs to hobble the last of the distance. Strong hands in gauntlets took me, frisked me down, and dragged me away towards the Eagle Lawn, where they had already started to build the pyre.

41

It was what I had feared ever since I was brought to Redwinter, and it was upon me now, but I didn't care so very much anymore. So many were gone, the life that I'd been building here had been shattered. The buildings were the same, and the air smelled of night blooming flowers just as it always did, and the cool Harran wind swept down over the walls to raise the same old gooseflesh on my arms and legs. But it wasn't the same place. Too much was missing.

Somebody began ringing a bell well before I got to the lawn. The same lawn where Ovitus had held his betrothal feast. There were spectators gathered around, a good two hundred Draoihn and their servants. People shouted things as I was dragged on by, a ring of burning torches. A flaming brand is an inefficient way to light an area when we had cadanum globes and lanterns, but I guess it was all about drama. The air brimmed with hostility. What a difference a few months make.

I saw familiar faces in the crowd. Draoihn Palanost, my wonderful teacher, had been weeping. She'd lost a lot of her former students today, and mostly at my hand, so I didn't think her tears were for me. Haronus LacClune watched me with grim eyes, the demon-scratch on his forehead glowing faintly in the night. He wouldn't be sad to see me go. Castus was beside him, but he didn't meet my eye. That felt like a betrayal, but then, I was the one who'd been lying to him the whole time. With what everyone now knew about me, I could hardly blame him. Princess Mathilde and her bodyguard and her young niece and a bunch of their entourage looked uncomfortable. I didn't know what relationship had survived there, but evidently she'd surrendered Redwinter after the grandmaster was slain along with half the Winterra. I suppose that was my fault. She couldn't have held it, not against the army Ovitus had brought with him, but at least she'd tried. I couldn't blame her for choosing survival now.

The retainers from the LacNaithe greathouse stood in a group. Tarquus, Ehma, Howen, Bossal, Potalia, Hehnry, Margen . . . The Draoihn would watch. I couldn't expect less than that. But the retainers seemed something more of an indignity. I felt so sorry that they'd changed my bedding, dusted my room, served me meals. I wondered how it must have felt for them, to hear that there'd been an enemy in their midst this whole time.

Until it does, nobody truly understands that it will happen to them one day. I looked for the Queen of Feathers. She'd asked me to live, and I didn't think I could keep our bargain for very long, if indeed I was alive at all right now. It seemed a cruel demand to make, even for her. I could feel my pulse in my neck. It was sluggish, the ghost who'd been charged with powering my heart growing tired. Thirteen ghosts left to me. Ovitus wanted to see me stand trial. He loved the law. Loved its little nuances and sub-clauses, and anything that fit within them was morally right to him. But there's a difference between law and morality. The law is made by the powerful to serve the powerful, to maintain a status quo and the easy transference of power. The rules of men are as fallible as those that make them, after all. But as usual, the Queen of Feathers had emerged and then disappeared. At least after this I was done with her. But then, I was done with everything.

The pyre. One of the trestles from the betrothal feast had been used for the base, and brushwood had been stacked up around it. Preparations for this had begun before they'd taken me.

'How long will this take?' I asked, that accent still tinting my voice.

'Only an hour,' Ovitus said. 'I'm so sorry that this happened to you, Raine. I'm so sorry that this is what you became.'

'You should be,' I said. 'It's at least partly your fault.'

'No,' Ovitus said. 'I'm tired of being blamed for things you've lied about. I pity you. But I can't stand for your lies. Not anymore. Whatever love I have for you, I owe it to the people.'

'You aren't sorry,' I said. 'You've never felt sorry for anything. Not even once.'

It didn't make a difference whether he heard it or not. He wouldn't have been able to comprehend it anyway.

I released the ghosts who'd been holding up my ankles. They were faded and worn down, doing a lot of the work. They went off to Anavia, or Skuttis, as their deeds would allow. I didn't replace them, I just sagged and let myself be carried instead. Eleven to go. Eleven lives to release and then I'd be gone from this place. To the freezing rivers of Skuttis, I figured. That's what *my* deeds allowed.

I wished the tunnel would be quiet, but it was calling to me. It hungered for me. It loved me.

They carried me up and bound me to the central stake. Those with the grave sight were stoned to death, but for a full blown Sarathi, it was the fire.

'The laws of the Draoihn are clear,' Ovitus called out to the assembled Draoihn, the few remaining apprentices who'd been too inexperienced to go to the Testing, men and women of the Winterra who'd survived the Soul Reaper, the common folk who laboured beneath them all. 'Raine of Dunan, who gave her oaths at the Testing, has shown herself to be in league with the enemy. In league with the Night Below. Today she committed a monstrous act, and slew three hundred of our brave warriors. Our friends. Our kin. Are there any that will speak in her defence?'

For a few moments there was nothing but silence.

'How do you know that?' a voice called from the crowd. It was Castus.

'Do you deny the Winterra were slain?' he asked.

'I don't deny fact,' Castus answered. Haronus LacClune looked furious, but he let Castus have his say. He wore the oxblood, after all. 'But what is the proof that it was her?'

Ovitus stood up beside me on the pyre, using it as a stage.

'I went out yesterday to meet with Van LacAud, to broker peace between our divided clans. I was there when she unleashed her power upon him. And when she killed Lassaine LacDaine, not only Draoihn but a member of the Council of Night and Day. There are others here who can attest to that.'

Ovitus gestured. Three men and two women of the Winterra stepped forward. They were honest, at least. I had done those things, and they'd been there among the rune-carved trees. I must have got the rest of them with the Soul Reaper. As they gave their testimony, I felt the blood beating in my temples, in my neck. Slowing. Ten, and then a few seconds later, nine ghosts remained. I let my wrists go. I didn't need them anymore anyway. The Queen of Feathers wanted me to endure this for some reason. Maybe she just wanted to punish me for having summoned her that time. It wasn't like she'd have had another chance to ask a favour of me.

Castus had nothing to say to that. He looked at me just once, but the Winterra were convincing. He ended up just giving a nod, and stepping back into the crowd. No use for me anymore.

'Raine of the High Pastures,' Ovitus said grandly. 'Will you admit that you have broken the law of the Draoihn and betrayed Redwinter?'

'I'll do nothing of the sort,' I said. 'Everything I did, I did for Redwinter. For the Crown. I worked at the behest of Grandmaster Vedira Robilar, whom you should have been serving also. I won't answer to a usurper, nor a traitor to the Crown.'

'These are rich accusations to come from a Sarathi, who has lain like a viper in our midst,' Ovitus shouted. 'Everything you've said since you came here has been a lie.' His eyes narrowed as he regarded me, and then he roared at the audience: 'Everything!'

'You killed your own uncle to take his power,' I said. I couldn't raise my voice to match his. Every ghost within me was weak. I made my words for him alone. 'You allied with the Night Below. You took a familiar. All because you're petty, and jealous, and weak. All that's happened, all you've done, is just because you were embarrassed. You see your needs as greater than those of everyone around you. I could have been your friend. But you don't have any friends. You can't see beyond yourself, even when it comes to life and death.'

My words washed over Ovitus like a spill of wave across a beach, momentarily there and then receding back until they weren't even memory.

'Friends?' he said. 'No, we are not friends, Raine. We never were, not truly. You've had a knife in my back the whole time.'

'That just . . . isn't true,' I said. But it didn't really matter what was true or not.

'The Sarathi speaks of her friends!' Ovitus yelled out towards the crowd. 'Let her final hour commence. Let those *friends* of hers come forth and speak on her behalf. Plead for her life. Plead for her innocence, if you will. I have staked my name on my words. Let those who would defend her stake their own names, or the matter will be settled and fire will cleanse the world of her taint.'

Another spirit left me. Eight to go. I wouldn't feel the fire. I'd go before then. I sagged against the bindings.

'Keep her upright,' Kyrand of Murr said gravely. 'She should see for herself that nobody will come to her aid.'

A tall man, an executioner in a black hood, clambered up onto the construction. He took my head in his hands, and pulled it back up to rest against the stake. His hands were warm against my cold, dead skin. I looked out across those assembled. Maybe Palanost would speak for me? No. I looked to Castus, and he had the dignity to look back at me and meet my eye, even as he said nothing. I gave him a sad little smile. He'd been good, when I'd needed him.

'The hour begins now,' Ovitus said. He produced the hourglass I'd given him as his betrothal gift, and placed it on my funeral pyre.

The sand began to flow, a steady stream.

We all know that it's coming—death. It's one of the few certainties in life. When you brush close to it, when you find yourself hurt or sick or on the edge of mortality, it's frightening. You get better, but the fear never really leaves you, because you know that one day, it's going to happen again. Maybe it'll happen a few times, and you'll get lucky, or healed, or somehow make your escape. But in the end, it's going to come for you. One day, you'll see it coming, and you'll know that this is it. This is the end. You don't know it when you're young, it's all too far away. But you get older, and then you know it, and then you never stop being afraid.

The sands poured through, and a fifth of the time passed in what seemed a blink of an eye. Nobody moved. Nobody came forward. That was the trap. That doing so would condemn anyone who tried, and when none did, the matter would be settled for all time. And then there was repentance; the chance that I might come to fear the fire more than I feared confession, as the minutes ticked by and the prospect of a friendless, lonely death set in. And then there was the healing: that by seeing how alone I stood, those around me would bond together, cast me out, and find their strength renewed.

The ghost who'd been working my left knee was so tired. I felt sorry for her, so I let her go. Seven, now. The night was cold, but the executioner's hands on my face were warm. Funny, that it was the man who'd set me alight who provided the only comfort I was to receive.

The pain in my chest had dimmed. The sharp edges were gone and it was just a dull ache. Better to die without pain, I supposed. I'd been ready to die. I just wished it hadn't been like this.

'There's still time to confess, Raine,' Ovitus said for me alone. 'If you do, I could—I could—make a case for exile. It doesn't have to be this way.'

'You're the one trying to kill me,' I said. My voice had gone back to its own way of speaking at least. 'I'm not going to beg.'

'A confession is not begging,' he hissed. 'I don't *want* to do this. I told you how I felt. I told you the truth of things. You can't think that I want this.'

'And yet you set it all in motion,' I said. 'You made it happen. You and your law. Have to follow the rules, right?'

He stepped up beside me and leaned in close, taking my jaw in his hand. His voice was a soft whisper.

'The rules don't apply to people like you and me,' he said.

Spoken just like the grandmaster. I was so tired.

'Ovitus,' I said. 'I think that maybe when you're powerful enough that you don't have to follow the rules, keeping to them matters more than ever.'

Ovitus released me and my head sagged forwards. The executioner let it flop. A horse was riding fast across the gravel paths, hooves crunching the stones away. People scattered from its path as the rider galloped into the centre of the Eagle Lawn.

'I'm still in time?' she asked.

For once, Ovitus was lost for words. I forced my head up. Esher slapped the rump of her horse and he trotted away.

'Don't do anything rash now, Esher,' Ovitus said.

'That's Draoihn Esher of Harranir to you, apprentice,' Esher said. 'And I'm fecking tired of people telling me to stop acting rashly.'

'You've been deceived,' Ovitus began. Esher responded by drawing her sword.

'Oh, will you just shut your whining for one damn day? I'm Draoihn Esher, born of Harranir, and I'm here to protest the innocence of Raine of Redwinter.'

My heart. My poor, broken heart felt a jolt of fire run through it as she spoke.

'Why would you do this?' Ovitus said. 'You were there, Esher. You were with us.'

'When you murdered Draoihn Liara LacShale? Yes, I was there.'

Ovitus skipped over that like he was hurdling a log.

'She doesn't want you,' he said viciously, jumping down from the pyre to stand opposite her. 'She never wanted you. She used you.'

'She's my friend,' Esher said. 'And I love her. You see, Ovitus, that's what you never understood about love. It doesn't have to flow both ways. You can love someone and want what's good for them and you don't have to ask for anything in return. You love them when they're strong, and you love them when they're weak. Asking for anything else isn't fair.'

Ovitus sneered at her.

'Only the weak insist that life be fair.'

I'd heard it before, what seemed a long time ago, from Castus. I'd said it myself. What a fool I'd been to think it true for a time.

The light of the torches glowed in her hair, and her blind eye caught the light like a mirror.

'It's the strong who insist that life be fair for everyone,' Esher said. 'I froze before, when I should have put a stop to it all. But I won't freeze now. I have the right to challenge you to trial by battle. I challenge you, Apprentice Lac-Naithe.'

My heart beat again, an irregular thump against the drained-out ghost. He'd been doing his best. I wanted to thank him. I wanted him to know he'd got me this far, to see this moment. The ghosts in my arms were all done. Four remained. Eyes, heart, lungs. It was only the executioner's arms around my waist and chest that were holding me up. I wanted to call out to Esher, to tell her that she didn't have to do this. That it had been enough that she came. I wanted to tell her that I loved her, and I was so, so sorry.

'You can't beat me,' Ovitus said. Baffled. 'I have three Gates.'

'What was it you said that time? "Sword-fighting is no business for a woman"? You think you can't take me on without a Gate? Why not let the Light Above decide who's telling the truth? Unless you're not man enough to fight me.'

Ovitus looked about at those around him.

'Why would I . . .' he began.

'Fight her, my *beloved*,' Princess Mathilde called. 'Fight her fairly. Prove what kind of man you are. No trances, no Gates. Just steel.' Her face was cold as ice.

Ovitus swallowed. He was no great swordsman, whatever pose he took. But he held out a hand, and Little Maran—poor Little Maran, still under his command—crossed over and brought him his sword. Ovitus drew it with a flourish.

'Very well,' he said. 'The truth guides my hand. May whatever creatures of the Night Below you've consorted with guide yours, and I will prove what I must.'

Esher. My beautiful, wonderful Esher, what are you doing?

Ovitus rose into a watchtower guard, blade pointed to the fat full moon above, as Esher dropped her sword back over her shoulder in the wrath position. No warm-up. No stretching or limbering. The sand in the hourglass trickled through. If she'd only come half an hour later, she would have been spared this.

I sucked in a breath, and it was deep and cold. I couldn't hold the spirit there much longer. Two, three breaths maybe. I took the deepest suck of air that I could, and held it. There was no pain anymore. It all goes away as you're about to die.

Esher came at Ovitus in a flurry of strikes. Had I never realised how good she really was? She flowed like liquid gold, rising high and low, and Ovitus fell back away from her swinging wild, inaccurate parries. I saw an opening and thought she'd take it and finish him but she slowed, settled back into a long-tail stance, her sword behind her.

Ovitus threw a big overhand cut. Esher just skipped back away from him. Judged the distance easily, even in the torchlight.

'You lied about everything,' she said. 'You did this. You did it all. You got everyone killed. You murdered my friend!'

She came at him again, her blade crashing against his, sparks biting blue in the night. She levered his blade to the side and poised above him, ready to send the thrust down into him that would finish him. But she held back and stepped away again as Ovitus staggered swinging wildly at a sword that was no longer there.

'She was just a dumb whore!' Ovitus yelled back at her. 'She never knew what she could have had.'

'That's what you think of all of us, isn't it?' Esher said. 'That's all any woman is to you.' And she flashed forward again. Chimes of ringing metal sounded louder in my ears than they should. I released the breath. Two to go. I just wanted to see the end, and then I could go. Then I could rest, and all the grief would go away. My chest didn't even hurt anymore.

'Breathe,' the executioner said. His grip tightened on me. But I wouldn't waste it.

This time Esher drew Ovitus's parry, stepped in and wrapped her arm around his sword. Held it there as he tried to force it to move.

'Admit it,' she said. 'I'm better than you.'

She kicked out, knocking him back but releasing his sword. Ovitus hit the ground, scrambled back to his feet. *No,* I thought, *please finish it now.* I didn't have the breath left. I didn't have anything left.

'Breathe, damn it,' the executioner said, but he didn't know.

Ovitus dusted himself down. He seemed to be thinking for a moment, then looked from Esher and across me to the executioner, and back to Esher.

'You're stalling,' he said. 'You're buying time.'

The executioner stepped in front of me, looking me in the eye as he lifted the front of his helm.

'Raine, for the love of the Light Above, for once will you do something I ask and just *breathe*,' Sanvaunt said.

I took a breath as I released the last of the ghosts. And the air surged into me, and I felt my hands, and my feet, and I looked down and the bloody wound in my chest was just an angry red mark against my skin. I felt my heart pulsing, growing stronger as Sanvaunt poured life-fire through me. I looked into his eyes and a little whimper escaped me. They'd both come back for me, after everything I'd done to them both. They'd come back.

'Get away from her!' Ovitus shouted.

'We're not done,' Esher said. And this time she attacked him in earnest. Ovitus parried the first attack, tried to counter and she'd already judged it, deflecting and driving her point at his chest. Ovitus's Second Gate boomed out into the world, a bull in a suit of iron bars, stung by a bee and Esher's blade flexed against it. Ovitus staggered back. Sheer fury contorted his face, twisting it into something that hated harder than the Night Below had ever managed.

'You think this means anything?' Ovitus roared. 'You think I'll let a Sarathi walk from here just because you spent more time doing pointless exercises in the dirt? You can all die together.' He snapped his finger at the Winterra. 'Apprehend her, and add her to the pyre.'

The Winterra shared reluctant looks. They'd been told the rules, and they'd seen how it had gone. Ovitus's fury turned on them too.

'If you want to be back in exile you only had to say,' Ovitus growled. 'Very well, I'll do it myself.' His Third Gate, Ulovar's stolen Third Gate, opened.

'I knew I couldn't hurt you,' Esher said. 'I just needed to give my other horse time to get here.'

'Your other horse?'

'Yes,' Esher said. She closed her eyes. 'I need you now.'

It emerged from a shaft of moonlight. A massive, perfect, powerful mare, eighteen hands or more, emerging from the darkness in all its shimmering, silver-light glory. She came at a full run, and Esher dropped her weapon and vaulted up onto its back as it charged through. Ovitus screamed his rage and let fly a blast of air that missed, ripping into a tree to bring it crashing down. The horse came up alongside the pyre, and I hadn't even realised Sanvaunt had cut my bonds.

'Jump,' he said, and we leapt into air. The mare swerved, caught us and then we were pulsing through the darkness at impossible speed, twice, thrice as fast as any ordinary horse could have carried us. We tore the night apart, speeding faster than a gale as we passed between Redwinter's greathouses, across her gardens and practice courts, past the grandmaster's residence.

'There's nowhere to go,' I said. 'We'll hit the wall.'

Esher looked back at me with pure joy on her face.

'Just trust the fecking horse!'

It swerved, tracking off towards the Blackwell and the gulf of space before its spire, and then it leapt from the edge. I clung to Sanvaunt's back as we sailed out into the night, arcing through the sky like a comet.

42

We fled into the night. And the night became dawn, and day, and summer and winter, and dawn broke though there had never been a night. I was aware that my arms wrapped around Sanvaunt, and Esher ahead of him, and I felt them more as warmth, and feeling, and there was so much love inside them and so much that was chipped and cracked or broken in half, or shattered, but the horse beneath us was a surge of love and power that kept us riding through the universe. It steadied us, even as it carried us away.

I was glad to be leaving the world behind us. I had never fit in there. Its people had doomed me to darkness just for being what I was, and now I was so much more what I was than I had ever been before.

The world beneath us changed and blurred, like water had soaked through a painting and made its colours run. They dripped and bled into one another, and then faded. The thing you learn about magic is that there's always a price. Nothing is ever as simple as it might seem. I didn't mind. It was better than burning.

'Hold tight to me,' Sanvaunt said. 'Just hold on and don't let go.'

I wish I could have heard those words before I made such a mess of things. Maybe things would have gone differently. Consciousness was fading away, heady at the edges. There was so little of me left that had the strength to cling on. There was no ground beneath us. There was no earth, no air around us. There wasn't anything. Or maybe there were circles, circles that spread out and around from every tiny thing that made up the world and the stars and whatever lay beyond. Spheres within spheres.

'It's beautiful,' I muttered.

'Stay with us,' Esher said. And then there was Sanvaunt, saying 'Where are we?' but by that point I was gone.

. . . . . .

I awoke to the smell of burning. Not hostile, but there, drifting in the air, distant woodsmoke. I blinked and looked up to see a broad, oppressive red sky. No sunset here, just red, blood red, dense but cold. There was a chill in the air, but no breeze. No wind. Absolute stillness. Absolute quiet. I had never heard anything like it, or rather, I don't think I'd ever encountered such an utter absence of sound before. My body hurt. There was a pulsing ache in my chest, where a sword had pierced me. It was sharp and unkind. Breath entered me, and left me again, and the cycle repeated. I concentrated just on breathing. I felt that if I stopped, I'd never recover it, but I tried to muffle the soft sound of my own inhalations. The world was too still for me to disturb.

I was so tired. Everything had run out of me, had dissipated into that vast crimson sky. There were no souls left to burn, except perhaps my own, and even that felt distant. If I could even claim to have one at all.

'She's awake,' I heard Esher say, and it was as though her voice came from behind a layer of blankets. Closed off, indistinct. Steps on stone followed, and then there was Sanvaunt over me.

'Can you sit?'

It was a question worth asking. I pushed upright. My hands and feet had fallen asleep, but as muscles pulled tight the blood began to return to them in a painful surge. My eyes weren't quite working right. The angles all seemed strangely off, like I was looking through whorls in a pane of glass.

'I can sit,' I said, and my voice was flat and dampened, as if by fog. Esher wasn't far from us. I took in the land around us, and I had no clever remark. No scorn to pour. I didn't know what to think.

We three, perhaps the only three in this desolate place, were atop a vast domed stone, jutting from the marsh. A vast swamp stretched out as far as the eye could see. Hummocks of earth, topped with brown grass and motionless reeds, wore moats of stagnant water. I had never seen a place so desolate, so devoid of life. Clouds of fog hung low across the earth, unmoving. I saw no sun. No clouds. Nothing.

'What is this place?' I asked. 'Where are we?'

Neither Sanvaunt nor Esher had an answer for me.

Amidst the endless swampland, the remnants of once-great structures rose broken and lonely. The ruins of a castle lay one way, walls collapsed and turrets fallen. In the other direction, pieces of a statue far larger than anything man should have been able to craft lay fallen. Here, a great hand of dark stone curled its fingers up from the murk. A half-submerged head watched us with a deep-set, round eye. I shuddered. They were not statues of men.

I couldn't have said how long I'd slept.

'Where are we?' I asked again.

'We're not anywhere,' Sanvaunt said, turning to me. He looked as worn as I felt, his cheeks sunken and the hollows beneath his eyes lying heavy and shadowed. Esher nodded gravely, but said nothing.

'This is the hidden realm,' I said. 'Isn't it? That's where the moon horse brought us. It carried us into the Fault.'

'I think so,' Esher said. 'We're not in Harran anymore. That's for sure.'

'How do we get back?'

'I don't know,' Esher said. 'The moon horse didn't stay.'

We sat there for a time, looking out over the swampland and saying nothing. Despite everything that had happened, every horror and battle we'd been through, I felt a sense of peace. I knew it wouldn't last. Not now, not with everything that had happened. But not every day is about tomorrow. Sometimes, it's sufficient just to exist, even when you find yourself far from home.

'You came for me,' I said at last.

'Of course we came for you,' Sanvaunt said. 'What else would we do?'

'Stayed away,' I said. 'Given up on me. I didn't deserve your help.'

'That's all in the past,' Esher said. 'It doesn't matter so very much now, does it?'

'Of course it does,' I said. 'I'm sorry. I'm sorry for being such a dreadful friend, to both of you. Whatever else I was feeling, that should have come first. I'll make it up to you. Somehow.'

There were no birds here. No animals. Nothing stirring in the water. It was a dead land. Even the blood-tinted sky seemed broken, cracked.

'Does anyone else feel like we were children, before all this?' Esher asked. 'Like everything changed so much, so quickly. It's like there was all this . . . stuff, and now—I don't know. It's just different somehow.'

'There was stuff,' I said. 'Lots of stuff. I'll tell you about it, if you want.'

'Ulovar is dead,' Sanvaunt said. 'And Liara, and most of our friends. We're renegades now. Whether we were right or wrong, we're outlawed. There's no doubt about that.' He looked around. 'I doubt it matters much, here.'

'We weren't wrong,' Esher said. 'We did what we had to.' She looked at Sanvaunt, and then to me. There was something she wanted to say.

'Just ask,' I said. 'I'm far too tired to keep secrets anymore.'

'What are you two?' she said. 'How did it happen?'

'I don't really know,' Sanvaunt said. 'Do you?'

I sighed. I could take a guess, at least.

'I died a couple of times. I could see the dead as a kid. Then one day, I had to save Ovitus of all people, and to do it, I had to go deeper. I think I'd been beyond the Sixth Gate before. I think perhaps I've always been slipping in and out of it, whether I meant to or not. But I pushed at it, and I got in. But there's balance in everything. What was it Palanost used to say about forces?'

'Every force has an equal and opposite reaction,' Esher said. 'Something like that?'

'Right. Something like that. Like when someone uses the Third Gate, they have to take the energy from somewhere else. I think that those who open the Fifth and Sixth Gates come in pairs. Robilar and her sister were the two sides of that coin, Kelsen and his wife as well. And when I opened myself fully to the Sixth Gate, it woke the Fifth in Sanvaunt. Opening onto death had to open something up to life.'

'Does it hurt when you use it?' Sanvaunt asked.

'Sometimes,' I said. 'But probably not in the way you mean. Does the Fifth Gate hurt?'

'Every time,' he said. 'But I can bear it.'

'A heart bond,' Esher said. 'That's what that creature called it.'

I reached across for her hand and for a terrifying moment I feared she'd withdraw. But she turned her own over, and locked fingers with me. I did the same with Sanvaunt.

'We're all heart bonded, whether it's magic or not,' I said. 'I'd given up. I thought it was over, and I was glad. You brought me back to life, both of you. I'm glad I'm not dead.'

'So am I,' Esher said.

Sanvaunt had a knapsack. He took out a roll of bandages, a pair of scissors, thread, lining them up with great care. He took out a little hip flask, then carefully repacked his bag.

'I don't know where we are, or where that horse left us, but I'm glad we're here. Wherever, whatever this is. Too many of us didn't make it.' He raised the flask. 'Here's to Ulovar,' he said. 'And to Liara, and Jathan, and Adanost, and Gelis.' He drank, and passed it to Esher.

'And to Vedira Robilar,' Esher said. She took a swig and passed it to me. I sighed.

'And to everyone else who died just because they got in the way,' I said. 'Poor bastards one and all.'

We drank our small toast, and it was all we could do for everyone we'd never see again. We sat quietly for a time, the whisky sour and thick on our lips, and when the bottle was empty, we gazed out across the Fault. The moon horse had carried us out of our world and into a layer below it. Not so far from the true world, not so far from the Night Below. I don't think my friends understood where we were, not truly. They didn't know who dwelt here. We had to find a way back. We had to put right the things that had gone so badly wrong. There were people who had to pay. There were scores that needed to be settled.

From a great distance away, we heard the sound of great bells being rung. A small tremor began to rumble through the ground, and we scooted back from the edge of the stone as ripples flowed across the inky water and little pebbles were set to dancing. We huddled together, as though shielding one another with our bodies. It soon passed, but the bells pealed on, and on. They rang from the sky.

'What does it mean?' I asked.

'The king is dead,' Sanvaunt said. 'The Crown is uncontrolled. The succession has begun.'

'So what do we do now?' I said. 'Everything's different.'

Esher put one arm around my shoulders, and another around Sanvaunt's.

'We run,' she said. 'And then we fight.'

Dramatis Personae

LacNaithe Household in Redwinter

Ulovar LacNaithe—Van of the clan, Draoihn of the Fourth Gate, holds one of the seats on the Council of Night and Day

Ovitus LacNaithe—Heir to the LacNaithe clanhold, nephew to Ulovar, cousin to Sanvaunt, holds the rank of Thail as well as being an apprentice

Sanvaunt LacNaithe—Draoihn of the First Gate, nephew of Ulovar, cousin to Ovitus

Raine 'Clanless' / Raine Wildrose—An apprentice sponsored by Ulovar

Esher of Harranir—An apprentice sponsored by Ulovar

Jathan of Kwend—An apprentice sponsored by Ulovar

Adanost of Murr—An apprentice sponsored by Ulovar

Colban Giln—An apprentice sponsored by Ulovar

Gelis LacAud—An apprentice sponsored by Ulovar

Liara LacShale—An apprentice sponsored by Ulovar, youngest daughter of Kaldhoone LacShale

Hazia LacFroome—An apprentice formerly sponsored by Ulovar, fostered at Valarane with Sanvaunt and Ovitus (deceased)

Tarquus of Redwinter—First Retainer, servant

Ehma of Harranir—Second Retainer, servant

Howen of Harranir—Second Retainer, servant

Bossal of Harranir—Fifth Retainer, servant

Patalia of Harranir—Fifth Retainer, servant

Waldy—Ovitus's loyal wolfhound

LacClune Clanhold

Merovech LacClune—Van of the clan, Draoihn of the Fourth Gate, holds one of the seats on the Council of Night and Day, father of Castus

Haronus LacClune—Draoihn of the Third Gate

Castus LacClune—Draoihn of the First Gate, living at Redwinter, son of Merovech

The Council of Night and Day

Grandmaster Vedira Robilar—Leader of the Draoihn order, head of the council, Draoihn of the Fifth Gate
Kelsen of Harranir—The king's personal healer, Draoihn of the Fifth Gate
Ulovar LacNaithe—Van of Clan LacNaithe, Draoihn of the Fourth Gate, usually at Redwinter, uncle of Ovitus and Sanvaunt
Onostus LacAud—Draoihn of the Second Gate
Hanaqin Clanless—Draoihn of the Fourth Gate
Lassaine LacDaine—Draoihn of the Fourth Gate, great-niece to King Quinlan LacDaine, commander of the Winterra
Merovech LacClune—Van of Clan LacClune, Draoihn of the Fourth Gate, father of Castus
Kyrand of Murr—Draoihn of the Third Gate
Suanach LacNaruun—Draoihn of the Second Gate, master of artifice

Rulers

King Quinlan LacDaine—King of Harran, bearer of the Crown, father of Caelan LacDaine
Prince Caelan LacDaine—Prince of Harran, son of Quinlan LacDaine, with the Winterra, fighting wars for the king of Brannlant
King Henrith II—King of Brannlant, father of Mathilde
Princess Mathilde—A princess of Brannlant, daughter of Henrith II
Lady Dauphine—Princess Mathilde's cousin and her companion

Rebels of the North

Onostus LacAud—Draoihn of the Second Gate
Akail—A woman from the far northern tundra
Lord Braman—A warrior risen to lordship in Onostus LacAud's service

Legendary Figures

The Queen of Feathers—A being of unknown origin who visits Raine

Hallenae the Riven Queen—Made war against the world, defeated at Solemn Hill by Maldouen and the last surviving generals. Hallenae was imbued with the power of the Night Below, which was bound and stored in five Crowns. Slain over seven hundred years ago, her defeat marks the beginning of the Succession Age.

Maldouen the Blind Child—Created the Lance and the five Crowns, which were used to defeat Hallenae and her armies, vanished thereafter

Empress Serranis, Lady of Deserts—A dread Sarathi ruler, defeated more than 4,000 years ago

Empress Song Seondeok—A dread Sarathi ruler who brought the world to ruin around 1,900 years ago

Grandmaster Unthayla the Damned—A Sarathi, unmasked and defeated in the year 456

Sul, a Faded Lord—The most active of the Faded Lords, and a constant threat to the Draoihn. Sul murdered King Dern LacNaithe in the year 370, and fought the Council of Night and Day to a standstill in 456. He returned to fight Grandmaster Robilar in the year 681, leaving her permanently wounded.

Alianna—Grandmaster Robilar's sister (deceased)

The Mystic World

The Draoihn

The Draoihn enter a series of existentialist trances that allow them to expand their consciousness into the world around it, become one with it and then affect it. To do so, they open a Gate in their mind.

EIO: The First Gate—the Gate of Self. Allows exceptional sensory perception by expanding the essence of one's self into the connected world around. There are about one thousand Draoihn of the First Gate, most of whom are sent to serve the Winterra, supporting the king of Brannlant's territorial expansion.

SEI: The Second Gate—the Gate of Other. Allows the expansion of consciousness into non-living matter in the physical world around the trance holder, and the manipulation of the Other. There are only one hundred Draoihn of the Second Gate, around half of whom work under Suanach LacNaruun working on artifice at Redwinter.

TAINE: The Third Gate—the Gate of Energy. Allows the expansion of consciousness through energy, the transmission of that energy and its redirection. As every scientist knows, energy cannot be created or destroyed. There are only thirty Draoihn of the Third Gate.

FIER: The Fourth Gate—the Gate of Mind. Allows the expansion of consciousness into the minds of living creatures the trancing Draoihn touches, enabling them to impact the thought processes of that creature's mind. There are only four Draoihn of the Fourth Gate—Ulovar, Merovech, Hanaqin and Lassaine.

VIE: The Fifth Gate—the Gate of Life. Allows the expansion of consciousness into the physical forms of oneself as well as other living matter. This is mostly used for healing. There are only two known Draoihn of the Fifth Gate, Grandmaster Vedira Robilar and Kelsen of Harranir, who acts as the king's personal healer.

SKAL: The Sixth Gate—the Gate of Death. The old power of the Sarathi.

Modern Draoihn are forbidden to even attempt to access it. There are no Draoihn of the Sixth Gate.

GEI: The Seventh Gate—the Gate of Creation. The Seventh Gate is purely theoretical, a concept used to understand how the Faded changed the world as they did thousands of years ago.

The Sarathi

Wielders of the Sixth Gate, they sided with Hallenae the Riven Queen, and enemies of the world, but are said to have betrayed Hallenae prior to the battle at Solemn Hill where she met her defeat. They are always enemies of Redwinter.

The Faded

A race of powerful and sentient beings, the Faded once lived alongside mankind. They were banished into the Fault by Maldouen at the beginning of the Succession Age. Very occasionally one of the Faded finds a way to escape that prison.

The Crowns

Prior to the Succession Age, the Riven Queen amassed such power that she could not be defeated. In their hour of need, the Draoihn were presented with an answer by the legendary blind child, Maldouen, who informed them of his labour to construct five great Crowns across the world, and that those Crowns could banish her most terrible allies—the Faded, the demons and dead things she had summoned. The Crowns lie in Harran, its imperial neighbour Brannlant, and the distant realms of Ithatra, Khalacant, and Dharithia. Vast domed chambers filled with magic, the Crowns' power must be ever bound to the mind of a mortal, or the dark creatures that were banished from the world might find a way to return. For the Draoihn of Harranir, the bond to the Crown is always forced on a would-be king, so that the ruler might understand that protecting the Crown is his greatest responsibility.

The Draoihn support the occupation of Harranir by its more powerful neighbour, Brannlant, because it leaves two Crowns under a single leadership. Khalacant is a realm ruled by the serpent queens, while the city of Osprinne lies in the distant empire of Dharithia. Ithatra lay beyond the western ocean, a voyage which has become too treacherous to make by Raine's time, and what has become of its Crown is unknown.

The Hidden Folk

Once, the Hidden Folk existed alongside the rest of the world, and this name was not given to them until after their banishment. When Maldouen created the five Crowns, most of the magical creatures of the world were banished into another plane of existence known as the Fault, while others were left in a kind of limbo, uncertain whether they belong in one realm or another. Those that do still have a presence were driven into the far flung, wild places of the world and are seldom seen. The Hidden Folk encompass a wide range of creatures, from the deadly, mermaid-like "Drowners," to the small and mischievous Powsies and harmless Snatterkin. Some compose whole species, while others are singular, unique beings.

The Fault

The Fault lies between the mortal world and the dark terrors of the Night Below. Some of those creatures, such as the moon horses, have ways of moving between the realms, but little beyond that is known of it.

The Hexen

Destroyed by the Draoihn during the Betrayal War, they burned the Glass Library of Redwinter.

The Knights of Tharada Taan

The knights drew their power from the Everstorm around Tharada Mountain, until the Draoihn destroyed it and ended their power.

Acknowledgments

For their assistance in bringing this story onto these pages, I would like to thank:

My agent Ian Drury, who finds homes for the stories I've always wanted to tell.

My editor Claire Eddy, who saw Raine's potential and took her forward.

My editor Gillian Redfearn, who helped Raine to grow and champions her still.

Sanaa Ali-Virani and the team at Tor, whose tireless work keeps the cogs turning.

My editor Brendan Durkin and the team at Gollancz, whose labours never go unappreciated.

Gaia Banks, Alba Arnau and all of the team at Sheil Land Associates Ltd., who have sent my words around the world.

The incredible doctors, nurses and staff of the NHS, who put me back together when the world had other ideas.

And finally, this book would never have got here without the assistance, suggestions and ongoing support of my first reader and editor, my inspiration and companion: Catriona Ward, who is all the colours of my heart.